THE LIGHTHOUSE OF KUIPER

BOOK ONE OF THE HELIOSPHERE TRILOGY

E. M. RENSING

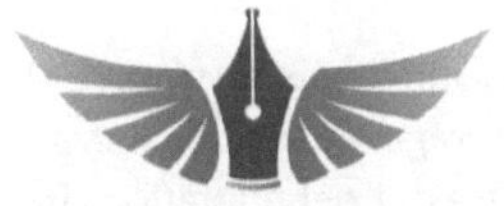

For my Dad

BOOK ONE
4VESTA

CHAPTER
ONE

"SO. MA'AM. WHAT DO YOU THINK?"

"I think it's a spider scat problem, Olin."

"This is not normal."

"I don't see why this matters."

"Not normal comes back to bite you in the ass, Lieutenant Chen. Hold the lamp."

And that was a direct response to their toolkit floating off. The female lieutenant took a better grip on the ceiling as her sergeant kicked off in the microgravity after it.

"You really should start calling me Tharsis, Olin!" she yelled. "Everyone else does!"

He stopped as he grabbed the bag, swinging himself back around in a low drift, and gestured towards her neck and the rank insignia there. "You outrank me, ma'am."

Fat lot of good her commission had done her. Tharsis stared at the jumble of ruined chairs below. Now little more than a convenient dumping ground, the floor of the old auditorium had been collecting broken scat for decades.

She hated wasting her people's time on routine maintenance inspections in the lower levels of base, but then, that was their job here. Maintain a post designed for thousands with a squadron of barely two hundred. If it hadn't been for Olin's patience with her, she wasn't sure if she could've put up with the assignment.

Tharsis had been working through yet another pile of paperwork that afternoon when her Transmissions Superintendent had shown up.

"Found something in Main Briefing," Olin had said. "Need you to go down with me."

Come down. To poke at wetware that wasn't theirs, in a place that nobody used. Again.

He'd seemed worried, though. Unusual for him.

So down she'd gone.

The spherical auditorium had been carved directly out of 4Vesta's crust. Inside the asteroid's mass, olivine-enrobed, neural-synthetic cabling grew where it would. The wetware honeycombed the interior of the 'roid like a fungus, forcing its way through the base walls on a regular basis. Amazing, really, that anything worked in the lower levels.

Even considering that, today's findings were unusual. Fist-sized, turgid nubs had broken through the walls in amazing number. Like demented mushroom caps, they glowed with pained maroon light, wiring inflamed, spread out across a space at least ten meters square.

Not normal, indeed.

But then, her eye caught movement.

On the floor. Between the chairs. Dashing through an open space. Not just dark but somehow absorbent, the shape consuming the light from their broad-spectrum maintenance lamp.

Olin fastened the bag to a maintenance handhold. Steading himself with another, the sergeant flicked the lock open on the canvas box, rummaging. "Something down there, El-Tee?" he asked conversationally.

Looking back, the space below was empty. "No."

"If you're seeing something, ma'am, we can always go get Tommy."

"I don't see things," she said, eyes still fixed on the spot. Had she imagined it? The shadows playing with her mind? "We don't need the cat."

He had the decency not to press. "So, what do you think of our tumors here?"

Master Sergeant Caleb Olin was unremarkable in most respects, a standard-issue career enlisted man who carried the extra kilos on his lanky frame with self-deprecating humor. He'd been at Humphryes for over a decade—the definitive expert on not only the installation's infrastructure, but the civilian sprawl beyond the guardhouse air lock. He did his job and did it well, but with a kind of quiet, world-weary attitude. The Arran Self-Defense Force did that to people, she'd learned. But the sergeant had taken her under his wing from the first, and she trusted his judgment more than her own.

"Tumors?"

"Definitely cancerous, mutation in the synthetic DNA. Energy surge, maybe, or radiation cross talk." He huffed. "That's what you get with this unethical wetware scat."

Tharsis grabbed a spare wrench that had escaped its magnetic anchor, tucking it away again. "I don't know. I mean, it seems to work for everybody here. And isn't it necessary for the grav-generators?"

The sergeant produced a small Cimmerian-glass jar. "First time you see a myling leaking out of a line, you'll understand why the Tenancy banned human-based biotech."

"Human-based biotech was a horror show, I know. But mylings aren't real."

"Not anymore, maybe, but the Euphemism's nightmares are well documented. Besides, even synthetic DNA can still produce umbran," Olin said, a tone of finality in his voice, a pair of stainless steel forceps and a huge chunk of medical-grade gauze in his hand. "Hold this," he said, and tossed her the jar.

"Wait, what are you—"

But before she could stop him, Olin sealed the forceps around the base of one of the nodules and ripped it out. A dull glow surged, then died. Suspension fluid sprayed out under pressure, soaking them both. A smell akin to rotten shark meat filled the space.

"Fuck," Olin cursed, and slapped the gauze down on the bleeding tear of the wall as another huge glob struck him on the cheek. "Jar, El-Tee, come on. Fuck."

The now slippery nodule, suspended in the 'roid's natural micro-gravity, almost got loose from the jar before Tharsis was able to screw the cap on. "Seriously? You're just gonna rip it out?"

"Need to figure out what's in that," he told her, and unclipped his tool bag from the wall, securing it back onto his work belt. "See what's been jumping through the wires."

"Can we do that?"

"Sure. Why not? Biopsy the cancer cells, isolate the type of radiation that formed 'em. Basic stuff," Olin said, and paused. "But I'm going to need some discretionary cash."

Tharsis groaned; so that was why he'd brought her along. "From Captain Hinden?"

"Technically, he is in charge now, El-Tee."

"Can't I just ask the Major instead?"

"Major Lanin ain't the boss no more," Olin reminded her, and dabbed away the last few drops of fluid from the rotten surface of the wall. "Change of command was last night."

It was clear that he'd killed the line; the neural carrier tissues were already necrotizing. Strange. She'd never known her sergeant to be so careless when conducting repairs on the Ibbie infrastructure. Normally, he was meticulous about cauterization, disinfectants, all those extra little touches biologic cabling required.

"Major Lanin doesn't leave until the rotator comes on Sevenday. Hinden's not going to care about this."

"You gotta learn how to deal with the man."

"You deal with him," she snapped back.

His amused smile turned sympathetic. "Let's get out of here before that thing bleeds on us again."

Despite its ostensibly prime location, Contingency Base Ewan Humphryes was far from an elite posting. Its existence was owed to the disastrous events of the Sixth Propagation, almost a hundred and fifty years before. One of the plug-and-play, prefab installations common to this region of the Heliosphere, it contained everything a station needed to rapidly deploy combat troops, both within and beyond the 'roid. Everything had been considered: gravity, filtered water, radiation shielding, air-locked gates with atmo sterilization scrubbers, an extensive manhole system, molecular welding around every nut, bolt, and joint, denatured wrapper defense systems, cattery and kennel facilities, dorms, chummer.

It was an effective design. But it had been built for far more people than it currently contained, expected to run on funding far exceeding anything the Inner Shoals Command could currently provide. INSHOALCOM handled that region of space between Mars and Jupiter, a relatively small region of the Heliosphere, yet one of the most densely populated. It was also one of the least fractious. Its Landlord was more hated, but less problematic, than many others. Whenever they could get away with it, whenever Mars's own Landlord didn't force the issue, Congress tended to cut Command's budget to the bone. And Mars's Landlord hadn't been public for nearly thirty years.

The Inner Belt wasn't a region of primary concern and it showed.

Projects started in the fat years after the Seventh Propagation were still undone, raw concrete subfloors exposed, walls left only half-painted, entire buildings held together with nothing more than the ingenuity of the guys in the fabrication shop. Gravity was kept off in all nonessential areas. Tired carpet, worn tile. Even the landscaping had suffered, the trees and grass long dead and nothing to replace them but bare dirt. Everything about Humphryes spoke of age, of dysfunction and emptiness. It was nothing, a tiny spec of Arran utili-tarianism in the vast archipelago-city of New Stockholm.

Yet there they were. Stressing the ancient, jury-rigged atmo scrub-bers to fill the cubic meterage with breathable air, wasting manpower on routine maintenance inspections, a hedge against the next war that never seemed to come.

Eight years in officer school, void-qualified as a female, and Humphreys was where she'd ended up. Tharsis hated the place.

Olin was pulling away from her, almost to the exit hatch that opened into the base proper, and Tharsis hurried to catch up. He hadn't bothered to turn on the shaft's lighting system. The lamp he was carrying was the only light in the darkness. Combined with the weightlessness of mig, which was the sensation of floating that the Arran mind could never quite ignore, it was almost scary.

Falling out of the shaft was awkward as always. As with the differ-ence between the heat of a late summer day and that put out by a carri-er's air cycling systems, the distinction between the natural mig and artificial gravity was uncomfortable. She barely caught herself, swinging up and around onto the bare dirt.

Tharsis lay on her back for a moment, staring up at the wrappered sky, letting her organs shift back. In the past year, she'd come to hate the weight of her planet-born body. The thick wrists, ruddy-pink skin, large breasts, pronounced facial features, bore witness to the lot she'd pulled in Mars's unregulated genetic lottery. It was an unfair comparison; she was still well within military weight standards, and she'd been told she was pretty. It didn't matter much. Not home on Mars and certainly not here. The local Ibbie women were painfully gorgeous. Far thinner and paler and more feminine than any Arran had a prayer of being. Custom-designed, purposeful phenotypes mixed up in prettily skinned home wombs.

She did keep her dark hair as long as she could manage, though. Her one little bit of pride in herself as a female, she supposed.

"Why do you even want to get Hinden in gimble-spin about this, Olin?" the lieutenant asked as her sergeant offered her a hand up. "He's not going to care. This whole base is an anomaly. It's so far off giddie as it is, it's a miracle it's still running."

"Doesn't mean it doesn't matter," Olin said firmly, and cut a course for squadron HQ.

CAPTAIN HINDEN WAS ALREADY MAKING himself at home in the major's old office. The place felt bleaker, despite the half-opened boxes of memorabilia littered across the floor, the stacks of dedicated report tablets on the desk.

Gone was the mini fridge, with its stock of cheap liquor and pressure bottles of cider. Gone was the battered lamb-leather couch. Gone was the laid-back man who preferred impromptu rugby games to briefings on Fiveday afternoons.

Present was the least-liked officer on base.

Captain Mikael Hinden was a thin, gangly sort of man, hair lank and dead even in its buzz cut, the rank tattoos on his neck dark against ashen skin. There was speculation amongst the lieutenants that he suffered from calcium depletion, organ failure, his self-vaunted time in the magnetic nightmare of Europa's Trilan Watch Base still taking its toll on his body. His might have been a pathetic presence. But there was a kind of power-hungry intention in him that made Tharsis's skin crawl. It was hard for her to look him in the eye.

Already, Hinden had covered the wall immediately facing the door with all of his various plaques and trophies—commission certificate from the Academy, graduate degree from Deimos Technical University, a signed picture of him with the Speaker of the House he'd gotten while serving on the man's communications detail, Company Grade Officer of the year plaques. Six of those. How he'd managed that feat, Tharsis had no idea.

"Arrogant little scathead," Olin muttered under his breath, examining one of the frames, but before Tharsis could correct him on it out of principle, the officer in question was waving them deeper into his lair.

"Yes, Tharsis, you've got five minutes before my next meeting," he said, feet up on his desk. "What's so damn important?"

"Umm," she began, the chaos of the office chasing her half-formed arguments from her mind. "Sergeant Olin found something growing out of one of the local wetware lines tangled up in our scat downstairs. Looks cancerous, sir. I'd like to request that we send the sample to the Titan lab downtown."

Hinden laughed. High and whiny. Tharsis could almost see him formulating his refusal. "Cancer? In the wetware? Since when do we care about the Ibbie's wetware?"

Olin pulled the jar out of his pocket. Holding it up, not handing it over. "I'd like to make sure we don't have a cross-talk radiation issue going on."

Captain Hinden brought his feet back to the floor and glared at the sergeant. Olin's expression didn't budge, and Tharsis had to bite back a smile as Hinden's own scowl wavered.

"We're off their power grid. Communications, too," the captain said, neat, as if saying it made it so. "No cross talk possible."

Tharsis stepped in. "Sir, I get that this isn't exactly on giddie, but I wouldn't have brought this up here if the shop wasn't sure it was important. I—"

Hinden cut her off with a flick of a bony hand. "You need to stop letting your enlisted men walk all over you. Remember when you let him," and Olin bristled, "talk you into proposing we spend half the base operating budget on Lighthouse repeater repairs?"

Scat. He was still pissed about being overridden on that? Major

Lanin had supported it. Command had even coughed up additional funding for it. "Sir," she began.

"I am not Major Lanin, and I've inherited a scat-ton of problems from him without you making up a bunch of new ones. You with me on that, El-Tee?"

Tharsis bit the inside of her cheek. "Yes, sir."

Moods switching with ionic polarity, Hinden grinned his unhinged grin at her. "Good girl. I knew you'd see it my way. So, you don't need the lab now?"

"What?"

Olin tapped the back of her elbow. "No sir, we'll get out of your hair," he replied with a smile, and all but hauled her from the room.

"Shut the door on your way out!" Hinden called. Tharsis's last glimpse of him was the man putting his feet back up on the desk, pulling a reading tablet out of a drawer.

"What the hell was that about?" she demanded of Olin, after the door clicked shut behind them. "I thought we needed this."

"We do, and we're going to get it," Olin assured her, and steered her back to the secretary's desk, where the harried Ibbie woman was almost hidden behind a projection field of requisition and manning forms, a forest of gaudily framed family photographs. "Hey, Cheria, hon, where's the boss?"

The Ibbie woman blinked huge eyes through the projection and dimmed it to minimum. "He took off, headed for the Wardog."

Tharsis glanced at the chronograph. "It's only 1600."

Cheria smiled. "He said something about wanting a head start on drinking it dry."

CHAPTER
TWO

LEAVING BASE THAT AFTERNOON, Olin quiet at her side, Tharsis was once again struck by just how alien a world 4Vesta was.

Back home, on Mars, in the Tharsan Highlands where she'd grown up, everything was open sky, sweeping taiga. The nearest town was twenty kilometers from her family's ranch, a journey never undertaken without good reason. The terrain didn't allow for paved roads, and the air currents coming off Olympus Mons were too harsh for all but the most massive of airships. Travel was a slow thing, by superjeep or pony, through newpeat and heather and low alpine grasses. The mist born off the oceans to the west crept inland, skirting the heights of the ancient volcanoes, settling in amongst the rocks and junipers, lingering in every hollow, every stream bed.

As a child, she'd disappear for days into those wilds, sometimes with friends, sometimes with nothing more than her pony and one of the family dogs, saddlebags loaded with dehydrated curries and her older brother's ultralight fly-tent. Off to the thermal pools or the endless snows in the foothills of the western Bulge, where the air lay thick enough to breathe, up to the edge of the snowfields themselves, far above the timber lines. Slept with a dog curled around her for warmth. Listened to the planet's synthetic magnetosphere sing as she drifted off, the only brush she'd ever had with the penumbra.

New Stockholm, capitol city of the Rallarhu's Inner Belt Coalition and jewel of the Heliosphere, offered no such solitude. The place was dense with humanity and ever shifting, built out on islands that twisted through the bind of barrier seas like icebergs in the Vastitas Ocean. Dense-packed and low-short, buildings on the islands were meticulously maintained to exacting Ibbie standards. Surfaces glowed, the natural curves in the still growing structures shining with starlight, the roads maintained at perfect smoothness, even when roots from the buildings occasionally broke through the strata.

There was beauty there, even if it bore none of the majesty of Mars's carefully cultivated nature. The undisputed apex of Ibbie architecture towered in the Old Town heights, where the Rallarhu's statue marked the spot where artificial land met artificial sky. Like the sky above Humphreys, New Stockholm's contained a thick layer of xeno-cyte wrapper, pressed and woven and fused, its radiation-hunger kept from the environment below by the will of its Landlord alone.

Looking back, up over the low rooftops surrounding Humphreys, Tharsis could see iron spires catching the light of the daydreamed sun. Every cell of New Stockholm's sky contained mitochondria spliced out of the Rallarhu's long-vanished human body. Her memories. Tharsis wondered if that was what the sky on Earth looked like. The sun was larger than it was on Mars.

Right now, that false sun hung low, the dream of sunset just starting to spread across the sky. It was always nice when the base's chrono was synched up with New Stockholm's Heliosphere Standard Time.

"You doin' okay, ma'am?" Olin asked.

"Yeah," Tharsis said, and shoved her hands in her pockets. Not on kiddie, but giddies be damned. "Hinden creeps me out."

"No help for it," the sergeant grumbled, and started walking again, down into a wilder, low-slung tumble of islands moored around Humphryes. "But you have to try to do things right, before you do things effectively."

In the decades since the base had been built, jutting out past the seal of the Vestan sky, the area around it had become a haven for foreigners; the district was a jumble of nationalities, everything from Cronuan students to Trans-Nep refugees.

Where so much of the rest of the city reveled in its glassy perfection, the international district was a mad scramble of vice and hasty decisions. The buildings had grown thick and close, the olivine facades pitted with doorways and windows, rooms like caves in some, the spaces between them sometimes wide as parks or narrow as slot canyons.

Billboards smeared the air with Jovian neon, advertising everything from oxygen bars, to Ionian sense-dep chambers built out on stilts over the water, to local whorehouses that offered every kind of bizarre biologic interaction the Tenancy would allow. Music spilled from every doorway, pattering out in the false twilight. Aromas from a dozen different cuisines filled the streets. It seemed that every floor, from the basements to the sixth-floor jump landings, had something to sell, items from all over the Heliosphere.

During the HST standard year she'd been there, the lieutenant had come to see the place as both exhausting and exhilarating. An illusory world cast bright against the memories she had of the stone-cold permanence of Mars. A lot of Arrans had trouble adapting at first to the crowds, to the noise, but Tharsis liked it. A balm against the chafe of Humphryes.

What she didn't care for was the Wardog.

In the abstract, Tharsis understood the appeal of the place. Good old Arran pub. From its scavenged wood interiors and DeimosNet wireless broadcasts that carried National League rugby on game days to the karaoke band set up on the back stage, it could have been found in any planitia town on Mars. It even had Mars-normal gravity built in, something that must have cost a small fortune. The owner kept it on the Arran clock, too. Twenty-four and a half hours, instead of the Heliosphere-standard twenty-four hours. Even when Humphryes was well out of time-synch, when their evening was the Ibbie's morning, the Wardog was open

It had been a given that the base officers at least pop in on Fiveday nights, and most stayed for far longer than that. It was the only real thing any of them did together, the only time they ever really got to dig out of the endless demands of sustaining Humphryes.

A slice of home.

The lieutenant had tried to get into the spirit of it, and for the first month or two she'd been here, it had been fun. And yet now, it wasn't. It wasn't what she'd imagined her first assignment would be like.

Wasn't what she'd had in mind at twelve, when she'd realized that one of her family's three daughters was going to have to shoulder the national service commitment. Wasn't anything her fourteen-year-old self had hoped for, heading off to the Arran Military Academy.

Most people loved it, though, and it was always packed.

Tharsis put her own irritation aside and poked Olin, who was drifting over to the open bar. "I'm gonna go talk to the boss."

"I'll find you," Olin promised, and turned back around, smiling at the Ibbie girl manning the liquor bottles.

Tharsis rolled her eyes and headed back.

Major Lanin, back when he was still commander, had held court at the Wardog on the weekends. That night, he was casual as always, a pressure can of cider at his elbow and wearing civilian clothes in place of support-troop grays, chatting it up with the rail-thin Arran expat who ran the place. He was unmistakably Arran: dark blond hair shot through with gray, the vaguely Asiatic features of the equatorial planitia regions, features stained ruddy from a childhood under planetary atmo. The void-born, by comparison, and regardless of skin color, all had a pallor to them no Arran could hope to match.

The major's first name was Trai, although nobody ever used it. His handle, hung on him on his first tour, was stitched in neat letters on the deepvoider patch on his left shoulder. "Trig, like trigger happy, cause I suck on the A-24," he'd always laugh. Nobody ever used that either. He'd always been The Boss.

Major Lanin had a wife and kids back at the family ranch, inwell, back home. They sent him care packages every month, cookies and sweets from Cimmeria that got passed around at briefings. His would undoubtedly be a long and unremarkable career, but he'd always gone out of his way to take care of his people, and Tharsis missed him already.

The major smiled at her as she slid into the seat next to him. "Ambera, how's my cable maintenance shop doin' today? RMI rounds down in the basement go okay?"

Anger rumbling anew inside her chest, Tharsis managed to smile back. Major Lanin was the only person on base who called her by her first name. "Fine, sir."

He gave her that look of his, sizing her up. "Whatcha got, El-Tee?"

She blanched. "Not really sure. There was something growing on a line, but it's probably nothing."

Olin sat down between them, plunking a couple of frothing steins down and tossing Major Lanin the jar. No preamble at all. "Wetware tumor. I need it biopsied."

Lanin's easygoing smile dropped away. He sat up a little straighter, turning the jar over in his hand. "You think it's a problem?"

"Yes, sir."

"So why isn't this on its way to the university lab?"

"Captain Hinden didn't want to cough up the cash," Tharsis said.

"Did you talk to him?" Major Lanin asked, serious now.

Olin grimaced. "I spoke with him about this, if that's what you mean."

"Not at all what I meant. We discussed this, Sergeant."

"And I believe I said he was a void-chewed sack of scat who isn't worth the carbon his DNA's printed on," Olin shot back. "He gets nothing out of me."

Lanin huffed a low laugh, then pulled a credit chip from his pocket. "Courtesy of the Arran taxpayer. I'll expense it when I get to my new assignment. Do what you need to."

"Thanks, sir."

"And talk to him."

Nodding, Olin snapped a quick salute and headed off, vanishing into the crowd.

The bass amps whined on behind them; a couple of the other lieutenants were gearing up for a round of bad karaoke. One of them—Andren Junia, an Academy classmate, the only other female officer on base—was already drunk, hanging all over Nyes from the MP shop even as he tried to get her back in her seat.

Tharsis's chest clenched up. Given a choice, their men never chose them. Not when there were millions of petite voider girls around, girls who amassed more sexual experience by sixteen than an average Arran woman managed in her entire life. Most military females went their entire commitment without attention from their male counterparts. Marriage between soldiers was practically unheard of.

Some ASDF women supposedly took care of each other when the hormone patches didn't take the edge off. Arran home rules didn't really apply to military females. But she and Junia had never gotten along, and Tharsis didn't think the other girl would take the suggestion very well, even if she herself had been interested.

"Hey, Ambera," Major Lanin said, breaking through her thoughts, and she wondered if he'd been talking to her that entire time, "you still with me?"

"Yeah," she said, wincing a little as the amps ground out a bass line from some Silicone Age classic. "I, uh, just thinking, I guess."

"Well, I need some atmo," Lanin declared, and grabbed the steins. "Come on, Tharsis, no fun drinking alone."

THE NEON-SWEPT roof of the Wardog was never quite as popular as the studiously grungy interior. That night, it was empty. Tharsis breathed out into it, settling herself against the low, crenelated edge. The anger roiling in her gut settled under that expanse of now dark sky. The starfield was always brilliant. No clouds, no miles of natural atmo to block the view.

People seethed below them, a mass of almost-humanity. Young and healthy children locked in home womb or school, the aged sent to daycare islands beyond the roil. Everything was provided to them, but participation in the workforce was both mandatory and assigned. Most threw themselves into it with frightening intensity. Despite that, though, Ibbie life was one of deep leisure, compared to what Tharsis was used to on Mars, engaging whatever kind of erratic hours and hobbies and habits they pleased. The environment was programmable, and therefore always pleasant.

It was what the people of the Inner Belt had requested of their Landlord. In return, she demanded balance, and what that usually meant was complete loyalty to the regime and a sense of group identity over self. Work assignments were involuntary, hereditary, but shared amongst family. Perhaps that last factor was part of the reason why it was so crowded: more children, less labor per individual. Over a hundred million people lived in the four major and twenty-four minor asteroid archipelagic city-states, half the estimated population of the entire Heliosphere.

So different from Mars.

"What are you thinking about there, Ambera?" Major Lanin asked her, pressing one of the steins into her hands.

The cider tasted bitter. "I don't know," she confessed. "Guess I'm just not in the mood."

"Nothing says you have to be." He clapped her on the shoulder. "What can I do?"

Don't go. She didn't voice it. "When is your replacement going to get here?"

Major Lanin leaned against the edge next to her, eyes down on the party spilling across the pavers outside the pub now. "Hinden's pinning on major in about six months or so."

"So Command's just leaving us with him?" The words spilled out of her mouth.

Lanin laughed. "I tried, believe me, I tried." He rubbed a hand back against his bare scalp. "Between you and me, I considered submitting a request to the Rossen."

Her eyes widened. The Landlord was a serious card to play. "Why didn't you?"

"No hard evidence of abuse or incompetence. Besides, it would have required the Wytt to do an investigation, and not even Hinden deserves that." The major hesitated. "And I figured the Landlord could have corrected the situation already, if he'd wanted to."

"He really hasn't shown his face much lately, has he?"

"Never has. Not since Ceres, at any rate." Major Lanin finished half of his own stein in one go. "I'd be fucking embarrassed about that too."

"Yeah," Tharsis replied softly. "Ceres."

In the early days of voidcraft, the Inner Belt's dwarf planet had been an essential port between the inner and the outer regions, as well as a prime source of water, oxygen, and hydrogen fuel. Technically under the control of Mars, she'd been heavily settled by Arran's entrepreneurs and their families, and had been the launch site of the exodus craft. When the Tenancy was put into place, the Rallarhu had volunteered to serve as that planet's Landlord. The Rossen had vouched for her.

The trust had proven false.

"Fucking monsters, the Landlords," Tharsis grumbled.

"What happened to them wasn't their fault."

"Fuck whose fault it was," Tharsis replied, shaking her head. "We shouldn't have to deal with it. With him."

"Can you imagine what he deals with? Regenerating back into his twenty-four-year-old body every time he dies, right down to the neural configuration of his memories." The major shook his head. "Think about it. Waking up in some med vat on Deimos tomorrow, thinking you're still in the thick of the worst war humanity's ever seen, and then having some asshole in an unfamiliar uniform tell you, 'You let your former commander kill a million people seven hundred years ago.'" He chuckled, humorless. "Nobody would handle that well."

The lieutenant sipped her drink. Wanting to say something about the whole fucking thing being unfair in the first place. Fuck the Rossen. He'd been a Chief Master Sergeant back in the day. He should have known better.

"They say he spends a lot of time on the deepvoiders, hiding in the ranks, still fighting the Toks," she said instead, and looked at her commander. "Did you ever meet him?"

"Really, I think we've had enough depressing political scat for the night without getting into that mess," Lanin said, and held out his hand. "But seriously, El-Tee, you're doing good work. Stick close to Sergeant Olin. He'll take care of you."

It hit her, then, that with his couch and his fridge and his humor gone, Humphryes was going to be a hell of a lot less fun. And it hadn't been much fun to begin with.

"Thank you, sir. For everything," she said, and shook back, firm as she could manage.

He smiled, patted her on the shoulder again, and then she was alone on the roof.

Tharsis listened to the strains of classical rock streaming out onto the streets below. Thought about heading down. Joining the throng. Getting drunk and singing along to those almost intelligible Silicon English lyrics and pretending like she wasn't dreading Oneday.

She flicked the gravity off in her boots instead and took the plunge off the edge of the building, three stories down, landing hard on the grease-slicked asphalt of the alley.

It was three blocks before she could breathe again.

CHAPTER
THREE

HEADED BACK TO HER LODGING, Tharsis found herself looking up to the thick bubble of the sky, wondering if the Rallarhu was up there, if that bio-fucked creature was watching her right now.

Landlords.

The final legacy of the Euphemism.

The details were hazy, so much lost to the confusion of those final few years on Earth, but few things were certain. More than a war, beyond a simple armed conflict, the Euphemism had been the result of nearly a century of unchecked technological progress. Off had come the controls of even the most indulgent of philosophies. Extinction cults coalesced, deep-green movements advocated human abandonment, purging of Earth, governments funded efforts to find what proponents called better intelligent life, laboratories labored to find ever more effective means of population control.

There had been no organization, no religion, no leaders, no plan. Just an unfettered riot against the existence of man.

Some had fought back—remnants of old national militaries, new coalitions funded by the same industrial families who'd had the foresight to fund Arran terraforming—but organized resistance had ultimately been futile. Too many people dead, too much of the international infrastructure of civilization decayed beyond repair. Once hallucination contagions were spliced into seed crops, all the fighting bought was time to escape.

There was already a small population living outwell of Earth, but when the famines and the nightmare plagues became too much, that population exploded. Military forces kept the lifts open, but from there, people had to find their own way.

Most settled on moons, or out in the major asteroid fields of LaGrange points. For those closer in, the gravitational influences of major planets wrecked havoc on Earth-born physiology. But those settlers had it easy, or so they thought, even as genetics were forcefully adapted, labor consolidated, populations enslaved.

By contrast, settlement on Mars had been more difficult. Living on a planet in the middle of terraforming was no simple feat. But those few souls hardy or adventurous or desperate enough to sign on for the Founders' onerous conditions, it had proven a hedge against the worst of the insanity.

Earth's philosophical sickness had still spread into the void. Student riots on Titan. Polarist activity spreading through the settlements of the Jovian inwell. Discoveries in Europa's adlivun depths that claimed nearly three brigades before nuclear fires burnt it away. The last gasp of the Euphemism.

Something had to be done.

The University of Titan had proposed the Tenancy. Totalitarian control. Undying. Unending. To halt the descent.

The first of the Landlords, the Wytt, announced his presence by killing nearly six million people—scientists, doctors, theorists, drug lords, anyone sympathetic to the Euphemisms's various ideologies— the day the decision was ratified. The rest proved little better. A depopulated Earth was placed under permanent watch. Scientific research was all but banned. Religion was viciously excoriated from most of the system. Economic systems were frozen.

Mars positioned its military forces against the lingering madness.

The Euphemism was stopped.

But seven Propagations on—an eighth due any year now—the Heliosphere hardly resembled the gleaming paradise once promised.

Mercury dead. Venus barely holding on. An empty Earth watched by a lonely woman who regenerated by giving birth to herself. Mars violating its own Constitution by allowing a dictator. The Inner Shoals, run by an Arran traitor whose portrait hung in every shop and home and facility, the starched blue of her collar unmistakable as the old Earth's resistance military. Jupiter with its nepotistic stranglehold on the Heliosphere's energy resources. Saturn, fancying itself above the milieu, leeching billions in resources from other inwells. Uranus and Neptune, half-empty habitats haunted by insane, lonely Landlords. The brain-dead pilot of Pluto. The frozen wastes of the Kuiper and their madwoman, who promised a utopia none had ever seen.

Tharsis pressed on, over the last bridge into the hostel district. Humphryes had dorm complexes, but the things were large, power-intensive. The squadron only kept one open at a time; when it was full, personnel were allowed to live off base instead. Tharsis had arrived at such a time and had jumped on the chance. The things everybody warned her about—*you'll constantly be out of time-synch, you'll need to watch what you say around the voiders, you have to sleep in a grav-bag all the time*—hadn't mattered. It had sounded like an adventure, and an adventure sounded good.

The only true concern was gravity. Humphryes was kept to the Arran standard of 3.73 m/s2. Ibbies, by comparison, kept their cities to the bare minimum required to hold the seas together, and even that was aided greatly by the sky-structures and general water tension. Local physiologies were adapted, but for the planet-born Arrans, calcium depletion and muscle atrophy were ever-present health risks. Tharsis had spent a few hundred MSD on a good graviton sleep bag and found herself somewhere that wasn't full of Arrans.

Nighttrippers.

A hostel, tuned to serve the mélange of low-budget, grav-shot travelers who passed through New Stockholm every year. It was a worn-out place, the seals around the doors showing their age, battered furniture and old cookware in the common kitchen that could barely hold together under standard prep pressures. Nothing matched, everything from the rugs on the bare stone floors to the ceiling air compressors looked as if it had been raided from the local recycle shops. There was a pub in the basement and a decent library with an Arran wireless terminal on the first floor, and nobody cared about the military rank tattooed across her neck. It had been love at first sight.

Coming in that evening, the el-tee smiled a little at the sight of the cobalt-skinned Iapetan behind the front desk in the foyer. Feet were kicked up, a tablet in a long-fingered hand, the sticker on the back —*Fuck Planets, Go Mig*—glowing blue in the halogens of the foyer. tDaer had been working here for at least the last Heliosphere-standard year, according to some of the other long-term travelers. Whenever the graduate student wasn't cleaning toilets or working on research, she had her nose in a book.

Hen, Tharsis silently reminded herself. The Cronuans were touchy about gender—their Landlord had done away with it centuries before, at the first settlers' requests. tDaer had, after a sinful amount of alcohol on a synched-up Fiveday night, tried to explain it. "I know it's not Heliosphere Standard, but not using the right pronouns makes you Martians look like hicks."

Tharsis had never really thought about something like that before. It had been her first taste of just how varied the human cultures of the Heliosphere were. Tharsis didn't quite understand it but tried to be sensitive. Didn't make the two of them friends, but tDaer was nicer to Tharsis than hen was to just about any of the others passing through.

"Hey, Tharsis, you look dragged. What's up?"

About to reply, she noticed the projector over the counter. On mute, in deference to tDaer's tablet, legible Ibbie script in the ticker. International news. Explosions at a recycling plant on Ennomos, more Arran military assistance being readied for Venus as the Dena threatened to shut down the argon scoops again, a Nalatok terror cell rooted out on Hygiea.

"Fuckin' Toks," she grumbled.

"So much for your people's much vaunted freedom of religion," tDaer commented without looking up. "The Rossen has 'em executed, doesn't he?"

"Homicidal behavior is not religion," Tharsis shot back. "Mars executing Toks is about as remarkable as Ibbies sending tax-dodgers to the sucksuck."

tDaer's dark eyes, just a little too big for hen's face, edged over the top of the tablet. "Bad day with that bloated gas-harvester of a captain?"

"Nothing more booze won't fix," the lieutenant grumbled, and tried to put it out of mind. "What are you reading?"

"HS Zero-Five-Two-Six," came the answer. "A whole lot of nothing."

"I still don't believe that you've read five hundred years of the Journals."

"Sometimes I think the rest of the Heliosphere knows you Martians' history better than you do," tDaer replied, and tapped the tablet. "Didn't you have to read this in school?"

"A little bit, as kids," Tharsis evaded. She was not about to explain her planet's lack of formal schooling to the academic-obsessed Cronuan again. "The Rossen's obligated to publish it. We're not obligated to read it."

It wasn't quite a lie. Not even the Speaker of the House could order Mars's Landlord to do scat he didn't feel like doing. The Rossen's Journals were published, most people thought, not in accordance with any mandate, but guilt.

For the first seventy years or so of Tenancy rule, things had been fine. Not great, but not horrible. Two generations on Mars grew up without war, and the memories of the Euphemism faded with each trip the planet took around the sun.

Until, in hS0079, the Arcna's initial broadcast fucked that peace to hell.

Until, in hS0081, the Rallarhu tore the sky off Ceres, killing a million people and launching parallel invasions of every other city-state in the Inner Belt.

The first and final moments of the First Propagation.

The details of what happened in those two years were hazy. In hS0080, when it became clear the broadcast was not going to stop on its own, the Flet himself had launched a craft to the Kuiper. To investigate. To hold the Arcna to the Accords. To stop the killing.

Reports varied on who had actually gone along, but it was a confirmed fact that the Rossen had led the expedition. It was also confirmed that he'd shot himself in the senate, rather than report what he saw, or explain why he'd ordered a military stand-down while the Rallarhu tore the Inner Belt apart.

A small book had been found in his pocket. One word in the whole fucking thing.

Noqumiut.

The Arran people were incensed. They wanted answers. They wanted insight. His regenerated twenty-four-year-old self, coming out of the vat for only the third time and pissed as hell about it, had agreed. Since then, the Rossen had kept a very thorough accounting of his actions.

Outside of school, Tharsis had never felt the need to read the damn things.

"Why not? He's your Landlord. You should know what he's done."

"I didn't vote for him," she retorted. "The Tenancy's a fucking stupid system anyway."

"Voting's a stupid system. Never understood why you Martians chose yourselves a Landlord who kept that antiquated scat around."

The Rossen had been a goddamn national hero. Once. One of the Founders. The man who'd held the planet together through the stress of colonization and those early civil wars. Tharsis had always believed, privately, that maybe he'd done what he could to preserve what they'd been fighting for. "Who knows?"

"You wanna go out tonight? I'm off shift in an hour or so."

tDaer always asked. The same thing. Every one of Tharsis's Fiveday nights. But it probably meant either drugs or illicit booze or one of a dozen different other illegal entertainments sold openly in New Stockholm. It didn't matter which one. The consequences for Tharsis would all be equally bad.

Tharsis never went, but she never said no.

"Come on," tDaer challenged, smile hopeful. "It'd be fun to spend some time outside of this piss-chute of a place."

Tharsis hesitated. That wasn't interest. Was that interest? Nobody was interested in her. tDaer couldn't be interested in her. Hen was interested in reading and traveling and talking and studying. Working on a doctorate. There was nothing a girl from the back country of Mars had to offer someone like that.

"I'll think about it," Tharsis promised.

"And I think you'll enjoy it," tDaer said, the edges of hen's mouth quirking up just so, and went back to the tablet.

CHAPTER FOUR

THAT NIGHT, for the first time in her life, Tharsis dreamed.

Of a planet, an unspeakable menace hanging in the background radiation of the universe. Of its song, an ancient, decrepit hymn, diving into her mind, wrapping around neurons, vibrating across synaptic gaps. Of metal pressing against her skin, her own blood boiling into the void, her life slipping as that song tore at her, demanding a—

A bang tore her from its depth.

She woke to the confines of her grav bag, the close pressure of its humming gravitational circuits oppressive. Normally, the sensation took her back to the soundless nights of the *Centrifuge* cruise at the Academy, that three-hundred-day trip to the Koronis training grounds meant to separate those who could stand deep void service from those who could not. More serene, she'd always thought, then the constant pressure of the artificial gravity on the base.

Grav bags were said to aggravate penumbra sensitivities, but she'd never been prone to it. She'd never seen the things that moved in the spectral depths of the space-time gradient.

That morning, Tharsis almost tore the bag getting the seal open, panting into the cool air of her room.

The bang sounded again, continuing.

"Hey, El-Tee, come on! You alive in there?"

Sergeant Olin.

"Field trip, ma'am! Get that lazy officer self of yours out here!"

Scrubbing a hand across her face, Tharsis tried to remember where she'd left her uniform. She rolled her eyes over to the row of recessed cubbies that served as secure storage in the room. Empty. Fuck. Everything tended to drift into the vents if it wasn't secure. Last thing she needed was another uniform getting sucked into the atmo intakes.

"What's the occasion?" she shot back as she unzipped herself from the bag and let herself float out naked, grabbing the bag's anchor cable for support. Twisting around, she spotted her errant piece of clothing. Three meters up, up in the heat chimney. "It's not like it's the fucking weekend or anything."

"Would you just let me in, ma'am, and we can talk about it?"

She jumped; Mars-born muscle easily made the leap to the ceiling. Her hair was getting too long again, she noticed idly, the dark strands of it drifting around her bare shoulders. Tharsis could never bring herself to cut it all off, like Junia had. As stupid as it was, it felt like the only thing she had left that separated her from the guys.

"You're staying outside until I get my uniform on!"

Olin was quiet for a moment, and then knocked again. "Are you sure I can't come in?" His chuckle sounded through the door.

"Fuck you," she snapped, grabbing her clothing at the top of her jump, letting herself fall slowly down, regretting her stupidity in not securing it properly.

Tharsis could still hear him laughing as she landed. "It's really not funny!" she yelled back but got dressed as fast as she could. Knickers, breast-binders, thermal undershirt, thermal socks, grav-suit grays. The lieutenant headed over to the control panel and punched him in.

"How you doin', El-Tee?" he asked casually, strolling in, hands in his pockets.

"You see my boots anywhere?" she asked sharply enough to cut through his humor.

"They're over there," and he pointed to where they were caught in a corner of the recessed desk area. He glanced back out into the hallway. "Fuck, where'd Tommy go?"

"You brought the cat?" she asked, and snapped the seals on her boot shut, wincing a little as the circuits connected and the field switched on, simulating a change of mass relative to the 'roid's own artificial standard. It let her heart pump, muscles move, as if she were in Mars-standard gravity.

"Yeah, he's gettin' fat, not doing any work."

The ASDF went nowhere without its four-leggers, and the cislunar cat variants were especially vital. At least one of the twenty-kilo, thick-furred animals could be found on every base, outpost, and craft in the inventory. Dogs deployed with combat forces, but cats were essential to keeping penumbra entities off base. Pest control. Humphryes's tom was a moody little bastard, though. Olin wouldn't have been messing with him unless it was important.

"We really need him?"

"High radiation zone? Yeah, we need him."

"Radiation?" She thought for a second. "The Lighthouse? We're going down there?"

He just gave her that look all senior sergeants seemed to reserve for an especially stupid junior officer question. "The lab's still working on that tumor we pulled outta the wall, but they got me the RNA markers. It indicated it was part of the main communication taproot for the city. Those are shielded lines. It wasn't cross talk. Something was multiplexing across."

Multiplexing. Only one option for that. "Voice?"

"Most likely. I can source it better at the antenna forest."

The lieutenant was going to ask him something else about that, and then caught the chronograph again out of the corner of her eye, the date displayed at the bottom, and felt her stomach clench up. That day of the month again. Of all the things she'd thought she'd be happy about leaving behind when she'd joined up, the reality was quite different.

Sometimes, she wanted to go back and slap some sense into her twelve-year-old self.

"Come on, how bad can it be?" she asked brusquely, brushing past him back over to the cubbies, pulling out the small stainless case with its unpleasant inventory of small hormone patches. Three were already used, three left to take, and then she'd have to turn the whole thing into medical, get her blood tested, and pick up the next round. She removed the next in the series, her back to Olin.

"Tumors only express if there's something abnormal coming

through the system," Olin began, and then stopped. The lieutenant could feel his eyes on her and was glad she couldn't see his face. "Come on. We're burning daylight."

"Go get the cat," she shot back, and eased the patch under her zipper and onto her hip.

THE PLAGUES of the Euphemism had been originally bred for pleasure, bringing out vivid visions in the infected. Gene hackers tweaked the active compounds, found ways to facilitate the sharing of everything from memories to entire interactive environments; bridging, some stories said, the collective unconscious itself. It was only one of the period's biological horrors, and far from the worst, but it had been the most insidious. Induced nightmares, insanity, mass suicides.

The genetic vaccinations required to settle on Mars, delivered via high-velocity RNA, had worked perfectly; certain perceptions were dampened, lessening the drug's influence on the mind. For most voiders at the time, already significantly genetically altered as they were, the effects of that were almost unnoticeable. A slight decrease in right-brain function, barely enough to bother anyone, or so the doctors had thought at the time.

But it had destroyed something in the Arran mind. Except for extreme cases, or after years of strenuous training, spontaneous interaction with the subconscious was gone. Only one of the many genetic sacrifices humanity had made, but the most profound experienced on Mars.

By the time the scientific community figured it out, it was too late to reverse the process. Voider settlers had undergone genetic modification as well. The Scient had already destroyed Titan's stockpiles of Earth-bred fetuses, along with its genetic databases. The last of the exodus craft had departed almost sixty years before. Even the few indigenous Earth-tribes remaining had undergone compulsory inoculation through atmospheric release. There was no source of comparative genetic neural code. The loss was mourned. Humanity moved on.

After a generation or two, though, adaptations began presenting, the mind reaching out in other ways. Not in but out, into reality's energetic depths. Into the vibrational penumbra.

In the region where Tharsis had grown up, penumbra sensitivity was the norm. Sightings of the dead were so common that parish bylaws governed the interactions. But for some reason, even the most gifted of females saw little once they started the mig-mandatory sterilization hormone regimen, and Tharsis had never been particularly gifted to begin with.

The dream in the dark should have been impossible.

It felt like a violation.

"So what are we worried about?" Tharsis asked, locking her door. "Why the cat?"

"Umbran are everywhere," Olin said curtly. "Antenna forests are always active, lots of energy to feed on."

"Yeah, like what?"

"Let's just find him, ma'am."

Tommy, it turned out, had planted himself at the door to one of the second-floor rooms, and wouldn't be budged. He hissed as the lieutenant approached.

"Who's room is that?" the sergeant asked.

"tDaer's," Tharsis answered automatically, wondering what it was hen had wanted to show her. Could it really be that bad? "Hen's just some grad student who works here."

The cat growled again, and batted at the recessed latch, smacking the wood, open-pawed. His blue-gray ruff bulged up around the edges of the ENEX vest, his own little rapid-deployment void gear pack. His entire back prickled up in anger.

Olin made a disapproving little sound in the back of his throat and snapped his fingers at the cat. "Come on, boy, you can harass the nice voider later," he told him in that bored voice he used with the enlisted troops. "What is it with cats?"

With a grumpy meow, the cat dodged past them, bounding ahead in smooth, fluid movements. He was out the door before they were, and closed the five meters to a small, bubble-headed aerospace craft in one leap. Landing on the radiator manifold, tufted ears twitching, the animal's purr echoed out through the hull.

"How the hell did you get the rockjump?" Tharsis asked, her grumpiness at being woken so early fading at the sight of the small craft. Capable of both endo- and exo-atmospheric flight, the little chem-props were essential short-range military transport vehicles. Completely mechanical, with plasma fields instead of a wrapper for shielding, they represented the limits of what Arran engineering could achieve under the Accord restrictions. The military kept their manufacture to a minimum, to reduce the risk of one being captured and the alloys being analyzed by the never-ending list of Mars's enemies.

One didn't just check out the keys from the guard house.

"Same way I got Tommy here. Major Lanin approved it." Olin smirked. "How else are we supposed to get there?"

"Captain Hinden's going to take this out of your ass if you break it."

"I know how to fly a jump craft."

"You sure? Should I go get my ENEX?"

"I promise I won't kill us, ma'am."

The hostel's discreet island was quiet, before what passed for the sun rose into what passed for the sky. Before the day cycle began. Olin made the spaceport's internal air lock with five minutes to dawn, and they were outside in the black well in time to watch the programmed light spread across the skin of the artificial sky, glimmering in an oil slick of color.

False, of course. So, unlike the fey steppe dawns back home. Reds, pinks, and purple-yellows filtered through the planet's ever-dusty atmosphere. The sunrises here were gentle, almost artistic, like drawings out of a children's storybook.

"Is that what a sunrise on Earth would look like, you think?" Tharsis asked. The cat looked up from grooming himself, polydactyl thumb twitching a little. His mind murmured out a reply. She strained to pick it up, but the edge of that dream was still cutting through her thoughts.

Tommy mewled as he retreated from it.

The sergeant gave the cat a curious glance. "Well, they do say the Rallarhu still dreams of Earth, so it might be."

"Was she actually born there?"

"All the Landlords were born on Earth. One of the requirements," he said, grudgingly. "Need some connection to the rest of humanity, bio-fucked as they are. The further we drift, the less trustworthy we are. Like your little Cronuan buddy."

"tDaer's not that bad."

"Voiders can't be trusted, not as far as you can pitch 'em planet-side. Especially Cronuans. They tell you they don't, but they all believe in Noqumiut."

"I don't think hen's into that."

"Ma'am, no disrespect, but believe me, they love the idea of the Arcna's perfect little self-contained utopia. They might disdain the more mythic aspects, but they love her ideas." He snorted. "Think she's out there, building a better breed of transhuman, or not-human, or whatever."

She rolled her eyes. "Aren't we all not-human these days?"

"The genetic adjustments that occurred on Mars were largely adaptive. Third-generation settlers didn't even require vectored modifications to deal with the gravity differentials." He tapped at a dial that was blinking out, adjusted another set of controls. The craft bellied into a slow downward roll.

"Yeah?" Tharsis asked, brittle, that dream still unsettling her. She never dreamed. It had to mean something. "What about the inoculations?"

"Ma'am, with all respect, it's not the same thing," Olin said, voice hard. "Those plagues had to be stopped. It all had to be stopped."

"So why didn't the Rossen stop the Arcna when he had the chance?"

The sky was rippling into a daytime blue, glowing out of the utter black of the void.

"No accounting for their behavior, the Landlords."

The asteroid body twisted up, taking the sky with it. The false, thick-woven wrapper vanished beneath the 'roid's curving cap of ocean, the deep Ceres-sourced waters smeared across the perfect sphere of its induced gravity field, held together by surface tension and wrapper and the Rallarhu's influence. The passengers in the rock-jump had one last glimpse of shimmering dawn, before the beauty gave way to the vast expanse of automated, Arran-contracted industrial wastelands of the underside.

"How long's the flight?"

"Two hours, give or take."

Olin switched on a deep-cast from Mars about the last National League rugby matchups, and they didn't talk for the rest of the trip.

THE LIGHTHOUSES WERE OLD. Older than the base. Older than New Stockholm. Older than anything else in the Inner Belt habitats. Representative of the apex of Euphemism biotechnology, nothing like them had been built in nearly eight hundred years, and nothing like them would be built again. The knowledge of their construction had died in the Scient's purges.

The boles were all different heights, some of them a kilometer or more in height, all rooted deep into the spongy rock. Grown of organic material interwoven into strong, flexible nanotube skeletons, some opened into bloomed focusing dishes, others branched out into multi-fingered receivers. They swayed in the lee-side darkness, permanently anchored in the 'roid's shadow, the radio nets reaching out to the farthest edge of the heliopause.

The stalks couldn't survive in completely airless environments, and the old engineers had accounted for this. The top edges needed the void to ensure transmission quality, but the thick boles needed the carbon exchange to keep the organic matter alive. Extensive root systems extracted carbon and other necessary minerals from the rock around it, boles exhaled waste oxygen into the surrounding environment. Single-celled exophiles contained in bark and soil translated oxygen and other waste back into carbon dioxide. Naturally generated magnetic fields created a downward static barrier, enough to hold the resultant atmo in, pressurizing it to survivable levels. The system was entirely self-sufficient.

The only variable that had to be painstakingly accounted for was energy; beyond Mars's orbit, solar radiation levels were too unpredictable to be relied on. Conventional fusion reactors were used in larger forests, providing warmth to the biologics, electrical power to the equipment, radiation to the synthetic bark layers. But those had to be refueled often. What powered the forests further out, in the Arcna's Kuiper Shoals, nobody remembered. Whatever secrets the Arcna was hiding in her own worlds, she hadn't deigned to share.

Sergeant Olin kept their little craft well clear of the radiation in the canopy, maneuvering through a shielded tunnel to a flat landing pad, set up on what seemed to be a canyon lip, overlooking the forest. A rough tin building lay just inside the translucent retaining wall. Small though it seemed, Tharsis knew it would house a tunnel leading deep underground to the power room and operation controls.

As he landed, Tommy pushed between them, staring straight out the front cockpit glass, ears flattening.

"You see something, boy?" Olin asked.

The cat made a chattering little whine and butted his head against the glass. Whined again, angrier this time, and pawed at the glass. Olin ran a hand through his thick fur, making a little shushing noise in response, but the cat just growled at him, flattening his ears down even further. When Olin popped the lock on the cockpit door, the cat slipped like quicksilver from the craft, the fur rising along his spine.

Tharsis watched him, nervous. "You think there's something out there?"

"Maybe, maybe not. We'll let him run around while we're working, let him scout out the place, bring us back anything significant."

The cat, as if waiting for this, bobbed his head forward, taking in the expanse of forest, and began prowling around the edges. A low warning growl rumbled out of him, menacing, chilling. Tharsis found herself falling into another place where the air was almost too thin to breathe, colder than death, another cat, another threat, a—

"You ready to head in, ma'am?" Olin asked, jingling the rockjump's keys in the direction of that little outbuilding. "Or you want to wait, see what Tommy flushes out?"

Something moved in her peripheral vision, and the lieutenant jerked her head around to the sight of a figure disappearing into a thicket of ASDF-installed tactical fleet repeaters.

Huh.

"Can you handle it without me?"

"No problem, ma'am," the sergeant said. "Keep your gravity on. The atmo peters out about five meters up and the static field won't hold you in."

"Roger that."

The cat's eyes were luminous under the eerie bio-blue half-light that reigned above the swaying antennas. Blinking once, he swung his head back around as something moved in behind again, growled, and bounded off into the dark between the pale boles.

For no good reason at all, she followed.

The cat was fast, weaving through the stalks of the close-range antennas with insane fluidity, body bunching and springing, throwing himself from ground to stalk to platform to stalk again, paws scrambling on organic metal surfaces, dust clouds rising, hanging.

Tharsis found herself trailing at an ever-increasing distance. She caught only flashes of color, the flow of clothing or hair, the dark shapes of whatever it was that the cat was after. She heard laughter from that figure and screeching rage from the cat, and of the two, the animal's voice carried more humanity in it.

After a breakneck minute or so of chasing both cat and quarry, the gray dust so thick now she could barely see, the lieutenant almost tripped on something soft and yielding. And there the cat was, underfoot, crouched, tensed for a strike, too focused on what was in front of him to even growl his disapproval at the slight.

Two figures. In the middle of an open space between antenna stalks. Illuminated only by the soft glow of the electromagnetic energy within the boles. One on its back, the other crouching over the first, digging a hand through its chest. Bones jutted out all wrong, violently elongated by mig and hunger, blurry, discolored, inhuman.

And the top figure yanked hard, and the other's belly ripped apart like rotten fruit, gore scattering like smoke. The top figure howled its triumph to the stars.

Unbidden, a snippet of prayer, one that everyone learned in basic, that hung in Humphryes's guardhouse, forced its way into her mind.

... be with me in battle, the strength in my blade, the integrity of my gear...

Tommy screeched, enraged, and pounced into now-empty space, stamping around furiously, practically biting his tail in an effort to get at whatever had been there.

Finally satisfied the thing was gone, the cat padded up to her. Purring, pleased with himself. "Good boy," she obliged, rubbing his neck. "Guess that's nothing I need to be afraid of, is it?"

His gold eyes, dilated to near black in the weak gloom of the forest, considered her for a moment. Then he bumped her with his head and padded off towards the rockjump.

Tharsis, after a moment, followed.

She mulled it over on the walk back. Umbran could be unconscious entities, or mere impressions of the past, things pressed and preserved in EM fields, in the background radiation of the void. But that had felt real, somehow. Real in a way she hadn't expected.

Olin was waiting for her in the rockjump, a frown on his face, Tommy curled up at his feet. But if the cat had told him anything, Olin didn't say.

"There's some kind of signal coming in on the long-range antennas. I couldn't make anything out, though. Encrypted, probably," Olin told her, as he started the craft back up. His voice was gentle. "You okay, ma'am?"

Her stomach churned, denial ringing louder than common sense in her mind. "Nothing that we need to worry about."

Olin didn't press it.

"UNIFORM? You had to go into fucking work today?" she heard as she slipped back inside Nighttrippers' splintered door that afternoon. "It's still your weekend, right?"

tDaer. At the counter. Reading.

As always.

"You wanna go out?"

As always.

And for some reason that she would never later understand, Tharsis nodded back. "Why the fuck not?"

CHAPTER
FIVE

"WHERE DID you say we were going?"

"What difference does it make? Trust me, it'll be great."

Tharsis looked up and around at the area they were headed into. Shoal Bar, the weird Trans-Jovian enclave near the edge of the hostel district.

Life was different past Jupiter's orbit, and it showed. Most people spent their entire lives in mig, their physiologies adjusting accordingly. Even the weak .2 Earth-standard gravity of 4Vesta could be a pain for them, and seal skins—specially fitted expansion garments—poked out from beneath sleeves and above collars. Their architecture was equally adapted to microgravity, more a series of tunnels and nodes than proper straight-sided structures. Passing into it, Tharsis was reminded of plaster molds of anthills she and her brother used to make for their schooling co-opt science lessons.

Shoal Bar had a reputation for being rough. It also had the highest concentration of off-limits establishments in the city. The mech brothels, however, were still a favorite of the younger enlisted guys who couldn't land Vestan girlfriends and didn't care about a disciplinary mark or two. The lieutenant had heard many a story about the apparatuses there, but she'd never tried it herself; sex was an obnoxious reminder of everything she'd probably never have.

They passed a crowd of Ibbie girls, giggling their way out of an oxygen bar, and tDaer pulled up, letting them pass into the tight curve of the street.

"How do you think the Ibbies tell each other apart?" Tharsis asked, watching them. "They all look exactly the same."

"They go for that. They head down to one of the gamete exchanges, run a comparison estimate through a quant, pick what they want, dump it in the home-womb. Whatever's in style this year, you know? Shake and bake baby," tDaer said contemptuously. "Even then, there are mistakes that get flushed. Nose too big, wrong digit ratio on the hands, vestigial tail."

"Tails?" the lieutenant asked, catching up, her brain stuck on *flushing*.

"Yeah, tails. Heard that was actually a popular thing a few generations ago. Why?"

Tharsis had never heard such a question asked and had no idea how to answer it. The mere thought of hurting a child made her ill. "Infanticide's a capital offense on Mars."

tDaer snorted. "And yet your people use women for breeding. Like animals. Where's the sense in that?"

That conversation, Tharsis had actually had with Mama about a year before her brother disqualified himself from service. One of those days when she'd been put in charge of watching an infant cousin, a burping little bundle of flesh. The day had ended with her in tears, blubbering in her mother's arms about how she never wanted to get married or have kids or anything.

In the years since, her thoughts on the matter had changed somewhat.

What had she known at eleven, anyway?

"It's what we're built by nature to do," Tharsis said lamely, and rubbed the patch on her hip.

"Scat on that," tDaer replied. "Saturn got it right under the Scient, clean and predictable, you know? No squirming little parasites being accidentally forced on anyone."

"Babies aren't parasites." Tharsis paused. "You know I can't get pregnant, right?"

"Yeah, lucky you."

"Lucky," Tharsis began angrily, and stopped herself. "It kind of

screws up your ability to find a man, when they all think you're sterile." While the hormone regimen was reversible, it wasn't unheard of
for former Arran military females to continue having problems after
the service. And that was without the problems that often came with
service out in the void. A lot of guys wouldn't take that chance.

"Well, maybe you should consider yourself fortunate. Lets you live
your life for yourself, instead of being exploited for some throwback
organs humanity doesn't even need anymore."

"That's not—"

"Fair? Come on, Tharsis, it's exploitative. Like this place, these poor
bastards, interchangeable pawns in the Rallarhu's bid to maintain a
stupidly large population."

"They can't all be interchangeable," Tharsis mused. "They must
have different dreams, different lives."

tDaer shrugged, then paused at a six-way spherical interchange to
examine the signpost in the center. "What difference does it make? The
Rallarhu wouldn't care, they don't mean anything to her. Built to serve
her purposes, not their own. Just like you, all wrapped up in your little
ASDF uniform, like a pawn on a chessboard."

Those words cut. "My family would care if I died."

"And you hate your family," the Iapetan pointed out. "Stupid thing
in the first place. You hate them, but you're stuck with them."

They came to a stop in front of a roughly circular door, set in the
middle with a palm lock. tDaer stuck hen's hand in it, the edges
sucking up a bit around, surface tension clinging. Psychoreactive silk.

"Look, I get that you don't have any choice in the way your Landlord's patterned your inwell," tDaer continued breezily, "and it's
supposed to be our decision as to what we do with ourselves. That's
our right as people, you know? That's what the fucking Tenancy is
for."

Tharsis thought about her family. Dad. Who'd probably slap her for
this.

The door creaked open, revealing a long, dark passage, curving,
falling into nowhere.

tDaer passed inside, and Tharsis, with only a moment's hesitation,
followed.

•   •   •

THE TUNNEL WAS as black as the quartz mines in Albas Mons, illuminated by nothing but a faint bioluminescence expressing in the darkness. The going was dim, but the walls were smooth, at least, springy to the touch, widening as they walked, the gravity dropping. A smattering of lights coalesced outside the tunnel surface.

"Boundary sea," the Iapetan said, pointing up at the translucent, hydrophobic weave, holding back nighttime waters and its eerie lights. "And its animals."

Although the sea, normally pushed back by the gravity differential, sometimes broke in wrapper-slicked waves along Humphryes's edge, the lieutenant had never seen it from below. She tapped the interior surface of the tunnel, lights rippling as tiny sea organisms scattered.

"Lovely."

"Dirty. Don't know why the Rallarhu brought them here."

"She did that?" Tharsis asked curiously, then floundered as mig reasserted.

"I mean, seriously, why?"

"Living oceans help regulate atmosphere. It's what keeps Mars alive."

"We don't use animals to regulate the environments out in the Cronuan moons. Flora works fine."

"No animals at all?" Tharsis thought about the ranch, the dogs asleep under her sisters' cribs and the cats playing in the hayloft and the hawks wheeling high over the flocks, looking for small, unwary things. "Wouldn't fly on Mars," she commented.

"Yeah, why is that?"

"You ever read *Wardog of Mars*? Everyone reads it in Sevenday School. It's about—"

"Thought you said your people don't have schools, that education's done at home by your families?"

"We have lessons after Mass."

And that got her an actual stare. "They don't bother to give you any kind of real schooling, but they'll make you sit there and soak in a bunch of spider scat about that religious whatever?"

"*Wardog of Mars* isn't a religious text, tDaer. It's more like Tyr's Journal."

"The fact that Martians anthropomorphized a fucking dog is insane."

"Sure, he's a dog," Tharsis said, not sure what nerve she'd touched off in her companion. "But dogs are important. That's what I'm trying to say."

"Again, I return to my first point."

The tunnel breached the thin edge of the sea, and they were pushing into what felt like a huge, empty space. It was dark, lit only by a few emergency lights blinkering off and on in a random pattern around them, and some strange white glow from below. The diffused light filled the space. Fifty meters from side to side, bowled out below and static-shielded above, the curve of the walls supporting thick bundles of lines that had to be for power, water, air exchange, chemical propellants.

"This is a port," Tharsis said, realizing.

"Yup, it's a hollowed-out island. The sky's stapled to the inner edge. Spits us right out of the atmo into the void. It was probably somebody's private cessna tie-up at some point, maybe. Mine now." tDaer pushed away from the way, gliding towards the illumination in the center. "This is what I brought you here to see."

Moored against the evernight of the void, bobbing like a sleeping cetacean, an object glowed, both too bright and too dark to properly look at. It obscured a perfect circular section of open void twenty meters in diameter. The Milky Way reflected off it in the negative, dark pinpricks where stars should have been.

Curious, Tharsis kicked off towards it.

Coming closer, she could see the outer surface was spiderwebbed with thin lines, gaps between perfectly fitted plates that arched in and out of one another, overlapping and subsiding with hairsbreadth effi- ciency. It looked remarkably similar to that sphere of Earth-mined white calcite her mother had, one of the family's most prized posses- sions, mottled and shifting, a cloud caught and frozen in stone.

It looked like a thing that respected no law of physics, that dwelt in its own reality, unmoored in time, an ancient thing from a far distant future.

Which in a way, Tharsis supposed, it was.

The last masterpiece of the Euphemism. The only human-based

biotech allowed to exist.

"God in Heaven," Tharsis whispered, still in shock, one of her hands reaching out for the surface of the craft of its own accord, stopping just short. "Where in the hell did you get a divedrive?"

tDaer laughed. "You can touch it. It's not going to bite."

Tharsis shook her head. She couldn't. Not something like this. Fully encapsulated divedrives were rare—and dangerous—and fodder for the worst of Mars's ghost stories. "Not worth the risk," she said lamely, against the Iapetan's disapproving glare, and used the little thruster in her boots to scoot out of range.

"These things are bespoke, fully tested and shielded, don't be an idiot!" tDaer teased, pushing up around the curve of the ship, up to the portion facing the void above. "Come on, Ang's not going to wait forever, and hen is a twitchy thing, let me tell you."

"Ang?" Tharsis called back, as she followed around the precipitous falling edge of the craft. "Who's Ang?"

She had her answer soon enough, however, when she pushed down through the open hatch, sections of hull broken eggshell subliming into each other, leading down into the interior of the craft.

"Who's this?"

"I told you I was bringing a friend today."

"You didn't tell me you were bringing a Martian."

"Tharsis is good people, Ang. Shut up and behave yourself."

Inside the craft, there was nothing. No divisions, no compartments, no visible control surfaces. Nothing but a dull white, spherical room, about four meters less in diameter than the exterior, utterly bare; there were no discernible control surfaces or discreet components visible. There were no indicators as to what was up, down, or anything at all from the craft itself. There was no gravity, but the curve of the wall tugged with light static force.

tDaer and another voider were sitting cross-legged on the comparative bottom. Waiting.

No good, Tharsis knew, pausing at the sight, could come of anything involving voiders and divedrives and midnight liaisons.

She still shoved in.

The Iapetan smiled at her as Tharsis eased herself into the sticky pressure of the curve, and nodded at the other voider, a young Jovian man with the jaundiced skin of that inwell, its rounded features and slitted eyes.

"Angakkuq," tDaer said by way of introduction, gesturing with a long hand at the Arran, "this is Tharsis. Like that's her travel name, and she's cool, so let's not fuck it up by getting hung up on those tattoos, okay? That okay with you, Tharsis?"

"Travel name?" The lieutenant found herself relaxing a little, despite that Jovian's gaze. "No, it's just, umm, not exactly a mark of distinction to be from the Tharsan Bulge. Got it hung on me at the Academy."

"What's wrong with the Tharsan Bulge?" Angakkuq asked, cocking his head. Jerky, animalistic movements.

"It's seen as a backwater. Not very populated," she replied, telling her nerves to take a hike. "Life's tougher in the highlands than almost anywhere else on the planet."

"Sounds like us," Angakkuq replied with a smile. "We're supposed to be fanatics. But me," and he spread his hands out wide, "I like the whole Heliosphere too much to worry about being attached to one little rock trapped by the mass of Father Jupiter."

"The whole Heliosphere?"

"And everything above and below it, outside of this shock wave of reality we're riding to oblivion," he replied, and smiled.

"So, Tharsis, I'm pretty sure we're going to break your seal tonight?" tDaer said.

"What?" she shot back, cringing a little at the crude euphemism. "Look, if you want to get freaky, I'm really not in the fucking mood, so—"

Ang perked up a bit, but the Iapetan just grinned wider. "Trust me, what we're doing tonight is way better than sex."

"And what is that?"

"Oobing," tDaer announced, and pressed hen's hand against the floor. The door behind them slid shut as a column extruded up, and there was a slight feeling of dropping, cutting loose from the static moorings.

Undocking from the static fields.

Too late to go back now.

Tharsis ground her heels into the hull. Bracing.

CHAPTER
SIX

HURTLING out to dive distance on conventional fusion-prop, Tharsis found herself drifting near panic. Tried to focus on anything else. The magnetized argon swirled through the orbits of fully deployed stabilization panels. How 4Vesta was falling away, visible only through a transparent window, tapped out of the hull.

Oobing.

It wasn't for no reason that the ASDF, not to mention Arran law, was vehemently against the practice of oobing. Dives were risky under normal operating conditions. Oobs were downright dangerous.

Hinden would court-martial her if he found out. Gleefully.

The Jovian named Angakkuq was rattling a small bag in his hand. "Calm down, Martian. I'm not gonna eat you or anything. Unless you want me to."

tDaer nudged him with a foot. Hen's arm was buried to the elbow in that punched-up control column. "Don't be a dog, Ang."

He tossed the bag up and caught it out of the air. Stones, had to be stones in there, judging from the sound. "Ah, that's right. That famous Martian repression. Is it really true your people are only allowed to fuck one person in their entire lives?"

"I think they call it marriage," tDaer threw back.

Tharsis sighed. "Why are voiders so interested in my planet's tics?"

"Cause you people are anachronistic throwbacks."

"We're what?"

"Not you, Tharsis." tDaer rolled hen's eyes. "You're a cool Martian."

"Umm, thanks?"

tDaer caught the Jovian's bag as he tossed it up again, yanking it away. "So, Ang, what do you have for us tonight? Something better than last time? I keep have nightmares about that color in lower clouds."

"No, no, no more trips to Venus. I was thinking Mercury tonight," he said expansively. He tugged the drawstring on his bag open and a few small grayish stones escaped into the space between them all, glinting with light bursting off tDaer's skin. "I got these off a dealer a couple weeks back. Late Bombardment Period, from the impact sites."

tDaer grinned. "Confirmed?"

"Two independent readings. Pure volcanic Apollion glass." He turned the stones over in his hand, letting them slide against his palm before letting them drift again. "Ought to show us something good."

Curiosity overcoming her initial concern, Tharsis reached out for one of those little rocks. "Can I?" she asked, and Ang flicked one over to her with a smile. Small and unremarkable, that pebble. "Why Mercury?"

"Mercury was once a prosperous mining and solar research colony," Ang said, "but in hS0124, the caravans of Mars, mandated and blessed by the Tenancy under the Accords, suffered a three-week engine breakdown and missed the gravshot pathway out there. The decay of fuel was far slower than that of their meagre food supplies, and by the time relief arrived, it was far too late. The colony's people had gone adlet, and they were lost. Their Landlord lives out there still, driven insane but unable to die, slumbering amidst the penumbra ghosts of his people.

"The story goes that the Naven, Landlord of Earth, visits once a standard year. She brings us back pieces of that long-dead world, in accordance with its Landlord's demands, to remind us of what was once there, so his people don't die," the Jovian continued, and then flicked at the stones, sending them spinning in all directions, up to hover above them in the unrelieved sphere in which they were all sat.

"No, I know that," Tharsis said, "I mean, why Mercury? How's this... work?"

"Well, what have you heard?"

"Probably the scat about the monks at the monasteries being required to skin-dive out to Pluto from Phobos in order to be accepted into the Golanites," tDaer snorted.

"You've got the University, we've got the Vatican," Tharsis shot back.

"But which one of those places isn't filled with crazy people?"

Angakkuq pursed his lips. "Come on, tDaer, can't there be room in this Heliosphere for more than your inwell's mindless worship of its Landlord?"

"What? We fucking hate our Landlord. But at least we don't worship the energy headwaters, like the Martians do, and we sure as fuck don't venerate the piijuit of Europa as martyrs for the cause," hen said, eyebrow raised, casting over to Tharsis for support.

Ang frowned. "But the Arcna—"

"The Arcna knows better than to be fucking around with that scat. It's why she led the expedition to create Noqumiut. Right, Tharsis?"

The lieutenant ignored it, looked back to Ang instead. "Umm, as to your question, the usual, I guess. If you think of the universe the way the Flet described it to Father Golan, not as a flat surface, but a very deep ocean—"

"Again, not scientific—"

"Yeah, tDaer, I get that, but it's an operating idea, right? Doesn't the Scient even agree that a certain amount of that's necessary? Glimpsing it in totality literally melted the Flet's body," Tharsis replied, testy. She might have learned her letters on the cleaver-scarred expanse of a ranch kitchen table, but it didn't make her an idiot. When tDaer didn't argue, she continued.

"Divedrives operate by pushing us down into those depths. Since energy is conserved, it can't actually stay down there. So, the craft is thrown back to the surface. It's similar to submerging an air-filled capsule in water. But because the universe doesn't exactly care where energy is, just that it is, the craft doesn't have to surface at the same spatial coordinates. The wetware subsentience can direct the craft to any discreet set of physical coordinates, given some kind of reference point. That can be achieved by a sample of stable atomic mass once present at that point, preferably for a few hundred years or longer.

And it's got to be a significant distance from any other large masses, like 4Vesta. Essentially, it conducts near-instantaneous matter transference to any point it has material for."

"A little too dry for my taste, but yeah, that's the basic idea," Angakkuq replied, expansive. "The Flet teaches us that there are no parallel realities, no flat sheet of space, as classic physics had once proposed. Instead, he has seen that there is but one continuous ocean, flowing from the moment of the Bang to the end of time. It's never-ending, surging down to where creation breaks against the nothingness of before and after, where even the smallest of quarks tears apart. The vastness of the supermassive black holes in the center of our galaxy siphons the crashing energy away, sending it back to the high dimensions to be purified and released into the flow once again. Every atom in our bodies is tagged to its proper order in that flow, and it matters not where we dance within it, only that we stay in step." He smiled. "It's a beautiful thing."

Tharsis had never heard it put quite that way. Arrans tended to be clinical about the entire thing.

"When we oob," Angakkuq continues, "we stay in the shallows, the chaotic region at the edge of the bow shock. Physical reality becomes translucent. You can see the energy of X-rays; you can hear the sounds of the planets crying out in their orbits. It's amazing."

"So the rocks from Mercury are navigation material?"

"They will guide us to when, and where, we will go. The Flet's spirit in the craft meditates on their crystalline structures, heads to where they whisper..."

"Seriously, enough," tDaer interjected, moving back down to the circle, stones in hand, and gave Tharsis a sympathetic look. "Those rocks, right? We see a three-dimensional point, discreet. But that's not what anything actually is. Space-time is a volume, and worldlines are the paths that matter carves through it. The craft can trace those worldlines back to whatever moment specified by the navigation processors. In this case, the eruptions of the Late Bombardment period."

"Ah," she said, catching on. "Same operating concept as the Vastitas Mission."

Recovering the ancient oceans had been the only thing that made Mars inhabitable. Water was essential for terraforming, and there hadn't been nearly enough locked in the crust. Moving Ceres would have been impossible, and asteroid bombardment nearly as difficult. Instead, the terraformers utilized dive technology to trace trillions of trillions of solar particles out into the Kuiper and beyond, find where they interacted with the correct type of water, and grab those molecules' contemporary position. That far out, time ran different; exact coordination had been essential.

"Exactly, but without the mass transfer. We can't surface," Angakkuq answered. "The energy requirements of temporal transfers are prohibitive."

"Flet didn't melt for no reason, after all," the Iapetan nodded back and laughed.

Quantum computing could model worldlines, but it couldn't track a particle's discreet movements, not even for the fractions of seconds required. Too, subatomic particles had a habit of transferring between energy levels, vibrating out of the bow shock, splashing up, crashing down into the chaotic regions. The behavior of matter was too complex for even a quant to account for all the variables, especially at scale.

The human mind, however, worked on a different set of parameters, parameters that weren't governed—or limited—by mathematics. A rock, to the human intuitive processing of the divedrive, could look the same, even if it were no longer comprised of the same quarks it had contained billions of years ago .

The Flet, back when he was still human, had volunteered his services to the terraforming initiative for the capture. Afterwards, he'd given permission for the development and integration of his nervous system into things like dive cores. Kept it all legal, under the Accords.

At least, that was the story.

Even Mars still utilized divedrive tech.

Tharsis wondered suddenly how in the hell a graduate student from Iapetus could afford a craft like this, rare as it was.

But before she could ask, something in the ship chimed, lighting up in a pattern on the part of the wall that curved up above them.

"Dive distance," tDaer announced, the white nanofibers flowing around hen's cobalt skin like loose clay in a riverbed after a hard rain. "Hand them over, Ang. Go time."

CHAPTER
SEVEN

IT STARTED IN DARKNESS, in iron. In a matrix of young stone, barely formed, not cooled, still on fire with the friction of accretion. It was everywhere—around and beyond and within.

The beginning of the planets clattering through her bones.

Nothing solid. There was nothing to touch or feel or smell or taste. All sense, all sense, all an impression on the inside of her mind. Nothing else. No one else. Just her, and the planet, and the sound of the magnetics working their way through the core, through the outer layers of thin crust remaining from the sheering force of those earlier collisions that still sang through the stone out to the surface.

Above her, the sun burned. Not yellow, not white, no color at all. Beyond color, she saw, her brain taking in the information of what it was across the entire spectrum of radiation it output. On—in—her skin, her blood, her bones. The light was consuming her, burning everything she was away, leaving nothing but ash. It loomed over the horizon, a hemisphere of utter destruction, and Tharsis breathed out, hot in X-ray.

The planet around her lay cold, a dead thing that somehow knew it was dead. The rocks beneath her feet sighed in their slow cremation. Figures gathered on the horizon, a ring of them, holding what should have been hands, where no hands would ever be, watching her.

Umbran.

This was their reality she was standing in now. In the penumbra. Their energy level. Their reality. Them.

They all looked up, turning eyes that weren't eyes and never would be to the sky that wasn't really a sky and never would be.

The planet around her screamed to an indifferent sun.

Asteroids. Or not asteroids, she thought, giddy from the magnetics rumbling her muscles like the strongest drink she ever had. Asteroids were a human construct, a human word, and these were before humanity. She was before humanity now, watching a world that had died long before the hand of God pushed one bacteria inside another to create ribosomes. This was the world before history.

Beneath her not-present feet, Mercury shook.

A victim of its own mass, its own gravity pulled in its attackers—slow, terribly slow.

One by one, rocks struck.

World breaking, exploding, matter turned to energy, energy turned to heat, heat turned to light, and the umbran creatures rode the brilliant bursts of color into the cold of the void.

It stretched, twisting out until covalent bonds burst into light that no longer could burn.

Then everything faded away again, final bursts of color from those ancient explosions before all went silent.

And Tharsis saw the edge of a darkness, a vast endlessness, utterly empty, a place where no things could live. Yet there was still something moving in it, moving in that unreality, moving, moving, moving closer...

But before those things could reach her, there was a ringing in her ears, and the taste of blood in her mouth, and the sound of a shrieking, inhuman laugh, braying as the craft around her tore apart, dissolving into an explosion that ripped through the absolute cold like the claws of a feral cat.

The lieutenant fell, and a long-dead world rushed up to devour her.

COMING TO WITH A HARSH GASP, Tharsis found herself in a dark space on a strangely soft surface, the carbon fiber rippled beneath her. Instead of the flame of the young sun, the space was now lit only by a soothing glow from the skin of the craft. Her Iapetan friend was floating weightless in the center of the divedrive's belly, stylus working across hen's tablet.

"Is it always like that?" Tharsis asked, nerves rattled, body unsettled.

Huge black eyes blinked over the edge of the device. "Sometimes," hen said. "Sometimes worse. Sometimes better. Always good. Like I said, better than sex. Or drugs."

"Never tried drugs," Tharsis replied with a yawn.

The Iapetan smiled and went back to writing. "We'll be back in port in about an hour. If you want to sleep until then, I'll wake you up when we're pulling in."

"I don't think I could. It's just..." She spread her hands, then dropped them. "Fuck."

"That's how I felt about my first trip out there," tDaer said, and reached down, patted the hull. Sunk into it. Tharsis cocked her head. "If you need it, touch the skin, then think a cmmand," hen explained. "The chemoelectrical sensors in the silk pick up neural impulses."

"Oh," Tharsis said, wondering, and found herself sinking into the surface tension. "Right. Euphemism tech."

"We lost some good things," tDaer said, and lapsed back into silence.

Angakkuq came out of his full lotus as they were docking. Didn't speak as tDaer opened the hatch. But his jaundiced yellow eyes turned to Tharsis as tDaer nudged her to her feet. Hen nodded without speaking, as if acknowledging some kind of binding secret between them.

tDaer and Tharsis headed back to the hostel back through Shoal Bar, moving slower, the lieutenant's legs still unsteady.

She had no idea how long they'd been gone, but as long as she wasn't missing work, she figured, what the hell difference did it make? She could count on one hand the number of things she'd done with other people in the year she'd been here that wasn't mandatory squadron fun. It was nice to have something, some experience, that was purely her own.

They stopped off at the Wardog for a bite to eat, despite Tharsis's misgivings about it. There was absolutely no mistake about who she was with—even if hen's skin wasn't enough of a giveaway, the way tDaer struggled with the place's higher gravity would have been. There wasn't a lot of love lost between Saturn and Mars.

"You sure I can't get you a beer?" tDaer asked, eyes to the board behind the bar. "They've got some good Nepo-sponsored microbrews. Fucking rich kids with way more money than sense, but you can't complain about the results."

Tharsis ordered a yam cider instead and shot a nasty glare over at a couple of young, enlisted soldiers from her cabling shop. Fuckers were staring. She didn't like how it felt. "Better not," she said.

"Baby steps." The Iapetan shrugged and dropped the subject.

**CHAPTER
EIGHT**

TWO SEVENDAYS after Major Lanin's departure, Humphryes was almost unrecognizable.

Oneday had become nothing but briefings. Planning for briefings, presenting briefings, sitting through everyone else's briefings, trying to translate Captain Hinden's meandering thoughts into yet more deliverables, for yet more briefings. Briefings where he would yawn, or ask far too many questions. Offer solutions to problems that didn't exist, and issue bad advice on the problems that did.

Most of the enlisted guys already seemed primed to blow. But they knew—as did Hinden, Tharsis was convinced—that the second they said anything, off to the tattoo chair they would go. Redding up a service mark, the visible sign of a loss of a rank, was accompanied by a drop in pay, or a dishonorable discharge in severe cases. Most Arran families depended on military pensions, the one reliable source of income on a planet with unpredictable weather and three-hundred-day winters. Nobody was going to risk their family's livelihood, so they had to sit there and take Hinden's scat.

With Mars's compulsory service requirements, bad officers were inevitable. Every Arran male was required to serve five years in the military upon reaching sixteen HST, eight Arran, years of age. For families that didn't have an able-bodied son, a daughter had to serve. Pulling from a planetary population of forty million, not everybody was going to be stellar. Hell, most people struggled to be average. But that didn't make it less of a disappointment that Hinden wasn't even bothering to be decent.

"The problem with that man," Sergeant Olin had told her that first Oneday morning after Lanin's departure, "isn't that he's a power-hungry bastard who knows it. He's a power-hungry bastard who believes he's a good officer. That's probably why they've got him out here. Less damage done, place like this."

Tharsis, remembering Major Lanin's comment, had joked that they should send the Rossen a request to review the situation.

"You'd be amazed at how much District of Lunae doesn't let the Landlord do," he'd replied. "The generals don't take kindly to being ordered around by an enlisted man."

"Don't they have to take his orders?"

"Sure, but what's he gonna do if they don't? Kill them all?"

"He could, right?"

"So what, he should? Come on, Tharsis. Most people aren't okay with random murder like that."

"None of the Landlords are human."

"Sure, I'd agree that most of them don't qualify anymore. But ours, he starts over," Olin had replied, slow. "Most of the others have lived every year of the past millennium. The human brain, the human soul, wasn't designed for that kind of load. It's probably the reason why they're all so insane." And he looked at her. "You sure you're doing okay, ma'am?"

Tharsis hadn't known how to answer.

At the time, she'd been stumbling through her day on autopilot, mind still out in the oob. The real world, the solid, immutable, boring world, felt too small. Like boots that didn't fit. She kept wondering what the walls or water or the fries on her plate would look like in an oob skip, how different the molecules might be, how strange the colors bursting through her body would look, if she would be able to feel the energy of the sunlamps drenching her in deep white heat.

She was in deep, deep scat if the ASDF ever found out about it.

Tharsis found herself resenting Humphreys all the more for it.

"Every trip is different," tDaer had told her, over cider in the hostel's media room, after they'd gotten back. "It settles down after a few times doing it. Then you can focus on other things."

"Like what?"

"Umbran, maybe?" tDaer asked, careful. "You see any of them?"

Tharsis thought of those formless gray faces turned to the heavens. "I thought voiders thought the whole thing was ridiculous."

"I'm just curious about it. Like, what are they? I seem to get a different answer from every Martian I ask."

Unsure if this was another dig tDaer was taking at her planet or not, Tharsis answered slowly. "Nobody's really sure. Some people think it's spiritual in nature, like ghosts or something, even though the Church is pretty clear that's not the case. Other people think it might be actual intelligent entities. Some people think it's human brain waves impressing onto them energy from beyond the electromagnetic spectrum, you know, the penumbra of space-time. That ocean Ang was talking about. I tend to agree with the idea that it's a perception thing."

"Yeah, I've heard that one a lot. So, you think there is something to it?"

"Some of it, sure," Tharsis said, uncomfortable now. "Neural tissue, synthetic or real, can extrude it. Most people back home can see when a life starts, or when it ends. We've got hard data on that. But that's just humans, right? It could just be some tic in our brains, you know, since the dreams stopped." Tharsis looked over at her friend. "Do you dream?"

"Not when I'm asleep."

"Why do you want to know about umbran?"

But tDaer wouldn't say any more about it.

It didn't really matter what it was that tDaer was after out there, Tharsis told herself. What hen wanted from her, or if it was just academic curiosity.

Didn't really matter.

Dreams had been coming with bruising force for her, every night since.

Tight yet endless, a space of obtuse corners too far away or too dark to be seen. She could hear people talking in indistinct voices that did not seem to quite form words, heard them moving sometimes, but as soon as the sounds grew closer, she'd yell, push them away. She wasn't sure if she was afraid of them or afraid of what they might see with her. All she knew was that she was afraid. Endlessly, apocalyptically afraid.

Was it her future? Somebody else's past? Some kind of warning? A punishment? Tharsis had never put much stock in that sort of thing. Her whole life, she'd never seen anything. To have it hit her like this, hard and fast and overwhelmingly present, was awful.

"Hey, guys, thanks for waiting. Serious problems, serious problems. Let's get going!"

Hinden's voice, that grainy, nasally, irritating voice, cut through the lieutenant's thoughts and startled her back to the here and now. Humphryes's main briefing room, and the brand-new Fiveday operations briefing.

Everyone was on edge; Hinden hadn't offered much in the way of direction, which meant he didn't know what he wanted. Which meant no matter what they presented, they were fucked. Tharsis glanced at the chronograph on the wall above the door. Fifteen minutes past start time. She'd been there for twenty-five. She wondered if he was trying to make some kind of point.

Sergeant Olin was across the table, on the enlisted side, attending at her request. Tharsis wasn't about to field a mountain of penetrating questions about the state of the cable runs without her most knowledgeable sergeant.

The briefing room, like the rest of Humphryes, had been designed for a complete expeditionary wing, with a full-bird colonel in command, and the trimming reflected that. A huge chevron of a table, real lamb-leather chairs, solid wood paneling on the walls, and a wrought silver plaque of the Archangel Michael in his flak vest hanging over the door. The integrated projection equipment in the center of the space represented what the very limits of holographic technology had been, fifty years ago.

It was a nice room, and under different circumstances, it was a nice place to be.

"Okay, guys," the captain said breezily, finally showing up, "let's get going!"

He came in. Headed straight for the head of the table.

But instead of sitting in the base commander's seat, the first chair to the right, he took the one at the head.

The seat nobody ever used. The seat present at every military briefing room table, Heliosphere-wide

The Rossen's.

For a moment, the entire room froze. Hinden didn't even seem to notice, though. He just flicked skeletal fingers across inlaid controls, bringing up the briefing slides Tharsis had spent three hours putting together with Cheria and Lieutenant Graben.

"Let's get into this. Who's presenting first?" He looked up at the room silently staring back at him and rubbed his hands together. "Come on, who's running this thing?"

Chief Anders, the base's senior enlisted man, sitting to the left, made a little harrumphing noise. "Umm, sir, I think that perhaps you forgot that—"

"Forgot what?" the captain said, irritated. "Come on, people, let's move! Sooner we get going, the sooner you all can get out to your Fiveday night partying and whatnot. Tharsis!"

The lieutenant dragged her eyes back up from where she'd carefully averted them, away from the chair. "Yessir?"

He waggled the remote at her. "How about we start with your little project?"

What? "Sir?"

"Lieutenant, come on, I'm waiting," he said in a half-teasing voice that was somehow more intimidating than simple yelling.

"I don't know what you're talking about, sir."

"Your little pet project!" he exploded. "Your stupid little obsession with that fucking comm line we aren't even responsible for."

Tharsis caught a glimpse of Olin's face through the translucent haze of the projection screen. The sergeant hadn't been forthcoming about the lab's final results, only that he was going to call in a couple of favors with an old buddy in signals analysis. See if he couldn't get better minds than his on it. His expression now was inscrutable.

Fuck.

"I'm not ready to rule out the possibility of a problem," she said lamely.

"Olin?" Hinden asked.

And the sergeant winked at her through the screen.

She wanted to give him a tight shake of her head, dissuade him from whatever was going through his mind, but that heavy Alban steel chair scraped back, and her window for action closed.

"I think what we should be discussing, sir, is what Chief was saying. That you're in the wrong fuckin' chair."

Olin. Standing now. Leaning on the back of his seat, gray sleeve pulled up far enough to see the top four stripes on his rank tattoos stretched taught over tensed arm muscle.

The mood in the room turned, a low murmur starting up. Chief cocked an eyebrow, a clear sign for Olin to sit down and shut the fuck up. Tharsis rubbed a hand over her face. There was going to be hell to pay over this.

"Can you repeat that, Sergeant Olin? For the class?" Hinden asked, folding his elbows up on the tabletop, laying his chin on his hands, the previous topic forgotten.

"That's the Landlord's chair."

"There are no lords on Mars, Sergeant. You know that as well as I do."

Olin tensed. "It bears remembering that Chief Ross is the one who first said that."

"I don't need a history lesson from you, Sergeant."

"How about a regulation, then, sir? General Order 1? *No member of the Arran Self-Defense Force, no matter his rank or station, may show disrespect to the Landlord of M—*"

"Holy Michael's ball-sweat, Olin!" Hinden interrupted. "Do you seriously think the Rossen's going to show up and get pissed at me because I'm in his chair?" He grinned. "Or maybe it's you, eh?"

"And what if it was me?" the sergeant demanded, over the rumble that was beginning to grow, spread. Angry now. "What if I was the Rossen? Telling you to get out of my chair?"

In the silence that followed, a micrometeor strike would have sounded like an explosion.

But the captain just burst out laughing. That reedy, whiny, horrible laugh.

"Now's who's being naive, Olin? Come on, Tharsis, we're burning tallow here! What's your answer?"

"Get out of his chair, sir, or I'm calling Command. See what General Cochrane thinks about your attitude," Olin growled, in a voice Tharsis had never heard him use before. "Or would you just like to stop being a coward, admit you made a mistake, and show the goddamn country some respect by sitting where you're supposed to sit, sir?"

The *fuck you* was palpable.

For the first time ever, Captain Hinden actually looked shocked.

The only sound in the room, for a moment, was the faint whirring of electricity passing through the projection bulbs, and then Chief Anders huffed out a slow, slow breath. "Thank you for the, uh, professional opinion, Master Sergeant Olin. Perhaps we can continue this discussion in the commander's office."

"Love to, Chief, but I've got scat that actually needs doing," Olin replied, icy, and strode from the room.

The lieutenant, with only one helpless glance at a shell-shocked Hinden, grabbed her tablet and ran after Olin. Graben would have to manage the brief.

HER MIND WAS on her sergeant. On where he might go and what she might have to say to him when she caught up. But headed out across the xeriscaping in front of the small headquarters building, the lieutenant saw something move out of the corner of her eye that had nothing to do with Olin.

Standing on unsteady feet in front of her was a child, the shape of it strange, unhinged, and loose, staring back at her with sightless, empty eyes.

She froze.

The thing started walking towards her, left hand out as if in supplication. But all the lieutenant could think about was that darkness, the screaming darkness from her dreams, and she found herself backing up, backing away, leaving the main path, and heading up in between two small outbuildings of corrugated tin.

The formless thing was right in front of her, cutting her off as she tried to turn a corner, heart hammering in her ears, panic drilling up through her blood. Reaching out, touching her with a frozen hand, fingers cutting like ice.

She scrambled back.

Blind.

Straight into Sergeant Olin, nearly knocking them both over. But instead of teasing her about it, he took one look down and wrapped an arm around her, holding her still.

"You're shaking like a newborn kitten, El-Tee," he said softly in her ear. "You okay?"

She huffed a small, humorless laugh into the rough cotton weave of his grays, holding on and hating herself for how much she needed it. "There anything behind me?"

He made a noise deep in his throat. "You seeing things?"

"If you don't see it, too, then it's not there," she replied with another small sigh, and, remembering herself, pushed him away. Tharsis couldn't remember the last time a man had touched her.

Judging from the look on his face, the sergeant knew he'd crossed a line there too.

Out in front of them, the base stretched another half kilometer to the translucent barrier of synthetic sky. Olin looked like he was somehow staring at something else entirely.

Tharsis didn't ask, though. Just stared at the spot where the umbran no longer was. "I don't see things."

"There's been a lot of death in this region," the sergeant replied, even. "A lot of death. Plenty here that's been smashed down into the penumbra."

She ignored the little probe and looked up. If one looked straight at the false sky, it was possible to see around that dusty projection of the Arran sky against the inner surface of the base's habitat bubble into the void beyond. Tharsis liked that better. Seemed more honest.

"I probably have to issue you paperwork now. So fucking thanks for that."

"Do what you gotta do. I'm not getting promoted again in this life-time," the master sergeant said, and turned his face up to the false ball of light on the sky. It put her in mind of Mercury's surface, the young sun screaming into the penumbra.

"You get the signal analysis on that tumor we yanked out of the auditorium?"

"I yanked. You supervised. Big difference there, El-Tee."

"I did get covered in goo. And you did just fuck us both with that little show in there. What, to avoid telling him what's going on?"

A strange silence dragged out before he replied with, "The lab hasn't found anything yet. At least nothing I'd be comfortable going to the captain with. But I think..."

"Yeah?"

"According to the data we pulled out of the Lighthouse, it's Trans-Neptunian in origin."

"And you neglected to tell me this?"

"You've been sort of out of it, ma'am."

That hurt. More than it should have. But, since there was nothing more that could be said about it, the lieutenant pushed off the wall, planning on making some excuse about needing to start on his disciplinary paperwork. As she was walking away, though, Olin shot one more thing over to her.

"Oh, and ma'am?"

"What?"

"Whatever you're seeing, whatever the problem is, I'm here to listen."

"I don't have a problem."

"Well, I'm always here to talk about your nonexistent problem."

She nodded and left before she could do something stupid. Like ask for another hug.

Or tell him about the oob.

You're never doing that again, she told herself on her way back to the office. *Not if you're seeing scat like that.*

She got back to the squadron. Cheria was tidying up, but the briefing room door was still firmly closed. Tharsis had no desire to go back in there. "Sorry," she said to the pale-skinned secretary, "but can you get me one of the form templates for disciplinary action?"

"Sure," the Ibbie woman said, and went back to her desk. Her hair fell in that solid sheet around her shoulders, flowing like water over thin shoulders. Even the simplest of her movements were graceful. Tharsis tried to shove the jealousy aside as she took the proffered silic drive from the secretary. "What happened, Lieutenant?"

"Somebody insulted the captain, but the captain insulted the Landlord."

The secretary paused, cocking her way in that way voiders always seemed to, like gravity made her move wrong. Frowning. "That is not good," Cheria finally said, and held out a chip. "The Landlords must be respected. How else do we keep habitats alive?"

About to answer, a small holographic plaque on Cheria's desk caught her eye.

AND IN THIS HEAVEN I LEARNED THE TRUTH

THAT WE ARE ALL OF US OUR OWN GODS

"That's from the First Propagation, isn't it? Very first transmission?" Tharsis queried, pointing. "The Arcna's declaration of intent?"

Cheria flushed pink and hit her hand on the unit, the quote smearing out into some other Ibbie pablum. "She speaks the truth through her Propagations as she understands it. None of us have the right to begrudge her her view of the world."

"That view of the world includes destroying Mars."

"The Landlords have the power of life or death over us. If one deems it necessary to kill, then it is not our place to question," the secretary replied serenely, fingers drumming nervously against a thin cheekbone.

"Convenient that she lets other people do the killing for her," the lieutenant commented wryly, but seeing the look on the secretary's face, she didn't press it. "Thanks for the template."

THARSIS HAD no intentions of going anywhere that Fiveday night. No oobing, not again, never again. Wasn't worth it. The lieutenant had a plan half-formulated that involved an old radio show and something cheap and salty for dinner.

But the second she'd settled down in a hammock in the hostel's shabby little media room, headphones on and pressure can cracked, there Angakkuq was.

Lounging in the doorway.

Tossing a bag from palm to palm.

"Neptune's rings," he explained. "An oldie but a goodie. We'd been planning on Jupiter's gossamer belt, but that's probably off-limits to you, eh?"

"Me?" she asked, surprised. "You changed plans for me?"

"Yup. You, Tharsis, traveler of Mars," he intoned dramatically, the humor registering only at the very end, and threw her the bag. "You're on the team now, right?"

"No, what? There's no team."

He didn't answer, eyes gleaming gold.

"You gonna tell me that last week didn't blow your mind?"

She sighed, and looked at him, and tried to tell him no.

Tried to believe that oob to Mercury hadn't been the best goddamn thing she'd done all year.

Twenty minutes later, borrowed Ibbie strip makeup taped over the rank on her neck, she was following Ang out to Shoal Bar, the voider telling her some crazy story about a trip to Titan Station that had almost gotten him killed.

Really, she told herself over her own unease, *what difference does it make?*

CHAPTER
NINE

"THERE ANY REASON why tDaer keeps calling you a Polarist?"

"I'm from the Trojans. We have a reputation for being unconventional."

"Yeah, but you're not all Polarists." Tharsis picked at a loose thread in her uniform sleeve.

"We're not all Toks," Ang corrected, patronizing, strangely kind. "As you call us."

The curving interior of the divedrive rose up around them like a wave, a distinct separation from the shimmer of the dark ice around them. Without that faint, off-kilter sensation that accompanied oobs, Tharsis might have been tempted to believe that they were really standing, moving, in that place.

That night marked Tharsis's fifth oobing trip with the voiders, but she could tell something was different. Instead of violently skipping up through the temporal gradient or lingering out of physical phase in some molten vision, they were tracking through in synch with some past point in the gradient flow that neither of the voiders would identify to her.

"An experiment," tDaer had said.

"A quest," Ang had added.

Like that clarified anything.

"Yeah, Tharsis, you know, your military didn't manage to kill everybody during the Big Scare on Europa. When refugees flooded out into the Lagrange regions, so did all the insanity."

"Europa was a paradise," Angakkuq said, heated. "The piijuit were to be the Arcna's chosen people before she was driven to the Kuiper."

"The Arcna had nothing to do with that." tDaer shook hen's head. "What happened on Europa was an abuse of science. The pinniped experiments never should have been attempted."

"Noqumiut promises us transcendence."

"Noqumiut promises us perfection of society, not soul."

"Where the hell are we, anyway?" the lieutenant asked sharply, cutting that off. A bead of sweat slipped below the collar of her issue ENEX. She'd started bringing it along on these trips at Ang's suggestion; unsealed, active layers safely dormant, the thing was hot. She could hear Hinden's voice in her thoughts. *Misappropriation of taxpayer-funded equipment.* He would definitely court martial her if he found out.

"Water world. Good places to contemplate the deep truths of the universe."

"Enough, Ang. Shut up and let me drive, you have no idea how weird this feels," tDaer interjected from behind, hen's hands sunk into one of the raised control surface, protruding, fist-like, from the craft's floor. "Are you sure your fragments were pure?"

"My supplier doesn't fuck up," Ang replied.

"Something special?" Tharsis asked again.

He grinned.

"Promised you, didn't I?" tDaer commented proudly. "I deliver what I promise."

Even delivered in the Iapetan's arrogant, dismissive manner, the words were almost touching. Better than anything Tharsis was getting from her squadronmates, at any rate.

Micromanaging had continued unchecked over the past month, no end point in sight. The young officer corps was starting to split apart under the strain of it, descending into unsettled hostility. Arguments began over the smallest things. Earlier that night, when Tharsis had gone by the Wardog, instead of the drunken din that normally marked the place, there had only been quiet, muted conversations. Small gatherings around half-empty tables. Cheria helping her Arran husband dry glasses behind the counter.

The most infuriating thing about it was that nobody else appeared to recognize it. Or, worse, would acknowledge it. The irrationally long hours, nonsensical tasks, and unpredictable mood swings were taking a toll on everyone. Tensions were clearly ratcheting up amongst the enlisted, and the chair thing wasn't helping; Hinden was still using the Rossen's seat. But when Tharsis had tried to talk to the other lieutenants, it didn't go so well.

"You do not fuck with the Rossen's scat like that," she'd commented to Junia the next Oneday after morning PT, trying to breathe through thin air and exhausted muscles, the base's half-dozen enlisted girls heading into the showers ahead of them. "Who knows where that fucker is?"

"He's not out here," the other female had insisted.

"Well, it's not like we'd know."

"I'd know. Every scrap of transmission that comes into this base comes through my command post. If we were getting the kind of volume of scat the Landlord's said to go through on a monthly basis, believe me, I'd see it."

"Hinden can't keep sitting there."

"Oh, and what? You care about the fucking Landlord now?"

"Fuck the Landlord. What is that going to do to enlisted morale?" Tharsis had replied.

"No, what you mean is that you think Hinden's adlet scat and you want a way to prove it. So, stop," Junia had warned. "Don't even try to get him on some stupid technicality like that. Don't make this worse than it already is!"

At least Junia would talk to her, though. The rest refused to say anything, even as they silently started shuffling into separate camps; those who supported Hinden's changes, and those who held there was nothing wrong at all. In an attempt, Tharsis thought uncharitably, to avoid any obligation to fix the problems.

But Tharsans prided themselves on pragmatism. The lieutenant from the Bulge had, in fact, looked into the process for reporting the captain. Spent the whole day in the base's silic archives, researching. She'd only found a labyrinth of regulation and red tape obviously intended to discourage the attempt. It pissed her off. The Rossen was supposed to be accessible to the Arran people; that was the whole point of him. Making him that unavailable was unacceptable.

They were alone.

Nobody was coming to help.

Humphryes didn't matter enough to bother.

tDaer's voice brought her out of her musing.

"We're getting there."

Around them, the world was still indistinct, the penumbra fuzzier than usual. But Tharsis could still pick out a form growing in front of them, solid in the liquid seas, a long tubular structure waving gently in the currents.

"Adlivun kelp," Ang explained, excited, tapping so hard at the hull that the scene rippled. "The leaves could grow up to a half kilometer long in some cases, manipulated into habitable forms through RNA growth templates."

"It's an inhabitation?"

"Road. Leading somewhere good," tDaer explained, and twisted hen's hand in the controls. Hen was sweating. "Hopefully."

"In its time, it was one of the biological engineering marvels of the Heliosphere," Angakkuq said, awe in his voice, and ran a hand against the hull, touching his own non-presence to the kelp beyond. The plant glowed in response to the contact. "The finest works of mankind, the Polarists wrought. Success torn from the very edge of what all others said was impossibility."

"Maybe pressurized kelp structures were impressive once," tDaer corrected, and shuddered a little as they reached a Y-junction. She navigated up the right-hand path. "Before we discovered wrapper."

"Wrapper is programmed off of something that may or may not have been alive in the first place. Proto-xenocytes, growing in tholin fields. Warped, alien. Horrific." He sniffed. "This kelp was pure, patterned from the base pairs up. And multicellular, might I add. Before Mars destroyed it."

Tharsis sighed. "You mean when the Polarists forced us to come in and put hundreds of thousands of dying children to death? Nuking a living moon to stop it from continuing?"

"What happened on Europa was regrettable. The Arcna would not have—"

"Regrettable? That entire colony's genome was warped past the point of survivability in a quest to become seals or whatever the fuck?" Tharsis shot back. "Regrettable isn't the word I would use."

"They were the children of the ocean, a new species, built to survive and thrive," Ang said, sad. "The Arcna could have perfected them, made them live, true and proper, if your people hadn't gone in." He sighed. "And she wouldn't have to speak to us now from the Kuiper."

"And maybe if she'd died in that purge, the Heliosphere—"

"Seriously, people, shut up. I'm trying to focus here!" tDaer growled.

Ang, stung, stared mournfully out the side of the craft.

On the strange flow of movement, taking them through the kelp halls, they went into something that could have been a town. Structures blurred into each other, hard surfaces and electricity and carrier signals and heat blending to smears of color that had nothing to do with visible light, more bizarre than beautiful. Like listening to a short-wave show played too slow and too fast at the same time, Tharsis thought, as it slid through her. Like one of those moving picture plays the Ibbies produced, being shown with the projector bulb half burnt out.

"It's not like she's wrong," Ang said, after long minutes.

"The Arcna?" Tharsis sighed. "What is she not wrong about?"

"What is she not right about? Your people see so much, but you don't comprehend."

"Stop lumping Tharsis in with the rest of the fucking Martians. She's not some judgmental, racist, mudcunt," tDaer said, hand still enveloped in that extruded control-pillar of hull. The Iapetan's dark eyes were on her. "I mean, seriously, right?"

Tharsis did not at all like the implications contained in her friend's words. But before she could reply properly, she noticed something.

People.

Surrounding them. Falling through the water. Some slow, some fast, the matter of their bodies passing through the space in slowly curling contrails of purest white light. The worldlines of blood and teeth and hair and eyes, their descent imprinted into the penumbra. Bodies falling. Energy fleeing. Soundless.

A set of eyes turned on her, light streaming from vacant sockets. One set. Another. All.

And every story she'd ever heard about the passing of the dead rushed through her.

"You brought me to a massacre site!" she groaned. "Where are we?"

"Ceres." tDaer looked up at her, steady. Unafraid. "You do see it, then?"

Rubbing a hand over her face, Tharsis fell back. "Fuck," she muttered, and tendrils of penumbra-pressed death energy flowed through the hull, smoke in strong winds. Ceres. Dear Christ. "Fuck you, tDaer."

"Let me know if you see anything interesting," the grad student replied.

They floated through the stream of the dying up into the sound of the ten-kilometer–thick ice sheets, groaning around them in impossible frequencies. None of the dead made any attempt to touch her, but Tharsis could feel them. Their questions, anger, confusion. She fought to keep her tears down, stop that foreign emotion flooding her.

So many of them. Too many of them. Killed by their own Landlord. For no reason. Nobody knew why. Nobody had ever known why.

Eventually, the death glow faded, the divedrive ghosting inside a small room. Not kelp, this, but reinforced titanium and carbon fiber. Through now smeared vision, Tharsis discerned the darkness of a world that had never seen sunlight, and never would. Not until the sun swelled into a red giant and devoured it.

The walls, equipment, the very atmo left little more than a shadowed whisper along the worldlines of the trillions of atoms it had once been built from. Ornate carvings littered the walls and great pillars rose to three meters above the floor, smeared in the same inconstant whisper.

It felt sacred, but unlike any church she'd ever been in—not the towering heights of Saint Peter's in District of Lunae, not the small mountain caves of her own parish, the flutter of silk prayer flags bright against driving snows. This, even through the disassociation of the oob, felt self-satisfied. Arrogant. Tiny and cruel. Privy to secrets that were best left unspoken, secrets with the power to devour those who sought them out.

They weren't just observing this place. They were inside it.

"This is it," Angakkuq said reverently, kicking carefully off into it, towards the central panel of the room. "This is where the ones who came before us came to talk to the heavens. This is the space she carved to store what was precious, to hide it from us. But we found it, and we took it from her." His face hardened. "This is what the Rallarhu sought to destroy."

"Stop the sermonizing and find the fucking things," tDaer ground out. Hen looked to be in a bad way. "Craft's starting to fight me."

"Right," the Jovian traveler said, eyes luminous in the weak light of the phased-out flow they were stuck in. He went to work prying open a panel.

Tharsis, unease mounting, tried to focus on the details. The little things. Tubing beneath the candlelight, twists of circuitry, the markings on hardwired radiation feeds...

"This is a Lighthouse," she realized.

"The control center that was lost in the First Propagation," tDaer confirmed. "The only control center. It does still exist. I thought so."

The Heliosphere's silic-based radio network had been built in pieces, cobbled together by a dozen different corporate entities of the Silicone Age, to facilitate mining and colonization efforts. But they hadn't been pulled into one cohesive thing until the final years of the Euphemism, when the Lighthouses were constructed. Radio relay stations were already scattered throughout the inner system, but the Lighthouses extended that reach from 4Vesta out to the frozen reaches of the Kuiper Belt.

The Arcna had claimed one of those Lighthouses, built her Noqumiut, broadcasted her Propagations across the entire Heliosphere. Or so it was believed. It had to be a Lighthouse. Nothing else had the transmission range, nor the subsentient encryption that could withstand even Arran quants. No other network even existed.

But nobody had ever been to the Arcna's world since the ill-fated expedition of the First Propagation. Especially after the destruction of Ceres, it was unlikely anyone would ever go back.

Even without her isolation enshrined, sacred, in international law, the planetoids on which the Kuiper Lighthouses had been built were almost impossible to reach, even for the best fusion drives available under the Accords. A trip could last a decade or more, depending on launch point, and long-term stasis technology had been destroyed during the Scient's purges. Any existing divedrive navigation material had long been lost or destroyed. Compounding the issue, nobody even knew which location she was at, or if she moved between many.

Noqumiut was an impossible place to reach.

Didn't mean the ASDF wasn't still wary. Didn't mean others didn't still try. Task Force Gabriel was in charge of guarding against any incursion from the place. Mostly, they dealt with pirates and unaffiliated can stations and assorted voider craft; Toks, mostly looking for their heaven. Jovian patrol craft could be found out there too, Tharsis had heard, but security in the Heliosphere had always been the province of Mars.

"Why are we here?" Tharsis demanded, wanting nothing more than to fucking leave.

tDaer ignored her. "Ang, fucking hell," hen snapped, "I'm losing my grip on it."

"Calm down," he hollered back, still ripping into panels and cabinets, frantic now. "It's got to be here."

Faint, far away, it seemed.

"Fucking voidburn, Ang, we're only going to get one shot at this. When the wetware figures out where we are, it's not going to let us come back!"

"I know that..." Tharsis heard, but the words trailed into static as the world deformed.

Turned to nothing but ice sheets above, the starfield blazing in the sky, a doorway of twisted organic metal around her that led seemingly to nothing. There was a craft parked above. Arran. Blasting out some kind of unintelligible warning.

There was a figure striding towards her. Towards the doorway. Naked, barefoot, dark against the blue of the ancient ice.

Hand raised.

A great whine rose from the ice beneath her, the burning scent of the void tearing into Tharsis, screaming, her very soul streaming out like wind across the tundra. Death lights shone in the dark waters around her, and all sense fled.

CHAPTER
TEN

THARSIS NOTICED a few things immediately upon coming back to her senses.

Her body was a mass of pain, joints swollen and popping.

The Arran-made ENEX was fully deployed around her.

She wasn't in the voidcraft.

That last one rattled her to the core, and she shot up, almost floating off whatever surface it was she was lying on. Microgravity. She caught a fingerhold at the last second, barely catching herself. Her eyes wouldn't quite focus, struggling against the bubble of the integrated goggles. Adrenaline was spiking into her blood, itching its way to her fingertips.

Biting hard on the silicone teeth guard of her rebreather, she concentrated on her lungs, on her heart. A trick she remembered from the Centrifuge and its horrible three weeks of outwell survival training. Her forty-nine hours spent alone on a sun-blasted spit of spongy 'roid.

Tharsis let the slight edge of oxygen deprivation take down the panic, slow the heart, calm the body. Let her mind flow around the problem. *Water around rocks in the stream. Wind around the peaks*, she told herself.

It almost worked. She hated this.

The earpiece of her deployed helmet buzzed. <Thank Tulukat, you okay?>

Ang. With no small amount of relief, Tharsis tapped her radio on.
<What the fuck?>

<Craft threw you out. Don't move, okay? We're coming to get you.>

But as her brain got past *how the fuck did this happen?* something new occurred to her.

<Did you dive the craft into that control room?> she demanded into the radio, tearing her eyes away from the planet in the sky above and scrambling for her wrist read-out. How long had she been out? How long did she have before the fucking xenocyte wrapper in her ENEX began eating her?

<It's a bit complicated, but—>

<You took me on a fucking dive to Ceres?!>

<I told you,> tDaer said, <we were doing something new tonight.>

<No, you did not tell me, or I would not be here! What the hell is wrong with you?> Tharsis snapped, still careful not to let herself lift off the surface. The planetoid's gravity was weak; she had no idea how far up she would drift if she let go of her tenuous connection to the ancient ice.

<Overreacting much?>

About to reply that it was not, at all, an overreaction, Tharsis looked behind herself and the words dropped from her tongue. The ruins of an antenna forest, the cracked fragment of the heat shield, tops of ancient antennas, poking through the ice, out to the steep slope of the horizon. But not three hundred meters from her, on the other side of a large mass, protruding up through the ancient ice, there was a figure. Just outside of the protrusion of what looked like rock. Featureless, without definition. Walking around the far side of the broken ice.

It couldn't be a ghost. Teams of priests had spent months on Ceres after the disaster, helping settle the dead. Even what she'd seen in the ocean had been far back in the flow of the temporal gradient, an echo, not intelligent.

Ignoring it was the best course of action.

Instead, Tharsis turned the gravity in her boots up, and followed.

To her surprise, the protruding mass wasn't solid. It was cracked apart, a hatched-out egg, exposed to the elements. As Tharsis maneuvered herself around, her arm caught on a worn edge of rock-hard, dead kelp bark. Moving fast enough to hurt, the wrapper layers in the exposure suit used her own momentum to displace it, disassociating the incoming substance through the negative space in her own flesh, sliding two pieces of solid matter through each other.

An involuntary shiver jittered up her arm as nerves temporarily stopped talking to each other, synaptic clefts interrupted. Tharsis gritted her teeth as she pulled herself free. Using the Cronuan xenomyocetic wrapper to eliminate micrometeor damage or stray cosmic radiation on the craft was one thing. With the heavy internal shielding, disassociations weren't felt by those inside. The way the ENEX translated the sensation, however, was downright disconcerting.

<How long have I been in this suit?> she asked over the headset, shaking her arm out.

<About an hour.> There was a pause, and then, <Oh, right. That. No worries. We'll get you before it starts going after your waste thermal energy.>

Fucking brilliant, she thought, and stepped inside the battered interior of what had been, only moments ago, such a carefully constructed little space. <How did I get blown out, anyway?>

<Not sure. No worries. We'll get it fixed before next time.>

<Next time? Who said there was going to be a—> and she stopped.

There, in the weak refracted light, in the eclipse of the node's shattered shell, was a man.

A soldier. In the same uniform as the one she'd seen in the antenna field on 4Vesta. Dark, torn, skin bruised, hair gone, some kind of pattern roughed over with red ink on his bare scalp. Huddled up over his knees, or maybe his legs were missing from the knees down.

The umbran-thing didn't look at her. Its mouth moved, its eyes stared, but she couldn't hear the words. Not intelligent, unaware. Residual energy then, but impressed into what? The dwarf planet was dead, abandoned, no EM fields strong enough to hold onto something like this.

What the hell was going on?

<Hey, Tharsis, you in here?> She rotated on a knee on the rotten floor to see Angakkuq, wrapped in his own suit, raise a hand in greeting. He stepped into the shadows with her, flashlight out, the beam piercing through the haze. <It's so broken up.>

<What did you expect?> Tharsis asked, distracted. The soldier apparition was gone. <Perfect condition after what, seven hundred years?>

<This was a temple of my people. Would you enjoy standing in a ruined church?>

<It's not the same thing.>

<You receive words from the headwaters of Udlormiut in your houses of stone and glass.> He touched the protrusion of the panel reverently. <But this is the first place her word was captured. This is the first place we heard her speak.>

<We don't worship energy flows,> she said, and an inexplicable flash of memory assailed her. Christmas, the whole family gathered around the hearth, storm winds whipping around outside. Something transcendent at the heart of it. When was the last time she'd been home for that? The Academy granted leave for that. Why hadn't she gone home? <We don't worship a human, either.>

<Polarists don't worship the Arcna. We aspire. She's an ascended being, enlightened,> Angakkuq replied, the bubble of his ENEX's goggles mirrored against stray cosmic radiation, giving nothing of his intentions away.

tDaer's voice crackled over the line. <Ang, focus. Can you see what we came for?>

<No. Nowhere.>

Silence for a moment, the line on mute. Tharsis got the distinct impression, though she didn't know why, that tDaer was spitting obscenities on the other end. <Okay, well, there's no help for it. Haul ass back here, okay? Let's get off this fucking ice cube before the wetware wakes up.>

<Roger,> Tharsis replied, and looked over at the voider. <Where is hen?>

The Jovian traveler started a bit in his own exogear. <The craft's on the other side of the ridge. Might be a bit of a push.>

<Fine with me,> she said, but lingered for a moment on the edge of the broken room. Hoping, for some strange reason, that she might see the soldier again. Damn, she thought, and left, following Angakkuq's easy bounds back with her own plodding steps, to where the divedrive was waiting for them. A few meters above the ice, it

was nothing to turn off the gravity compensators and jump lightly up.

An opening yawned in the hull. A tight-chambered air lock, molded in place of the divedrive's usual entrance.

As they settled in, Tharsis noticed movement beyond the circle of white hull. A great multitude of small, dark figures, misshapen and awkward, eyeless, soundless, watching.

That little boy from before. Standing in the center. Eyes locked on her.

She didn't say anything about it to Angakkuq. Just closed her eyes until the door slotted into place, and the pressure rose enough for her to pop the hood.

tDaer, mercifully, didn't ask.

Instead, the Iapetan just watched with a vague interest as Tharsis tore off her ENEX as quickly as possible, the second they were through. Still naked, to save time, she punched the suit's storage locker open up out of the hull. A curved door section rose up and she carefully deposited the suit back in its protective suspension fluid. Once deployed, the outer layers would degrade in atmo. The goo stopped the reactions that led to damaging radiation release, effectively resetting the biological components to full dormancy.

"You, uh, you good?" tDaer finally asked.

The lieutenant punched open the adjacent space, where she'd stashed her civilian clothes, and shrugged them on. She didn't like the way the grad student was looking at her. Nobody ever looked at her that way. For some reason, it pissed her off, almost as much as being hurled onto the surface of Ceres.

"This craft burped me out like waste through a cell wall. Am I supposed to be okay with that?"

Angakkuq had his own voidsuit tied casually around his waist, eating one of those perfectly spherical, synthetic apples they sold everywhere on New Stockholm. Naked too, his body spoke of a lifetime of poor nutrition and low gravity. He resembled a plucked, starved chicken. "What good is life if you never experience a little bit of danger, now and then?"

"Ang, snow leopards are dangerous. This, on the other hand, was fucking stupid." Tharsis smoothed the last hook and loop strap into place around her hip, turned back to tDaer. "Do we have to dive to get back to Vesta? Should I put my exogear back on? In case it does it again?"

"That shouldn't have happened," tDaer conceded, and paused. "And, umm, we aren't headed right back to 4Vesta. We blew something in the propulsion system," the Iapetan replied, completely flat. "Argon's leaking."

Tharsis groaned. "From kicking me out?"

"Don't worry," Angakkuq said quickly, "I've got a guy we can go see, get this taken care of, no problem, no issue, don't worry about it, okay?"

She held out a hand. "I have to be back to work in forty hours, or my boss is going to have my ass thrown in lockup for being AWOL."

"Can't throw you in jail if you aren't around, can he?" the Trojan quipped and threw her a wink. "Don't worry, Lieutenant, we'll get you back for your shift on Oneday."

CHAPTER
ELEVEN

THE CRAFT, tDaer said, was far too underpowered to do anything like open transparent windows in the hull. Or process the atmo. Or provide heating. Even the usual inner illumination was too much of a strain for the divedrive to maintain on its damaged reactor. A few small float-lamps, deployed from one of the storage lockers, cast only isolated spheres of light into the darkness. Even the normal whisper of propulsion rattled wrong.

"Never been so happy that dive cores operate on their own weird physics," tDaer muttered, "but we still have to use conventional means to make it through the inwell. I can push out the stabilization panels into a sail configuration, fall into the gravity well and steer us into port."

"And where's that?"

tDaer didn't answer. Angakkuq just closed his eyes and pushed his lower body a bit deeper into the surface tension of the hull.

The second dive was jarring, uncomfortable. But there was nothing to see, nothing to feel, and before long, the stabilization panels deployed, and they were falling into open void.

The remaining hours, with gravity in the pilot's seat, passed slowly. tDaer curled into the column, obviously not wanting to be disturbed, and Angakkuq settled into some weird meditative state. With the glow cast upwards against him from the small electric lamp jammed into the floor in front of him, he looked like some kind of carven spirit-figure from that room they'd seen under the Lighthouse.

Tharsis sat alone with her own thoughts and tried to control the tiny ripples of fear that only seemed to grow in her throat with each passing minute. Until the seemingly distant impression of movement stopped, and the sound of the panels clicking back into place indicated some kind of dock.

tDaer pulled hen's hand out of the navigation panel, the cobalt skin of hen's neck cast a waxy-gray. A few stray drops of red escaped from raw fingers into the open air, the Iapetan's face more annoyed than pained. "That was the exact opposite of fun," hen announced and slumped back. "But we're in."

"And where is in, exactly?" Tharsis asked again, testy. Her body still hurt.

"Amalthea. The craft needs repairs to its power systems, or it's going to die. And there's nobody in the Inner Shoals with that kind of expertise," tDaer explained calmly.

Tharsis just closed her eyes. She didn't have the energy to protest. To point out how very, very much she was not allowed to be anywhere near the Jovian inwell. "I don't have my passport," was all she said.

"Doesn't matter," Angakkuq said cheerfully, shuffling himself out of his indentation. He pushed free and slapped her lightly on the shoulder on his way to the hatch. Five trips, and Tharsis had started to recognize the telltale hairlines that ribboned through the interior. "I've got connections."

"You guys don't understand," she protested, "I can't be here."

The hatch slid open, and a wave of dry, cool air surged in, changing out with the stale atmo they'd been breathing for the past few hours. Tharsis hadn't realized how hot the hold had become with the craft unable to use the panels to vent excess heat.

"Seriously, calm down, I've got you covered," tDaer said, packing a ripstop backpack from some storage locker as Angakkuq floated outside. "I shot a message off through the radio, let him know we were coming and that we have a Martian with us." Hen tossed the lieutenant a second, smaller bag, sealing the panel shut again. "I think you'll find the hospitality here pretty fuckin' good."

"Who's waiting for us?" Tharsis asked, and pulled the drawstring on the pack. It contained an Arran-made grav bag, dehydrated meal packets stamped with discreet Arran certification markings, a toothbrush. Didn't make any sense, unless… "Did you plan on this?"

tDaer pushed up off the hull, propelling henself towards the hatch, ignoring the question. "Come on. We really don't want to keep this guy waiting."

"What guy?"

THARSIS LEANED her head against the window of the monorail car, headed away from the port towards some destination tDaer had been uneasily unspecific about, and tried to catch glimpses of what was passing below.

They had indeed made it through security without an issue. Ang had flashed some badge, chattered a little guttural Jovian to the port inspector, and they'd been ushered through into the terminal proper. No fuss at all.

The world around the car seemed far too bright and shiny, for all the stories she'd heard about the Jovian moons. Founded as mining colonies in the heady, last years of the Silicone Age, the misshapen satellites formed the basis of the Onias monopoly on the international hydrocarbon trade. Chemicals from Jupiter's clouds were harvested and refined into propellant and plastic bases. Base materials, mined from moons and asteroids alike, were fed into the vast factories of the Arran merchman fleets and Ibbie workhouses. The wealth amassed by the Onias was staggering; his palace on Themisto was legendary.

The inner moons, the foundation of that resource-rich empire, were far from affluent. Jupiter was a monster, magnetics intense and inimical to life. No habitats could be built on the outer surfaces of moons like Amalthea, and humans instead clung to life in the shielded caverns of the icerock interior.

Every aspect of the Jovian system was the personal property of the Onias, the Landlord citing the Accords as the basis for his absolute ownership of every aspect of life on over sixty moons, and dozens of void habitats, that made up his empire. The original union contracts of the first workers had turned into indentured labor, then into slavery, then into tribal fundamentalism over successive generations, as the fight for space and resources had become more severe.

The Onias wasn't a single individual, like the Rossen. Instead, the Onias was more a collection of personality, memories, knowledge. When the last Onias died, that mental template was implanted in a boy from a carefully cultivated gene-line. Those males who were unneeded or failed compatibility were still useful, politically. Through these little princelings, who were scattered across the vast inwell and granted wealth and influence far beyond any other Jovian, the Onias maintained power.

Communities were said to do anything to secure Onias gametes for the home-womb and a status-raising Nepo child. Muddled the region's internal politics horribly. Genetic ties to the Onias conflicted with tribal ties to moon and people, to philosophy and belief. Despite the official Accords ban on organized religion beyond the Arran inwell, thousands of different quasi-spiritual factions thrived in the Jovian inwell. Polarist, and otherwise.

Violent habitats, these.

Yet the world sweeping under the monorail's run felt ordered, parklike. The first cavern had contained a smooth sweep of shallow sea overlaying the rock in all directions, pillars of blue-green algae reaching a meter or more off its surface. The spaces they were moving through now were filled with rounded buildings suspended by thick cabling systems, glowing with yet more algae. Water droplets, they seemed, on spiderwebs. The place seemed more akin to the stories of Themisto than the darkness and chaos of the accounts of the Propagation battles, fought in the dark hearts of starving moons.

She mentioned this, and tDaer nodded.

"True, but these are all Nepo neighborhoods. Prime real estate. Close to the atmo generators and aurora passages," hen replied and gestured vaguely at the sea. "We're headed into the nightside."

"Nightside?"

"Where the majority lives. And slaves away for the Onias," tDaer replied, condescension thick in the words.

"Somebody has to do the work," Angakkuq replied in his usual amiable tone. "How else would we support the Landlord if there was no labor?"

"The entire point of the Tenancy is to support the people, give them what they need, allow them to live full and enriching lives, not the other way around."

"To Ang's point, how's that work if nobody's working?" Tharsis interjected. "If the economy ground to a halt, wouldn't everyone just, I don't know, die?"

tDaer just smiled, patronizing. "Well, that's the argument the Rossen used to get it approved or whatever by Mars, but that isn't what the truth of it is. That's not what he's really after, slaving people to their labor."

Irritated by the dismissive tone, the lieutenant shot back, "And your theory?"

"Doesn't matter what I think, right?" tDaer tossed back, sarcastic. "What difference do better ideas make to Martians? Your planet could have been a paradise before the Donovan family came along with their little regressive religious vision for the place."

Tharsis kept her eyes outside the car, the next station coming into view. "They were trying to preserve something the Euphemism was destroying," she replied, quiet.

"Yeah, something that needed to be destroyed," hen sniffed.

"Do you ever fucking stop?" Tharsis demanded, suddenly sick of it. "What the fuck is your problem with Mars? We don't tell you how to live, why should you give a clogged-up piss chute what we do?"

"I don't," tDaer said, and it sounded honest. "But you do, don't you?"

The simple question rippled through the lieutenant, although she didn't quite know why. "You don't know anything about us," she grumbled.

The next stop was theirs. They unhooked from the seats and grabbed their bags and Tharsis soon found herself on a static-cling platform, watching the car pull away into the gloom.

Angakkuq had to code them through the dropway down to what he said was the station's main level and the exit to the streets, the sphincter below them opening only with his palm in the reader. They continued through, out into what felt like a main avenue of some kind, a bored-out tunnel, its light packed in discreet units.

There seemed to be no gray zone, no twilight, between the darkness and the light, no transition at all between the two. Bright patches guarded doorways and facades, outer walls, and guarded entrances. The rest of the street was left to the moon's native shadows, deep and ancient things. There was no sense of space. It felt, to Tharsis, very much like being inside a termite mound.

"Narrow-spectrum illumination," tDaer explained. "It takes less power to run, less interference from the magnetics."

"I thought the what, kilometers of crush and the sealant and whatever the hell else was supposed to protect from the magnetics."

"Once electrical's involved, anything can happen," hen said. "But come on, we don't want to lose him."

Tharsis lost track of how long they were moving, how many twists and turns and dives and long runs it took to catch up, but when they finally did, on the edge of a carven, sealed icerock facade, she was surprised by what was above the door.

"Nighttrippers?"

"Yeah, hen has a whole chain of places. Hen likes the name or something. Who knows what these people are thinking sometimes, huh?"

"Wait, who?"

The layout, Tharsis noticed as they dumped their scat in an empty room, was essentially the same as that of the New Stockholm house. Same shabby, worn-out furniture, same unmatched tile flooring. Same, same, same.

Except for one major difference, discovered when tDaer threw a couple of loitering Rheans out of the top area that should have been the stargazing deck—her absolute favorite thing in the New Stockholm branch. Instead, Amalthea's Nighttrippers boasted a massive zero-line skyviewer. She'd seen things like it back on Mars, chambers cut out of raw rock, configured so one felt like one was standing inside the sky.

It wasn't stars or sun or rainy afternoon that was projected down into the room, though.

"Aurora's permanent this close to the planet," Angakkuq explained, over bites of pre-tubed amino acids. "Father Jupiter talking to us through the light."

tDaer gave Tharsis another of those looks that was clearly meant to indicate shared frustration. "It's all pretty basic, really. We get it at home. But you know the Jovians. They've got an entire viaduct system built for it."

"You take no joy in life, do you, tDaer?" he shot back, wounded.

"I take joy in things," hen replied, and circled a finger around to indicate the tired space. "It's just, you know, this is what we get. This world. Why do you feel the fucking need to make it something that it's not? Planets don't talk, nothing lives in the penumbra, it's all just pathetic make-believe." And she huffed. "Where the fuck is he, anyway, Ang?"

"Can't rush family. We're on his schedule. His rock, his rules."

Tharsis ignored it as best she could. Anger and adrenaline both spent, exhaustion was beginning to catch up with her. tDaer lapsed into silence. Angakkuq had just started on a second tube of whatever that gray stuff was before their mystery host showed up.

"What, in the name of Jupiter's magnetic asshole, is this?"

Jovian, but nothing like Angakkuq. Where their backpacker was pale, thin, obviously stunted, this man was a hulking brute. Not that he was tall, nor broad, nor especially massive. But there was an aura about him, heavy and imposing, that seemed to fill the aurora's chamber and push its threads of projected light away. It was impossible to see the jaundiced tint of his skin, because every visible bit was gold. For a moment, Tharsis couldn't figure out what that was, and then it hit her. Everything, even his eyes, were tattooed.

Onias markings.

Nepo.

"What's your problem, Riqan? I told you we had a Martian along for the ride…"

"Martian, yes. Fucking moon-nuking ASDF bitch, no." He turned yellow-tinged eyes on her. "Lieutenant? You mind leaving? I need to discuss what the fuck happened to my craft with the people who are actually involved."

Afterward, thinking back on that moment, she couldn't figure out why she didn't head to the nearest Arran consulate. Suffer the consequences of what she'd already done. Get out of the scat.

But.

"Who said I wasn't involved?" she shot back and settled into the ancient sofa.

"Fine. You stay. tDaer," and his attention snapped back to the primary target, "we need to talk about you breaking my toys. You're supposed to be learning how to operate it, not fucking it up."

He launched into a lecture about what was wrong with the divedrive and how much fixing it on a tight schedule was going to cost him. However, the discussion quickly disintegrated into Franco-Jovian: the Nepo mentioning something about the last shipment and Ang falling into their native tongue. tDaer listened to it for about thirty seconds before announcing, "I don't have time for this scat. Tharsis, how about some fuckin' sleep?"

The lieutenant was more than happy to follow hen out.

In the scoop of the commandeered dorm room, in the soft illumination of the not-quite-light that suffused the moon's interior, hen's mig-born body seemed angular beneath its thin cotton tunic. Tharsis found herself wondering what was beneath it, what the Iapetan really was under all those layers of blue skin and sarcastic indifference. Not male or female, they claimed.

Not really human.

But then, neither was she. Nobody was.

Not since the Euphemism's quest to make something more of the species had left them so much less.

What difference does it make what we do when we aren't even anything? Tharsis wondered. It scared her, that she didn't have an answer for that.

"I am sorry," tDaer said, without a trace of hen's usual cockiness. "I wanted you to see it."

"Ceres? Get fucked," Tharsis replied, staying in the interstitial of the door. Between hall and room. Guarded against some threat she didn't understand. "You had no right."

"I know, I know, the craft kicked you out, but how was I supposed to know it could even do that?" tDaer protested.

For a moment, it hung, strange and unfamiliar. Tharsis didn't want this. She wanted a cold cider. A long nap. A commander she didn't dread. She wanted somebody to look at her the way tDaer looked at her and to not wonder what in the hell was going on.

"Fuck it," tDaer muttered, and surged in, wrapping those spider-long fingers around the back of Tharsis's neck, yanking her into a kiss.

There was no warning, no indication of any kind, and the Arran completely froze up, too shocked to respond. But then tDaer stroked up into the base of Tharsis's braid, caressing with a gentleness that the Iapetan had never demonstrated in the year they'd known each other.

Hen's lips were surprisingly soft, and Tharsis tried not to think about how long it had been since the last time she'd kissed somebody. She pulled back, but tDaer didn't give her a centimeter of space.

"I like you without your uniform on," tDaer whispered against the skin of her cheek. "Makes you look like you."

"The uniform's still me, though."

"Doesn't have to be," the Iapetan said. "You ever thought about that? Being who you want to be, instead of who they tell you?"

Tharsis didn't at all care for the smile tDaer was giving her. "Did you bring me a grav bag?" she asked, pointedly avoiding the question.

tDaer finally backed off, jabbing a thumb at the back corner of the room. "You sure you need it?"

"Yeah," Tharsis said, moving away. "Pretty sure."

It took her a long, long time to fall asleep, discomforted in the endless night.

CHAPTER
TWELVE

TOO MANY THINGS, Tharsis found herself thinking over the course of the next sevenday. Too many beautiful and terrible things out there.

tDaer.

Amalthea.

Those bodies, falling into the endless seas.

And Tharsis wasn't sure if it was fascination or repulsion she felt at the memory of it all.

"Matter transference through a hull?" Tech Sergeant Santos asked, when she put the question to him, Oneday morning. Technically an MP, he ran the base's small orienteering club and had a near-encyclopedic knowledge of navigation theory. She'd gone in early, to catch him on the tail end of his shift, almost two hours before reveille, and they were both yawning. "Forcing anything through any voidcraft hull would fuck up the mechanics pretty bad."

She rolled her eyes. "I understand that, Sergeant."

"Okay, well, let me think." He paused. "The hull is a technicality, not a necessity."

Tharsis leaned on the edge of the entry desk. This early in the morning, the normally bustling room was quiet: no twittering Ibbie girlfriends, no soldiers waiting on drug breathalyzers, nobody arguing with the guards. Just her and the sergeant and Tommy, perched on the counter; paws tucked up and keen, slitted eyes surveying everything.

Half dreaming, she could sense, mind wandering off into the penumbra, more curious than concerned.

"What do you mean?"

"Well, you don't technically even need a craft…"

"I'm not talking about skin diving."

He drummed his fingers, nodding along to his thoughts.

"The hull's a point of focus for the wetware. Tells it, essentially, the volume of mass to be moved: atmo, people, cargo, whatever. Minus that focus, scat can surface in a place where it already is. Fold up its matter along the worldline's temporal axis. Exist, basically, in parallel with itself, which violates the fundamental laws about conservation of energy. Even a fraction of a second of that kind of folding causes massive destabilization at the subatomic level."

Tharsis nodded. "And then things blow up, right? Like those sections of the coronal mass collection arrays, during the Vastitas recovery mission?"

"Exactly. You need a comparable energy reserve in order to maintain stability in a mass transfer. That's one of the big reasons they positioned the *Undine Glory* that close to the sun. And they still had issues." He shook his head. "When it moves things, it moves them exactly as they are, internally. Shoving things out of the hull would, fuck, I don't even know."

"So you can't, I don't know, fall out?"

"No, no way. The wetware can't imagine that kind of thing. It's intentionally programmed like that." He stopped, clearly mulling it over. "But, if the Flet imposed his central consciousness, I mean, who knows?"

Tharsis's chest tightened. "Can he do that?"

Santos stopped again, fingering the ID card she'd handed over when she walked in. "Maybe," he said, and looked out the window, laughed nervously. "But, umm, that's all just speculation. Of course. Even skin diving's a wildly unproven theory. Who knows if the Golanites actually pull it off or not? Why do you ask?"

"Just curious."

"Oh. I thought it might have something to do with our guests."

Tharsis followed his gaze to one of the upper windows of the guardhouse, the hatches that sucked along the top of the artificial sky's terminal curve. She'd seen it, walking in, that craft. Hanging low over the base, over the tops of the fronting islands, fuzzy through the daydreamed Ibbie sky. Some general with his private cessna, she'd thought. Here, though, the sky was still in its night cycle. She could see the hull configuration quite clearly.

Her brother used to have a painting of one pinned up over their study area. What he'd wanted to serve on. What he'd been working for.

Enoch-class deepvoider craft were the forward operating bases of the Arran fleet. Crews were small, missions were long, classified above top secret. Nobody quite knew what they did, but rumors abounded; the Rossen preferred those assignments, Command was using them for interstellar recon missions, they knew where the Arcna was.

"God in Heaven," she breathed.

For one crazy, terrifying moment, she wondered if they were here because of her.

"Yeah. Deepvoider. Can't remember the last time one of those showed up here. Ought to be a fun day," Tech Santos said. "Anything else I can do for you?"

"No. I better get to work."

The cat followed her out of the guardhouse.

Tharsis had no idea what the animal wanted. Judging by how his tail was twitching, high and irritable, he had no intention of explaining himself. But once they'd gotten out of view of the gatehouse, her ranch-raised senses caught something from his thoughts.

question.curious.human-from-mountains.

"What?" she asked aloud, without stopping, eyes on that craft and gut roiling.

The image of a host of umbran—smaller, malformed, watching— fell into her head, as the cat nipped lightly at the skin above her boot, curious.

"You've seen it, then," she mused. "What is it, boy? Can you tell me?"

No answer. His mind had wandered again, as cat's minds so often did, off to the warmest corners of false sunlight and his nightly patrols and the scent of a strange dog in his territory.

"Scat-ton of help you are," Tharsis grumbled. He meowed his agreement, sitting back on his haunches.

She gave him a look, trying to ask why he wasn't coming any closer, but the fur stood on his back and his teeth bared in an angry hiss. Tharsis turned to see Master Sergeant Olin, coming towards her, smeared pressure mugs of coffee in hand, a strange dog at his side.

It looked nothing like the sleek Tyrannus shepherds or old Belg Malinois breeds often favored for fast-intercept military actions. Built like a bear, thick and powerful, he sported a tight-clipped, dark coat and heavy jaws. The dog's head reached well above Olin's waist. Aonian Ovcharka, Tharsis realized, surprised. She hadn't seen one in years. They were notoriously difficult to manage, good for ranch work and surface infantry auxilia, but usually unsuitable for the tight conditions found on military craft. Aggressive, it was said, with anybody who wasn't pack. But this one had an ease about him that belied both his stature and his breed.

A small group of people was huddled around the main entrance of the squadron building. Hinden, with his back to her, spoke with animated sweeps of chicken-wing arms to three men in high-necked blacks, the heavyweight uniforms of deepvoider combat troops.

"What the fuck's going on?" she whispered to Olin as he passed her one of those mugs. Boiled ag-platform coffee beans, unfiltered, real nasty cowboy scat. His usual.

The sergeant smirked, bitter. "He's regaling them with that one story he loves so much, you know, about the double transit of Ganymede and Thebe on Trilan, when the base got invaded by a horde of pinniped umbran from the depths."

She hid a yawn with another sip of Olin's noxious brew. Her stomach burned, but the jolt felt good. "Did you get him off on that story?"

"Fucking right I did, ma'am. Needed to get to you before he did."

The gravity dropped out of her gut. "What do you mean?"

"Remember the auditorium?"

She took a sip of coffee to hide her relief. It burned. "Oh, right. Hell."

"Oh hell is right," he said and started walking again. "Let me do all the talking, okay?"

She barely had time to nod before Captain Hinden caught sight of her, and the drone of the all-too-familiar story stopped.

"Ah, Lieutenant Chen, good to see you finally in," he asked in a false-nice voice as she threw him a salute, using her surname like a cudgel. He was pissed about the deepvoider. "Took you long enough, eh?"

"She does live off base, sir, and it's not even reveille yet," Olin shot back, and turned to one of the enlisted blacksuiters. "She's the one who caught the problem I sent you, Yip."

"It was a good catch," the other sergeant said, and scratched the nape of his neck with one huge hand. His wrist-rank was circled twice in red, cut through with a vicious scar. "Based on her data, Colonel, it deserves a closer look."

The colonel in question, to the sergeant's left, nodded to her.

"Lieutenant Chen, I'm Colonel Cambel of the AMS *Barachiel*, along with Lieutenant Hans Morray, my comm lead, Tech Sergeant Christofer Yerpoli from our Marine detachment, and the pack lead of our canine recon unit."

"He's a handsome boy," Captain Hinden laughed, nasal.

"He's one of the best war dogs in the service, sir," the last of the blacksuiters, Morray, shot back, clearly irritated. He looked every bit the soldier, from his close-cropped copper hair to the rank on his neck, standing out with a double combat honor, inked gold on the first wing. Rare for a comm guy. "And he outranks you."

"El-Tee," the colonel said sharply.

"No disrespect intended, Captain Hinden," the lieutenant added.

But beside Olin, disgust was boiling undisguised off the dog, too thick for any Arran to miss. All eyes turned on Hinden, Morray smiling a little. But Tharsis was the only person that caught the pat Olin offered the big animal.

It really was weird.

Hinden cleared his throat. "The el-tee's at your disposal for whatever you need. Sorry again about the inconvenience. Can't imagine the fuel cost."

Tharsis kept her face as neutral as she could. "Anything you need, sir."

"Not a problem, Captain," the colonel replied, easy, collected;

disappointing, really, in its lack of criticism. "We run down every lead we get, no matter how tenuous. We're grateful for the tip."

"And we can always use a bit of shore leave," Yip said.

"We've been at dry dock for the last month," Morray said, grinning.

"Exactly. Time for a break."

Tharsis didn't miss his commander smirking back.

A team, these guys. A real, honest team.

What would that be like?

"I couldn't take the chance of us missing something important," Hinden blustered on, either too oblivious or too obstinate to realize he'd been snubbed. "Even if it was just a mistake on our part. Now, sir, can I show you to your lodging? I'm sure the rest of your boys would appreciate—"

"Showers?" Colonel Cambel laughed and laid a hand on Hinden's shoulder. "Lead away, Captain. I'd like to pick your brain on the current political situation here in New Stockholm. We're getting some intel on the Rallarhu's recent behavior I'm finding a bit troubling."

Tharsis didn't relax until the two of them were well out of view, Tommy trailing after them. "Come on," she said, gesturing, "underground's this way."

Morray, however, was still watching his commander's retreat.

It was Yip who asked, though. "Guy's an ass," he stated flatly, and looked to Olin. "How's he keep this job?"

"Welcome to Humphryes, the politically expedient base that not even the Rossen could fix," her master sergeant drawled, the dog nuzzling his palm for a pet. "Ma'am, you ready?"

Tharsis forced a smile, stomach roiling.

Her nervousness only grew more pronounced on their way down to the auditorium, even the blacksuiters' casual banter with Olin dying off as they hit the darkness. It seemed thicker than before, more oppressive.

Fear. Pressing on all of them.

When they came to the bottom of the well, she had to grab for the wall, trying to catch her breath. It felt as if the air was being forced from her lungs. High altitude, low pressure, trying to suffocate her.

She started at a touch at her shoulder, Olin whispering in her ear, "Stick close to the dog, El-Tee."

But before she could ask what he meant, he pushed past her, unlocking the door into the auditorium proper. "I hope you're ready for this," he announced to the group. "Last time we were down here, it stank to high heaven."

"I think we can handle a little stink, Sergeant," Morray said.

The big animal pushed his nose up into Tharsis's hand, and she instinctively ran her palm down, gripped at the loose skin and thick fur of his ruff. Her heart was starting to race, the world fading, blurring. He whined at her, but whatever he was trying to communicate was lost when the door opened, and as promised, a terrible stench assaulted the little party outside.

She turned to ask Olin how it had gotten so bad in the last month, if the wall had become infected when they'd cut the tumor out, if a wall could get an infection, but he was gone.

The dog, the party, the room—

She was the only thing in the universe.

The darkness was older than time, a living entity, a predator lurking in its stronghold. Absolute, impenetrable, and she couldn't move for the weight of it, pressing in against her skin with the atmospheric intensity of a gas giant.

Silence. Profound, primordial silence.

Broken by a laugh. If one could call it a laugh. Quiet, subtle, the ghost of sound. Growing. Tighter, louder, closer crawling under the skin, infecting the blood. Twisted, twisting, in ways no human voice could ever twist.

Turning into an all-out scream of pure, unadulterated fury.

Accompanied by a dozen more, blasting out from all directions.

Weapons fire, then, screamed orders—*shoot for the head, the head goddammit!*—panic, so much panic.

Deathlights, illuminating a—

"Lieutenant?" she heard, far away. Almost that same voice that had spoken before. Impossible for it to be. No fury now, no anger, nothing but concern. Mercy. That darkness, she thought wildly, was the opposite of mercy. The place where mercy went to die. "Tharsis!"

A warm nose nuzzled her shoulder, present, solid, real. She grabbed at the owner, struggling to breathe. To surface up from whatever that had been.

"You okay?"

Olin had a firm grip on a chair beside her. Her body had flung itself into the cold concrete floor. Into those fucking chairs.

The lieutenant dug her fingers deeper into the dog's fur,. "Fucking penumbra," she managed.

"What'd you see?" Morray asked.

"Why?"

The blacksuiters exchanged a look, and Olin laid a hand on her shoulder. "Tell him, ma'am."

Tharsis ground her teeth, shifted into a more comfortable position. Tried to keep herself from floating off. The dog moved with her, pressed against her. She stared at Olin, trying to figure out where he was coming from with all that. What they weren't telling her. What he wasn't telling her.

"How would I know what it was?"

"You've been seeing things."

"I hear military women typically don't," Yip said. "It's the drugs they've got y'all on."

Tharsis bristled. "We all know how dangerous it is to conceive in mig."

"You worried about getting pregnant, ma'am?" he asked, grinning again. "You and that Graben kid doing some penetration testing?"

"Yip," Morray warned.

Tharsis rolled her eyes. "Like I'd want to fuck that little scat smear."

"Yip, stow that scat," Olin said, and the other sergeant spread his hands in mock apology.

"How would I amuse myself if I can't harass the el-tees?"

"She's my el-tee, mud dick."

"Yip's an ass, very true," Morray said, interrupting, and pointed above them at a new spiderweb of cracks. Mutated wetware crumbling through the plaster. "But that's a problem. And if you're seeing things, that makes it a bigger problem."

"Why's it matter what I saw?" Tharsis challenged, tired. Tired of Humphryes, tired of military obtuseness and double-talk, tired of the visions and of being tired all the time. "Is this a fucking interrogation or something?"

"Something might be riding the lines from Noqumiut," Olin replied, emotionless.

The word hit her. Hard. "Noqumiut? You're saying this is—"

"We are not saying that. Not until the Landlord declares it. Until then, per Colonel Cambel, this is fucking classified," Morray interrupted, getting in front of Olin's words and offering her a hand up. She let him pull her into something approximating upright in the microgravity, grabbing on his arm to steady herself. He had to caught her elbow to steady her, and smiled when she looked at him.

There was something about it that reminded Tharsis of tDaer, everything that hen had offered earlier. A connection.

The civilian girls on Mars might dream of a man like the one in front of her, but her sterile military ass didn't have a prayer with someone like him.

What had she gotten back for that sacrifice, anyway? What good was any of it?

Fuck them, she thought. *Fuck this.*

Morray was still looking at her. Concerned. She didn't like that at all. "You good, Chen?"

Irritated, she brushed him off, legs shaky but holding under her. "The less I have to talk to Hinden, the better."

They left it at that, nobody speaking at all on the way back up to the surface, the blacksuiters headed off to Humphryes's small lodging facility, the alpha at their heels, leaving Olin and Tharsis alone at the shaft's small outbuilding.

"You know," Olin said at length, "the Rossen's dog is said to serve on deepvoiders."

"Like that's actually true," she replied, not in the mood for one of Olin's spider scat lessons. "It's just a story that fits, makes dogs more important to Arran society."

"If you think dogs aren't critical to our military forces—"

"What the fuck are we talking about?" she blurted out, cutting him off. "What is any of this? You talk like you know these guys, they tell me there's probably a," he held up a hand, and she caught herself, voice dropping, "a big fucking problem, and now you're acting like everything's normal. What the fuck?"

"I do know them," he replied.

It deflated her rising ire. "What?"

"Yip and I were corporals together. My first assignment was the *Turiel*."

Dots connected in Tharsis's mind. "He's the one you called about the signal."

"Yes."

"And you knew I was seeing stuff?" she pushed.

Eyes hard, caught up in studying the night sky above them, he didn't answer. "We can leave the report until later this morning. We'll work out a story, okay?"

She sighed, pulling her arms tight around her chest. "What kind of story?"

"One Hinden'll believe."

"I'd like to know what's going on."

"I'd like to know what you're seeing," Olin shot back, commanding in a way she'd never heard him before, and it took her aback.

"I'll see you at work, Sergeant," Tharsis replied as dismissively as she could, and strode away.

She still had a few hours before she had to report in for work. The thought of waiting it out in her office was highly unappealing.

Humphryes, for all its artless corrugation, still had a decent little chapel. It was a rambling construct of pointed arches and heavy stained glass and shelves of half-melted beeswax candles, built into a false hill and turfed across the roof. Expeditionary-style, the kind built during the first days of Mars by the first settlers, much like the one in her own parish. A comfortable place, she'd always found it, and that was where she headed.

So early in the day, before Mass, one solitary single oil lamp, burning in Michael's alcove, flickered in the space. A flame, lit from the Vatican's military chapel, the same flame that burned on a thousand bases across the Heliosphere. A flame, legend held, brought down from the slopes of Olympus Mons by Father Golan, given to him by an angel during his war against the umbran that rode the oceans back from the depths.

She didn't know if she believed that story. Not anymore.

Sinking into a pew, Tharsis folded up on the kneeler, head in her hands.

She had no idea what to do. No training, no wise words, no prayer came to her. Her feeble prayers, for Michael, for the saints, for God, died unformed on her lips.

Maybe there was no peace to be had.

Not if those things were coming from Noqumiut.

The shining spires of New Stockholm stood empty under the false dawn, as she left the chapel hours later. Hollow forms, shells without yolks.

How do they live like this? Tharsis wondered, bathed in synthesized sunlight that offered no warmth at all. *How do any of us live like this?*

CHAPTER
THIRTEEN

THE *BARACHIEL* DEPARTED TWODAY. The moment it left radar range, Hinden dropped a cubic meter of paperwork on Tharsis's desk. Dragged her into his office that afternoon and explained everything he wanted done with it, in excruciating detail.

"... and I want it by the end of the day," he concluded smugly, and pointed to some poster he'd tacked up on the door. Stylized drawing of a piss chute. *Are You a Floater or a Sinker?* It was the kind of thing he found funny, inspirational.

She loathed that poster. But Hinden had it there for a reason, and the next person in her chain of command was stationed half an AU away, so she took the point. Ate lunch at her desk. Wore out a stylus. Didn't make her usual daily round to her work centers. And still had to go back to Hinden at 1700 to ask for more time.

Tharsis felt like she'd been contaminated somehow, the way he smirked at her.

Sliding back into Nighttrippers that night, ignoring the happy chatter from the common areas, all Tharsis could think of was taking a shower. A hot shower. She needed it, to step into the uncertain heat of water and scrub the top layer of skin clean off.

After a stop at her room to throw on her ancient, Academy-issue robe and grab her shower kit, Tharsis could smell the harsh chemical undertones of bathroom cleanser flooding the hallway. About that time of day, she remembered, cleaning time.

Scat.

But it was just tDaer in there. On hen's knees in the shower bay, scrubbing away at an ancient stain in ancient grout that was not going to come up.

The lieutenant watched her friend for a moment, thought about what it would be like to live like that; nothing to her name but a back-pack. No tattoos. No family. No responsibility.

But no amount of wishing was going to cancel out the service she still owed, promises she'd made. Everything on Mars boiled down to duty. When she was a girl, she'd thought it'd be grand. As a woman, it was just suffocating. At least a husband and children would have loved her. To Hinden, she was just something to help further his tin-pot ambitions.

"You alive in there?"

She startled and found the Iapetan staring at her with those inky eyes, neck pulsing faintly. "Pardon?"

tDaer sat back over hen's heels, stripping gloves off, tossing them away to squelch wetly against the shower wall. "I said, you alive in that skull of yours? You look weird."

"Don't you have a master's degree?" Tharsis interrupted, not in the mood for whatever it was tDaer was about to say. That darkness, that sound, was still there. She couldn't get it out. Couldn't understand the look in her friend's eyes. "Didn't you tell me that?"

"I have two, actually. With honors. About average for the Daer line, but," and tDaer cocked hen's head, "you want to know why I choose to scrub fungal growths in some scatty hostel? Instead of doing what-ever one's supposed to do with one's academics?"

Tharsis bit her cheek. "I don't know, I guess."

"Everything back home is all theory, talk," and it sounded honest, in a way in which tDaer wasn't ever honest. Liked it pained hen. "Works for most of us and that's fine. It's not my place to judge what somebody else derives meaning from, but it doesn't work for me."

"So what, you'd rather be scrubbing showers?"

"I'd rather be doing something that matters."

"They told me I'd be doing something that matters," Tharsis said slowly, and sank down onto the bathroom floor, dirty water immedi-ately soaking into the edges of her uniform. "But I go to work and I try, but it's all just, I mean, what difference does it make if Humphryes is here? If I'm here on Humphryes? It's fucking useless."

tDaer was quiet for a moment. "Means something to your family, doesn't it?" And for once, there was no judgment, no condescension. Just honest curiosity.

Tharsis thought about the *Barachiel*, and her brother, and laughed a hollow, empty laugh. "I'm talking about me." She let her head fall back against the wall, sighing. "You give up your whole life, and this is all there is."

A shifting noise and a soft touch on her knee pulled her eyes down. "This is all there ever is," tDaer replied quietly, so close their noses brushed. "There never can be anything else. And that's by design. It's all lies, Tharsis. Fucking lies. They lie and they fucked it up and nobody's where they should be and it's not fucking fair."

Something in tDaer's words set off every alarm in Tharsis's head, as if Mars itself was screaming at her to not listen. But all Tharsis could think about was the stench in the darkness, the war that was coming, how pointless it all seemed.

And, seized by something she didn't understand, Tharsis pitched forward and sealed her lips against tDaer's. Her hands grabbed for purchase on threadbare work clothes as thinner, longer ones twisted into her uniform.

She hauled them both up to their feet, pushing tDaer back against the shower wall, kissing hen with all the desperation welling up inside of her. tDaer went with it, let Tharsis lead for the moment, lips and tongue and teeth submissive.

For a moment.

Before hooking a leg around, flipping, pressing pelvis to pelvis, back to wall, as hen started working the uniform's zipper down. Tharsis didn't even have time to shrug out of it, either, before a hand slipped down. Up.

"Jesus, tDaer," she gasped, those fingers hitting the wetness building there, sliding into her. Her head hit the tile, cushioned by her hair, falling from its bun.

"Calm down, it's okay, I've got you, go with it, come on, just go with it."

Dimly, Tharsis realized with a flush—tDaer chuckling, kissing her again—she had no idea what she was doing. But her body seemed to understand what tDaer was doing to it, manipulating it with the same intensely bored focus hen piloted the divedrive with, and she could feel her own response growing in her belly. Hotter and brighter and more.

Until it hit her. Full. Blossoming in the uncolored glory of a magnetic explosion.

Her knees gave out under the force of its blast.

tDaer was right there, as she hit the shower room floor, holding her as she drifted back into herself. The lieutenant blinked, hearing a laugh that could have been hers, far, far away.

"You needed that," tDaer observed, smug and sweet.

Tharsis nodded, a little breathless. It never felt like that when she did it herself. Not that she was going to admit that to the voider. "Yeah, yeah, that was good."

"Just good?" tDaer sniffed and ran those impossibly thin fingers back through the Arran's tangled dark hair. "I'll have to try harder next time."

"Next time?"

"Fuck yes, next time. Right?"

"Sure," Tharsis said, not sure at all what she was feeling, eyes firmly on the ceiling. Mold up there, she noticed. As if cataloging it would somehow make the rest of this make sense. She wanted a shower. She wanted to go somewhere that wasn't Humphryes. "If you want."

"Well, yeah. Why wouldn't I?" tDaer shifted, eyes glowing like the black heart of a neutron star. "Why do you keep throwing that scat out there?"

The lieutenant sighed. "Arran men don't… they don't like us."

"Fuck them and their stupid opinions. It's disgusting," hen said, and moved back into Tharsis's space, swinging a leg up over hers, straddling her, pressing a hand to her belly. "That whole planet is fucking slavery. To dirt. It's insane."

At those words, home, home sprang to Tharsis's mind. The red dust of the planet, the wild storms that battered the shutters, the snow and the seas and the struggle to eke out the most spartan of livings from it all. The need to protect it. The fanatical pride most took in the task.

"This is freedom," her father had told her once, on a campout in the high slopes, before she'd left for the Academy. "This is freedom. And this kind of freedom is what keeps us human, Ambera. Don't forget that. Don't let anybody tell you otherwise."

"I've got something I'd like to show you," tDaer whispered in her ear, breaking through those memories. "I need your help."

"Sure," she whispered.

But when tDaer took her back to hen's room to show her what hen had been talking about, Tharsis wished she hadn't asked.

THARSIS FOUND herself at the Wardog that evening. A quiet seat, far end of the bar, as far away from the few other officers that were in here on a weekday night. The radio was up—rugby season had started back home—but conversation was subdued.

The place hadn't been the same since Major Lanin left. Nothing had been the same. It all felt very distant, like it belonged to another life.

A life where one Lieutenant Ambera Chen hadn't heard what was in tDaer's grainy recordings, squirreled away in the mess of hen's tiny dorm room as if precious.

Quiet, at first. Almost silent. A whisper, rising to a plea, to a whining scream, one word contained in it all, echoing coldly around the spare little dorm room.

... come... come to me... you must...

It was the voice from the past. From the darkness.

Everyone in the Heliosphere knew that voice.

"I picked that up about a year ago, while I was working on my doctorate at a Tethyan campus," tDaer had explained. "Took me forever to decrypt it, but I could see the source of the signal. Knew I had to keep trying. And there it was. There she was. The Arcna."

"This is new?"

"I need something," tDaer had pressed.

"What?"

"A complete copy of *The Book of Shoals.*"

The enormity of that request went through Tharsis's mind again, there at the bar, and she had no idea what she should do about it.

Another Propagation. Another fucking war. Coming. Proof of it coming, right there, on some Cronuan grad student's tablet. A Cronuan who wanted Tharsis to violate the Accords for hen.

It was probably the reason for hen's interest in her, that scat in the showers, which was an infuriating thought.

Tharsis knew she had to go back to base. Report it. Confirm Colonel Cambel's suspicions. Get it up the chain as fast as possible before things started blowing up. But then Hinden would get the credit for it. Promotion, decoration, bragging rights.

That thought was inexcusable pettiness, and Tharsis knew it. She knew better.

She didn't know what the hell to do.

"Anything else you need, El-Tee?" the owner asked, swiping his cloth in front of her half-eaten basket of yam chips, ordered an hour ago. "Another cider, maybe?"

Tharsis tipped the empty glass in front of her with a tired finger. She didn't remember finishing it. Didn't even remember how many it was.

Getting drunk. With a Propagation starting.

What the fuck was wrong with her?

"I'm fine, Chris." Her whole body ached. "Just tired."

The expat leaned in, glancing at the radio. "I've been seeing a lot of that these days with you military kids. Since that Hinden took over up there."

"Major Lanin was a lot better," she agreed, silently wishing the gregarious man away.

"Commanders come and go, El-Tee. I've seen oh, eight of them pass through Humphryes since I opened this place. Good or bad, they all try to change everything, but the system trundles on. Always does. You younger officers are too young to know this yet, but Hinden ain't the end of the world." He nodded. "Don't get caught up in it."

Tharsis scrubbed a hand across her face. He wasn't leaving. Why wasn't he leaving? "It's my first assignment. I guess I thought it'd be, I don't know, different?"

"Especially stop worrying about it if it's your first assignment," he told her, and then chuckled a little. "Keep yourself attached to a good NCO, and you'll be fine. Like that one man you've got, Olin."

She snorted. "Hinden doesn't like him any more than he likes me."

"Good NCOs usually piss officers off. It's their job to let you wing-necks know the difference between what can be done, what's being ordered to be done, and what should be done," Chris said. "If Hinden knew what an asset he had in that man, he'd lay off."

Tharsis ran a finger around the rim of her empty glass. "What do you mean?"

"I was stationed out here at Humphryes, you know, a decade or so ago. Did my six, met a nice local girl, liked the 'roid and decided that was it for me," Chris replied. "But Olin there, he had drive. 'This is my life,' he used to say, 'there's nothing else for me.' I tried to tell him otherwise, but he'd started out on the *Turiel*, and I guess that set it for him."

Tharsis tried to fit that in with the man she knew. Blacksuiter, like the boys off the *Barachiel*. Serving with clear-eyed honor and distinction. No sarcasm, all duty.

It didn't seem to fit.

"He's a good man, kiddo. Listen to him."

"Yeah, but—" she began.

But at that moment, the radio went dead, the news feed cut off the monitors, and Humphryes's Big Noise, pumped into the bar courtesy of the same ASDF-issued speaker stack located in every Arran estab-lishment, household, and craft on 4Vesta, crackled to life.

On automatic override.

<—*We have confirmation, I repeat, we have confirmation that Lecides Base in the Hilda Archipelago is under active fire from unidentified enemy forces. Casualty reports will be provided as known. We repeat, Lecides Base is under attack*—>

The quiet of the room that had descended with CP's words was shattered by the sound of falling glass. Tharsis turned to see Chris's daughter struggling to pick the pieces up and put them back on her tray. Nobody moved to help.

Chris turned up the volume.

<—*We repeat, Lecides Base is under attack. An official statement from HOMECOM is expected shortly. Lecides Base is under attack. Conventional*

Tharsis thought about the divedrive, and the *Barachiel*, and tDaer's recording. The first words of the Eighth Propagation, calling somebody, something, out to Noqumiut.

And, leaving a twenty-five MSD coin next to her half-finished glass, she left for base.

Whatever the consequences for herself, HOMECOM needed to know.

"WE'RE at WARNCON YELLOW now, but the moment HOMECOM declares RED," one of the technical sergeants, Winters, was explaining, "even an insignificant little place like Humphryes is going to get turned upside down."

Under normal circumstances, Tharsis had no business being in the command post. Under crisis conditions, her presence was actively interfering with the more classified reporting operations. But the CP held the radio terminal that could talk to the *Barachiel*, and so that's where she had gone.

Tharsis squinted at the flashing wall of indicator lights, the MSLS communications array. Long-range fleet ULF to VHF: a hideously complicated piece of engineering. The silic encryption unit alone had an entire room to itself. In theory, she understood how it operated. Any cadet at the Academy could describe the basic functions.

But if she'd learned anything in the past year of active duty, it was that the older something was, the more thoroughly, the more off-giddy, it had been tweaked. Places like Humphryes rarely got refreshes on their equipment. The thing might as well have been fully bespoke, with all its modifications. She had no idea how to operate it.

"Measures are in place for that, though, right?"

"Sure," Tech Winters replied, and glanced over at the private on the console before continuing, "but no matter how many curfews we set or how much bandwidth we reserve, it ain't going to do us a damn bit of good if the base gets attacked."

"Yeah, but our sky shielding's still effective, isn't it?"

"Base perimeter maybe, but personal exogear's fucked."

"What?" she asked sharply.

"I examined our own stuff this morning. It's a good four years past its expiration date."

Tharsis swallowed; that gear included her own. "Why's it so old?"

"We're not funded for it. Acquisitions keeps redlining it out on the base budget every year to make room to fund some commander's pet rock garden at Hygeia."

"Really?"

"Naw, I'm bein' sarcastic, ma'am," Winters drawled. "The money probably went to something more pressing. But still, if I were you, I'd double-check my ENEX." He glanced around, bidding her sit down as more people started filing through the mantrap. "What did you need again?"

"The *Barachiel*, that deepvoider that was here a couple of days ago. I need to get her on an encrypted channel. I've got a follow-up report on the thing they were investigating."

"Right now?"

"Right now."

"Give me a minute, ma'am," and the sergeant nodded, gesturing her down to the MSLS array's chair. But before she could get herself settled in, Junia—just through the mantrap at the double titanium doors—spotted her.

"Jesus Christ on a rocket ship, Tharsis! The fuck are you doing in my command post?"

Tharsis groaned internally. Last thing she needed was a damn cat fight. "I need to use the encrypted UHF."

"No. You don't."

She narrowed her eyes. "I'm not asking."

"How about we step into my office?" Junia asked, mock-sweet, and threw open the door to a small, attached kitchenette off to one side of the console.

"Get it spooled up for me," Tharsis ordered Winters quietly, and followed.

Squeezing in, Junia was barely able to reach around Tharsis to slam the door shut. The narrow counter area had just enough free room for a pressure percolator, microwave, and gravity sink. The rest of it was stacked high with empty boxes and spare bits of keyboards, exercise equipment, office supplies. A hundred years of junk that couldn't be thrown away. Every structure on base had a room like it.

"I need the MSLS."

"Why?" And Junia lifted the top from the percolator, peering inside, wincing as the scent of stale grounds filled the tiny space. "Not trying to be a bitch, but you don't get to just waltz down here during an emergency and use the radio. I've got inputs coming in from all over INSHOALCOM, and my guys are struggling to keep up with passing the scat to Hinden as it is."

Tharsis leaned back against the counter, irritated. "Why isn't he down here, anyway? What's he doing, picking his fucking nose?"

"How the fuck should I know?"

"I don't know, Andren, have you called him?"

Junia glared. "I don't tell you how to fix the goddamn cabling, don't tell me how to run my command post."

"I'm just saying, Hinden should—"

"Agreed, but don't sit here and think you can give me advice. You let Olin go fucking AWOL—"

"Whoa, stop, what?!"

"We've had a scatload of static coming over the lines tonight, Tharsis, so I called the cable shop to come out and look at it. Olin wasn't there." Junia paused. "As far as I can tell, nobody's seen him for days. There's not even a record of him leaving base. AWOL, Ambera."

Holy hell. "Have you told Hinden?"

"Unlike you, I'm not openly insubordinate to the boss's face." Junia dropped her voice. "And my sergeants don't piss in his oatmeal by calling down a deepvoider and then fucking disappearing."

Mind racing, Tharsis grabbed for the first thing she could figure. "That's why I need to call the *Barachiel*," she blurted out. "Olin left with them."

Junia's brow furrowed. "What?"

"He's on that deepvoider, Andren," and Tharsis realized, as she spoke, there might be some truth to it. "How else could he have gotten off-base without going through the guardhouse?"

"Right, because some bitter-ass gray-suiter enlisted man's a help out there."

Tharsis reached. "He's black-rated, Andren. He's served on deep-voiders before."

It was the other lieutenant's turn to stare. "Olin?" she asked, incredulous, and began fishing in a cabinet for the coffee. "Look, stop lying, you fucked up. Deal with it."

"I'm not lying here!"

"Deal with it and don't drag the rest of us down with you because you can't accept the reality that you've got a scat assignment and scat people and a scat boss—"

"And what? In a fair world—"

"Fuck fair!" Junia slammed down a kilo tin of coffee. "What difference does it make? Fair? Did we go to the same Academy? Do you understand anything? Hinden's the fucking commander. Why do you do this to yourself?"

Tharsis sighed. "I need the radio, Junia."

"You need the radio? I need a damn good reason."

"That's classified."

"Spider scat. My clearance is higher than yours."

She closed her eyes. Admitted as much as she could. "They found a signal, Junia. They're worried it's from the Kuiper."

Junia stopped cold. "Confirmed?"

"Colonel Cambel classified it," she shot back. "To me, and Olin. I can't tell you."

"And Olin's gone. By Michael." Junia still looked hesitant. "Okay. Ten minutes."

"Once the call picks up," Tharsis countered.

"Fine. Just keep your head down, okay? On the off chance Hinden shows up, I can't guarantee he won't roast your ass for this." Junia blanched. "And if you can get Olin on the line, I'll take the AWOL thing out of tonight's report."

"So you didn't tell Hinden yet?"

"Like I said," Junia said, and a small smile twisted her lips, "I haven't been able to get ahold of the man."

Junia got her coffee on the stove, and Tech Winters got the frequency binders out and had the private talk Tharsis through the spool-up procedures. They were ten minutes into programming the silic when the CP doors banged open, Hinden sweeping in with his usual blusters, Graben tugged along in his wake.

Tharsis froze. The private looked at her with an odd expression on his face. A very calm Winters just came over, reached between them, and removed the frequency binder. Tossed it under the console, out of view.

Just in time.

"Ah, Tharsis, not who I expected to find," Hinden said eagerly, rubbing his hands together as he poked his gaunt face around the corner. "What are we doing down here tonight?"

"Just wanted to get a head start on recalling people, sir," she lied quickly, shooting a quick look at the private to keep his mouth shut. "I've got a couple people out on leave."

"Who said anything about emergency recalls?" Hinden laughed, in that careless way of his, and Tharsis had the sudden, irrational desire to punch him right in the face. Hard as she could. "I appreciate the initiative, sweetie, but it's my job to make those kinds of decisions around here. I just heard the news on the radio. According to General Cochrane out at Hygeia, they've apprehended the individuals responsible for the attack."

"Toks?" Winters asked pointedly from the main control console.

The captain just gave him a patronizing look and kept going. "They're going to stand down from Yellow. All good. So, Tech Winters, would you mind putting out a Giant Voice announcement about that? Don't want everybody dragging their ENEXs around for no reason."

Tharsis didn't miss the sergeant's facial tic at the mention of the expired safety gear, but his tone stayed even, professional. "And was the general going to be pushing that information down through official channels?"

"You think I'm going to ask a general what she's planning on doing?"

"Sir, we've got procedures."

"Fuck the procedures. I'm giving you an order."

"Sir, the giddies very clearly state that—"

"What are you doing down here again, El-Tee?" Hinden said, cutting the sergeant off mid-sentence and turning back to Tharsis. "Who's out on leave?"

"Olin asked me for some time last night. I figured I should get him back here," she said. "He knows the base infrastructure better than anyone, and if we've got issues—"

"We don't, because there's nothing going on," he said, cutting her off again, and shrugged. "Tech Sergeant Winters, declare WARNCON WHITE."

"Can't base a military decision off something you heard on the fucking civvie shortwave," Tharsis grumbled to herself, almost grateful they weren't at a large base. Man like this, he'd get them all killed.

"What did you say to me, Lieutenant?"

It was low. Dangerous. Venomous.

But there was no helping it. Not with the words out of her mouth.

Tharsis swallowed the knot rising in her throat, and answered, "Nothing, sir."

"What did you say?" he repeated, biting off every word.

She was fucked. "I, uh, I said you can't order them to take the base back to white because of something that was on the civilian broadcasts."

He folded his arms, a vein starting to twitch in his forehead. Man like that, his uniform too baggy for his skeletal frame, it should have been amusing. It wasn't.

"And you know so much about protocol. That why you're calling a deepvoider? Again?"

Glancing back over her shoulder, the last of Tharsis's gravity dropped away.

The MSLS was finally up. Message box open. The *Barachiel's* code clearly displayed in the address window.

"Sir," she began, desperate.

"I run this fucking base," Hinden sneered. "Not you. You are not authorized to be messing around with this equipment. So, you are going to leave here this second and report up to my office, and I'm going decide if you need to spend some time in lockup."

A cold wave crashed straight through her. What? Based on what? "Sir."

"Don't fucking argue with me, Lieutenant. Out. Now."

"Sir, I need to make this call."

"I don't give a fuck what you need. I am giving you an order. You understand me?"

She understood. She did. She really did. But exhausted and fed up and far past her breaking point, something in her just snapped. "You have no fucking idea what's going on here!"

"Lieutenant—"

"What if we've got a fucking Propagation starting up, and in your arrogance you think that you know so much fucking better than—"

"Lieutenant!"

The realization of what she just said washed over Tharsis, and she stuttered to a halt, face burning. Everyone in the room was staring at her. The controllers, a couple of people from the briefing room, Junia, just out of the kitchenette, face a strange shade of gray.

The captain almost smiled. Cold. Triumphant.

"My office. Now."

Eyes stinging, Tharsis knew there was nothing she could do to save the situation. Not even the truth—he'd only accuse her of lying or have her arrested for diving without orders.

So, she did the only thing she could do.

Threw him a salute, and headed out, her chance to contact the *Barachiel* gone.

Hinden made her wait in his office—at attention, no less—for two hours before he showed up, a cruel mix of anger and enjoyment playing across his sallow face.

He let her have it.

All of it.

Four months of base-restriction. A Deny Promotion note on her next performance report. The possibility of administrative discharge.

Tharsis stood there and took it. There was nothing else she could do. The tears she was dimly worried about mercifully didn't come. In their place, a furious heat crept up her neck and flamed out across her rank.

"... and lastly, Tharsis, Master Sergeant Olin hasn't shown up to the squadron today," he finished, a nasty little smile still firmly affixed to his lips. "Is he really on leave?"

It would have been easy, so easy, to throw her sergeant under the bus, do to him what the captain was doing to her. Take the pressure off herself, keep the situation out of free fall.

But she couldn't. Not to Olin. Not to any of her guys.

"Yes, sir," she lied, praying he wasn't going to push it. "He requested it a while back and I approved it. Sorry if I didn't get it in the system, but..." He glared at her, and she summoned every ounce of will she had left to keep her own eyes steady on his, level, respectful. "I'll get it in immediately."

He sniffed. "You'll have a few things to sign tomorrow, El-Tee. Other than that, I don't want to look at you for the rest of the week. Get out of my sight."

"Yessir," she replied, the words clipping off, and saluted as he made to go.

He didn't return it.

She closed her eyes as she left the room and didn't manage more than two steps outside the door before it slammed shut, and she let herself collapse against Cheria's desk. Shaking.

If she got discharged, if she didn't serve out her full six years, one of her sisters would have to step up. Her little sisters, who sent her happy, silly letters sometimes about the cute boys in the parish and barn dances and local gossip. They deserved their innocence. No point in more than one woman in the family becoming damaged goods. And there was no way she was going to last her remaining four years at Humphryes without stepping wrong around Hinden.

One more wrong move. That's all it would take. One more.

But even as she contemplated the consequences in front of her dangerous little thought began forming in the back of her mind: *what difference did it make?*

The secretary came around the edge of her desk, rubbed her back. "You okay, Lieutenant?" she asked quietly, accent clipping the words.

"He's gonna red me up," she replied, voice eerily calm in hot ears. Nothing she'd done over the past year—over the past seven years—meant anything now. Nothing she'd sacrificed since she was fourteen years old meant a goddamn thing. "Fucking stupid giddies about respecting that bastard."

"It does not matter what kind of man he is. Giddies are law, and the foundation of law is the Accords, and everything the Accords say is in accordance with humanity's survival."

"Right," Tharsis replied dully.

"If you broke giddies," Cheria replied, with the iron-edged sweetness only an Ibbie could muster, "he should punish you. People who break the law do not belong in civil society."

What difference does it make? Why does any of it matter at all?

It haunted her, all the way back to the hostel. And when she got there, she headed straight for tDaer's room and let herself in.

"You really need it?" Tharsis asked hen, numb. "*The Book of Shoals?*"

"Yeah, I need it," the Iapetan replied. "But you sure? I get it, it's a scat thing to ask. Fuck only knows what your boss might have to say."

"You think I give a caked-up piss chute what he thinks?" she retorted. "You working tomorrow?"

"Why?"

"We'll hit the embassy then."

Dark eyes regarded her for a moment, and then a long hand opened out to her. "Sounds good," tDaer said, and Tharsis, not much caring at the moment, closed the door behind them.

CHAPTER
FIFTEEN

IT WAS a quiet trip out to Old Town the next day, both of them wrapped up in their own thoughts.

Tharsis had expected to feel some kind of regret, hesitation, about agreeing to do what she was about to do. Breaking not just federal law anymore, but the Accords. If she got caught, it'd leave her open for execution by the Rossen. But after her trip to base to sign that paperwork earlier that morning, she just felt weirdly numb.

The paperwork was as bad as she thought it would be, but it still earned her a sympathetic word from Chief Anders when she went up to drop it off. The secretary was, predictably, less consoling.

"This is a just reprimand package," she'd said as she handed it over for palm-print acknowledgement. "You should be thankful for it. Happy, even."

"This life is not about being happy, Cheria."

"What else matters?"

Tharsis hadn't been able to come up with an argument against that. It wasn't exactly what Arrans believed; happiness on Mars was a symptom of a life well-lived for other things. But with the embassy gates in sight, Tharsis found herself wondering why she couldn't have it. What was wrong with wanting it?

"I hate this place," tDaer grumbled, as they emerged from the twisting tunnels of Old Town's buildings, into Helion Plaza.

"Yeah," Tharsis replied. "Me too."

The main square of Old Town stretched for half a kilometer in all directions, radiating out from the statue of the Rallarhu in the epicenter. Grand structures each sat on their own islands around the edge, intricately carved or painfully smooth, in a dozen different architectural styles from across the Heliosphere. Embassies, all.

Mars's lay behind thick, carbon fiber gates. Atmo shields, like Humphryes's but far better quality, curved up to completely enclose the relatively low, squat building within, horizontal civilian flags waving proud in the drift of the microgravity. The red circle set in the deep blue background, the rim of white and eight angulated rays in the lighter blue above.

"I can't take you in," she told tDaer as they reached that wall.

The Iapetan ran a blue hand back through hen's short, downy hair. "I'll be here."

"I'll be quick," Tharsis promised, and slid her hand into the reader.

The embassy was empty, unmanned since the Seventh—and last and worst—Propagation. Locked against anybody without Arran DNA and still claimed as sovereign territory, such Department of State sites served as both a refuge and evacuation point in case of a crisis. Traditionally, there were weapons caches, reinforced cellar safe rooms, explosives, gas, independent environmental systems, everything an expat community might need to stay safe until military relief could arrive. Since the Seventh Propagation, most had dive cores.

Some had umbran.

Laughter echoed down the grand entry as she pushed the doors proper open, out from what looked to be a side hallway a few meters down. The sounds of ghosts. Once people, past-moments, never to be erased, a memorial to the civilian war dead.

The place had been Tok-bombed multiple times in peacetime, gassed, even taken for a fortnight during the Fifth Propagation. The Seventh Propagation had seen the Embassy's entire population of 163 men, women, dogs, children, puppies, pulled from their safe rooms. Their mutilated bodies had been paraded through the streets like rotten balloons.

The Rallarhu had sky-hooked every Ibbie at the scene, but even that failed to appease Arran national anger; last rites couldn't be said over any of the murdered. Nobody had been able to retrieve the bodies for burial, and with the Tenancy bans on religious expression outwell of Mars, no ceremonies could be performed.

Tharsis had never before really considered what that might have meant.

She shivered and hurried on.

The reading room was a round space on the top floor, and Tharsis found her way to it readily enough. Its purpose in the Embassy was simple: providing access, via the dive core in the basement, to restricted library collections hosted on Deimos.

Per the Accords, the Tenancy carried the responsibility of censoring cultural material. Graphic-interface silic networks, virtual-reality tech, recreational hallucinogens, had all been banned Heliosphere-wide, in an attempt to curb the worst excesses of the Euphemism. Beyond that, Landlords had the authority to expand restrictions within their own inwells and for their own citizens.

Mars, under the Rossen, had the fewest such laws. The only work that was outright banned from outwell distribution was *The Book of Shoals*, the ADSF's compilation of the entirety of the Arcna's ravings. The books banned by every other Landlord could have filled a room far larger than the one in which Tharsis now stood. Nothing had escaped; thousands of works of history, religion, scientific discoveries, philosophy, even fiction, could only be found on Mars.

Providing any of them to a voider—whether it was the younger *New Standard Tri-Testament*, or the classics, like *The Republic* or *Beowulf* or the Silicone Age's *Fairy Tales of Middlearth*, never mention *Shoals*— carried an automatic death sentence. Not because Mars wanted it that way, but those were the terms in the Tenancy Accords.

And so it was that Tharsis found herself spooling through the database silic with more than a little hesitation, data-chip in hand.

"It's always you young kids, isn't it?" a voice said behind her. "Always thinking there's no third option."

She started.

Behind her was a figure. An umbran. Unlike any she'd ever heard of. Male, tall, lanky. A uniform hanging loose on his frame, not the gray or black of the void-deployed. Kelly-green, covered in patches she didn't recognize, left side obscured. Ancient, she realized. Silicon-Era.

For a moment, it studied her. Every square centimeter of her. Everything she'd ever done, everything she'd ever do. Cutting through her, straight to the worldline of her soul, and the pain of it was unbearable.

For a moment.

Before it melted away, back into the penumbra.

Heart in her throat, Tharsis saw the file already up and on the screen.

Two terabytes, downloading to her chip, and she hadn't so much as finished typing it into the search feature. Or approved the upload.

Briefly, staring at it, she considered going down to the basement, pulling up the dive core, trying to figure out how to contact the *Barachiel*. But she didn't know their identifier codes, and had no idea how to operate the damn thing anyway, and so it was too easy to dismiss the idea entirely.

The terminal chimed, pulling her attention away for a moment.

File ready and uploaded.

A mob was gathering in Helion Plaza, pouring in, as Tharsis exited the embassy gates. "What the fuck?" she asked tDaer, who just made a disgusted little noise in hen's throat.

"Sucksuck," the blue-skinned voider replied. "I forget they do this scat on Fourday."

"Why is it public?" Tharsis asked as emotion from the crowd lapped at her. "I know it's necessary, but the Rossen doesn't make a spectacle out of it."

"Neither does the Scient. You report into the clinic on Titan, get a lethal dose of the blue stuff, drift off into whatever end your mind wants to imagine. No panic, no fear, nothing but the fade. But this?" tDaer said and spat. "Ibbie pomp and circumstance. I swear, they enjoy her killing them."

Their conversation was interrupted by a vast speaker array crackling to life, a living twilight descending, fog-like, into the square. The gravity started shifting down, the crowd starting to rise. Music blared out across the otherwise dead silence of the square, something pompous and strange, an orchestra missing pieces of its full variety, the percussion far more varied than anything an Arran composer would dare even try.

A platform rose in all white from the center of the plaza, elevating the Rallarhu's statue. Unformed wrapper oozed up around it, from it, as the sky tunneled down and opened the space to the void. Tendrils twisted to life, alien formations rising and falling like breeze-whipped nubs of lake waves. Readying themselves.

Tharsis poked tDaer. "Let's get out of here."

The sucksuck—the Rallarhu's periodic exercise of executive privilege—was infamous around Humphryes, and not just because of who its perpetrator was. There were stories about sky-hooking; the Rallarhu dropping directly down to eject into the void some person who displeased her. But even with that, her vast police forces handled most of the minor offenses themselves. On the spot. Violators of major laws were brought here, and an utter spectacle was made of their deaths.

The going was slow, the huge plaza filled with bodies. Footfalls were hard to reach. Tharsis, not nearly as nimble as her void-born friend, soon found herself lagging far behind.

Struggling for the obscurity within the high buildings and narrow passages of Old Town, Tharsis heard the music swell, felt that weird bioluminescence of the wrapper growing, penetrating the crowd now, rendering everyone into gray blobs of inconsequence.

Behind them, in the center of the square, the sky was falling to earth.

Tharsis was knocked off balance by a stray push, thrown higher above the ground than what her boots alone could recover, and as she tried to lose altitude in the near-mig, she had an uninterrupted view of what was happening in the center of the plaza.

The sky draped like a sheet on laundry day across the encircling spires. The statue, still discernible beneath the waving sheets of energy-hungry xenocytes, was coming to life. A consciousness was gathering, concentrated into that form's surface.

Beginning to move, the Rallarhu's vessel did not mimic the motions of bone and ligament and muscle. Rather, it seemed to flow in and back out of itself, arms fading into the sides to push back out at the shoulder, fingers retracting into the hand-space and reasserting in a different configuration to stretch palm-open to the sky.

Sightless eyes turned their attention to the crowd, to the places where it was parting now, men and women—and children, the Arran lieutenant saw with another chill—pushed through. Naked, beaten, stumbling. Up to the base of the platform, towards down-winding tendrils of raw wrapper, attracted to the thermal energy of the human body, both devouring and decaying with its touch; the same biological functions that rendered exogear dangerous, awake, unleashed.

Flesh caught fire in the intense radioactive grasp of the raw wrapper, as those people were dragged into the platform. Through the sky. Into the void, silent, screams impossible.

Ashes drifted free.

Tharsis could see an auric brume rising from the crowd; emotional energy, escaping into the penumbra. A bright rose-red pink, horrible beyond belief in its beauty. The roar—of pain, from those on the execution stage, and of excitement, from those in the audience—was deafening.

The lieutenant sacrificed what little momentum she had to knock the tiny boosters in her boots on and went for it.

tDaer wasn't hard to find, glowering under an empty cafe's awning, the spots on her neck incandescent. Eyes flat, hen reached out as the lieutenant came closer, pushing hen's long, thin fingers through the Arran's more substantial ones, holding on, breathing hard.

Something strange in hen's dark eyes.

"They're the lucky ones in a way, aren't they?" hen mused.

Behind them, deathlights rose, curling smoke spreading against the lifting ceiling of the false sky, brighter than the blue daylight glow reasserting itself there, ash floating off into the void beyond. Tharsis felt like weeping.

"Shut the fuck up, tDaer."

The lights continued all the way back to the train station.

"Who gave these fucking Landlords the right to do this to us, anyway?" Tharsis asked when they finally got in a car, trying to block out the cheerful chatter of the Ibbies, fresh from the sucksuck and giddy.

tDaer leaned forward in their facing seats, strange fire in hen's dark eyes. "See, Tharsis? Now you're catching on."

THE NEXT THREE days passed in a haze.

Tharsis knew she needed to go back to Humphryes. Fucking report what she knew. Deal with the consequences as they came. But Hinden still had her on leave, and judging from the looks she got when she went to the Wardog the night after the sucksuck, looking for Junia, he'd made some kind of statement about her to the rest of the officers. Nobody was going to risk getting redded up to help her, and so Tharsis tried to put it out of her mind.

Concentrate on figuring out what tDaer was after.

Most of the Iapetan's project passed completely over the lieutenant's head. Still, she understood enough basic theory on radio transmission—and enough of the Heliosphere's military history—to see what tDaer was trying to do.

The Arcna broadcasted on numerous frequencies in different voices, only some of which could be properly deciphered by the ASDF's quants. With Shoals, tDaer seemed most interested in the sections still encrypted. tDaer had hen's chemical-hybrid silic processors stripping through the terabytes, looking for the pre-conflict sections and running them through the wet-base algorithms from hen's lab on Iapetus.

"Location," tDaer kept saying, "we need a location."

"Location for what?" Tharsis asked again, during a break on the third night of number crunching. They'd been operating on no kind of set schedule—not for eating, sleeping, working, or fucking—and she found it all oddly liberating.

"Tharsis, I'm not sure—"

"It'd help if I knew what we're looking for."

After a moment's more hesitation, a blue hand waved across the silic array, raising a projected map of the Heliosphere into the center of the tiny room. "We know the signal bounces off a few dozen discreet repeaters seeded through the Kuiper before it hits the first major relay on Pluto. But the interesting thing is in how the signal moves once it hits there." Hen entered a few lines of command code, and the projection shifted, a spiderweb of tiny threads of light arcing across the Heliosphere.

Tharsis nodded. They'd spent a year on diagrams like that in her military strategy classes. "It targets specific locations. Passes certain messages to certain Nalatok cells before anyone else gets them."

"Right," tDaer said, waving hen's hand in command, and the lines disappeared. "What I found was that the earliest signals, like the one I intercepted, have been blocked at Pluto."

"Blocked by what?"

"I don't know. The university's data is incomplete. I was hoping I could mine the intended destination out of the data in *Shoals*. Seems to me that the key to figuring this mess out is knowing who in the fuck she's trying to contact."

"Why does that matter?"

"Tharsis, I've spent a year working on this—"

"Do you want my help or not? What are you looking for?"

"Fine. Look, remember Ceres? The Lighthouse?"

"What, like I'm going to forget almost fucking dying out there?"

"Shut up, you were fine. But according to some of the Nalatok cells," and hen hesitated again, "the last known set of navigation stones was kept there."

"Where?" And Tharsis groaned, comprehending. "The Kuiper? Noqumiut? Motherfucker, you can't just go out there."

"Of course we can. What did you think the Arcna's talking about? It's time. She's going to show us Noqumiut. She wants us to see it," came the reply. "But that navigation resource is gone. I was hoping I could extrapolate—"

But before hen could finish that sentence, the silic chimed. Compiling complete.

A fresh thread squirmed across the projection field. Gold and thin, bisecting the system.

"I thought you said it was being blocked," Tharsis said, eying the line's termination point.

"No, it's being redirected," and tDaer pulled up a second field on the projector, double-checking the numbers. "That's the Second Propagation right there, umm, hS0145."

"A full year before it began," Tharsis muttered to herself, and then, to tDaer, "What about the others?"

Another line of code and ten more minutes of escalating anxiety brought up the Third. Fourth. Seventh.

All directed at the inwell of Earth.

tDaer, silent, stood up, heading for the door.

"Where are you going?" Tharsis asked, before hen could leave.

"Gonna give our patron a call."

"We can't go to Earth."

"Sure we can. Gravity's a little harsh, the air's completely unbreathable, but there's probably something that can handle that."

"Even if you, a voider, were still physically able to set foot on the surface, the scat is very illegal."

tDaer's face clenched up tight. "We're sitting here with an illegal copy of *Shoals*. On the very off chance we get caught, what the fuck are our Landlords going to do? Kill us twice?"

"This is stupid."

"Don't you want to know what's out there? What she's discovered? What she's built?"

"What difference does it make? Nothing's going to change."

"Everything will change! Everything! That's the point of Noqumiut, Tharsis!" And hen grabbed her. "These Landlords, they failed us, they took Noqumiut away, and now nothing's the way it should be. Doesn't that bother you?"

The lieutenant sighed and pushed that hand away. "You know it fuckin' bothers me."

"I thought you were with me on this," tDaer whispered, still holding on, more desperate now. "I need you with me."

Tharsis rolled her eyes to the ceiling, to the dusty duct work, the faint whir of the hostel's atmo circulators. It was insane, what tDaer was proposing. Nobody went to Earth, not without permission, and not without consequence.

But her gaze dropped back down to the projection still orbiting slowly in the center of the room. There was something there, she knew, something strange she couldn't put her finger on. In the route of the signal, maybe, or the source, the purpose, of that diversion. Why it had happened six times before, but not on the First, or now, in the developing Eighth.

Maybe, she told herself, knowing it was self-deceptive spider scat, *maybe if you had a little more to offer in terms of intel…*

"I might be able to stand the gravity for a few hours," Tharsis replied, and untangled herself from tDaer's arms, moving away.

tDaer didn't respond for a moment, and then grinned, reaching out and pulling Tharsis back in for a kiss. "I'll be downstairs in the comm room," hen whispered against the Arran's lips. "Shut this down for me, okay?"

Sitting back down on the floor by the silic as tDaer left, Tharsis flicked the tiny blue symbol for Earth, scattering its light, breaking its form.

Wondering what in the fuck she'd just agreed to do.

CHAPTER
SIXTEEN

THE SUN CAME UP FAST at the equator. Bright. Hot.

It made her long for the sunrises of her first life. The slow roll of high desert. The chill of night giving way under the softest tendrils of light creeping through atmospheric dust, cast in a thousand different shades.

How long had it been since she had gone back there? Watched it again? Too long. Maybe she would manage it this life.

The little girl, who was not a child, watched the sun crest the eastern rim of the ocean now.

Something was coming.

She could have said something, but the people here didn't always understand. They cared, of course, but they didn't always listen. She was too young, they thought. Too small. Too fragile.

Sometimes others came to visit her. The ones who understood. The ones who remembered her. She had known them all, over the years. They didn't treat her like a child, the other Landlords.

Perhaps she had been. A child. Once. Long ago. Before the weight of centuries accumulated. Before the past crushed in so deeply that not even her still developing four-year-old brain could keep it from her.

She didn't always understand the things she could remember. They came to her in dreams and whispers, in sense-recollection and a sense of déjà vu she could never fully shake.

Perhaps it was something reaching out from back then. The past. Some old moment, arriving anew.

Time was funny that way.

The people around her may not have understood, but they did care. They cherished her for what she was. She was one of the only children here. She was little, and she was free. She walked where she pleased, in the remnants of the city-state of Singapore.

She remembered what it was like before, a city of glass and steel, an engine for trade. International, yes, but also interplanetary. The grand silhouettes of the Lifts still stood in the southern sky, but the rest of the towers were gone, brought low by hubris, by fear.

What remained was a small core of a few historic buildings from the first British settlement, and many more that imitated the style, white wood and stone against the unrelenting green of the jungle beyond. Some of the old green spaces had been left, parks and such, as well as gardens. There were a few other agricultural centers, spread across the planet, that grew more temperate-climate crops for the small human population, or for export. Singapore's fields were maintained more as a community activity.

She'd had the dream again. Last night. The dream of a walk she had taken, perhaps, in some past life. Gray stone, white snow, brilliant under an endless night. Gravity all wrong. Something ahead she didn't want to face. Didn't want to see again.

The place where she once stood and would stand again.

Someday, her hands said, fingers flicking through the words before, again, *someday we will change it*.

It was coming. But that wasn't what was waiting for her today.

The girl walked along the seawall, her little feet carrying her along a route she had walked many times before, in dozens of lifetimes, her little hands open to the morning sea air.

The daily kingdom of clouds, new and huge, was already building out across the warm waters.

Memories walked with her.

Maybe today she would find out what their intentions were.

Then she saw them.

Then she knew.

Something new. Something unexpected. Different.

The Naven smiled.

"HOW IN THE hell did anybody ever live on that thing? Crawling around its surface, eating scat growing off its ground. Disgusting. We shouldn't be here. Nothing of Noqumiut should be here."

"If you don't want me to miss the next orbital pass, Ang, shut the hell up and let me concentrate," tDaer announced, hand buried in the chemo-neutral control panel, voice far more businesslike than usual. Hen was sweating with the effort of holding the craft still. "Craft's bucking pretty fucking hard."

"We shouldn't be synched with the planet's gravity. We're in a fucking oob, tDaer."

"Of course we're synched." tDaer glared at Riqan the best hen could, hands buried in the controls. "Or we need to be. Do you see the surface or not?"

"I want you to stop bitching about the craft," their Nepo sponsor told her with a yawn. "Do you have any idea how many strings I pulled to get you this thing?"

"It's like a child, Riqan. A mentally challenged little child, that any decent society would put out of its misery, that you have to charm and cajole and whatever. That's what happens when the fucking Golanite monks split neural stem cells too many times."

"And you can't manage a child?"

"I've done enough TA work to understand that nobody manages children."

Angakkuq leaned his head against the transparency encircling them, sighing. "You're from a planet. What do you see out there, Tharsis?" he asked quietly.

Tharsis hesitated. Hung in the higher energetic flows above them, a hazy swirl of blue and green and white blurred through the penumbra. Taking up almost the entire open section of the hull, its corona grudgingly bled into the blackness of the void. The sun whispered a stream of glowing dust around the planet's ionosphere, crackling against the protective shell of that natural magnetic field. The light thrown off by the energy exchanges seemed to pass right through them, swirling and twisting like clouds through the space described by the craft's belly.

Earth.

She had only ever seen it in textbooks, in photographs, in the artwork smuggled to Mars in the last days of the Euphemism. Birthplace of humanity, mother to billions. All but abandoned now. Even if the people of the Heliosphere were allowed to return, most couldn't. Genetic drift meant most people alive couldn't handle the environment. The people in stasis on the exodus craft were the only ones left who possessed the right biology.

"I had a great-uncle who came here. Penumbra-sensitivity exception," Tharsis replied softly, pitching her voice under Riqan and tDaer's growing argument. "State Department got him three months of in-vat gravity adjustment at Diana Base, sterilization regimen, and a one-way ticket down the Singapore Lift. He died after a couple of years, but he used to send my Gran photographs." She dug her heels deeper into the hull, remembering that little album, its pictures, grayscale and grainy, condensed to fit into bandwidth allotment, of a vanished world. "The photos were always beautiful."

"I've heard Arrans can still get gravity-fitted," Ang replied, and frowned a little, his thin face scrunched. "But what's penumbra sensitivity got to do with it? I thought the point was to bring people here for the Naven's restoration projects?"

"Some people are too keyed into the penumbra to live under generated magnetics," Tharsis said, and nodded back up at the blue-green above them. "Our species was built to live there. For some people, it's the only place they can find peace."

"Oh, come on," tDaer groaned, up over the top of her. "Who the fuck would want to live there? Nothing controlled, no way to protect from thousands of variables trying to kill you. It's no wonder humans evolved into such beasts."

"I don't think so," Tharsis countered, and, realizing Riqan was staring at her, hurried to clarify with, "because its ecosystems are billions of years old, perfectly attuned to supporting life."

"In the dirt and disease," tDaer replied, shaking hen's head. "The Euphemism got it all wrong. You could never make something new down there, not in a space you couldn't control. That's why it never worked."

"The Euphemism was an attempt to wipe out humanity, tDaer. The transhumanists of the day—"

"—were right," Ang interrupted, eyes shining with a strange light. "The problem wasn't the experiments not working, it's that we didn't go far enough, we didn't do enough for it to work. The Arcna's going to show us how to make the piijuit live, how to save even your people, maybe, who can't live without this place."

Why do we need to be something different? Tharsis wanted to ask, but thought better of it.

Riqan cleared his throat, loudly, contemptuously. "I like the idea of no more talking. Wouldn't want another fuckup like Ceres. You're fucking lucky I got a good deal on the maintenance contract for this craft, Cronuan, or I might have pulled the plug there and then."

Tharsis saw tDaer flinch a little, but hen didn't respond.

"That's what I thought," Riqan said. "Get us down there. I want to grab this scat before Diana Watch figures out that we're here."

"Grab?" Tharsis asked a little too sharply. "I thought the plan was to check the receiver stations here for—"

"You think I'm risking a trip into Earth's inwell for a data upload?" Riqan snorted.

Uneasy now, the lieutenant put her hand up and felt the planetary magnetics slide like mist through her flesh. She closed her eyes for a moment, ignoring the voiders. Ignoring that little voice in the back of her mind, screaming at her. For a moment, it was just her and the iron currents and the new glow of an unfamiliar day.

Tharsis caught herself formulating a prayer to Michael, to watch her, keep her safe, and admonished herself. Let it go with a sigh.

Mars's guardian didn't help traitors.

He wasn't going to save her from this thing that was watching her. She'd damned herself with this.

"We're over Singapore. Let's go see if your intel's right, Riqan," tDaer announced in that same bored, clipped tone.

Singapore? That hadn't been discussed last night either. Tharsis looked over at Riqan, looked for an answer, but none came.

Before she could ask, the world beyond the hull went white.

. . .

"SIR? WE HAVE A PROBLEM."

"What is it?"

"Call from Diana Watch. A Jovian-registered divedrive just surfaced and vanished in cislunar space."

"Purpose?"

"Unknown. But considering—"

"Granted, El-Tee. Put out the word to the rest of the task force. It's the Rossen's game now, and we play it the way he wants. Go back to Ops. I'll go wake his lazy Earthborn-ass up."

THE NEXT THING Tharsis saw was something that should not have been there.

A little girl.

A little girl with white-gray hair and red eyes was staring at her. No fear. Smiling.

She was standing on the edge of a small park, it seemed, rain-fat grass impossibly green beneath her, a cool breeze whipping off a distant ocean. Beyond her, the high canopies of a thousand different species of tree waved over low wooden buildings painted white and bleached by the sun, the sound of birdsong rising from the shadowy depths.

In the distance, cables reached up, thicker than a skyscraper back home, the sea-bitten white weave of nanotube reaching for the lowest of orbits, tens of kilometers above. The last Lifts on Earth. The last Lift over the last city. Singapore. One tiny island in the center of all that vastness of blue. A speck of rock in an ocean wider than Mars's diameter.

Earth.

The little girl cocked her head, rabbit eyes wide. Luminous.

"There she is," Riqan said, taking a step forward. The little girl's intense gaze snapped over to him. Something in her eyes changed. He smiled, golden tattoos wrinkling. "The Naven."

"I heard she had red eyes. I didn't believe the stories. But they're true," Ang breathed. "A real piijuit."

Tharsis wondered what experiment, what twist of nucleotides, could have produced a woman who gave birth to herself, asexually cloned daughters, carrying memories centuries into the future. But she was young, she was so young, and whatever Riqan had planned—

"Fucking hell, Riqan," tDaer snapped behind them. "You didn't tell me she was a kid."

"Doesn't matter," he said, and laid his hand against the hull. He began to press. "Just keep us synched."

"Riqan…"

The girl blinked once and then, still silent, fled.

"Fuck," he growled, and withdrew. "Catch her."

"Riqan," tDaer warned.

"Catch. Her."

THE NAVEN KNEW she couldn't outrun them. They weren't really here, after all. Weren't present in any real sense of the word.

The memories percolated up, bubbles through her boiling fear. The divedrives, the way they moved, what he'd given up to make it happen. All of it, all of it she had kept all these centuries. She remembered his first real dive. How lost he'd become and how hard she had worked to bring him home.

She'd been his navigator, after all. There to help when nothing else could.

This thing chasing her wasn't him. Not fully. He wasn't present, or he would have stopped it. She tried to call out to him, mind reaching out across the void, but he didn't come. Instead, she fled through the city, reality rippling behind her, unable to do anything else.

But she took a wrong turn, and her little legs were only as good as any four-year-old's would have been. She found herself on the edge of the seawall, the great tumble of boulders that separated the town from the ocean beyond.

It was still early yet. The streets were still largely empty.

She was alone. And nobody could have helped, even if they were here.

The Naven collapsed, gulping air, lungs burning. Tears leaked from her eyes.

They were there. In front of her.

"Hand it over," the man covered in gold said. *A Nepo*, her past whispered to her, *a bud from the branch of genetics that rules Jupiter*. She bared her teeth. "You know what I want. Do I need to cite the Accords on this? I have claim to it."

The Naven touched the pebble slung around her neck. Something from the past, something simple. Just a pebble with a hole drilled in it. But it was how the journey across the blinding white began, the walk under the starlight. Grief whispered to her. Pain. Guilt.

That one, the dark-haired girl. The tormented one.

Memory whispered of her, too, although the Naven knew they hadn't met before this moment.

Time was a funny thing.

The man whose neural cells animated this craft had taught her that.

The walk through the white pulled at her.

She was too young. Too little. Whatever she was meant to do out there, wherever it was, whatever it was, her body was way too small to manage it. Not this time. Not this time.

Someday, she felt her older self's hands saying long ago, *someday we will change it.*

Someday we will change it.

This had never happened before. Not in all her memories had somebody come looking for her.

The Naven picked herself back up, wiping her eyes with one hand. She let the fingers of the other trail along the outside edge of the hull.

Someday, we will change it.

THARSIS PULLED BACK a bit as the ancient girl, still silent, stood there. Right in front of her.

Holding a pebble, unslung from around her neck, hanging off a simple hemp cord.

"Riqan, what's going on?" Tharsis asked.

"She's going to hand it over," he said, breathless. The normal bored tone was gone, his words saturated in excitement now. "She's really going to do it."

Those red eyes were locked on Tharsis. "What?" she asked, fear rippling down her spine now.

"The last navigation material," he said. "The way to Noqumiut."

"Wait, wha—" Tharsis began.

But before she could finish her question, the craft screamed.

Every surface inside turned into some kind of sonic amplifier. It bucked, rocking as if something had exploded. Ang and Riqan were both thrown around, dashed against the hull. Neither moved. tDaer held on, blue skin now cast a pallid gray.

The Landlord's form blurred, the skin of the divedrive not quite letting her through. Trying to push her out. She was clearly fighting it, struggling. Tharsis realized what was happening, but the words that left her mouth froze in the air.

Time stopped.

Through the hull both hand and rock came.

Through the penumbra, twisting across trillions of subatomic worldlines.

Straight in.

Mass transfer across space-time, from outside the hull, without the Flet's permission.

tDaer yelled something Tharsis couldn't hear.

For a moment, it seemed as if everything was aligned. Secure. But then something slipped, fell apart, broke loose. Some tether was broken, and the little girl was swept away.

Instead of falling neatly into Tharsis's palm, the pebble slid into the flesh of Tharsis's wrist.

The last thing Tharsis felt were tiny fingers against her skin, dissolving as reality folded in on itself for a fraction of a second.

The world dissolved in quantum hellfire.

For a moment, Tharsis saw it. The land blowing outward, glass and chrome and trees and birds ripping apart to nothing. The deafening roar of nuclear explosion. Salt-encrusted white tearing itself apart, blue electrical fires arching out from the shattering core, a mushroom cloud rising, rising over dark smears of reef set like jewels in glittering seas.

There was a moment before it was gone. Winked out.

All sight, all sound, all agony.

Gone.

Tharsis was alone.

Naked over the planet.

The reeking nothingness of the void—its rarified freeze, the vacuum seeking to fill itself with every drop of air from her blood—roared loud in a human mind that wouldn't accept what its nerves were telling it. Hands wouldn't move to the controls of the suit, lips wouldn't seal shut, eyes wouldn't blink, wouldn't focus. The sun shone in a thousand wavelengths above the horizon, bombarding her body with energy no human skin had ever been designed to endure.

The vapor of her breath boiled on her tongue, her lungs screamed as the vacuum fought its way in, the surface of her skin started ballooning out, seeking in vain pressure to hold it in.

She was going to be the first person to die in cislunar space in over seven hundred years.

If she'd had the atmo, she could have laughed at such an absurd thought.

But before the void could blow the life from her body, the xenocyte layer in ENEX, dormant in the atmosphere of the craft, screamed awake. Lightning-fast, the inbuilt rebreather slid up over her face, the hood and gloves slamming around and over her head and extremities. Squeezing, sealing.

Too slow to prevent damage, but at least enough to keep her from dying. Fucking expired scat. The lieutenant felt every muscle in her body scream out as fresh oxygen hit through her blood, cramping, relaxing, fading into shock that took over, tingling down from ravaged skin as gravity swept her into an orbit away from the unbearable burn of explosion below.

Eyes sealed up, she could see it. The mushroom cloud, spreading. The energy release produced by the Naven moving matter across the gradient flow.

It didn't make any sense. The Flet and the Naven were said to have been incredibly close once. Hadn't he known? Couldn't he have diverted power in the craft, sucked it from somewhere, stopped that?

Stopped her?

Fuck. Why hadn't Tharsis stopped them herself?

Because of her, a Landlord was dead.

Tears condensing on the inside of the ENEX's temporary goggles, the saline of it stinging void-burnt eyes, Tharsis forced her face into the direction of her orbital spin and let herself fall, skimming over the upper layers of Earth's ionosphere, stray particles hitting and disassociating through until her entire body felt numb.

Her arm, the one the Naven had touched, burned.

An hour passed. There were only so many orbits she could take before her path degraded into an entry angle or her atmo ran out. Her oxygen flow was too low; even with efficiency breathing, it was as thin as that in the highlands, and her lungs had been badly burnt by the void. She couldn't reach her reserve tank. Her limbs refused to take commands from her brain, and ASDF gear didn't have the expensive control systems that would have allowed her to do it with a constriction of pupil or twitch of fingertip. So, she exhaled into it and tried not to think of home, of the hypoxia that would inevitably overtake her.

On the next pass, her body safe in the wrapper, she disassociated through almost a kilometer of ship hull. Too lost in the numbness of her failing exogear, she couldn't catch the tether that was thrown out to her by the crew.

Three more orbits like that, through the same craft, again and again, and she started to lose sense of things. Her nervous system was rattled, horribly, by the effect of the wrapper, and even though survival instincts started fighting back for her, it was too late. Her vision began to narrow, tunneling as the air gauge on her wrist flashed red.

Too—

BOOK TWO
TRANS-JOVIAN

THARSIS WOKE TO PAIN.

White-bright pain smeared through boiled tissue, her entire body still tingling from the assault of disassociation. Her ENEX was gone, at least, and she held up a quavering hand, trying to discern with ruined eyes if the gear had done any permanent damage.

That movement, however, tilted her equilibrium completely off-gimble, and she found herself violently retching out the entire contents of her stomach into the surrounding air. Stomach acid burned through her already ravaged throat.

"Shh," a voice said, steadying her shoulder with a touch, "you're okay." A wet cloth burned on her forehead, on her lips. "You're okay, Lieutenant Chen. Can you understand me?"

She coughed, immediately regretted it, and that soothing voice kept going.

"Managed to catch you in a static net, so you're probably feeling like scat right now. We've got a vat filling for you right now. You're going to be fine. We've got some of the best medics in the fleet."

Tharsis tried, but the words wouldn't come. It felt like somebody had taken steel wool to her throat.

"Diagnosis?" a second voice asked.

"Early stages of cerebral edema, plus severe void burn on mouth, skin, and possibly down into her lungs. Estimated seven to ten seconds exposure."

"She's lucky she's not dead."

They sounded familiar, those voices, but she couldn't place them. Trying to focus, Tharsis was unable to see anything but that little face, smiling at her, that hand, dissolving in front of her… fuck, what had she done? How many people had died because of her? She needed to tell them, needed to tell them…

"She's lucky if she manages to stay that way."

"The Rossen pissed?"

Third voice. Familiar. Entering. "What the hell do you think, Doc?"

"Holy fuck, sir…"

Moisture trailed out of the corners of her eyes, a fresh wave of pain slithering through her skin.

All those people. That little girl.

Her arm burned.

There was a sharp jab, then a coolness. A hand on the inside of her elbow, rubbing the skin. It felt nice. Calming. So tiring.

"I'm sorry about this, Tharsis. Really, I am."

Tharsis felt a tube pushing down her throat. Soothing, sticky gel flooded over her raw limbs, darkness and quiet and cold. She let it take her away.

WHEN SHE WOKE AGAIN, she half expected it to be in an interrogation room.

What she found was worse.

The kitchen of her family's ranch house.

Except it wasn't.

Bead-board walls and tile floor and sealed stone countertops and beat-up butcher block table and old induction range were all in their places, but they were still wrong.

All wrong.

Looking at that table, Tharsis didn't see what it was. No. She saw what it meant.

She saw the first scrambled eggs of spring coming out of the cast-iron skillet onto chipped stoneware plates. She saw Mom's measuring cups, teaching her fractions. She saw Dad's hunting rifles and the cleaning kit and the mess of little red rags, stained dark with cleaning oil. She saw bread baking and holiday gift wrapping and the bolt of cadet-blue wool from which she and Mom had cut her first Academy uniform.

She saw Dad sweeping the breakfast dishes off the surface and laying his only son down as the crockery shattered. She saw her brother trying not to cry and failing, Dad tightening the tourniquets on his ravaged leg as the doctor cut what was left of his pants away, administering anesthetics, dousing bone saw-wire with iodine. Their dog, fur caked with drying blood, humiliated by his failure to protect his alpha's pup, huddled in the shadows. Mom, pulling her from the room, flour-dusted hand slapping down over little eyes and dragging her from the room, so she wouldn't see the doctor start cutting.

"Interesting."

A figure. Male. Shifting, indistinct as an umbran, featureless, or at least, containing no features she could easily determine. He was white, and not the void-pale of the Jovians, nor that of some fair-skinned person in midwinter, but true white. Like a mushroom grown underground. Empty, void-filled eyes.

Tharsis recoiled, stumbling backwards off a seat she wasn't even aware she was in.

"None of that," the man said from across the battered farmhouse table, and gestured back to the again-upright chair she'd just fallen out of. "I'm not what you fear. Eyes are just very difficult things to get right. If I were to dream some up, they would most likely scare you more." The walls around them rippled with her uncertainty, and he cocked his head. "Is there something you wish to ask me?"

Her throat didn't hurt. Her skin wasn't on fire. She could speak and did. "What is this place?"

"Top layer of your mind, a memory you carry close." Something glimmered in the abyss where his eyes should have been. "If you tell me what I need to know, I won't have to go deeper."

Fuck, she thought.

Fuck, the walls around her whispered.

The Wytt.

A nightmare among a people who couldn't experience nightmares, his story was well known on Mars. A university on Earth, back in the Euphemism, had been conducting research on almost every aspect of human consciousness, seeking to change those things they found impure. One such experiment had resulted in a single human awareness permanently locked inside the collective subconscious. A parasite within humanity's soul, the master of the depths once plumped for their horrors by the hallucinogenic plagues.

The Wytt was now their gatekeeper, the only member of the Tenancy with neither territory nor people. Yet, if one of their number asked, he could kill her without effort. Lock her inside, show her things, until she threw herself into the void or overloaded her nervous system with fear or simply starved to death.

"Well, you don't have to worry about that, Lieutenant Chen," he told her, coming around the edge of the table and offering her a document. On old-style parchment and everything. Stamped at the bottom with the huge federal-blue chop of the Rossen.

Her gravity dropped away.

"Under Section 13-D of the Tenancy Accords, I am contractually obligated to perform noncoercive interrogations, memory mining operations, and act as assistant to a priest or shaman in the administration of last rites for a person in a coma or other compromised mental capacity, for or upon Arran citizens at the Rossen's behest. He has approved me for the first, in your case." A pale hand pushed the thick document across the table to her. "I prefer it to be delivered hard copy, in the waking world, before we come here, but I was contracted to get the information before this craft arrives back at Deimos, and considering your comatose state…"

The Rossen? the walls echoed. *Deimos?*

"I'm in a coma?"

"Yes." The Landlord of the mind's interior blinked. "Induced. I'm not seeing any brain damage, which is a bit of a miracle, I daresay."

Tharsis stared at the vellum, unable to draw any meaning from its strong, flowing letters. In her heart, she knew she deserved whatever was on here. She'd broken the law; she'd provided classified material to a voider, she'd entered cislunar space without official orders, she'd been party to the destruction of Singapore. The death of the Naven.

The Landlord who, from all accounts, was the only one in the Heliosphere to never execute a citizen, who spent the short time between her rebirths working to remove the detritus of the Silicone Age. A woman, a little girl, who'd never hurt anything.

Guilt swelled to bursting in her chest.

She heard her brother screaming, the doctor taking his leg.

"Good. Reflection. Self-examination. Makes my job easier," the Wytt interrupted. "Please read the documentation so we can begin."

She bit her lip, looking up from the blue seal to the flood of memories around her. All the memories—good, bad, horrible, beautiful—she'd forgotten were held in the small, warm space of that kitchen. "Do we have to be in here?"

"You chose the location," the Wytt said, and now there was a notebook spread out in front of him on the old table. "I've answered your questions, Lieutenant. Will you answer mine, or shall I inform your Landlord you need another dose?"

Tharsis glanced around the facsimile of a kitchen, all the dreams born and lost in the warm little space, and set her jaw. "Yeah. I'm good with that."

CHAPTER
EIGHTEEN

"SHE SAW THE FLET? How is that even possible?"

"His consciousness can bounce around the divedrive neural nets. It's uncommon to see him, but far from impossible."

"So how the fuck did this happen?"

"I doubt the Naven, at four, knew about the temporal incongruity between the surface and low Earth orbit—"

"I mean, if he was there?"

"I don't know. Maybe he didn't wake up in time."

"And this, this all you can get me from Chen?"

"I can only pull what's there."

"So what? She did it for shits and giggles? I don't buy that."

They weren't actually talking, the Rossen and the Wytt, striding out across the vast ASDF medical campus of Swift Crater. The Wytt was, for lack of a better definition, a hallucination, but one the Rossen didn't need any additional help to see. He might not be able to see what most Arrans did, but when it came to the places where the Wytt dwelled, he'd been experiencing that shit since he was twelve. The blue scarring on his arms ensured he never really could turn it off. Euphemism tech. Heinous shit.

He had injected the lieutenant with it though, before leaving the *Barachiel*. As the Landlord, he was one of the few people alive allowed to authorize its use.

Made him feel unclean, watching the blue spreading out on her skin.

He'd asked the Wytt to go easy on her. Now, he wished he'd requested something more invasive, more painful.

What the fuck had she been thinking?

The Wytt nodded. "She's angry, and she's alone, and she's more than a little hopeless about her future. It's a bad combination."

"Hopeless about her future?" Mars's Landlord snorted. "Hopeless? Jesus fuck. What's there to be hopeless about in her life? Fucking Hinden?"

"I know," the Wytt replied. "Caleb Ross, Landlord of Mars, knows all about hopelessness, doesn't he?"

The Rossen glowered but fell silent. He'd had hope once. Back when he was one of only a dozen children saved from the ashes of a ruined rural town in Wyoming. Do some good, kill some bad guys, get revenge. A good plan. Before his squadron got captured. Before he woke up in a vat on Deimos, a pack of doctors telling him it was over seven hundred years in the future, everything he knew long turned to dust, an entire planet depending on him.

A strange last name on a fresh ID.

OLIN.

They didn't know how it worked, they'd said. Only what it did. The subgenetics that guided his particular brand of immortality had tagged his body, down to the electrical impulses in his brain. Upon brain-death, Caleb's body reverted to the state it had been in at attainment.

Right down to the most base receptors in his hindbrain.

There were theories—dozens of them—on how to reconstitute his memory, but invariably, they had all failed. So, he was stuck in a vicious cycle. Dying, regenerating, forgetting. Waking up with the knowledge, memories, nightmares, experiences, and anger of a twenty-four-year-old corporal, instead of the centuries he'd actually lived. The same personality, the same set of values, the same morality, the same core beliefs, carrying down through the centuries.

Caleb wondered sometimes if that meant he was nothing more than a meat robot. What the fuck had the First Planetary Congress been thinking? Nominating him? Agreeing to any of it?

"They didn't have a choice," the Wytt offered, reaching back through fresh scars, picking the thought from his mind. "The Jovians would have used it as an excuse to crush your planet."

"I know, I fuckin' know." He pinched the bridge of his nose, trying to keep his mind in the game. "Help me out here. What did her interrogation space look like?"

"Family kitchen," came the reply, and the squat buildings of the medical facility around them shifted, overlaid with a comfortable sensation of curried sweet potatoes and waxy crayons, fading into blood and screams and severed flesh. The Wytt volunteered it, before the Rossen could even ask. "Her older brother was attacked by a snow leopard on a hunting trip when she was eleven. He was thirteen. They amputated his leg, and the family's service commitment fell to her."

She'd never told him. Explained a lot. "Why'd she see what rides the signal? Or the Flet, for that matter? Why her?"

"I can't speak to the Propagation." The Wytt's words felt clinical. "But nobody sees the Flet unless the Flet wants to be seen."

"So he wanted my lieutenant to go down there, pick that scat up, blow up Singapore, kill the Naven?" The other Landlord said nothing, and the Rossen tapped a finger on the window. "The Flet loved that little girl like family."

"We all have something for which we would sacrifice anything."

"A child? I wouldn't sacrifice a child."

"Believe what you want, Caleb," the Wytt replied, and the other Landlord melted from view.

"Fucking drugs," he muttered, rubbed the dead stain on his arm, and kept going.

The fast burn from Earth's inwell to Mars's outer moon had taken the *Barachiel* almost sixty hours to execute. Deimos hosted the bulk of the ASDF's void command headquarters, and the hospital here was well equipped for injuries like Tharsis's. Able to sustain a gravity environment for better healing and eliminating the need for potentially dangerous planetary surface transfers, it was a joint-run effort between the military and religious charities, providing a level of care the federal government couldn't manage on its own. The Rossen's regenerations were managed here, whenever possible, in a purpose-built, secure facility. No better place to stick his wayward lieutenant while her body knit back together.

The guard at the door scrambled up to salute when he walked in, spotting the subdued gold-embroidered patch of the Tenancy velcroed to his shoulder where his unit patch should have been. For added emphasis, he'd rolled his sleeves up. The Rossen tossed the salute back with a confidence he didn't feel and headed up to Tharsis's room.

She'd nearly bought the farm out there, skin blistered, and eyes burst near-out. There'd been something in her arm, too, they'd said, a constellation of shrapnel too deeply embedded for removal, some of it fused directly into the bones of her wrist and hand. No need to put her through bone grafts until he figured out if he needed to execute her or not, he'd told the docs.

They'd had the good sense not to protest.

Now, her body lay submerged in a soup of amino acids, lipids, and fixed-state antibodies. A light electric current was running through it, pulsing at random intervals, forcing her skin to heal itself. Intubated and wired-up, a jungle of tubing snaked out of the tank's pale red goop.

She looked very, very small.

"It's a good thing they didn't shave her head," a familiar face commented from a chair beside the vat.

Her hair was slicked back into a ball at the base of her neck, dark strands loose and running through the gel every which way. It made her look a little like an octopus. "She does have a weird hang-up about her hair," the Rossen agreed.

"Military girls. They all have something they try to hold onto," Major Lanin said, and eyed him. Maybe nervous, maybe amused. It was hard to tell with him sometimes. "But look at you. Back in the blacks. King of the planet."

That girl could have been beautiful, he'd thought, the first time he saw her, unable to identify exactly what it was that was wrong with her. Then he'd thought her bitter, frustrated, and maybe that was true. Considering what happened to her brother. How disappointed she'd become, how disillusioned.

A shame. What she'd done to herself.

"Blaming yourself, Caleb?" Lanin chuckled, mirthless. There was a book spread out on his lap—a Tri-Testament Bible, open to *Acts of the Apostles*, and the Landlord wondered if he'd been reading to himself, or to her.

"Some of it's probably my fault." The Landlord rubbed a hand across his tired eyes. "I seriously underestimated the effect Captain Hinden was going to have on morale."

"As much as it pains me to say it, sir, she made her own choices."

"Yeah, we all do, don't we?"

For the Rossen, the Bill of Ratification mandated that he report his presence to the commander of whatever base he was stationed at. Sometimes, it was easy. The commander of the *Turiel* had shaken Caleb's hand and told him he'd be treated like any other corporal. Major Lanin, who'd served as a lieutenant on the *Turiel* during Caleb's first assignment there, had laughed his ass off and then asked if he could get Humphryes's budget doubled.

Caleb hadn't yet gotten around to reporting in to Captain Hinden.

Some men just couldn't be trusted.

"What are you doing here, anyway, sir?" he asked. "I had the report classified."

"HQs hold secrets like plastic retains atmo," Lanin replied with a laugh, the way he always did when he was lying. "Thought I'd pop down and see if the weirder rumors bore out."

Bullshit, he thought. "Morray tell you, then?"

"The lead doctor, actually. We're classmates. He figured I knew her," the major said without missing a beat. "I figured somebody should be here with her."

Caleb shot him a look. "I haven't written this kid off. I haven't been ignoring her."

"Wouldn't think that you had, sir," Lanin replied, dog-earing the open page in his Bible before shutting it and getting up. "You've got your responsibilities, just like she had hers." He glanced back down into the vat. "Will that scarring come off?"

"Vat should take care of it. Mine stays because of whatever the fuck they did to me," Caleb told him, and thought of something else. "I may need you to come back to Humphryes with me, Major. We need a decent officer there, with what's coming."

"Things that bad?" And, when Caleb didn't say anything, his old commander nodded, slow, almost reluctant. "I appreciate the faith in me."

"You came here to check on her, didn't you?" the Landlord replied.

Caleb lingered, after Lanin left. Sat at the side of the tank in the half-lit room. Took in the sound of machinery beeping. Thought about what he was going to do about the whole ridiculous mess.

He liked to think of himself as a practical man, a pragmatic man. He wasn't beholden to nostalgia; his last winter in the harsh storms of Wyoming, his years fighting a losing war for the planet, had been filled with too much horror for him to look back at his past with anything other than disgust. And he'd never indulged in false hope.

He held no illusions that humanity could ever achieve one of those perfect states that they'd all seemed to think the Landlords could create for them. Even Mars, which had been founded as a constitutional republic, as a safe haven from the machinations of the Euphemism, was a failure. His very existence invalidated such fundamental principles.

But at the same time, the Heliosphere was trapped, barely functioning. Nothing could change, nothing could advance, nothing could be different. The transhumanist movements had failed. In horror or despair or mule-headed ignorance, nothing new had grown. None of those loose ends of human nature had ever been tied up, no matter what the other Landlords pretended. No matter what the Arcna screeched, safe in her mystery kingdom.

While Caleb didn't fully believe that the return of natural-state humanity would restore sanity to the Heliosphere, it had to be a step in the right direction. He'd grown up in the old world, and he understood that biology alone didn't make a man human. But even he held out hope that the people who'd departed on the exodus craft could, upon returning, help. Pull their progeny out of this Tenancy-induced stasis. Maybe, if they came back, humanity could move forward again, without fear or hesitation. Remind everyone of who they were, who they could be.

The Heliosphere desperately needed that.

Get the fucking genetic code back too. Go home to Earth. Remember what it was like to live at the mercy of things bigger than oneself. Lose all this fucking pretentiousness.

And if the Flet, the Naven, were willing to trust Tharsis, he couldn't do any less. Couldn't afford not to. Not with the Eighth Propagation coming on. The ASDF had no chance of decrypting that signal until the Arcna wanted them to hear it.

But he couldn't afford any more foolishness. Not like Ceres.

Even if that meant trusting a girl who'd killed a Landlord. One of the few he'd counted as a friend.

"Sorry, kiddo," he murmured quietly. "Looks like you're not getting off so easy as dying this time."

CHAPTER
NINETEEN

AFTER THEY WASHED the last of the biological healing gel off her skin and tossed a robe at her, Tharsis expected that the Rossen would show up. Condemn her. Rub her nose in all the scat the Wytt had pulled from her head.

But he didn't come. Not right away.

They gave her a private little recovery room instead. Small and narrow, but quiet. No windows, no view of the home world, which she was grateful for. She'd never stand on its surface again. Seeing it would have been torture.

The one saving grace about Deimos was Major Lanin, still in the mandatory post-outwell recovery period before heading back down to the surface. His new posting. He gave no explanation for his presence when he showed up, offered no insight to her fate, but he was there. Wanting to know how she was feeling. How she was doing. If they'd taken care of the scarring from the injection, and how he knew about that, she didn't dare ask.

He even brought her a couple packets of curried yam soup his wife had sent up in her last care package to him. "Better than hospital food," he said, and there was something like pity in his expression as he passed her one. "How long were you in the void without your suit sealed up?"

"I don't know." Her stomach ached. The vat might have healed the worst of the dermal injuries, but she couldn't shake the sensation of being lost in the void. Painkillers weren't helping. "Doesn't matter. I should have died out there."

"You wanna go like that? A million kilometers from home, from your unit, from the people who care about you?"

"Who cares about me at Humphryes? Hinden? The rest of the fucking el-tees? Huh? You think that's a place where anybody gives a scat about me? About anybody else? It's not like this assignment must be for you, all nice and meaningful."

"I'm going to be running a lot of drills, getting pissed on Fiveday nights. Pretty goddamn boring, if you think about it."

"But it's not pointless," she said. "Right?"

Her former commander's eyes softened. "Nothing's pointless, Ambera. You gotta get over thinking that everyone's out to get you."

She stared down at the meal, ashamed by the kindness in the man. She didn't know what to say. How to even start to explain herself.

She just kept seeing that little girl. That little hand, pushed through the hull. That tiny little hand, dissipating into red vapor, the entire world catching fire.

"Brought a uniform for you," Lanin said, handing her a paper-wrapped bundle. "No patches, no name tag, but there it is. Best I could do for you in a couple of hours. They were out of stock on female grays, but the boots are your size. Shouldn't be any seal issues."

"Female," she muttered, and didn't meet his gaze. "Female. Not even good enough for a woman. You have any idea how wearing that gets?"

"Tharsis." There was a hint of warning in his voice. "You need to let this scat go, or it's going to eat you alive."

She'd finished her soup and pulled the uniform on over the mess of her arm—swollen and blotchy, the Naven's fingers still tingling as they dissolved against it—and settled in to wait.

"Evening, Lieutenant Chen."

She'd fallen asleep, if that chronograph over the door was any indication.

Maybe it was a dream or something.

It wasn't the Landlord standing at the foot of her bed, looking pissed as all hell, but her sergeant. Her asshole, AWOL sergeant. Hands in the pockets of void blacks, sleeves rolled up to the elbow.

The obvious question, *the where the fuck have you been?* died on her lips.

Wound around both elbows and pulling upwards towards his shoulders were indigo patterns. Intricate tattoos that weren't tattoos at all.

Holy mother of god.

A quiet man with humble ambition, she'd always thought of Master Sergeant Olin.

Nothing like the Chief Ross from the stories. That proud, certain man who'd helped found the nation, who'd kept it together all these centuries.

"This is a fuckin' joke, right?" she groaned.

"Let me put it this way, ma'am," he said, unzipping the one-piece and shrugging out of the top, "I was eleven when I got these for Christmas, and I assure you, it was as far from funny as it gets."

There was no mistaking what was there. The sergeant's chest was completely covered in deep blue scars. Curling and winding and spreading. Across every square centimeter of skin.

Any schoolkid on Mars could have identified it. Dermal scarring from the old horrors, the bacterium of the Euphemism. The scat colonized under skin, releasing hallucinogenic toxins directly into the muscle and nervous system, permanently damaging the tissue above it. But the inoculations had taken care of that, wiping all but a few carefully cultivated strains out. Nobody had been scarred like that in over seven hundred years.

Tharsis felt faint. Of all the places that fucker could have been hiding, of all the lieutenants' lives he could have been fucking with...

"Ambera," he—Olin, Chief Ross, the Rossen, whoever the fuck he was—was saying as he pulled the blacks back on, "I move through this world as unobtrusively as possible. It's the only thing that keeps Mars from descending into the same fucking mess as the rest of the system."

"Right, and that works out so fucking well," she grumbled without really meaning to.

He leveled a finger at her. "Stop," he said, in a tone she'd never heard him use before. "Fucking stop. I'm not going to be lectured by a selfish little girl who let herself get sucked into this Nalatok insanity..."

The words stung, but Tharsis could feel the anger starting to build, and really, what difference did it make? He was going to execute her anyway. A man she'd worked with, liked, admired, relied on, trusted, was going to execute her. "Do you think I would have if I'd known what hen was trying to—"

"—like giving *The Book of Shoals* to some random asshole university brat from Iapetus because she fucked you! Are you that goddamn blue in the cunt that you'd—"

"Like this was about sex!" she yelled back, stung. "You, of all the goddamn people, ought to know that I wouldn't do that!"

His eyes narrowed a bit, the way they did when he was tracing out a fiber path in his mind. "But you still knew. You knew something was wrong, that it was going somewhere wrong, but it wasn't worth caring about. What difference did it make? What could possibly go wrong?"

"Right, and all the fucking stress of the last few months doesn't have any part to play in this?" she protested.

He exploded.

"That's voider talk, El-Tee!" His voice took on a mocking quality. "I'm no better than the sum of my parts. I'm just a machine that reacts to the environment. I can't help anything I am. It's all somebody else's fault! But you know what? Other people's mistakes are not an excuse for yours!" He roared the last sentence and slammed a fist on the table.

It popped her anger like a soap bubble. Tharsis sagged. "I..."

Drawing his uniform back over the legacy of a long-vanished world, her sergeant sighed. "I had Colonel Cambel explain a version of the situation to Hinden before we left. I told that fucker directly that I hadn't had time to discuss it with you. But he probably thought he found a way to neutralize you, and he used it. I'm sorry about that."

She closed her eyes, sinking back into the thin hospital pillows. "Fuck."

"Put it aside, Ambera," he said. "You're better than this."

The lieutenant rubbed a hand down her tingling arm. "What if I'm not? I'm a scat-stain of an officer. What the hell am I supposed to be better than? Who?"

"You know, I've heard this scat from somebody else," he replied, letting his long frame in its unfamiliar blacks fall back against the nearest wall, scarred arms folded across his chest, very far away. "She was like you. Young. More focused, but we were a people in a world-ending crisis."

There was something hypnotic about the story, the little singsong lilt in the words as he spoke. Reminiscent of the way he always was in the squadron, when he was shooting the breeze with the guys, giving her some casual advice about how to handle this or that problem. It hurt.

"Eliza Rallison, right?"

He nodded.

"The Rallarhu's a fucking inhuman monster."

"She was a fine woman, Ambera, and a fine officer. I would have done anything for her." And he looked down at his arms. Sighed. "She threw herself into the uniform on the faith that we could still save our world. But she fell. She fell, Tharsis. I've lost the memory of exactly how, but," and his eyes pulled up, locked with hers. "I don't want to see that happen to you."

Shame boiled hot in her blood, and she could feel herself shaking. "Jesus, Olin, it just... I killed a little girl. She was just a little girl, and she's vapor now. She vaporized in front of me."

The bed next to her dipped, a stiff-garbed arm wrapped around her shoulders. And for a few moments, Tharsis tried to fight off the tears, the wave of grief that was threatening to carry her out to sea.

For a few moments, it felt like sympathy.

Just a moment.

Then the tentative hug was gone. The sergeant was gone.

The Landlord spoke.

"You know what I'm supposed to do now, don't you?"

Tharsis nodded. "I know."

"Too bad. Dying's easy, Tharsis. This is going to be substantially more complicated."

CHAPTER
TWENTY

CHECKING the address for one last time on her palm, Tharsis licked the ink and rubbed it off on her cheap, borrowed leggings. Right around the corner, and none too soon for her still healing body. Her arm ached.

The Rossen—and she was struggling to think of her master sergeant as that rat-bastard—had been painfully blunt about how this was going to work.

"You get me the algorithms the Cronuan used to decrypt the message, any other intel you can manage. You're on temporary amnesty only. Once you get what I need, you will report in to the nearest base, and I'll deal with you from there. You fuck me over, and I will know. Your family's service commitment will fall on one of your little sisters. You understand me, Lieutenant?"

"Clear as quartz, sir."

After taking the grav boots Lanin had brought for her, Tharsis had scrounged a couple sets of civilian clothes from the clinic's lost and found. She'd even found a tunic with a high neck on it. Not high enough to fully hide her rank—the damn things were purposely placed to avoid concealment—but enough to make it look like she was trying. The rucksack contained the only things the Rossen had been willing to issue her: fresh ENEX, grav bag, water decontamination tablets, a hand-forged combat knife in a flexible ceramic hip sheath that would get it past imaging equipment.

That last had given her pause.

"You don't expect me to come back, do you?" she'd asked, rubbing her thumb over the dark, reflectionless surface of its Alban steel blade.

"We'll get you home," the Rossen had said, sounding more like her old sergeant. "This isn't about sending you out there to die. I need you to believe that."

"I'm sorry, you know. About everything."

"Yeah? Me too. Make it right. Okay? Go out there and make it right."

"I won't fail you on this."

"Forget about me. Don't fail yourself."

The Rossen hadn't given her a plan. Nothing workable. "The less I do for you, the better," he'd said; but Landlord or not, she knew her sergeant. He hadn't been sure what to say.

But she'd remembered one of the flyers from the messy bulletin board in New Stockholm; there was a Nighttrippers on Phobos. Just outside the library. She caught a civilian shuttle over to the other moon and went looking for the place.

An open-source research facility, the Phobos Library was an important node of Heliosphere academia. Originally created to house the Rossen's Journal, it had expanded its charter over the past seven hundred years to include archives of nearly every book, poem, monograph, essay, news report, or thesis produced by Arran or pre-Euphemism Earth cultures. It was weak on foreign source material, though, and its religious archives were DNA keyed for Arran access only.

Beyond its walls, a tumble of private libraries and stores sold texts —most illegal outwell—from dozens of different cultures, supplementing study programs. Some were Arran-owned, but most were run by voider expats; the whole area was, therefore, a strange mishmash of different architectural styles and building-bound gravitational constants that levitated pebbles in the byways between. Tharsis found herself stumbling through it, until she felt the tug of the moon's natural microgravity from a section that was purely international.

From there, it was a brief push to a raw rock doorway, carved into the top floor of a Jovian-style building. Nighttrippers was spelled over it in Standard English and Jovian scripts.

The lieutenant had no idea what to expect. The address in the clinic's local directory had listed this place as a long-term researcher's hostel, but there was none of the easy, comfortable familiarity of the New Stockholm branch. Instead, austerity ruled. Taking a turn that would have brought her to the common lounge area at her own hostel, she instead found herself in a wide, thick chamber, roughly spherical, with most of the internal surface covered with bookcases. The volumes were held in with small bars positioned on hinges across each shelf. At the bottom, a small flat landing held a cashier's desk and lounging hammocks.

Another of the private libraries, then, and a physical depository at that. It seemed a little unusual. Outwell standard was digital. Bound books tended to be bulky and difficult to produce, and voiders tended to avoid products derived from biological materials, like the animal leather or tree paper traditionally used by Arrans for physical publications. But those books on the shelves around her, she noticed, were all plastic. Plastic covers, stretched plastic film for paper, the ink no doubt completely synthetic.

The Systems of Udlormiut; Crystalline Grids of the Heliosphere; Stories from the Piijuit.

"Fucking Polarists," she muttered, plucking that last off its shelf dock for a closer look.

"Can I help you with something, Martian?"

She craned her neck, a yellow-skinned Jovian floating above her, but it wasn't until he came closer that she realized the color represented a full-body tattoo.

"You have a problem with something?"

"I'm looking for somebody. Riqan. You may know him."

The Nepo bristled. "I don't know who you're talking about."

"Yeah you do," Tharsis said, pushing, raising her voice. "Riqan. Onias Family from Amalthea, funds this chain of hostels, along with a couple of side projects."

Gold-inked eyes narrowed. "There's nobody here by that name, Martian."

"Don't jerk me around, Jovian," she snapped back. "I've got something he needs, and I need to get in contact with him. Now."

The Jovian stared at her for a moment more, before pushing over to the small desk. Up in the entryway, the doors slammed shut with a loud clang.

"What's your name?"

"Name they know me by is Tharsis," she replied.

The Jovian didn't answer that. "What's your story?" he asked, then waved a hand at her rank tattoos. "Lieutenant?"

She sighed, and hunched into herself, and started telling the story that she'd come up with—found by a Red Cross rescue ship, brought to Deimos for treatment, gone AWOL the second they pulled her from the vat.

"I'm not going to fucking prison for that asshole to execute me," she finished, putting as much heat into it as she could. "No way."

"I'm not the consulate."

"Fuck, I'm not asking to defect. I'm asking to help finish what we started on Earth."

He raised an eyebrow. "And what's that, Martian?"

And there was no other option but to tell him. "You heard about Singapore blowing up, right?" The Nepo nodded. "It was energy released from a worldline fold. Something was pushed through the hull, and I need to get it to him."

He smiled, bland. "So, Tharsis, help me out. Your little girlfriend, she get any freaky scat done to her cunt?"

"Is that necessary?" And she sighed. "No."

It hung for a moment.

Finally, the Nepo held out his hand, fingers spread in Jovian style. "I'm Nanuk, Amalthean Family liaison here in the Mars inwell, and ten percent investor. Pleasure to meet you."

She shook back, puzzled. "Investor?"

"You'll have to forgive me my suspicion," he continued, "but it's not often you find a Martian as open-minded as the one described in the last quarterly report. I'll make arrangements to get you out of here immediately. You're welcome to stay in the dorm upstairs tonight." The Nepo spread a hand around. "Feel free to poke around the reading room, if you'd like. I find these texts a comfort, and they would likely do you a world of good. But take the way out back if you leave. Let's avoid any questions from the cops."

"No problem," she nodded back, and he was gone again.

The rest of the day passed slowly, uneventful. She pulled a few of the books down to read and saw a lot about crystals and energy matrices and the shape of the universe, but very little of anything of substance. They read like books written for children, really, and she found herself longing for a tablet and a file of *The Odyssey*.

It was almost sad, she thought as she plowed through the shelves, how little they allowed in. How much they cut out. What was the difference between stories about a talking dog or a sea monster or an intelligent race of umbran who lived forever, and the books here about the projects in the depths of Europa or the transmissions of a raving madwoman from the edge of navigable space? Why was one deemed violent, and one deemed enlightening?

Finally disgusted with it all, she left to go get supplies.

DIETARY STANDARDS HAD DEVELOPED in the first days of Arran planetary settlement. Earth's grain supply had been compromised in the Euphemism, vectors for the biological pogroms. Large meat animals, like the now extinct bovines, hadn't survived the freighter trip from Earth. Only a few places on Mars were capable of supporting old sugar crops like beets, tropical regions nonexistent. The Arran diet, therefore, consisted largely of cold-hardy grain, alpine potato varieties, and hardy sheep, goats, and pigs. More sensitive fruits and vegetables had to be sourced from the temperate Sabaea region, or orbital ag-platforms.

Voider nutrition analogs—vat-meats, congealed carbohydrates, synthetic sugars—were seen as abominations. The aversion ran deep enough to prevent more Arrans from taking positions on voider craft. Ex-pat communities often cooperatively ran ag vessels of their own.

That night, unsure of when her next good meal would come, Tharsis splurged on a decent dinner at a Bulge-style steak house. At the little attached specialty food store, she bought a few weeks' worth of freeze-dried staples, along with a small bag of hand-pulled honey toffee, something most people in her parish could only afford on special occasions.

That night, the normally delicious treat tasted like ash.

She just kept seeing that girl. That arm. That mushroom cloud, soaring up into the void.

Her sergeant, sitting next to her bed, ancient grief on his face.

You fucked up, Chen, her mind kept whispering, *you fucked this up big time.*

That night, tucked into her gravbag and anchored on the small room's hammock post, rucksack packed and ready to go for the morning, she found her mind wandering. Back through the penumbra. Through the city, off the moon, out to some depth of the void that she couldn't identify. A dark planet, a tiny moon, frozen and cold on the edge of the system, the starfield burning above her.

"What do we do about this?" a man was asking a woman, his voice a haze. "What the fuck do we do about this?"

"What choice do we have?"

"There's always a choice."

"Only a choice of who we're going to damn."

The voices rose, dark shapes against the light of the stars beyond them, two people sitting on the edge of some vast crater filled with the sharp glow of antenna radiation.

"There has to be another way to—"

"Stop it. We can't fix it. We can't save him. We can't save anyone. All we can do is—"

Tharsis woke in a cold sweat, the shards of rock embedded in her arm vibrating for some reason she couldn't understand. Unable to sleep, she laid there in the confines of her bag until Nanuk came to get her for the ferry.

CHAPTER
TWENTY-ONE

THE ROSSEN'S instructions to the *Barachiel* before putting in at Humphryes were succinct. No talk of a Propagation. Of an active Landlord.

Not yet.

Not until he got what they needed first.

Slipping now from the gate in civilian clothes with Tyr and a small platoon of Marines at his heels, Caleb Ross said a quick prayer that nobody had cleaned out that Iapetan's room yet. Projectile weapons were disallowed by the Rallarhu, but his team was all packing blades, well concealed but close at hand. Just a small group of Arrans, dog alongside them, headed to the international district. *Nothing to see here,* he thought to himself grimly.

Tyr, sensing his nervousness, pushed his head into his hand.

Seeing his old dog was bittersweet at best. Tyr, like Caleb, was a salvage from the wreck of the Euphemism, from a gene foundry deep in the Norwegian mountains. Most of the animals his platoon had found there were ruined, some so psychotic they'd chewed their own skin off trying to escape the piss-soaked twilight. What they'd been trying to make there, nobody had been able to figure out. Common sights, in those late years of the war.

Only one little male pup had been left relatively unharmed, eyes barely open, cowering under a desk next to his dead littermate and mother. Caleb taken the puppy with him. Fed him on condensed milk and what bits of ration-meat he could spare. Kept him tucked in his uniform top, where the pup could stay warm. Defended him, when the other guys wanted to kill him, just to be sure.

He and Tyr had bonded. Loyal to the last.

Evidently, the dog had been used as a test run for Caleb's own manipulation, but as far as the sergeant could tell, the animal bore him no ill will for the experience. Tyr's contentment at having his old master around practically bled out of him. He still trusted him implicitly, even if they had spent the last decade apart, current identities given no special consideration by the fucking assignment algorithms.

Now, he strode easily beside Caleb in full K9 combat kit, ears pricked, growling at the shadows.

Dogs, as a rule, hated voiders. Tyr was more aggressive than most.

If anything got ugly, the team was going to need those instincts.

A preemptive sweep team from Humphryes had been out of the question. Caleb knew everyone in the MP shop; subtlety was not their strong suit. He couldn't risk anyone else finding out that Tharsis had handed over what she'd handed over, and he didn't want anyone else facing down the Rallarhu. If she decided to take an interest.

The Accords demanded no cooperation within the Tenancy, past what was already prescribed. The Landlords weren't necessarily on friendly terms with one another, but they coordinated from time to time. The Naven had kept an eye on depopulated inwells, the Scient maintained exhaustive records on scientific research, the Onias held yearly trade summits on Themisto. International security measures largely fell on the Rossen, and by extension, Mars. The other Landlords routinely decried the very existence of the Arran Self-Defense Force, while Congress whined about the expense, the danger, the human cost, but most of that was political theater.

Propagations were cyclical, but low-level terror activities, Nalatok or otherwise, were a constant threat. The Rossen kept the ASDF's intelligence services focused on every Jovian connection in the region. Nepo-owned properties were notorious centers for smuggling operations, Tok cell confluences, and all manner of shady scat that the Jovian princelings were so fond of indulging in.

But last year, when Tharsis had come to him for advice on a place to live, Nighttrippers hadn't popped up in the intel. It had looked completely clean.

And so, he'd recommended the place. To a newly minted lieutenant.

She was on her way to the Trojans, the intelligence folks had told him. Outside ASDF surveillance range. Putting her out in the field was a calculated risk. For both of them.

He should have executed her.

He didn't even want to think about what could happen if word got out that he hadn't.

"Don't fuck me again, El-Tee," he muttered to himself, and the hostel rose on the end of the street.

"Excuse me, sir?"

Right. Them. And he turned to Morray. "Tyr and I are gonna handle the grab. Run interference, but keep your boys calm, this isn't some fuckin' Lagrange colony whose Nepo mob boss doesn't care. You understand?"

"Crystal, sir," the lieutenant replied, jaw set in a thin line.

"We are not in the Trojans," Caleb repeated, just in case; Corporal Olin had cut his teeth in those godforsaken ruins of civilization, and he understood what service out there could do to a man's trigger finger. Last thing he needed was a tense situation getting bloody.

NIGHTTRIPPERS PULLED INTO VIEW.

The Rossen breezed through the front doors, past the check-in desk, some dyed Ibbie manning the place. Gestured to the lieutenant to grab her and kept moving. He took the stairs two at a time, Tyr bounding ahead. He could hear his team yelling, pulling people out of the common areas, securing the bottom floor. If alarms had been tripped, they had ten minutes before 'roid security forces arrived.

He put it out of his mind and kept moving.

tDaer's door was triple locked, two of which, Caleb didn't fail to notice, were not part of the door's original configuration. Thirty seconds in the floor's patch panel disabled the original lock, and a ten-second application of thermite took out the other two.

The room was a disaster, full of odds and ends of various, unidentifiable things, but all of it clearly undisturbed. Working fast, Caleb pulled a stack of notebooks and removable tablet drives from the mess, an Arran hard drive Tharsis must have swiped from supply. The books and drives went into Tyr's side bags, and as Caleb buckled the last strap, he noticed something strange.

A dimensional-projecting interface unit, one of those units of plasma and light that the Cronuans favored for complex data manipulation.

Probably password protected, rigged to wipe itself at a faulty log-in attempt. The Landlord pulled a screwdriver from his pocket and went to work on cracking out the memory.

Yelling in the hallway. Close.

Caleb just grunted, "Tyr, take care of that," and kept his attention on the hard shell of the computer's case. If he could just…

A loud thud echoed from the corridor as Tyr had his fun, and the case popped open.

Instead of a conventional silicone matrix, like he was expecting, there was a perfectly spherical ball of translucent glass the size of his fist. Stained dark from the nodule suspended within. Tiny ports pricked across its surface like the quills of a porcupine.

The Landlord stared at it, old memories of centuries before infecting his thoughts, memories of unregulated wetware processors leaking consciousness, mylings screaming out into the wider world, tearing the life energy from his squadmates' bodies in pain, in rage. Children, beating little hands against the glass of their tanks.

Shaking off the old nightmares, he snipped off trailing tendril connectors, the glass surface automatically curling closed to prevent bleeding.

Outside, beyond the hostel's walls, an entirely new noise started up.

Sirens.

Caleb tucked the sphere into his jacket, careful as he could, and whistled to his dog, trying to send him what calm he could. Tyr was one of the best trained there was, but the animal's blood was getting up. Last thing they needed was him tearing some innocent backpacker's throat out.

<Sir?> Morray's voice rang over the radio bud in his ear. <We've got trouble.>

"They won't do scat without the Rallarhu," he replied in kind. "Do not engage."

THE NEXT STOP was Tharsis's room. There wasn't much there, and he wondered, looking at the spartan little space, if he'd somehow contributed to what she'd done. If she had felt so isolated that tDaer had seemed like a better option than her own people.

He put everything but her tin of birth control patches into Tyr's other side bag.

She made her own choices, he told himself, but wasn't quite convinced.

A crowd had gathered outside by the time he and the dog made it to the front door, the team from the *Barachiel* fanned out against police, coming through the crush, pushing it back.

Mars's Landlord looked up to the sky. Rippling, twisting, thickening.

Scat.

"Sir," the lieutenant whispered quietly, "do you want us to—"

But the kid didn't get a chance to finish his question. A blinding flash of light surged down from that artificial ceiling of air to slam into the street before them. For a moment, Caleb could make out a pillar of wrapper, slowly pinching off, contorting, and when it separated completely, there she was.

The Inner Belt's Landlord was nothing like the woman he had once known. The protean sheen of her outer surface could only approximate texture and color—skin, hair, nails, lips. Her eyes were pits. Empty, grasping things. Despite his resolve, it shook him.

In that moment, Caleb couldn't help but wonder if any of the Tenancy could truly call themselves human anymore. If they even had souls left to make such a claim. If they were anything more than shells, filled with the petty ambitions of people long since turned to dust.

"I gave no permission for this," his old captain snapped, face flowing across a justified head, voice echoing, wind in the streets.

"I authorized it," Caleb replied, resting a hand on Tyr's bristling head. The dog, it seemed, recognized her, too.

"Rossen." Flat, cold. Nothing of the urgent warmth his old captain's tone had so often carried. "Animal."

"Eliza," he acknowledged, and had to grab Tyr's collar to keep the dog from going for her, fury howling through his thoughts. Caleb didn't blame him. "This was a retrieval operation, well within my authority under the Accords."

The other Landlord shifted, an unpleasant sight, like icing melting off a hot cake. "Retrieval of what?"

"Misappropriated national security information." Without knowing what she knew herself, he couldn't afford to give anything away. "Which is now reappropriated."

Silence.

"Acceptable," the Inner Belt's Landlord replied stiffly, and gestured to her own security forces to stand down. Caleb nodded to her, and shouldered Tharsis's kit bag.

A tunnel automatically opened in the crowd as he gestured his men forward. The Rallarhu's gaze landed square on him as they passed. A sudden urge swept over Caleb with the force of a tidal wave. To demand what the fuck she was thinking, why she'd done this to herself, what had happened to her to make her into this.

He ground his teeth and just kept going.

BACK AT THE STAGING POINT, the solitary hangar on Humphryes, the team made quick work of the haul. He passed the wetware over to Morray to be taken up to the *Barachiel* for analysis, along with one of Tyr's saddlebags. "Anything you can pull off 'em," he explained, handing the pack over. He kept the other. "Let's see what this bitch was working on."

"You think there's anything on here?" the lieutenant asked, and hefted the bag. "The glance I got at that crappy little office indicated somebody blew the system."

"She wasn't tied into the hostel net. You know how paranoid the Cronuans can be about their research."

The el-tee nodded at the other bag. "Tharsis's stuff?"

"I've got it."

"Sir, she could have—"

"I've got it," he repeated, more forcefully. The lieutenant nodded, acknowledging the dismissal, and snapped off a quick salute.

"I'll get the guys on it immediately, sir."

"Good," he said, and didn't leave until they were all loaded into the rockjump, headed back out to the deepvoider.

Tyr made a soft little woof at his feet, satisfaction carried in the sound. Caleb had often wondered what it was like for the current generations of Arrans, able to comprehend those signals so much more clearly. He was glad this animal, at least, tuned him in.

"Good boy," he said absently, and headed out, across the dark base, for the barracks and the room he'd left behind weeks ago. His own familiar quarters, as close to home as things got anymore. Better than the commander's suite, or wherever Lanin might try to stick him. Damn thing probably reeked of Hinden.

Space was tight, especially with his seventy-kilo dog trying to find a comfortable place to stretch out, but they'd had worse together. Settling in against the back wall, Caleb started going through the bag he'd taken from Tharsis's room.

There wasn't much. Reading tablet, compact spectrum camera, rolls of analog picture film in sealed, dark canisters. A small tin of challenge coins that began and ended with her time at the Academy, nothing awarded since. Spare uniforms. That gold velvet dress she'd worn to the Christmas party, that awkward night when nobody had recognized her.

Standard, for an unmarried female soldier.

At the bottom of the bag, though, was a glass-sealed photograph. Small, barely bigger than his hand. A cluster of smiling people—children, adults, farm dogs—all standing in front of a heavy stone ranch house of curving walls and grass-tufted roof. There was a note on the back, inked in a hand he recognized from dozens of maintenance reports.

They need you to keep going.

Suddenly feeling like he was intruding on something private, something Tharsis would not have wanted him to see, he cinched the whole lot up and laid it aside in a storage cubby he'd never bothered to fill himself.

You'll give it back to her when she gets home, he told himself, and hoped to hell that was a promise he could keep.

CHAPTER
TWENTY-TWO

TRIPS FROM MARS to Jupiter could range from weeks, for fast chem-prop or fusion drive craft, to months, with slower, cheaper plasma engines. Tharsis had been expecting a fast-run ferry or something like that.

What she hadn't been prepared for was a 0350 rockjump trip out to a refinery rig.

Resource extraction platforms were the largest craft in the Heliosphere and comprised the bulk of the civilian voidfleet. Notoriously slow, the vast craft were driven by the most energy-efficient of ion drives, the majority of reactor capacity saved for driving the machines of industry carried in their bellies. Mining models could be in excess of ten kilometers long, with engines and communications equipment considered, and crush-cavities capable of swallowing and digesting asteroids up to a half kilometer in diameter. The one she was headed out to, the *Ariane*, was considerably smaller.

"Six kilometers from nose to tail," the rockjump pilot explained as he waved his only female passenger up to the cockpit. He was trying to keep her away from the rest of the contract labor in the back, and she was grateful for it. Rough crowd. "We handle petrochemicals. Plastics, foams, gaskets, seals, that sort of thing."

"And you have passenger accommodations for, uh, for me?"

"You'd be surprised how many people we have looking for cheap rides to the outer orbitals. We get women every so often, too. We're familiar with the needs."

"Guess you can't house us together, right?"

"Ma'am, we try to avoid taking you ladies onboard at all. Tends to cause problems. No offense."

"No, I get it." And she did, she really did. The civilian fleets never employed females, not even as prostitutes. Pregnancy in mig carried serious risks: miscarriages, fatal birth defects. The civilian world had no access to military sterilization drugs, and no power to enforce their application. Industry best practice was to not mix crews. "We've all seen what happens."

Their goal was anchored on the night side of the planet. The pilot kept his attention on the controls unless she asked him questions, but before long she ran out of anything he could readily answer that she wanted to know, and watched the planet roll by beneath her, a spinning ball of southern red and northern blue, the Tharsan Bulge falling under swift twilight.

Her father, back when she was little, maybe five, had taken a contract on a mining rig as a security foreman. Tharsis had bawled her eyes out the day they'd seen him off at the train station, her older brother trying his best to be stoic about the whole thing, and her mother keeping her grief hidden as best she could. Dad had dropped to his knees and wrapped her up in a hug and promised he'd be back as soon as he could. She'd been too little to understand the distances or danger involved.

It had been a long Arran-standard year without him. He'd come back with stories, little trinkets from his trip to Jupiter's outer worlds, and upwards of three hundred thousand MSD, almost enough to pay off the remaining mortgage on the ranch.

Her mother had just been happy he'd come back alive.

Piracy was an ever-present problem for the rigs, especially in the region her father had been mining in, Jupiter's Lagrange regions. Despite the fact that the Onias Family maintained mining and security agreements with Arran companies, rigs were largely on their own. Most maintained swarm fleets for defensive purposes, as well as security personnel, same as a deepvoider might.

"We're headed to the distribution center at Thermisto," the pilot told her, when she asked. "We change out crews here, deliver Mars's percentage of finished goods and refined fuel, get a good dry dock overhaul, head back out. We spend the trip out there working on the Trans-Jovian orders and drop the stuff off. The Landlords make the decision on what they want next and in what quantities, we take that order to Metis, pick up raw hydrocarbon from Jupiter's gas harvesters, and start the cycle all over again. And the other inwells don't have to do scat for it. Kind of a fucked-up system if you ask me."

"Don't we make a pretty healthy profit on it?"

"Sure, but you have any idea what the fatality rate on these craft can be, industrial accidents, void events, all of that? We do all the work, we take all the risk, and they get to sit on their asses and collect the goods."

She thought about New Stockholm, the jewel of voider civilization. Everything in that city had been built by craft like the Ariane. Utilitarian raw products teased and smoothed and massaged by the endless, obsessive efforts of Ibbie industry. The bulk of international manufacturing occurred there, in their vast zero-G forges, but nothing happened without the labors of the Arran mining fleet.

She thought of tDaer, railing against it all on one of those pre-oob drops.

"What would happen if we didn't, though? Mars doesn't have those resources in any sufficient quantity, not to keep the military equipped, anyway."

"Kiddo, if we didn't keep the rigs cranked to capacity at all times, we wouldn't need a military."

"You mean, they'd stop hating us?" The pilot gave her a weird look, and Tharsis scrambled to clarify. "I mean, resource extraction seems to be a major factor in the tensions between us and the Jovians."

"No, I mean the only thing that makes the rest of this system survivable is us. Take this fleet out of the picture, and the whole thing collapses. Which is funny, considering how the Arcna keeps trying to do that." And he grinned a little. "Nobody ever accused the Arcna of sanity, though. Or any of these seal-fucking voider Landlords. Biting the hand that feeds them." He paused, glancing over at her, and waggled a finger at her neck. "Your commander know you've gone AWOL?"

"I'm just traveling," Tharsis replied, and tugged the collar of her tunic up. It was something she hadn't thought about, how she'd be seen, what people might think of her, and she didn't like the sick feeling it left in her stomach. "Nothing more than that."

The old pilot tugged his own high collar down, showing a spread of captain's wings outlined in the red of dishonorable discharge. "Sometimes, you gotta just get away from it."

"Yeah," was all she could say to that, and they were silent for the rest of the trip into the refinery rig's hangar bay.

The *Ariane*, she noticed as they docked, was a perfect specimen of Arran astroengineering. Massive, thick, heavy, built with utility in mind, a few spare touches of artistry that showed in the flare of the exhaust manifolds or the curves of ever thickening icerock cluster shields. Hazardous processes were housed on the underside of the craft, outside the protected interior, handled by robotics, poisonous by-products vented into the ion drive's wake. Factory systems that required human labor, as well as the navigation, living, and engineering sections, lay within the shielding. The engines seemed relatively small, while massive petrol tanks, split into two-hundred-meter sections, bulged like insect eyes from the sides and bottom of the craft.

Tharsis regarded the whole thing with trepidation. Nervous, she waited for the group of laughing, joking contract laborers in the back to disembark before getting out herself. She retrieved her duffel from the back of the cramped cockpit and, waiting, clung to it like she might have clung to her rag doll, back when she was a little girl.

"You're gonna be fine, kid," the pilot said as he popped the cockpit seals and deployed a short rope ladder for their exit. He held out a hand. "Wherever you're headed, good luck."

Throat tightening for some bizarre reason, she shook back firmly and left as quickly as she could.

A crew member was waiting for her at the exit, to take her bag and show her to her quarters.

"It's empty right now," he explained at the door. "We had a few reservations, but everybody cancelled after that explosion on Earth. I guess parents are worried about their kids getting caught far from home with a Propagation kicking off."

"Have they officially announced that?"

"No, but it's all over the shortwave. Why the Landlord hasn't come out and said something yet is anybody's guess." His voice dropped. "They're saying the Naven died."

Guilt clenched in her throat anew. "Really?"

"Gossip. But anyway, let's see, with you… I've got a transfer for you, scheduled for a sevenday from now, at Ennomos. Is that right?"

Ah. Trojan territory. tDaer was probably meeting her with the divedrive. And she wondered, briefly, why Nanuk hadn't said anything about that to her. Weird people, Jovians. "Yeah, yeah, that sounds right."

"Take any bed you want, and you're free to have meals in the regular chummer. Lads are on shift, so it's always in operation. I'd try to avoid it during peak times. With this gang, you never know who's going to push something with, umm…"

Tharsis sighed. "Yeah, I get that."

He handed her a key. "That'll get you in and out. It might go without saying, but none of the crew are allowed in this space for any reason. Commander's rules."

She closed her hand down around the key, looking around the empty, dark space of the little reading nook. Lonely after the crowds of New Stockholm, but Tharsis felt an overwhelming exhaustion rising in her, and she was grateful for the solitude.

The crewman shifted. "If you don't need anything else, ma'am, I'll leave you to it."

"Thanks."

After the crew member was gone and the door locked behind him, Tharsis headed in, resolving to explore the strange little space before doing anything else.

Dorm, library, star-viewing lounge, toilet, all a bit worn, and not in the pleasant way that Nighttrippers had been; this place felt almost abused. There were a few little touches of color: the ratty old shower door inserts, a few bundles of artificial flowers here and there, the spines of the old print books in the few bookshelves. No umbran, though, and amazingly, there was a cedar-lined soaking tub, sealable for mig conditions.

Turning the hot water all the way on, she went and got her compressible towel and powdered soap from her bag, stripped down, and padded naked back into the room, watching the steam rise. She switched it off and stepped in, feeling the heat sting her still-healing eyes. It still felt good, the warmth working into the ache, soothing away the mindfuck of the past few days.

Tharsis closed her eyes and let her hair trail down across her naked shoulders and didn't move from the tub until the water went cold.

CHAPTER
TWENTY-THREE

"YOU SURE YOU want to handle this thing this way, Caleb?" Lanin asked from the dorm room's only chair. He'd come over on the rock-jump before reveille, breakfast in hand. He looked rough, and Caleb felt vaguely bad about that. Hot bunking on a deepvoider was never comfortable, officer quarters or not.

He's getting his old apartment back today, the Landlord reminded himself, and squinted down into his coffee. Spout was plugged.

He hated disposable mugs. He hated the fact he was wearing a set of uniform blacks with the subdued gold symbol of the Tenancy in place of his unit shoulder patch. He hated that he'd spent an unsettled night dreaming about his old squadron, their craft, the Captain Rallison he'd known and the monster he'd seen in front of that hostel.

Fucking void. It had turned the entire species insane.

"You got a better idea for dealing with that arrogant little scat-smear?"

The major speared the last protein patty off his tray, chewing thoughtfully. "He is an intractable son of a bitch, that's for damn sure."

"My point exactly." The spout was completely plugged, Caleb decided, and laid the pressure mug aside. No point in getting his uniform splattered, trying to force it open. "Do everyone else a world of good, knocking him down a peg or six."

"We both know this isn't the right way to do things. That really how you want to start this scat out with a planet that hates you?"

That stung more than it should have. Caleb had been avoiding this moment for over twenty years now, ever since he'd woken up in that Deimos clinic, a bevy of worried uniforms watching him on the other side of isolation glass. He hadn't believed them at first, thinking it some new kind of hallucinogen. But Tyr had been there, and Tyr, like all animals, was an infallible authority on reality.

Doubt gave way to anger, an anger that lasted a long time. Through all the tests and briefings and apologies and questions and language lessons and duty requirements, until they'd shipped him out to the *Turiel* and left him to a commander who couldn't have cared less.

Lieutenant Lanin had cared, though. Didn't know anything about him or his situation, and he'd never inquired. What he had asked, though, was for his new corporal to get his attitude under control and his work ethic in line.

Sometimes, being called out was instructive.

Caleb didn't say any of that, though. Nodded at the tray Lanin had brought for him instead. "What is it with you, sir, and feeding everybody?"

It got him a wry smile. "We all have a different way of getting through to our subordinates," Lanin replied. "And maybe I don't want our Landlord passing out because he hasn't eaten in the last eighteen hours."

"It been that long?"

"'Fraid so, sir."

"Huh," the sergeant replied, and tossed one of the patties to Tyr, who caught it midair, swallowing without so much as chewing. "Let's get going."

"Briefing doesn't start for another half hour."

"Yeah, I know."

With morning PT over, the bulk of the base's personnel were already at work, and the outer streets were mostly empty. The pair of soldiers still stuck to the outer walkways, the circuitous route that followed the base perimeter. Tyr trotted a ways ahead, nose to the air, stretching his paws in the Arran-standard gravity. The binding ocean peeled away in smooth, liquid curves from them, exposing lifeless rock. A reminder of what the 'roid had been before the colonists, the floating cities.

"What was it like?" Lanin asked, breaking his thoughts. "Back then?"

"I don't know," Caleb answered distantly. Those last years had been pure chaos. The media infrastructure had been so broken down by the final assaults, news had become more a matter of rumor and supposition and the odd shortwave broadcast than anything else. "Habitat construction had been going on for decades, but I never made it out this far. Not before they did what they did to me."

The major snorted.

"Most people didn't buy into the voluntary extinction the Labs were selling back then," Caleb replied. "But it only takes a few zealots to get a disaster rolling. There was this sense of invincibility back then. We were gods, cracking the secrets of life, moving forward into a glorious future to be created in our image."

"Didn't every major religion in the world denounce that kind of research?"

"Nobody cared, sir. Bein' a god yourself lets you ignore all the old ones." The path curved away from the edge of Humphryes's sky wall, pulling back into the heart of the base, and Caleb whistled Tyr along. "First time I ever saw a holy man was when the army rolled into town. Chaplain, young guy, obviously'd seen some shit in his day. Found me at the pit and told me I was gonna be okay."

"What pit?"

Caleb smiled bitterly. He could still feel that shotgun in his hands, smell the cordite, his father's blood. The way his mother had looked, hanging from that tree. Hunger and cold, friends dying with green snot caking their faces. The smell of it, a soldier with a green strip of fabric around his shoulders, talking in some language he didn't understand. How that soldier had held that little boy Caleb had once been, let him cry.

Lanin paused in the threshold of the squadron's small headquarters building when Caleb didn't answer. "Didn't mean to pry."

"Don't worry about it," the Landlord said, and clapped the other man on the shoulder, pushing him inside. "I'm sorry about this. Taking you away from your family. I know you were looking forward to being inwell of Mars again."

"The wife understands. She ain't happy, but she understands."

"Good," and Caleb nodded once, tight. "You wanna lead the way, sir?"

Lanin grinned back, real and genuine, without a trace of his earlier introspection. "I'd be honored. Maybe we'll luck out, and that fucker'll be sitting in your chair again."

He was, it turned out.

Caleb had originally intended to interrupt that insane morning briefing. The one Hinden insisted on dragging out for an hour or more, every day. March in there, throw him out of his chair, embarrass the scat out of the man.

But Lanin was right.

Wouldn't be the done thing.

Instead, Hinden was alone but for Lieutenant Graben, the harried executive officer dutifully editing something in one of the projection fields. Both men looked up as the briefing room doors banged open. Major Lanin marched in, straight for the head of the table. Caleb leaned up against the doors, gave Tyr a hand signal to take a seat.

"Major," Hinden said from the Rossen's chair, strained. "Didn't know you were here."

"Got recalled. You know how that goes."

"Yeah? Recalled by who?"

Lanin slid into the empty base commander's chair, fiddling with it. "Hmm, looks like it's still on my settings. You been using this thing at all?"

"This is my base now. You have no business interrupting morning stand-up prep to—"

"Stand-up?" Lanin said, words humorous, voice hard. "Stand-up takes fifteen minutes. Graben, how long does this scat normally last?"

The lieutenant answered automatically, obviously unsure of how to handle this. "At least an hour, sir."

"An hour? Mikael, did you not listen to anything I tried to teach you?"

The captain was turning a strange shade of red. "Major, unless you have some kind of orders authorizing you to be here, you need to..."

Caleb peeled himself away from the wall, Tyr, hackles raised, placing his bulk in between him and the captain. "He's here on my orders," he drawled. "He's reassuming command of Humphryes, effective immediately. Your squadron commander certification is denied. Forever."

"This some kind of joke, Sergeant Olin?" Hinden demanded.

"It's Sergeant Ross, actually," Caleb said, and Tyr growled, "and this is not a joke. You're relieved of command, you abusive little weasel."

"You can't possibly mean—"

"You have a deepvoider on your doorstep and phosphorous bombs detonating on in the Hygiea cluster," Lanin said, "and you're telling me nothing's going on? That there's no way the Landlord's showing back up?"

"Him?" Hinden asked, incredulity completely genuine.

"Yeah, him," Lanin said

At the sound of a cough, Caleb looked up.

It was Lieutenant Nyes in the doorway, briefing notes in hand and his senior NCO in tow. Frozen.

Hell, Caleb thought.

At least he'd made an effort to keep this private.

Major Lanin, however, didn't miss a beat. "Nyes, please escort Captain Hinden down to lockup. He's to stay there until I make a determination as to what to do with him."

"Sir?"

"Don't make me repeat myself," Lanin said with a yawn. "This is awkward enough for everyone as it is."

Caleb stepped aside to let the security chief deal with the shocked captain, taking a seat in his liberated chair.

The rest of the base leadership team filed in shortly thereafter, pregnant questions dying at the sight of Master Sergeant Olin in the Rossen's chair. Lanin kept quiet, making a little show of arranging his own notebook, until the last seat at the table was filled.

The major didn't give anybody a chance to say anything, and launched right into it.

"Based on the developing situation, our Landlord's requested that somebody with a greater degree of command experience pick back up here at Humphryes. Our mission is facilitating movement of troops and equipment for forward deployment operations. We're going to make sure we're prepared to execute that. The Rossen's got a lot on his shoulders right now, and we're going to support the fuck out of him. Hinden's stand-up sounds like a fantastic idea."

He tapped on the table, pointing at the briefing projected up in the center. "I'd like quick two-minute status updates from each section right now, and I'll get with each of you later on in the day to get the details." He pointed at Junia, way down on the end, and made a show of fussing with his watch. "Andren, why don't you start us off? Two minutes. I'm timing you."

"Sir," she asked as she sat, "why is Sergeant Olin in—"

"—the Landlord's chair?" he finished for her. "Because he's the Landlord."

A murmur went up around the entire room.

Across the table, Chief Anders started chuckling.

"What?" Junia blurted out.

"That's a minute-fifty, Lieutenant," Lanin warned.

Caleb settled deeper into the Landlord's chair as Junia started talking.

Fucking seat was even more uncomfortable than he'd expected.

TWENTY-FOUR

THE SEVENDAY PASSED UNEVENTFULLY on the *Ariane*. The quiet of the travelers' quarters provided a respite Tharsis wasn't sure she'd actually earned. She perused the collection of books, ate when she was hungry, slept when she was tired, and tried not to dwell on what was coming. Whatever was coming. Her nights were filled with nothing, no visions of anything to bother her, and for all that, she was grateful.

But the last night, the night before they were due to make rockfall at the Trojan transport hub, she saw something. Something new. A lightless city of hollow skin shelters and grunged-up rocks, the one that the Naven had been walking through. Quiet, it had been then.

Quiet now, it was not.

Little sounds. Chittering. Gnawing. Scraping. Grunts and squeals and cries ripped—it seemed—from the throats of dying birds, rising from the stink of the uncured hides around her.

She was walking, but her feet were not her feet, her eyes were not her eyes, and she couldn't control where any of it was directed. Where any of it was searching. And she had no idea what she was looking for in the haze that suffused it all.

Behind her came a rush of air in the still, oppressive space. Her body hit the slime of the rock, splashing it up around her. Pain screamed through her, a hand in her hair, jerking her neck dangerously up, and a rough stone blade just traced her jugular, blunt teeth catching in the skin...

She was on her side, retching into the filth. A wet nose snuffed at her back and at her hands, cleaning the gunk out of a bleeding gash the length of her arm, and she heard her voice—the voice of the person whose memory she was inhabiting—whisper back to the animal.

... it's okay, boy, it's okay, you got the fucker, good boy, I'm fine...

Olin's voice. The Rossen's.

"You'd better eat that, kiddo. Last real meat you're likely to get for a while."

Tharsis looked up from her numb contemplation of a plate of sausage and eggs in the main mess to see the pilot from the rockjump standing across the table from her, holding a tray of his own.

"You mind?" he asked, and she shook her head, gesturing him down to the empty bench. "We'll be in range in the next few hours. You ever been here before?"

"No."

"Well, if it makes you feel better, the captain usually takes a route that avoids the graveyard space."

"Graveyard space?"

The pilot sobered a bit. "From the attack in the Fourth Propagation. Thousands of people in the upper levels of the colonies were blown out voidside. Bodies are still out there."

Tharsis blanched.

He stopped. "I'm guessing you saw something last night?"

She dropped her eyes, desperate to change the subject. "So what'd you do?"

"What, you mean...?" He gestured with a laden fork vaguely in the direction of his neck. "Involved a woman, a couple of sheep, the commander's rockjump, and a hell of a lot of alcohol. How about you?"

Tharsis popped a piece of sausage into her mouth. It tasted of nothing. She didn't feel like she had any right to lie about this. "Kid died. Among other things."

There was a long, long silence from the pilot.

And he got up, taking his tray with him.

Tharsis sighed; the sooner she got off the *Ariane*, the better.

. . .

TECHNICALLY within the control of the Jovian Orbital System and its Landlord, the Trojans were a strange patchwork of Nepo depots, refugee tribes, and pre-Euphemism habitats. Mars regarded the place with equal parts suspicion and pity. Formal governance had all but fallen apart after the Sixth Propagation, when the Arran military had been forced to fight a bloody 'roid-hopping campaign against Tok forces. Casualty rates had run as high as ninety-eight percent on some rocks, the population believing suicide was preferable to capture.

Almost all surface 'roid colonies were gone now, warfare and radiation taking their toll. The deeper habitats and artificial platforms remained, poorly shielded and under-pressurized. Still, the Trojans were key hubs between the inner and outer system. Here, the *Ariane* would take on water and lubricants, off-load spent fluids and reactor fuel, passing it off to one of the recycling facilities that made up the bulk of the regional industry.

The disembarkation tunnel was a smooth hollow of ten-centimeter-thick glass, insulated with translucent aerogel. As she grabbed a handrail, Tharsis felt eyes turning to her. A great crowd assembled but unaware. Dead. *Graveyard space*, she reminded herself, and cranked up her speed, headed for the spaceport's International Arrivals hall and all its vision-shattering bustle.

Tharsis hoped she wasn't going to have to leave the port; she didn't have her passport, and she doubted her ASDF ID card would go down that well. All Nanuk had told her about how this was going to work was that somebody was going to meet her there.

tDaer, she'd been thinking, this whole trip back. Tharsis had no idea how she felt about that. The dive to Earth, the conversations, the sex, the hints of mania around the Iapetan's eyes, none of that was her. She couldn't understand why she'd let herself take part in any of it.

Anger, the Wytt had told her before he'd left that facsimile of her family's kitchen, *is like a sickness in you.*

She wandered slowly around the huge spaceport's central lobby, shops and bars and food vendors packing it to the bulkheads, still expecting to see tDaer pop up at any moment.

But it wasn't tDaer who found her.

"Tharsis! So, you are alive! Praise Tulukat!"

She mustered up an unwilling smile. The last person she wanted to deal with right then was the skinny Jovian and all his interest in all the wrong things. She still felt bad, the way his thin face fell when he saw her expression.

"You look disappointed," he observed.

"I wasn't actually, umm, expecting you," she said honestly.

"Ah, yeah, tDaer had some calibrations hen was working on. The signal's starting to shift. And I had to pick a few things up anyway."

The station passageway twisted and pulled, glide paths snaking circuitous routes through large, enclosed halls and past hangars a kilometer or two wide, open to the void. But rather than follow the brightly illuminated characters indicating the direction of the Trans-Jovian terminal, Angakkuq steered Tharsis down a long corridor, headed for what felt like the interior of the 'roid. Footfalls, shallow steps carved into the walls, from there to wherever their destination lay.

"We've still got a couple of hours before the craft's gonna be ready to go," he explained.

Tharsis adjusted her kit bag's straps as it tried to lift away in the mig, throwing off her momentum. "What's the holdup?"

"Well, it's still not at a hundred percent, not after what, err, happened over Earth."

"And?"

"And we had to take on some cargo. Nothing too serious, but, umm, important, yes," Ang replied, and kicked off a large foothold set in the thermal-sealed wall, gliding up another, narrower passage, characters she didn't recognize cast into silver plaques around the entry.

"That the stuff tDaer was talking about?" Tharsis asked, as innocently as she could.

"Maybe," he replied, wary, and rolled over on his back off the next push, eyeing her. "I'm not sure what tDaer's told you, but, it's important. I think. Why would the Arcna ask for something if it's not important?"

The curved passage narrowed considerably, almost impassible in the last meter or so. Tharsis had to shimmy to push her bag through, stretch an arm in front of her to grab the lip on the other end and pull herself through.

Into the center of a great hemisphere scooped from raw icerock, protected from the vacuum of the void beyond by nothing more than a thin static field, swirling like the skin of a soap bubble. Live flame flickered inside sealed glass bottles, their smoke venting into the wider space. Shadow dominated, moving and twisting, and she was almost instantly suffused with a sense of overwhelming dread.

"Holy god," she breathed, and grabbed onto a handhold in the curve of the room, forcing herself into a hollowed-out seat-dip. An umbran ghost drifted above them, echoed eyes frosted in death. "What is this place?"

"The kiva. A place where we can both descend and ascend, becoming one with the tuurngait. Mylings, or ghosts, I think you'd call them."

Tharsis didn't bother pointing out that Arrans considered those two things very different. "A place of summoning, then?"

"Welcoming," he corrected. "They can come, and we can talk to them in places like this. The layers of the multiverse, becoming as one. Like one of your, umm, churches."

Tharsis wondered what her Gran would say to her if she could see her now. The old lady had disagreed with much that the priests used to say at Mass, but on this, she'd always concurred. Never talk to them. Never interact with them. Not unless you had to. Nobody really knew what umbran were, but there were risks to talking to shadows, whatever their origin. Frivolous conversation could open doorways for darker things.

She could feel eyes on her, that question waking unknowable things in the half-light of the flickering tallow lamps. Full of intention. Not at all human.

A church this was not.

But if she wanted to stay in with these voiders, she'd decided on the *Ariane*, she was going to have stay with them. With everything, anything. Give them no reason to suspect. "So you come here to talk to your gods?"

"There's only one headwater, the origin of the multiverse's energy flow, Tharsis," he said with a patronizing smile, "and we don't worship it."

She rubbed a hand across her face. Of all the damn conversations to be having again. Burned deep into Arran life, religion wasn't something that actually came up all that often back home. It wasn't something she thought about much herself. It simply was. "We don't worship an energy state either, Ang. Or the energetic flows or anything like that."

"Oh? Then what is it?"

"I don't think I could rightly explain it," she replied lamely. "God's, umm, above nature, not a part of it."

He smiled an amused little smile at that, visible through a swirl of the strange smoke. "How can anything be above nature?" he asked. Ang's eyes drifted off into the shadows of the room. She followed his gaze to the ghosting of a figure in the center of the round space, the outline of limbs and emaciated body smudged in the smoke. "We don't have to worry about nonsense like that. Tulukat speaks to us. We know it's real."

"Tulukat?"

"There are no gods," he replied slowly, "no things beyond man. Just us, and the energy flows, and the things we create from it. But the energy speaks to us from beyond the skin of reality. You've seen it too. Down in the oob."

Tharsis sighed. "So where does the Arcna come in?"

"Before, as we spread to the moons and the 'roids and the planets, the Arcna toiled in the darkness of Europa's Adlivun Labs, taking parts of herself, creating the piijuit. Embodying the principles of the Tulukat, she made life where life had not been. That's why she is the Arcna. Mother goddess, fertility goddess."

"You said—"

He smiled. "It's an honorary name. She is ascendant, bringing us the knowledge of perfection. That's what Noqumiut is. The ascended place. The place where we shall make ourselves in our own image, no longer bound by the shapes forced on us by Tulukat."

Tharsis tried to wrap her head around that all. Arran history books claimed that during the Euphemism, old animist systems were twisted up with the new transhumanist philosophy. An attempt to make it somehow more palatable. Sometimes, as on Europa, the entanglement had been quite literal. Usually, she'd been taught, it was merely a convenient facade. New horrors masquerading as ancient wisdom. But what Ang had just described was something far more complex than name-grabs.

"That's the difference between tDaer and I," he continued. "Hen believes it will be a place in which hidden knowledge will be found, knowledge that can be wielded by those intelligent enough to grasp its meaning. My people believe it a physical state, attainable by all."

"What kind of state?"

"The evils of human nature extinguished," he said instantly. "Peace. No killing. No hunger. No want. No work, no labor or strife or anger of any kind. We shall ascend from the Tulukat's meat-shells, be in the very matrix of the stones, the hum of the starfield."

"Why all the violence then, if peace is the goal?"

Ang sighed a little. "Not all of us approve, you know. We're not all part of it. I know we cannot help the evils of our flesh, but it is sad."

"We have splinter religious groups, sometimes, but the Vatican always excommunicates—"

"Oh, no. We would never do something like that."

"Why not?"

"The Propagations teach us that everybody experiences the Arcna's revelations differently. All ideas must be considered if we've a chance at Noqumiut becoming a wider reality. We have no right to condemn another for how they might hear the message and bring it into being."

She rubbed a tired hand across her face. "If everyone's operating on a different version of reality, how can you ever reach some kind of harmonious state? Not everybody gets to be right."

He was silent for a moment.

"I used to be an engineer, you know?" He ran a hand through the haze. "Glaukos was poor, barely able to hold its atmo in, let alone hatch babies from the incubators. It was my job to give back to the people who gave me life. I studied hard as a child, apprenticed myself to a recycling center as soon as I was old enough for the radiation-proof gear. I fought to get certified as a fusionman, but it wasn't enough. It wasn't nearly enough. A life serving money is no life at all.

"But when I was at the reactor facilities on Agelaos, somebody gave me a copy of the First Propagation." His voice dropped, softened, sweetened, awe in his words. "She… she spoke to me, Tharsis. She told me things I've never understood before. It was a revelation."

Fuck, she thought. Of all the damn people to get mixed up with.

"I joined a Nalatok kiva. And when Riqan of the Family came looking for one who could help him, I…"

"Help him with what?"

He didn't answer that. Let it hang for a long time, the sound waves dying, joining the mists around them. "I know what I'd like to find out there. What are you looking for?"

"I don't know," she said honestly. "But I can't go home. If there's a better world out there, we should try to find it."

Angakkuq laughed.

The sound fell dead in that dead space.

She was glad to shimmy back down the tunnel, into the free, cold air of the main passages, and carry on, back towards the port.

The divedrive looked surprisingly stable when they reached it, bobbing gently in its static harnesses, a segmented tunnel hooked to the underside, obviously depositing cargo. Not a scratch on any of those tightly closed stabilization panels.

Ang plunked himself down in a worn hammock just behind the edge of the atmo-wrapper. "Should be done loading in a little while."

She nodded. "Loading what?"

He just smiled. "So, did the Naven say anything to you? We heard you screaming, but…"

"Navigation material. That's what the explosion was, energy transference back across the gradient," Tharsis replied quietly. "Shoved it into my body, too deep for the med folks to take out," she said, leaving off where it was. An arm, after all, was imminently detachable. While she would have put dismemberment past Ang, she did not share the same faith in their Nepo benefactor. "I've got the navigation material."

He grinned. "Amalthea, then?"

"Amalthea."

CHAPTER
TWENTY-FIVE

"NOT A CHANCE IN HELL."

"Do it, or you're off this trip."

"Go fuck yourself, Riqan."

"Remember where you are, Martian! This is my rock!"

"tDaer, fucking hell, did you know about this?"

"What do you want me to say, Tharsis?" tDaer sighed and didn't meet hen's friend's furious gaze. "It's hen's moon."

Riqan, smiling, waggled the package hen was holding.

Burn bags. Normally used in clinical situations to take off irradiated or necrotized skin. The chemicals penetrated the dermis and removed everything underneath it. Not fatal, not even dangerous, if applied correctly.

tDaer couldn't understand why the Martian was in such a snit over it. Not when it was the price of getting hen back on the trip.

tDaer couldn't remember much from those chaotic hours after the oob. Hen had seen nothing on Earth, nothing but a ruined, irradiated city. Felt the strange sensation of being watched. But Tharsis had seen something, Tharsis had spoken to something, Tharsis had started screaming.

The sound hadn't stopped until the craft had ejected hen somewhere over the planet.

It had been a horrible fight, tDaer's hand nearly torn apart by the neuroreactive controls. They'd been dragged halfway across the system before hen'd finally managed to wrest control away from whatever had fucking possessed the craft.

They'd surfaced near Jupiter, a full HST day later. The craft hadn't shown them anything of what had happened back there on Earth, and even though Riqan had gotten it bumped to the front of the line for emergency maintenance, not even a full download of its central brain revealed anything.

"The Flet was in control," one of the techs had suggested, scraping polyps off the main wetware circuits. "That's the only thing that explains these growths. I wouldn't be surprised if the monks out on Pluto aren't having to change a few power cells right now, compensate for the energy he pulled to do this."

So, of all of them, a conscious decision had been made to forcibly remove Tharsis. Only Tharsis. Execution, perhaps. Made sense, after hen saw what had happened on Earth, narrated on the news feeds with genuine shock.

Half the city of Singapore had blown apart in a massive energetic release. Like a nuke had been dropped on it. Something had been pushed across the penumbra, manifesting out of alignment. Folded back on its own worldline. Pushed through the hull. tDaer had torn the craft apart to find it, but there was nothing.

The only possible answer was that Tharsis had it.

Hen's data on that was sound enough to convince Riqan to grant the request from Phobos when it came in. To bring Tharsis here. Get hen back.

And it'd been with a strange sense of anticipation that hen had agreed to Riqan's one condition. tDaer was worried about the project, but hen was more worried about the Martian henself. Which struck hen as an odd thing, worth exploring further; tDaer had always been on hen's own. Good Cronuan independence, that. Tharsis, however, was turning into something entirely new.

"Tharsis will do it," tDaer had promised.

This reluctance really did confuse hen.

"You have any fucking idea how deep these things are set?" the Martian snapped, gesturing at the rank tattoos. "Do you know why? So your fucking militias can't burn them off of us when we're captured!"

"Nobody's captured here, Tharsis," Angakkuq offered earnestly.

"Yet," Riqan added in a mock-pleasant voice.

"Why?"

"I want to know I can trust you."

Tharsis sputtered. "Trust me? I'm AWOL, I've violated the Accords, I'm as far outside the system as I can get. I am here. For this. And you don't think you can trust me?" Hen turned scared eyes on tDaer. "Come on..."

The grad student just snorted. "It's disgusting, the way your people mark you up like that. Like they fucking own you. Doesn't it disgust you?" It was a dig, but hen had been curious about it since Tharsis had first shown up at Nighttrippers looking for lodging.

"And you don't want to be on base? It's easier," tDaer had asked, back then.

"I don't like easy things," hen had replied, and smiled.

A Martian finally worth getting to know.

Now, Tharsis just looked furious. And terrified. "tDaer..."

The Nepo tossed hen the packet, golden cat-eyes narrowing dangerously. "We can always opt for vivisection to get the navigation material out of you."

"I think you mean dissection."

"I know the difference."

Hen stared at the foil-wrapped packet, and tDaer had the oddest urge to reach out and hold hen's hand. Wouldn't do to show that kind of weakness in front of a Nepo, though; one way or another, the Martian was losing flesh tonight.

Tharsis's teeth gritted. "I'm not catching some weird voider infection for this."

Riqan held up a second, blue-wrapped packet. Fast-heal med pack. "I'm not a sadist."

"Fine," Tharsis said. Hen unzipped the top of hen's tunic down to the top of those full breasts. The ASDF ownership tags ran in a stylized wing pattern from the inside edge of the collarbone to curl around the tip of the ear on both sides. Tharsis had tried to explain their significance to tDaer once.

Back in the Euphemism, military personnel were branded when captured.

Barbaric, really. The kind of thing, tDaer found henself thinking,
that wouldn't be allowed in Noqumiut.

Tharsis unfolded the packs. Hesitated only a second. Slapped
them on.

The stench of burning flesh filled the room, but no noise. Not even
a whimper.

Riqan pushed back in hen's hammock, smiling cruelly. "Twenty
seconds ought to do it, don't you think, Martian?"

"F-fuck you."

That was the point at which tDaer couldn't stop henself. Hen
pushed over, touching the Martian's shoulder, vibrations of pain
wracking that heavy planet-born frame. Tharsis reached up and caught
hen's void-slendered wrist in a death grip, squeezing hard.

The Martian had gone a strange shade of gray by the time Riqan let
tDaer rip the pads back off hen's neck. The skin was brutalized, red
and oozing as if from severe radiation exposure. But Tharsis, unstable,
sweating, still took care to fold up the used pads neatly, put them back
in their pouch, and hand them back to their sponsor.

"H-Happy now?" hen asked, lilting Martian accent jarring with
pain. Hen was trying to get the med pack open now, but hen's hands
were shaking so badly hen couldn't manage it.

"Here, you're going to ruin 'em," tDaer said, and took the package
away. Peeling off the protective paper, easing gel packs up over
ravaged skin, hen didn't look the ashen-faced Martian in the eye. What
exactly did one say to one's partner after something like that?

Tharsis sighed as the medicated poultices were smoothed against
the ravaged skin. Hen sagged back. "Are we d-done here?"

tDaer looked up at their sponsor. "We're done, right Riqan?"

The big Nepo nodded, and pushed up, staring down at hen with a
condescending little smile on hen's face. "Sure."

Hen left, and Angakkuq filed out after, leaving just Tharsis and
tDaer in the small room, alone.

"Tharsis, look, I didn't know hen was—"

"Fuck you too," the lieutenant shot back, and pressed shaking
hands against the med-pad. Hen's voice was steadier as hen spoke

again, the painkillers in the gel going to work. "Just get me somewhere I can pretend I'm horizontal before I puke everywhere."

The air in the room had taken on a distinctively nauseating smell. One that tDaer thought might make hen ill if they sat in it for too long. "No problem."

tDaer took the Martian back to the little private room where they'd dropped hen's bag earlier, turning the lights on, stripping the Martian's tunic off without disturbing the packs. Tharsis seemed determined to deal with hen's trousers henself, though, rolling them carefully up and stuffing them deep into hen's bag. The Martian was moving slower than hen normally did, heavy muscles fatigued, left arm pocked and swollen red.

The Iapetan graduate student almost felt guilty about it; Riqan was a brute, somebody tDaer could have gone hen's whole life without knowing. But hen needed the funding. A grant request to the Scient could have landed hen in the execution chambers on Titan, for attempting to violate the Accords.

While the Scient's were kinder methods than most, dying was dying. Dying. Becoming nothing more than a data point in the Scient's computer, every thesis and action and belonging in hen's lab analyzed and evaluated and judged. The base genetic template turned over and tweaked again. Some new little baby being cooked up, the new Daer. But not tDaer.

The grad student had never been comfortable with it, the idea of nothing being hen's, not even hen's own genome. The Scient promised them absolute freedom, but the freedom to be what?

Nothing, hen thought, and snorted. Hen might have hated Riqan, but at least the Onias was always clear about what hen was. There was, in fact, fascinating honesty in hen's brutality. And it wasn't tDaer's place to judge Riqan's methods. They stayed out of each other's business. Besides, tDaer needed the Nepo's money more than an explanation.

Tripping around the Heliosphere after hen's bachelor's was done, tDaer had done hen's postgrad work for hen's first MA on Phobos. Easier than taking a four-month rig trip back to the Cronuan orbitals, it seemed a good idea at the time. But hen had only been disgusted by it all, the ugliness of Martian culture.

Disgusting, that anybody had ever agreed to live that way, in the dirt and disease, depending on everyone else for survival, no independence, no solitude possible. They slaughtered animals for food and hated their Landlord with a passion, thinking they could better order their nation without him. No real education system. Intelligent life arranged around biological barbarities: genders slaved to each other, men hard and women soft, fetuses carried within the body like parasites, everyone held down within sticky webs of unchosen, unwitting familial interconnections. Utterly anachronistic, Mars, oblivious to its own horror.

But Tharsis had never been like that, not even when tDaer had first met hen. No, that Martian had been unwilling to live like that, rejecting it outright, and it made sense that hen would come back here. To them. To Noqumiut. To henself. To tDaer.

Has to be liberating, tDaer thought, *to finally burn that stain away.*

"Does that hurt?" hen asked.

"I'd like to say I've had worse," Tharsis replied, easing a gravbag out of that rucksack. "But it's pretty fucking bad."

Down the hall in the media room, Riqan and Angakkuq were listening to one of the Arcna's broadcasts. Coming through, now, on Amalthea. Its low-level ULF had been ghosting through Trans-Jovian space for months, barely distinguishable from galactic background noise in casual analysis. The last sevenday or so, the signals had started cutting in.

<We can solve the problem of humanity, my friends,> the Arcna was saying tonight. <We may become perfect. We have the authority to make ourselves perfect because we take it for ourselves. Do not listen to others when they say it otherwise. Do not listen to anyone but yourselves.>

Almost a year and a half ago, the Iapetan had decoded it. Heard the Arcna's voice, as if for the very first time. Speaking to hen across the vastness of the Heliosphere—just to hen, it had seemed, a secret that they were sharing together. A message that not even the ASDF had ever recorded.

Come to me and I shall show you the truth.

In that moment, tDaer had known. Whatever hen needed to do, hen would do. To get there. To meet the owner of that voice. To hear the wisdom of one who had long watched humanity. Find the answers Noqumiut would hold.

Be the Daer who finally mattered. Be more than a moldering thesis in Titan's libraries.

"Did you only... you know, because?"

Tharsis, spreading out hen's bag in the hammock. Sad, almost resigned. tDaer couldn't quite bring henself to say yes. At some point, it had been about that. Maybe. But not for months now. *More*, hen thought, and wondered again what that might mean.

"I still wanted you," tDaer said, hoping that would cut across the difference, and shut the door. Pushed back to the sleeping hammock beside Tharsis, savoring the slight snap of static cling, holding them loosely in. Proud, tDaer realized, hen was proud of what Tharsis had done there tonight. An odd feeling, but good. "You were still intriguing."

Tharsis went quiet. Silent for a long, long while, and the Iapetan was almost certain hen had fallen asleep, when hen spoke again.

"She was four, tDaer."

"Who? What do you mean?" tDaer asked, letting long fingers play over that throat, teasing at the edges of the med packs.

"She's dead, the Naven," Tharsis replied quietly, an odd expression on hen's face. "Died in the explosion, shoving this scat into my arm. You knew that, right?"

"Of course." Fuck. What? No? They'd killed a Landlord?

But Tharsis just sounded haunted. "On Mars, children, family, it's all we've got. Children... children are what matters, only thing, and I can't even—"

Shushing hen, not wanting to listen to any more talk about dead Landlords, Mars, children, tDaer pressed a kiss right to the unburned hollow of hen's throat. Skin constricted. Breath caught.

"You'll see how much better it is," the Iapetan promised. "After they're all gone, the insanity will be over. Nobody will be forcing your people to live on a planet anymore, socializing you to believe that's the best way to live. You'll be free to make your own choices. Not bound by anyone else's... what?"

Tharsis was smiling a little, a pained and sad smile. "You think that's what we're gonna find in Noqumiut?"

"That's what the Arcna offers. Our perfect world."

"Right," Tharsis murmured, curling tighter into henself.

"We'll both see it together," hen promised, and hesitated. "I'm glad you're back."

The Martian shut hen's eyes, words muttered, heavy with sleep. "Yeah, me too."

tDaer smiled. "You're a hell of a lot warmer than anyone I've slept with before."

"Cause that's what matters. Temperature." Hen was slipping off already. That was probably good. Probably hurt hen less. It was a strange thing, watching Tharsis in pain like that. A knot of anxiety was tightening, deep in tDaer's own chest.

You care about hen, tDaer realized, and thought about what it would be like to be with hen, a long-term partner. Cronuans did that, sometimes.

They'd have to talk about physiology, of course. Tharsis compensated better than most, but hen's body in its current configuration was clumsy in mig, and fertile, which wouldn't do at all. Maybe, when this was all over, they could get some decent Cronun adaptations into hen. The Tenancy funded visa programs like that; the Scient had some very nice independent facilities on Enceladus.

When it was over. When they made the world the way it was supposed to be. No limits. No restrictions. Nobody forcing their own subjective moralities on anyone else, those stupid planet-born beliefs that said there was something sacred about the human form, human mind, spirit, that had to be preserved.

Tharsis would like that. Who wouldn't? Having the rot of that planet-born biology ripped out.

When they found Noqumiut.

Become what it was the Arcna knew they could become.

Hen laid there for a moment more, waiting for Tharsis to slip fully under, before wriggling out. To the kitchen and the radio and the message—that pure, unadulterated, uncompromising message.

CHAPTER
TWENTY-SIX

THARSIS WOKE—DISORIENTED and alone—into a nightmare.

Barefoot on ground cold enough to burn away skin. Icy dust rustled between her toes.

Where the fuck was she?

Turning around, trying to find some kind of bearing in the eternal night around her, Tharsis noticed a light. A light, burning like the final star left unclaimed by the entropy of Armageddon.

Something new, in the now familiar darkness.

She had to get to it.

The going was slow, or impossibly fast. There was no way of knowing how long it took her, pushing off, landing again, pushing off, in great bounding leaps that took her unknown distances into that space she couldn't see. But the oppressive darkness lifted as she neared that source, revealing the ground she was standing on.

A Lighthouse control center, same as the one from Europa, except that this one was retrofitted: torn apart and rewired by hand. Soldering clumped on metal components, biological casings bulging with cancerous growths, mechanical pieces twisted and broken. A gang of preschoolers hardly could have damaged the innards of such a complex system so utterly.

In the center of the room there was a creature. Naked. Almost human. Long hair swayed in mats around wasted shoulders, obscuring nothing; Tharsis could discern every rib, every sagging bit of skin, and it stank. A monster of the Euphemism, it seemed, one of those things that had rampaged through the unconscious, unrecognizable as anything other than reality.

In its eyes—

Tharsis shot straight up, jolted into the waking world by some horrible knowledge dissolving before it could solidify in her mind. In a blind panic, she tore at the loose confinement of the sleeping hammock and threw herself out. Her bare back hit the nearest wall, stunning her still.

The Arran lieutenant scrubbed a hand over her face, letting intrude on her senses the soft glow of the room's night-light, the close comfort of the walls, the sound of tDaer huffing in sleep. Sweat cooled on her skin, chilling cold. Tharsis went over to her rucksack.

Touching the bandages as she pulled threadbare clothes mechanically on, she felt sick, beyond the lingering pain from the burns. The thought that somebody would think her capable of betraying her country without a second thought, of doing it happily, horrified her. Almost as much as tDaer's reassurances that it didn't matter, the Naven's death didn't matter, nothing mattered but this mad quest to find Noqumiut.

The whole thing was insane.

She strapped her knife carefully to her thigh. On Mars, nobody left home without some kind of personal protection, but Cronuans hated the mere mention of weapons. It would probably disappear from her bag if the Iapetan caught sight of it. And that would be bad, especially if something broke loose. The average voider, like tDaer, with lighter bone and thinner muscle, wasn't necessarily a threat. Riqan, however, was a different story. Half of his DNA was Earth-bred, and male, and huge.

Get the algorithms and get out.

She donned the rest of her clothes quickly, grimacing a little at the cold permeating the material, her body working hard to warm them up as quickly as possible. Just as she was finishing up with the zipper of her tunic, though, she heard a noise echoing out from the central chamber of the house.

The radio, she thought, and, securing the last strap on her boots, gravity disengaged, headed out to see what was on.

The sounds echoed through the central chamber, and while it wasn't easy to identify which tunnel-doorway they were coming from, she knew the voice.

Tharsis stopped short. Fuck. The Arcna? Already?

<... in the beginning, there were only individuals, none better and none worse than the others, all equal, all beautiful of mind and body and spirit. But then we discovered manipulation, and the weak sought to force their personal realities onto all. I say to you now, let no other manipulate you. You are strong and they are weak. Your ideals are truth and theirs are lies. Do not tolerate their tyranny of the mind. We must stop these false ideas from spreading their misery...>

Tharsis frowned.

A long pause. The sound of whining laughter echoing through it.

<... gather together, and destroy the ideas that would destroy your own...>

The Arcna's voice. Had to be old recordings. Very old. Tharsis didn't recognize the content. Somebody must have left a player on somewhere.

<... destroy the ones who destroy your ideas, for our ideas are sacred. Destroy the ones who enslave you for petty, pointless ends...>

Or maybe it was the new Propagation. And that was a chilling thought. The Arcna never called for violence directly. Never.

<... kill your enslavers...>

"Fucking Landlords," she grumbled to herself, and slipped off to find the shower room. The med packs had gone turgid, solidifying, signaling their work was done, and she wanted the things off. Wanted to see what she'd done to herself.

Pulling the thick gooey compresses off her neck was surprisingly difficult, and disgusting, once she managed to dislodge them. The med-packs were cloudy: blood, ink, dead flesh, suspended in the matrix.

Her neck was bare. New pink skin, wrinkled, puckered. No ASDF wings. No rank.

Her whole life, the fate written for her on the kitchen table in her brother's blood, just gone. She'd hated it, or so she'd thought. But it had been hers, and now it was gone.

The lieutenant wanted to cry at the sight. But she could still hear the Arcna's voice drifting up from wherever that stupid radio was on. And she had more pressing matters.

Tharsis hit the dark tunnels outside the hostel, sucking at a high-protein packet of twice-boiled beans as she pushed to the train station. The food helped settle her stomach. And she needed to replace some of the massive caloric loss of the rapid healing process.

She caught the transport back to the port through the glittering beauty of the Nepo neighborhoods, head on the window. Tired, though she couldn't quite manage to doze off.

The Arcna never talked about killing. But then, did she ever really need to?

The other Landlords performed their own executions—messy and short-range and public. Honest, in a strange way. Even Mars accepted that. Hell, the Rossen had killed senators before, to prevent legislation that might have brought back the horrors. There was purpose in it, even if that purpose was terrible. But the Arcna never raised her own hand against another. Just inspired others to do the killing for her, in the name of Noqumiut.

Death upon death. All for words in the darkness. A dream where all wrong, real or otherwise, could be made right.

The car glided into the wide plaza in front of the bustling spaceport, trundling towards the station on the far end. The people below looked like ants. Ants in an anthill. Nothing human in any of it.

Just get the algorithms and get the fuck out of this place.

PEEKING around the edge of the little check-in desk as a pair of Arran rig workers signed in in front of her, Tharsis couldn't see anything out of the ordinary.

She didn't know what she'd been expecting, but gravity was a welcome respite.

Amalthea was too small to have an embassy, but there was a steady flow of Arrans through the region, thanks to the extraction fleets and the Trilan Watch Base. The port had a small but useful rest stop, run jointly by the Dominicans and the ASDF's civilian auxiliary force. She'd looked it up before leaving Deimos. It was a place that served as a lounge, cheap lodging, rest area, prayer room, umbran-free zone, and gathering space for Arrans abroad. They were also possessed of an encrypted military communication suite.

Tharsis, a little off-balance, handed over her ID card slowly, hoping they weren't going to ask for the passport she didn't have. The new skin on her neck burned.

"Lieutenant, huh?" the attendant said, glancing up at her. Tharsis could feel his scrutiny. The new scars on her neck burned.

"Medical problem," she lied quickly, and smiled over the sting.

The young man behind the counter nodded, and handed her back her ID. "You been here before? Need a quick tour?"

Tharsis peeked around the corner again, into the large room that made up the bulk of the little refuge. Sleeper hammocks, ad hoc kitchen facilities stocked up with instant-heat food packs, reading shelves full of battered old books.

"I'm just looking for the comm room," she said. "Thought I'd drop my family a letter, let them know I'm okay after," and she gestured at her neck. "You know, they're worried."

It got her a sympathetic smile. "Radiation burns?"

"Yeah, something like that."

"Happens all the time out here," the volunteer told her, and gave her back her ID. "Arran exogear isn't always up to scratch. You'd be amazed how many injuries we see coming out of the Jovian inwell. Not to mention the mental strain. I used to work at the USO on Europa. Some people, I'm told, never recover from their time at Trilan Watch."

"Yeah," Tharsis replied, Hinden coming to mind. "I know a captain like that."

"You'd think Command would spring for the expense of better gear for our soldiers, at least out there. An hour under those Jovian magnetics is not nearly enough of a margin of safety."

"That seems a little short," the lieutenant agreed. An hour, that's all her suit would buy her if something went wrong? She put it from her mind. No use borrowing trouble, as her Gran might have said. "Umm, so, that, uh, the comm room?"

"Third door down the hall thataway."

CHAPTER
TWENTY-SEVEN

"WHAT IS IT?"

"Sir, you told me to call the second she made contact."

Caleb rubbed a hand over his face. That. Right. Fucking intercom buzzer, waking him up out of a perfectly good dream. "Be there in a minute."

Sliding tired fingers off the talk button, with the scent of her hair still echoing out of aborted REM, a wet nose bumped his bare leg. The Landlord sank down over his heels, scratching the big animal behind one ear. "At least you haven't changed."

Tyr's tail beat loud in the small space.

The Landlord dressed as quickly as he could, exhaustion threatening to engulf him. He'd been averaging maybe two hours of sleep a night since he'd sent Tharsis off: the inevitable consequence of emerging from obscurity. He'd yet to announce it to the Arran people, or check in with Congress, but the rumors had been getting around.

Part of his promise to the Republic of Mars was that he'd keep himself accessible. He didn't mind that if it meant keeping his people free and his government constricted. But he loathed being the final arbiter of the planet's collective morality. At the very least, they should have been able to police things themselves.

Caleb had never quite understood why he'd agreed to it. The Founding. He'd been in his late fifties, when the First Planetary Congress began debating the Accords, so that was history lost to him.

But he remembered the conversations that had far preceded it, the ones about Mars, what it could be. Back when he was a corporal, the things they used to talk about in the barracks and on missions, trying to imagine a world after the war.

There had been so much hope, back then, that there was still something to be saved. The better parts, the functional parts, the parts that let a man stand on his own goddamn feet and build his own goddamn life. Caleb had hoped, as so many had, that his birth country's way of life could be salvaged on Mars.

They'd been so close.

"Seven hundred years, boy," he told Tyr, the dog's concern pressing in on his mind, sudden and thick. "Long time to be telling other people how to live their lives."

The dog just beat his tail on the ground harder, and Caleb smiled ruefully to himself as he sealed up his boots. "Must be easier for you, huh? Dogs run in packs."

The dog sent back a sense memory—cold metal and ruthless reek and dead fur and a set of gentle, gun-rough hands pulling him out into the light, telling him not to be afraid.

Caleb shut down his mind. It was familiar, Tyr's memory of the day they'd packed him from the lab. Something the dog used to communicate reassurance. But in that moment, Caleb didn't want the reminder.

THARSIS WAS EATING lunch when it started. Onigiri. In the back of a little convenience store in the international terminal. A ball of platform-farmed rice and boiled shrimp, squatting Ibbie-style in the small dining area in the back.

Crackling above the tinny music.

Mixing, and then overtaking.

<... is it not in these late years that we may see what has become of us? Our beauty and promise? Where is it? I shall tell you. It has been destroyed by the selfishness of a few who do not deserve your lives, the lives you use to serve them...>

The lieutenant stopped mid-chew. A grain of rice floated off the top of the ball.

The signal was already overriding encryption on the moon's radio stations?

<… they enslave you, forcing you to harvest their gas and mine their soils and do all the things they will not. Are they not rich enough? Do they not owe it to you to erase such tyranny? Must you starve while they feast on your labor? My friends…>

Everyone else in the store had stopped, some nodding, others merely listening.

Tharsis finished her meal in two bites, swallowing without tasting, and pushed back up to her feet, out of the store.

<… what have your self-styled masters given you but pain? They must be stopped…>

Tharsis picked up her pace, pushing out into the open spaces of the terminal.

Commotion behind her. Police, armed with concussive weapons and dressed in riot suppression gear, speeding towards the little store under heavy thruster. The crowds of the port's shopping atrium scattered like fish from a seal, yelling and cursing in a dozen different dialects, and Tharsis noticed a few locals pushing to the walls, fast.

No yelling. No time for yelling. In a matter of ten seconds or so, the police had entered, re-emerged, pushing a cuffed shopkeeper in front of them. The man appeared unconscious, bobbing aimlessly, a thick stream of dark blood leaking from his mouth and nose. From inside came the sound of smashing.

The Arcna's voice was still rising, echoing, cackling, indistinct from a dozen different shops now. Unintelligible angry cries from a hundred different throats. The indifferent roar of static discharges from a squad's worth of energetic suppression weapons.

The crowd clinging to the walls, not part of the situation but still watching, fled.

Away.

Towards.

A violent crimson-dark haze blurred around them, leaking out of the penumbra into Tharsis's field of vision. Aural, like the sucksuck, deeply stained with malice. A growing emotion, one she'd never seen before but instantly recognized.

"Faster, Chen," she muttered, and pushed off the next footfall with everything she could muster, and the next, the next, building up momentum and moving fast.

Another three police squads roared up to the grand entrance of the port as she pushed out, on the upper edge of a streaming mass of humanity fleeing the rioting within. Heedless of collateral damage, security forces began blasting an inward path through the crowd. People poured up into the monorail station, but the gates had come down, cars stopped and entrances locked. The major push-tunnels out were being systematically closed, huge jaws clanging shut with crushing force.

Panic was settling, a crushing yellow-gray fog filling the penumbra. Tharsis locked herself firmly down against it, willing her eyes not to see it, her lungs not to breathe it in. Casting around, she found a small pushway still open, far away from the masses starting to howl, tucked back into a corner of the plaza, the signage indicating it to be a surface street.

She hesitated for a moment, but the sound of projectile gunfire was echoing loud now. It was a choice between an unknown and a Jovian gun.

Tharsis dove into the pushway and took off.

Fifty meters down the small tunnel, it slammed shut behind her. But she, at least, was free of whatever death light was building up now on the other side.

Thank Michael, she thought.

The trip back was long, but quiet. No mobs, no gunfire, no screaming Arcna. She'd found herself in some kind of tertiary connecting road, dumping here and there into bulbous hollows of neighborhoods, weaving in and out of larger byways, a torturous and uncertain route. It was signed, at least, and after a dozen interchanges and untold kilometers, Tharsis found herself shadowing a rail line back to the nightside station.

tDaer was there when she finally dragged into the hostel, almost seven hours after she'd left. The Iapetan threw an arm around her, and Tharsis felt almost bad about how much better that made her feel.

Better, until Ang found them.

"Riqan wants everybody in the kitchen. Now."

· · ·

"THIS ISN'T MUCH."

"Yeah, well it's what was sent."

Caleb shot Junia a hard look. A hard-nosed giddie junkie, that one, who drank significantly more than was healthy for a woman of her mass. He hated it when officers got like that, especially the females, coming off like caricatures in their attempts to fit in. He remembered those same kinds of problems back when he was a young corporal, and that was in the middle of one of the nastiest wars ever fought. Why it was still going on was beyond him.

He wasn't sure if that was his fault. Probably. His planet, his military, after all.

But none of that was his current problem.

Tharsis's message was, well, disturbing.

ARRIVED AMALTHEA, NEPO NAMED RIQAN DEFINITELY INVOLVED, FINANCING PROJECT, GREATER EXTENT OF PARTIC-IPATION THAN ANTICIPATED. NO ACCESS TO ORIGINAL DECRYPTION EQUIPMENT. KUIPER LOCATION STILL UNKNOWN. CONTINUING WITH MISSION UNTIL OTHERWISE DIRECTED.

And there, at the end, was the real kicker.

ARCNA CALLING FOR KILLING. POSSIBLY EXECUTION OF NEPOS.

"Don't mind the el-tee," Winters told him. "She's just pissy because Chen got in her face, trying to call you a sevenday ago."

"Winters, shut the fuck up," Lieutenant Junia said wearily.

"And because none of your message traffic has been going through us," Winters added. "How have you been getting all those reports you're supposed to track?"

"Embassy core comm," Caleb replied automatically, distracted. "I have a terminal in my barracks room."

Junia looked like she'd just swallowed a lemon. "You're running an uncleared network through this base, around official channels?"

"I am official channels."

"Sir, I understand that, but—"

"The only reason you even know what's going on right now is because the Embassy silic can't handle these decryption algorithms," he told her. "Standards matter. But there's a big difference between following giddies like a bureaucrat and knowing when to break 'em. I've got no time for bureaucrats. Get what I'm saying here, Andren?"

Mouth in a thin line, she nodded. "Yes, sir."

The *fuck off* in her tone was clear, but before he could call her on it, Winters snapped his fingers.

"Hey, sir?"

"What?"

"Message from Trilan," and the sergeant flipped a switch on the console, a hazy image dropping from the ceiling's central projector.

Plunging the room into a stunned silence.

It was a video of makeshift incendiaries inside the base boundary. The screeching sound of the Arcna's voice, calling for death.

Caleb cleared his throat, knowing he needed to say something. Anything. "Get me HOMECOM," he ordered Winters quietly. "I'd say the Eighth Propagation's on."

"In force," the other sergeant muttered, and left to go spool up the MLSL.

A SMALL CROWD had gathered in the kitchen: a party of Cronuan travelers, Ang, Riqan. The staff Tharsis dimly remembered from the night before were gone, Nighttrippers empty above them. Over the microwave, Riqan had a two-dimensional projection screen cranked up.

<We want to reassure everyone watching that Public Security has the situation well under control,> a female reporter was saying, a big smile plastered across her tattooed face. <Our Landlord is magnanimous in his application of force, striking out only against those who would dare threaten his communities. He wants to take tonight to remind all tenants of his great system that violence is never the answer.>

<That's right, Amani,> the male reporter replied to the cameras. <The whole nation could do with a reminder tonight, that the Onias, and the Family, always has our best interests at heart...>

One of those Cronuans, Tethian, judging by the heavy piercings and garish clothes, glared at the projection field. A thick silver ring twitched in a thin-plucked eyebrow. "Don't these people ever shut up about their money-grubbing Landlord?"

"Just because your fucking world doesn't have an independent economy doesn't mean mine can't," the Nepo said, but it sounded distracted. The Tethian sniffed, and babbled something to tDaer in lyrical Crono, who replied in kind.

"What is this?" Tharsis asked the Jovian, voice pitched under the argument starting up around them.

"Private Family channel, quant-encrypted." His knuckles were white against the table he was leaning on, a thousand AU from the arrogant man of last night. "The Onias is worried."

"I thought the Jovian security forces were some of the best in the Heliosphere."

He chuckled, mirthless and angry, eyes still affixed to the screen. "You ever wonder why the Family funds the Toks?"

"Cause your people starve to death while your DNA set rapes this inwell dry of resources?" tDaer asked, in Standard English again.

"That was a rhetorical question."

The picture on the projected screen switched to a broad-spectrum shot of Metis. Plumes of gray-white atmo were escaping into the void, fires licking through them, debris flying off as outer surfaces buckled, exploded.

<The Onias wants to reassure everybody that this situation will be handled appropriately and with all correct measures. Family is encouraged to get to their panic rooms as soon as possible...>

"What?" Tharsis asked.

Riqan's sallow features didn't twitch. "Fumigation. Probably."

"Fumigation?" she sputtered, stumbling over the word. "Like, what, for termites?"

"What are termites?"

"Insects that burrow through and destroy structures."

"Perfect analogy. Mobs have been known to tear through structures before." He smiled at that, a predator's expression. "It's pretty weak stuff, the interior matrix of—"

Before he could finish, the news report flickered, once, twice, and then off. Going to white static on the projection.

The Arcna's voice booming in its place.

<... these worlds of yours are pitiful shells of what could be... Take back what is yours, what should be yours... The promise of the Landlords, to free you all from the unfair shackles that have always held humanity back... No hunger, no war, no strife, just peace, all equal, unchanging, and beautiful... I know the answer... I have always known the answer... Dethrone, destroy. Kill them, kill them all...>

Just then, Tharsis caught the faintest edge of reddish-black penumbran haze. Same as the port. Creeping in under the door. Stealing through the sealed icerock floor.

"We need to get off this moon," Riqan mused.

"We can't just waltz out the front door," tDaer said, staring in the direction of that sound.

"There has to be another way to the port," Tharsis said.

Riqan shrugged. "There isn't. And if things get chaotic, if they fumigate, I can't guarantee we have enough atmo for the panic room here to outlast it."

"But you're a Nepo," one of the Tethians said. "Wouldn't the Onias equip you with what you need to withstand this?"

"We're still citizens. What's your point?"

Tharsis looked around the room, at the little group assembled there. She wasn't responsible for any of their lives. She wasn't under oath to protect any of them. She bore them no loyalty. But she didn't want to die here, didn't want anyone to die here, and there had to be a way of getting them all out. To safety. Outside, off, the moon.

And she remembered the viewing room.

"Riqan," she said quietly, surprised by the calm she could hear in her voice, "those viaducts, the ones that pump the aurora in. They go to the surface, right?"

"Why?"

"Can we use them to get out there? Go overland?"

The Nepo, after a moment, catching up, started laughing. "That is some insanity if I've ever heard it."

Ang looked disturbed. "You have any idea what kind of radiation Father Jupiter pumps out? We wouldn't survive an hour out there in that."

"The viaducts are mostly shielded from that, aren't they?" Tharsis pressed. "Otherwise, it'd bake everyone. Can't we take them out to the port?"

tDaer shook hen's head. "No way. How would we even navigate in..."

"No, she's right. The aurora ducts do span a significant way through this part of the habitat. They're barely pressurized, but exogear should handle it. We should be able to get at least half the distance, underground," Riqan said, and he looked at Tharsis, gold eyes blazing. "Martian, you ever do a long push through mig?"

"Cruise year," she replied. "I can keep up."

He nodded in assent. "Everybody in the upper chamber in five minutes. Only what you need and nothing more."

They all got ready in silence, as quickly as possible. Back upstairs in the rest of the hostel, noise in the streets was swirling through, at a decibel level not even tDaer could ignore.

"What the fuck is going on?" the Iapetan muttered, staring out the window, pulling the elegant sweep of Cronuan-grown ENEX over the hard lines of hen's body.

There was nothing beautiful about the Iapetan. That body was viewed by its owner as a casing for the mind, and little more. Cronuans routinely indulged in modifications—surgeries, implants, tattoos, genetic restructurings—but for whatever reason, tDaer had never undergone any alterations. Hen's body, the Arran realized, was a starting point for a project never begun.

Not the time, she told herself.

Easing the Rossen's knife into an exterior hip pocket, Tharsis pulled her exogear on over her clothes. Arran gear didn't need skin-to-slick contact, even if it was recommended; she had no other way of hanging on to that knife.

"You seriously think this is necessary? I mean, we're on their side. If they just understood that..."

Tharsis pushed up to the window, peering out.

There, at the end of the street. A horde of Jovians, armed with rough bits of metal, long poles and huge screwlike things, components ripped from a craft or factory or god only knew where else, hammering on the sides of the buildings, screaming.

"You think a fucking mob is going to sit down and ask nicely what your politics are?"

tDaer didn't say anything, some crushed expression flashing across hen's face, and pushed out of the room. Tharsis sighed and took off after hen.

Riqan caught up with her in the hall, though, killing her momentum with a touch to her arm. He was clad in a matte-black, reinforced ENEX and carrying a pair of odd-looking weapons.

"Rock machete. You know how to use one of these?" the Nepo asked quietly.

Tharsis took the proffered blade cautiously. Dark with a synthetic diamond edge, the blade was curved for optimum swing-force in free fall. It would have been too heavy for Mars, far denser than anything they'd ever used on the ranch.

"Sure, I can use a machete. What's your point?" she asked and tried to hand it back.

"Keep it." He passed her a thigh-strap sheath. "Lieutenant."

She bristled. "Just 'cause I'm in the military doesn't mean I'm combat trained."

"Didn't mean it as an insult, Martian," he sniffed. "You trust any of those scat stains to swing it if they needed to?"

Tharsis sighed, and sheathed the blade, securing it to her leg as they headed down to the chamber. "This scat cut through wrapper?"

"Not really. But mass and force still counts for a lot, and the blade is lethally sharp. Control the swing, keep it slow enough, and it can get through."

The sense of things had changed, Tharsis noticed, as they joined the small group assembled in the upper observation deck of the hostel's top floor. Gone was the bemused detachment from downstairs, silence replacing the laugher, and the sound of the Arcna's voice was pounding, indistinct, but chilling nonetheless, through the very stone.

The room was vibrating.

"They'll be tearing through walls," Riqan said, touching the back of his hand to one of the walls, and drew himself up to his full height. "The aurora vents are mostly vacuum. ENEXs up, breathing masks on, radios on channel four-alpha-six, and don't fall behind. I'm not getting caught by those animals out there." He palmed a small spheric charge from a bulging bag at his hip, and, without waiting for a response, Riqan slapped it on the glass ceiling and wrapped a hand into a hammock. "Everybody grab something."

Tharsis grabbed onto a handhold by the door and slid her rebreather up over her face. She closed her eyes as Riqan started counting down. Tried to focus on breathing. Tried to calm her mind. Tried to—

There was a sharp snap, a rush of suction.

Her suit sealed itself over her face.

<Ten seconds to equalize,> Riqan announced, through the wireless. <Nine, eight…>

The building shook, violent, knocking everyone in their holds, throwing the suspended furniture whirling around the room.

<What's that?> tDaer demanded.

<Mining solvent!> Riqan yelled back, and let go, let the suction drag him up the shaft, everyone else following suit. Tharsis was last to let go, fighting back planet-born panic, barely managing to keep herself from crashing into the long vertical rise, rattling up like a bullet in a misfit barrel.

The shaking subsided as she hit the top of the shaft. Looking around, Tharsis saw a long tunnel reaching off in both directions, the hollow space lit by nothing except the faint glow of their ENEX and the occasional burst of magnetic interference. It was just over a meter in diameter and uneven, barely enough room to maneuver across its series of handholds, chipped into the raw matrix at long intervals.

She grabbed onto one away from the vertical next to Ang, steadying herself. The goggles on his exogear were mirrored, her own reflection bouncing back.

<You okay?>

<Yeah.> She had to remind herself to breathe, the oxygen from integrated compression tanks scraping cold and dry over her throat. <Everybody up here?>

A small chorus of yeses echoed back over the quiet static of her earpiece, and Riqan grunted up over the top of it. Tall body folded in the tight space and encased in that dark exo-armor, he looked predatory.

<Which way is it, Ang?>

The slimmer Jovian flicked his fingers in sequence, a map of the moon shining out of the palm projection web held between his spread digits. Stats rippled across the static surface. <We go left. Magnetics are within safe margins right now.>

They moved out along the long, uneven ladder of the handholds, the voiders mercifully slow in the tight space. Tharsis was glad for that. In a full-out sprint, they'd leave her far behind. She was meters behind them, catching up only at junctions where Angakkuq had to stop to determine which turn to take. Direction and distance lost all meaning. They passed other shafts, most dark, the air too thin to transmit sound, but through a few, Tharsis could see indistinct movement.

She could hear the Arcna's voice every time she touched the rock.

After what seemed like an hour, but was probably only a few minutes, the light ahead went from faint threads of green-yellow to dull blue, growing stronger by the handhold.

Riqan had stopped, him and Ang on the edge of that glow, cursing quietly in Jovian, her goggles casting their silhouettes harsh in her vision. They were both holding on in strange alignments, and she felt her stomach lurch, her planet-born brain demanding direction, horizon. The lieutenant only barely fought it down.

Then she saw it. The space in front of them.

A vast field of transparent olivine glass, pocked and bunched, suspended from rough rock by threads of steel and ice, cables protruding through, bigger around than her body. Shadows danced within it like sunlight in deep water.

<What is this?> she asked.

<Parkland,> Angakkuq said, frantically scrolling through map layers. <The Nepo area.>

Frowning around the hard rubber rebreather, Tharsis adjusted the polarization in her goggles to let her see through the glass, into the spiderweb of nodular structures.

The pools she remembered from the monorail were boiling, pulling apart, scattering in directionless rain. People were scattering everywhere, and it was only possible to tell where the mobs began and ended based on the blood. Manufacturing oil blasted out of thick hoses, vast arcs of incandescent flame, splattering the screaming crowds, pounding on exterior walls of houses.

People were being dragged out.

<Fuck,> Tharsis breathed.

Riqan ran a hand up the glass. <There's a fucking kilometer of this, and they might be able to see us through it.>

<There's no other way?> tDaer asked.

<Everything routes through here,> Angakkuq confirmed. <The port's two kilometers on the other side.>

Tharsis checked the timer on her suit. <What are the magnetics like above us?>

<Half strength.>

<You running out of ENEX time, Tharsis?> tDaer asked.

<We're all running out of time,> Riqan grumbled. <The port'll be locked down, but I don't know how long they'll be able to hold it. If that gets overrun, they'll—>

<Fumigate?>

<We need to cross this now.> He loosened his machete in its sheath and started pushing up, the rest of the voiders following.

Tharsis took a few deep breaths, steadying herself, fighting her mind back down as it started insisting that the challenge in front of her was a cliff face, that she couldn't possibly scale such a thing. "Your mind needs reference points. It'll search them out," she remembered her instructors on the Centrifuge telling them, "so work with it. Find something you can accept."

She found herself thinking, of all things, of home. About the hot springs that fed the pools in the cracked and gaping knees of the Three Sisters, those ever warm, quartz-clear waters. She and her brother would ride out there before the first snows, strip down, go swimming. Diving there, it was almost like floating in mig...

<You okay?> tDaer asked, dropping back down.

<I think so,> and to the Arran's relief, when she opened her eyes, the world had shifted. A long, narrow horizontal plane stretched out in front of her. <Yeah. I'm good.>

But tDaer wasn't paying attention. Hen was watching that scene beyond the aurora chamber, mobs tearing the fishbowl world apart.

Something about that chilled Tharsis to the bone.

<tDaer,> she said, switching over to a private channel.

The Iapetan's lean body rocked. <What?>

<There are kids down there, you know.>

< Nepo kids. Who'll just grow up to be abusive bastards like the rest of them.>

A plume of stray cutting oil splashed across the glass in front of them, sizzling.

tDaer didn't flinch.

<Come on,> Tharsis said quietly, and reached out, tugged at her once friend's shoulder. <We need to get moving.>

Shaking henself, tDaer turned a suit-blank face to the lieutenant. <Right,> was all hen said, and started pushing off through that vast aurora chamber, faster in the wider space, hot after Riqan.

Time to sprint.

Tharsis kicked off the closest support pillar as hard as she could.

In that space, wider and deeper than the squeeze of the vents, the reverberations from the noise beyond were more pronounced, the thin atmo more unstable. Throwing herself forward as fast as she could, her muscles screamed for more air. The oxygen flow in her suit was designed for light activity; there was no way to open the valve wider without risking hypoxia later on. Tharsis caught one of the anchoring chains, breathing as deep as she dared, only to feel it shake beneath her hand. Glancing down, her goggles highlighted cracks spreading out from the glass yoke, and the half-melted teardrop structure below snapped loose from its other moorings, jerking dangerously.

<They're pulling the ceiling down!> she yelled, switching back to vox.

A hundred meters ahead of her, Riqan paused against one of the support pillars, looking up. <We're not going to make it.>

<Options?> she panted back and watched another system of cracks spreading through the glass. Blind panic surged over the adrenaline already pumping through her veins. Tharsis realized her arm, holding onto that cable, was shaking uncontrollably. The timer on her suit read forty-three minutes since seal-up: the longest, the hardest, she'd ever gone in mig.

<Ang, find us a way up. We'll risk—>

But a shattering sound filled the thin air, vibrating through her bones, half the ceiling shearing loose like ice from a melting glacier. A roar rose, like a flash flood; the region below them was depressurizing, equalizing with the vacuum of the aurora ducts.

The lieutenant managed to dodge a chunk of rock coming for her head. But it put her right in the path of another. She retched at the sensation of disassociation, but the xenocyte wrapper did its job; the shrapnel ghosted right through her chest. It was hideously unpleasant, and the momentum from the moment of impact still knocked her back to the hard rock wall. Stunned, she held on there for a moment, keeping herself from floating away.

Breathing.

In. Out. In. Out. In…

And she saw it. One of those burn-mobs, watching her from less than ten meters away.

She bolted.

Tharsis had never been especially good at free fall navigation, but at that moment, instinct kicked in. Fighting through the shower of broken glass and snapped cable, she barely avoided the reaching, grasping hands. Below, the Arcna was screaming through the moon, and the mobs were screaming with her, the penumbra clouding with gray killing-fever.

When the lieutenant finally had to yank that machete out of its sheath, the world blurred. Low-grade Jovian exogear, wrapper mostly dormant in the venting atmo, was no match for gravity-born muscle and the heavy edge of the machete.

She wrenched herself away from a crowing, jeering Jovian, only to get grabbed from behind. Swinging the machete around in a wild arc, she sank it so deeply through the man's arm that the blade got stuck in the rock behind. Blood sprayed as the severed limb floated off. Her stomach roiled at the sight, but she didn't dare stop. Slicing through bone and atmo bottles and goggles, she won herself a small space. But it was like digging a hole in beach sand.

More hands reached for her, more faces hidden behind the insectoid ENEX masks of the local laborers leering at her, more blood filled the space around her. She hacked and shoved and kicked her way through, oxygen burning her lungs with every breath, goggles smeared with bodily fluids she couldn't wipe off.

Hands grabbed her and yanked. Hard. Throwing her back into a half-hidden alcove.

She brought the machete up again.

<Calm the fuck down!> tDaer yelled at her and jabbed up. <We're going out!>

What? <What?!>

But there was another explosion, another drag, and Tharsis found herself careening backwards through a long, dark space. She caught a flash of the surface, mottled and pitted gray-blue icerock, scarred from generations of meteorite impacts, a line of white stars beyond. Barely a glimpse, before the line on her exogear snapped tight, jerking her back whiplash-hard. A Jovian body shot past.

A prickling sensation skated across her skin. Under the suit. Candle-licks: hot, not entirely there. The lieutenant had never felt it before, but knew what it meant.

Glowing above her lay Jupiter's vicious southern hemisphere. Stretching beyond the limits of her peripheral vision, storms of red and blue and gold raged.

<You dead?>

Tharsis shook herself and started pulling herself down the line, back towards the moon's surface. <How far out are we?>

Ang held up the holographic palm pad, widening the field to maximum spread. <Two and a half kilometers, thereabouts.>

<We need to get moving,> Riqan said, and held up his arm as proof. There was blood boiling off hard armor and his gore-splattered machete, sending up red smoke, sparking bright with interference.

The implication was clear.

Clipped together, thrusters at full bore, the trip across the scarred surface of the tiny moon was terrible. The monstrous bulk of the planet loomed behind them, murmuring, caressing.

Tharsis said nothing and focused on keeping up.

They cut propulsion a few dozen yards from the rim of the port. Blowouts had obviously occurred there as well, translucent jets of atmo trailing out into the void, curving around the moon, sweeping away in the rarified winds off Jupiter.

<By the mother,> Angakkuq breathed into the radio.

Tharsis tried to ignore it. <Where's the divedrive?>

<I'm not sure.>

She checked her time. <I've got five minutes. Anyone else close to their limit?>

<I am,> one of the Tethians—silent until now—volunteered.

<Me too,> tDaer admitted grudgingly.

<There's eight square kilometers of port-space here,> Riqan said, dark against the angry orange whorls of the planet. <How are we supposed to find it?>

<I can try raising it on the radio,> tDaer said, and squatted down, unslinging hen's small, flat bag.

Tharsis watched hen fumble for a moment, the panic from earlier starting to solidify behind her solar plexus, the drain of adrenaline beginning from her tired limbs. A prickling on her skin was starting to scorch, light bursting through the fluid of her corneas.

She thought of the apparition she'd seen, back on 4Vesta. Remembered something Gran had showed her, long ago, on a snowy winter day after church. *You can tell them to leave or ask them to come. It's a matter of will.*

Tharsis tried.

Flet! she screamed in her own head, willing the words to carry down into the penumbra, through the song of the planet's wind, reaching the craft, *Flet, we need you. Send the divedrive up here. Bring it to us!*

Nothing.

She tried again, putting every gram of force she could into it.

Jesus fuck, Flet, get your worthless ass up here right the fuck now! Or the Naven died for nothing!

Again, nothing. The timer on her wrist read-out was headed into the red.

Tharsis was almost too tired to care.

But just then, before she could gather herself for another try, the divedrive rose out of one of the pits, ion props bursting into life, the wide jigsaw of stabilization panels forcing out into their subtle orbits, static tethers trailing behind in threads of umbran-gold.

Across the moon, towards them.

The lieutenant breathed out, laughing from pure relief, laughing harder as tDaer turned hen's mirrored eyes on her.

An air lock opened in the outer hull as it anchored itself above them, and the exhausted party from Nighttrippers threw themselves into the hollow.

The last sight Tharsis had of Amalthea, before the carbon white closed them away, cocooning them into a small, gloriously warm air lock, was a jet of glass and air rocketing out from the interior.

As she hit the heady density of the atmo, Tharsis wrenched the ENEX hood off her face, breathing deep lungfuls of warm air. Her body was screaming for oxygen, her hair clinging damp around her neck, adrenaline draining cold from her blood, that image of Jupiter imprinted on her corneas. Her arm ached—fuck, how it ached.

But she was alive.

They were all alive.

And she saw herself again, swinging down on a voider arm, bones tearing apart.

A chicken on the butcher block.

Tharsis barely managed to roll over on her hands and knees before her stomach rebelled completely.

The craft opened a small vent in response to her vomiting, sucking the vile gunk out of the air. She coughed out the last few drops, throat burning and belly on fire. "Thanks," she forced herself to whisper, patting the silky-smooth hull. She forced herself up to sitting, fighting unsteady fingers to strip her exogear off.

tDaer, ENEX rolled down and tied around hen's waist, steered them away from the moon, out into the outer orbits, dive distance from the massive gravity of the gas giant. The xenocyte layer in hen's suit was dying in the atmo, breaking off in fat, oily globules.

Ang tapped the wake side of the hull transparent.

Behind them, Amalthea was on fire.

How many children would be dragged from their homes today on other moons, in other habitats, for no greater crime than the gametes that had formed them? How many people would join the mobs, caught up in anger that wasn't even theirs? And when would that anger turn outward? When would the Onias get back in front of it, deploy his police forces with knock-out gas and hollow-point bullets?

How many people would die that day, that sevenday, that month? There and every other moon around Jupiter? In every corner of the Heliosphere?

All because that bitch decided to turn the radio back on.

Tharsis turned her eyes from the planet, looking around her. Everyone was all in bad shape. Angakkuq was a frightening shade of gray, blood bruises mottling his paper-thin skin. Riqan was working a fresh med-pack onto a wound in his arm, the first already too laden with blood to do any good. Everyone's gear was smoking.

"Your suit's fucked," tDaer finally observed, hand swallowed by the craft.

Tharsis looked down; it was. The magnetics had torn loose the metallic components, small rips in the inner layers, the outer pocked black from radiation burns. How many minutes, seconds, had she had before exposure?

"Hell," she breathed, shaky, and stripped the thing the rest of the way off, sweat-soaked civvies clammy against her skin. "I didn't even notice."

"Yeah. I figured. Actually, it looks like everybody's gear is fucked." The entire back of hen's scalp was scabbing over, looking painful as hell. "Aside from that, everyone okay?"

"Except for the part where a fucking mob is tearing my moon apart? Slaughtering my brothers? Lovely. Perfectly lovely," Riqan replied testily. That pack around his arm had migrated up to his elbow during the dive. "Get us to Titan, tDaer. Now."

"We need new gear. My vote's Iapetus."

"tDaer, I'm not checking myself in to some student clinic on a second-rate moon."

"And Titan produces second rate suits. My inwell, my call," tDaer snapped, and dove the craft.

There was no hint of any kind of movement that day. Nothing unexpected. Just the hull winking opaque as the ion engines cut out, into that black where nobody, nothing else existed, whirring back on, pulling them up into a vast sweep of ice and rock.

Tharsis just closed her eyes and prayed there weren't going to be any more surprises.

CHAPTER
TWENTY-NINE

"IF YOU DON'T MIND me asking, sir, why'd you bring me?"

Major Lanin yawned over the whine of the rockjump's engines spooling down. He hated it when the kids got mouthy. "You got somewhere else to be, Lieutenant?"

Morray, all smooth professionalism and fresh-polished boots, eyed the embassy gates with the well-practiced wariness of a first tour spent in the Lagrange Shoals. "With everything going on—"

"Both I and Cambel are authorizing you to have a night off. Shut up and enjoy it."

Congress had finally caught wind that the Landlord had resurfaced. Activated, as one of the angry cables passing around the dive nets had put it. An explanation was owed, and they were here to offer that explanation: civilian dive convergence with District of Lunae, straight to the floor of Congress, to the comm room of every State Department facility outwell of Phobos. The shortwave news stations had been blowing up with speculation all day.

Caleb was nervous as hell about it, not that he would admit it, and Lanin had offered to come along for moral support.

He'd dragged Morray along for an entirely different reason. Lanin remembered his own education on the *Turiel*; the veneer of civilization was only ever just that. Fragile. Easily broken. Impossible to restore once it was gone, except through the harshest of force.

It was easy to forget that the illusion of its permanence was what kept civilians sane and kept the military fighting.

"Look, Hans,"—that was the kid's name, right?—"we're here because the civvies deserve to know what the hell is going on. So, get some food, enjoy your shore leave, and stop whining about how we don't have anybody to shoot in the face yet."

The lieutenant smiled, bitter. "What am I supposed to tell these people?"

"Let 'em be proud of their boys in uniform," Caleb suggested, "and say everything else is classified."

"Just get the dive core spun up," Lanin said, "and leave the civvies to us."

Outside the small craft, the Rallarhu's voice echoed from the speaker stacks of Helion Plaza, from that monstrous statue, reading children's stories. Her way of keeping the Arcna off her airwaves. It wouldn't hold the Kuiper's Landlord off for long. Nothing ever did. The Propagations slid around everything but physical line cuts with an ease bordering on sentience. Caleb didn't like what that implied— some kind of organic wetware in play, out there in Noqumiut—but of course, there was no way to prove anything.

"Bitch," Morray muttered as they got out. He turned to Caleb. "Why don't your people stop this?"

"My people?" Their Landlord snorted, and Tyr, by his side, growled. "We're not some kind of cabal, Morray. We don't scheme together. We don't even like each other." He paused. "The closest we come to anything like that is the clause in the Accords that obligates us to kill each other when we step out of line."

"Like when the Rallarhu took over this region?" Morray asked, mock-innocent.

Caleb fixed him with a hard, hard glare. "You have no idea what you're talking about."

"And neither do you, Caleb," Major Lanin interrupted. "We don't know what happened on Noqumiut, but the woman you remember is not the thing that animates the sky here."

"I know what she's become."

"What about the Arcna? There any credence to the stories?" Morray asked. "About what she is?"

The veteran sergeant scoffed and waved them in towards the gate. "You mean those old blacksuiters' tales about her being some kind of malevolent umbran?"

"Spread throughout the entire Lighthouse network? Yes sir, that's exactly what I'm asking about," Morray said, and the lieutenant lingered as the gates chimed open, staring at the statue. "We've all been on deep runs before. We know how inhospitable the Kuiper is. Do you really think there's some kind of living civilization out there? Noqumiut? Really?"

"There's more a chance of that than what you're suggesting," Caleb replied.

"All I'm saying is couldn't we just destroy her by destroying the network?"

"Stow that scat right now," the Landlord said, flat, and there was something in his voice that was downright ancient. "Maintaining that network is a lynchpin of the Accords, and even if it wasn't..."

"What, the old humans are going to come back from the Oort and save us?"

Caleb's eyes hardened, and Lanin got in front of it, trying to wave the lieutenant off it. Down that road, the major knew, lay badness.

"Shut your mouth, El-Tee."

"The Arcna has free license to kill us, and you and General Rallison just fucking le—"

"Morray, you are drilling a hole in your hull. Stop before you hit vacuum," Lanin suggested, and prodded him into the embassy.

Neither of them missed the way their Landlord lingered, eyes on the statue of his former commander. His fingers tangling in the thick ruff of Tyr's neck.

Lanin couldn't fault him for it. Had to be hard.

The embassy was full that afternoon, bustling with expats: children playing in the stairwells and halls, adults clustered in side rooms, talking and drinking and swapping theories about what might be going on.

The largest group, Lanin discovered as Morray headed for the basement's dive core, was in the kitchen, making a late communal lunch. One of the wives spotted him the second he stuck his head in the door. The round of happy *hellos* and *didn't know you were back in towns* were more appropriate for a barn raising than the last safe haven in a crumbling heliopolitical situation, but it still cheered the major to hear it.

"So, Sergeant," one of the women asked Caleb, "you and the alpha are off the divedrive?"

The Wardog's proprietor, Chris, was manning the stove. He raised an eyebrow at the sight of Olin in blacks, but Lanin shook his head. Wasn't their place to say a damn thing.

The sergeant hesitated. "The dog…what are you talking about?"

"Is it true what everyone's saying? That the Rossen was aboard? That we're the ones who'll see him in person today?"

Caleb shot Lanin a helpless look. "I…"

"It's all over the 'roid," another woman piped up. "His little raid on that hostel."

"That wasn't in the news."

"Rumors travel fast."

"Would you lot leave the sergeant alone?" Chris said, ladle in hand, and nodded at Lieutenant Morray, slipping in through the door. "And as for you, kid, when was the last time you had anything that wasn't flash-frozen rations?"

Taken by surprise, the young man actually smiled. "Long time."

Chris laughed and tossed him a pressure can of beer.

The conversation turned away from the subject of the Landlord, back to other things, as the soldiers dug into the lamb stew the barkeep dished out in heaping portions.

New Stockholm had a small but healthy expat community, mostly established businessmen who'd been stationed there to protect their companies' interests in the convoluted mess of Accords-mandated trade. While it wasn't strictly recommended, wives and even children often joined them. The segmented nature of the island archipelago made it possible to maintain Arran-normal gravity in a home compound, and the risk of radiation there was far lower than most places. The embassy offered both safe haven and escape, in the event of some catastrophe.

In case of a Propagation.

Right now, the facility seemed to be functioning as intended. Local families had been drifting in piecemeal over the past sevenday or so, bringing what they could carry. "Just in case," somebody said when Lanin asked, and the ensuing laughter was nervous.

He made a mental note to issue official evacuation orders soon.

Everyone had questions about business and mobilizations and whether or not their older sons back home were in danger of getting remobilized. Lanin kept his conversation short and indistinct, between bites, knowing he wasn't giving them the reassurances they needed. Mars walked a knife's edge: ecology fragile, magnetosphere generators vulnerable to conventional attacks. Propagations weighed on everyone.

"Major, any idea as to when the Landlord's going to get off his ass and get to work on this Propagation thing?" the man who'd spoken first asked.

"The Jovian inwell's always on the verge of anarchy," Lanin replied with an ease he didn't feel. "Fucking unstable people, Jovians."

"Couldn't agree more," Morray said, cutting through the rising mess of voices, "but the situation's far more complicated that you might think."

"So, where the hell is the Rossen?" the civilian asked.

Lanin sighed. "Probably off somewhere trying to do his job, same as any other soldier."

A woman at the small stainless-steel table, a young child asleep in her arms, shook her head. "I don't buy that for a second. He can't die. What kind of risks is he taking? How is he in any way like my sons who are out there?"

"Ma'am, I would suggest—"

"What, you boys have this place wired for sound?" she sneered. "Is he gonna send the Wytt after me for speaking my mind?"

"I think we're lucky we even have our minds to speak, to even have this kind of conversation—"

"Lucky?" the woman demanded, near hysterical. "Fuck lucky! Who is he to decide who lives and who dies? To make our children die for him?"

"You'll have to forgive her, sir," another said quietly, reaching over to pull her into a hug. "Her oldest boy is at Trilan."

"And our fucking coward of a Landlord can just go gallivanting off, and what's it to him? He doesn't even have to live with the guilt of it!"

"Guilt?" Caleb said, angry, snapping, and shoved off the wall. "What the fuck does anyone raised in this last seventy years of peacetime know about guilt? Or death, for that matter?"

Lanin knew his sergeant; he was spooling up for a rant. He sighed into his drink. "Caleb—"

"Fuck that," the Landlord snapped, and drained the rest of his cider. "You want to talk about guilt? I killed my own father with a shovel to keep him from taking a meat cleaver to my little sister. That's guilt. I've torched gene-foundries full of half-alive things. You ever seen an umbran burn as its body dies? You carry that. You dream about that."

The whole room was silent now.

"I have no idea why I shot myself to forget fucking Noqumiut. But I can tell you, it wasn't over guilt. I've got plenty of that already. But ma'am," and his attention turned back to the now stunned woman who'd spoken before, "your boys are not out there to die for the Jovians, or me, or anything else. They're not there to die. They're there to fight. Defy this bullshit. Because that's who we are, that's what Mars is, and we will be here long after the Kuiper stops howling. Seven times that insane bitch has failed to kill us. We're going to make it eight."

The Landlord stopped abruptly then, as if realizing what he'd just said, just done, and didn't meet anybody's eyes.

"Thanks for lunch," he told Chris, and slapped his patch back on. "Morray, let's go get that core comm spooled up. I've got to go talk to fucking Congress."

In the stunned silence that followed, Lanin felt all eyes turning on him.

He just got up and fetched himself another beer from the industrial-sized fridge in the corner.

Somebody finally dared asked. "Was that—"

"You know," Lanin said, cutting it off, "if the First Planetary Congress had voted for General Rallison instead of him, we'd probably all be dead by now." And he snapped the bottle top off with his Academy class ring.

CHAPTER
THIRTY

"SO THEY JUST…"

"Give you a lab? Yeah, after undergrad. I love this place. Beats the dorms any day."

The University of Titan had been founded in the last century of the Euphemism, a triumph for the scientific community. But early objectivity gave way to partisan research and hidden agendas and things turned bloody—as so many things did. The university had nearly been destroyed by a cadre of over-motivated graduate students in a series of bloody riots.

But that had been centuries ago. In contemporary times, the Cronuan inwell was officially neutral in international affairs, concerned only with enforcing the Scient's restrictions. Major fields of study were broken down by moon, each containing dozen of campuses, specializing in all manner of subjects. Iapetus, tDaer had said, with the largest seeded tholin fields of any of the moons, focused primarily on biological engineering.

"What does that have to do with your signals research?" Tharsis had asked.

"The signal's biomechanical. The Arcna's made some really impressive progress, despite the restrictions in the Accords. It's something of a curiosity around here. You'd be amazed how supportive my professors were."

The campus they'd set down at was a segmented mess of broad-diameter connecting pushways and nodular semi-mobile habitats. The intention, tDaer had said, was that the entire campus could be reformatted and reconnected at will, the configuration changed constantly. Only a few components—thermal radiators, atmo scrubbers, the student union with its libraries, cafeterias, and clinics—were permanent.

The divedrive was anchored safely at one of those permanent builds, a rudimentary port half a kilometer away now. Since the facility wasn't currently connected, they'd taken a shuttle up to the union entrance. The Jovians had bunked down there, the Tethians catching a ride at the port back to their own moon. tDaer had been relieved. "Don't want the Nepo stinking up my nice lab," hen had explained.

Tharsis wasn't exactly sure what the grad student had meant by that.

The personal habitat—lab, or craft, or whatever—they were in now was far from nice. It was one large, open room, terminating in a padded nest beneath huge, curved windows. The space was crisscrossed with pressure support columns, woven tendrils of the same carbon silk that comprised the divedrive's inner hull.

But whereas that surface was always gleaming white, this was dark with age and use. Equipment was arranged haphazardly, tied up and locked in. A rough, inbuilt bathroom facility lay at the far end, and a small food-preparation space looked like it hadn't been used in years. It seemed a testament to the Cronuan obsession with byzantine form and obscure, purpose-built engineering. Tharsis had no idea what any of it did.

"It's a bit of a mess right now," tDaer explained, kicking off hen's shoes and shoving them into what had to be a waste receptacle. The rest of hen's thin clothing, wrapper-chewed and radiation-singed, followed rapidly. "I kind of left in a hurry last HST cycle. Didn't have time to get everything tidied back up."

Tharsis crouched into a more stable position by the pillar to strip down. Disposal was in order for most of her clothing. Her boots were mostly okay, at least, and she slipped her combat knife into one of those when tDaer turned hen's back. "So how's this work? Your space, make what you want?"

"You should have seen the scat I cleaned out of here from the last Daer. Hen had some good theories, but they were woefully underdeveloped. Had to start all over again. I was a little scared, let me tell you, knowing I shared those genes." And hen smiled, proud. "Glad to say I'm not as dumb as the last one."

"Last? Oh, you're, umm, clones, right?"

"Yeah, from the Daer sequence. Sort of like a family, I guess, but far less annoying than those massive gene groups your people have to deal with."

"Who was the original?"

tDaer made a face and kicked over to one of the cushions, closer to the window. "Never really wanted to know. I'm a better version. The Scient makes improvements, every generation."

To Tharsis, settling in, it seemed a lonely thing, barbaric, with no family, no connection to those who came before. Mentioning such a thing to tDaer, though, would have drawn cries of blasphemy. "This the giant experiment you talk about sometimes?"

"Basically," tDaer said, and tossed Tharsis a white box scrounged from some cubbyhole.

First aid kit. "I thought the medical facilities were good here."

"They are, but it takes forever to get in. I'm too tired to put up with that scat tonight."

"Whatever you say," she muttered back and popped the lid, taking quick stock of what was inside. Less extensive than the selection of bandages, splints, gels, and med-packs that the Iapetan had been keeping on the divedrive. It'd do; they'd been very lucky out there. Another ten minutes might have killed them all.

"Check the dates. I grab stuff when I can."

Three of the packs were dead, the remainder viable. "We're good," Tharsis reported, and sucked air as she got a full view of tDaer's body. "Michael above."

"What?" tDaer asked, and then looked down at henself. Hen's torso was littered with ragged, blistering burns. The Iapetan touched the edge of one of them with a fingertip. Boiled skin pulled back, pus oozing out. Tharsis managed to catch it with a piece of gauze as it rolled out into the air in thick, sticky globs.

You need to send the Rossen a report, the lieutenant reminded herself.

"You sure you don't want to go to the clinic?" she asked.

"It's not that serious. A few days of regen bandages and a couple rounds of oral antibiotics, and I'll be fine," hen replied, but hen's voice held none of its usual confidence.

"We're getting you a better suit before we head out to the Kuiper," Tharsis told hen, and eased a pack directly onto the worst patch. "We're both getting better suits. Whatever model you had, we're upgrading it."

"The one I was wearing should have been sufficient."

"Obviously it wasn't."

tDaer was quiet for a moment. "That's all we get."

Tharsis pressed a pack to a long, jagged rip across the Iapetan's spine. "What do you mean?"

"Base models are free of charge. Anything… scat, careful, you buy upgrades yourself."

"Can't be that expensive."

"It is when you're broke." Tharsis gave hen a questioning look, and tDaer huffed. "The Scient provides what we need. Beyond that, you have to apply for it." The next pack, destined for the constellation of blisters spread out across tDaer's head, went on. "We, ahh, I'd need a grant for an upgrade. The Scient's not going to give me the funds for a Kuiper trip. I never would have gotten Riqan involved if hen would have."

"Weren't you getting paid at Nighttrippers?"

"Sort of. Not enough, though, especially with exchange rates. Stingy fucking Nepos."

"Your back's a mess. Everything that wasn't covered by your pack is dead."

"Necrotizing?" tDaer made a little noise in the back of hen's throat. "The med packs'll take care of it. Eat it right off. I'll be fine."

"Like maggots."

"Maggots?"

"You do what you have to do in the Bulge. Nearest hospital's half a day's ride from my home parish. Why do you think my brother got his leg amputated on the kitchen table?" she replied, careful to not explain what maggots were.

"I'll see if Riqan will put up the cash," tDaer said, and let loose another quavering breath. As Tharsis pushed around to start on the burns on her chest, hen's huge eyes turned to the world beyond the window. "Back when I first got this place, I'd burn an entire month's worth of hydrocarb to get to an outer orbit. Scrounged myself up enough stuff for a good little nest, and I'd just lay there for hours, watching. The rings, the other moons, the way Saturn looks at sunset…"

That was something Tharsis could understand. She'd loved that when she was a kid, the sun setting through the thick dust of the western sky, disappearing behind the massive bulk of the Three Sisters, scattering color across the encroaching night.

"What do you think it's going to be like? Noqumiut?" tDaer asked.

Tharsis smoothed the last pack on, right between the rise of the Iapetan's slight breasts. *A horror show*, she thought, but couldn't say that. "Not this."

"It'll be better. I know it. It has to be."

"I don't know. This is pretty amazing," the lieutenant began, and stopped as a long-fingered hand brushed against the rise of her bare hip. She could feel her body trying to shy away from it, but when she looked back down at the Iapetan, hurting like hen was, the Arran didn't have it in her to say no. She hated this situation, hated what everything had turned out to be. None of this was what she wanted. She missed the friend she'd thought she'd had.

"You'll rip those," she warned, pressing her hand down on that last pack.

Fingers wound into her hair, tugging her down. "They're designed to cling. It'll be fine."

"tDaer…"

"Shut up, Tharsis."

SOMETIME LATER, after a combination of med-pack sedatives and oxytocin had pushed tDaer far, far out into the ocean of sleep, Tharsis dug herself out of their warm little cocoon.

She had work to do.

With the Arcna's words already chewing through entire moons, Tharsis wasn't sure if Mars's Landlord even still needed the algorithms. Anyone could hear the Kuiper's Landlord now, after all. But that wasn't the only use for that data. tDaer had based it off the very first signals hen had intercepted. It might bear insights on the nature of the signal, how it slid around security nets. Maybe even help reveal where it came from.

The Iapetan's lab was daunting, a disaster of disorganization. Memory boards, wave analyzers, neural-chem translators, projectors, cabling and wiring and raw silicone circuitry. There were a few unique systems, but even those had been cobbled together from parts that Tharsis at least recognized. And after about half an hour, it started making sense: tDaer had built henself some kind of jury-rigged, synthetic wetware processor.

The realization didn't help anything. Wetware was hardly Tharsis's area of expertise, and even at that, she was no technician. Two hours in and Tharsis was no closer to identifying the system components she needed. Frustrated, the lieutenant flopped down in the center of tDaer's junked-up floor, staring out at the eldritch gold of the gas giant beyond the bay of windows. There had to be something, some connection, some energy gradient, that would tell her where in the hell the algorithms were stored.

Maybe I could just ask hen, she thought, and dismissed it. There was no way tDaer was going to just hand over research like that.

But as she was ready to give up for the night, the hairs on the back of Tharsis's neck prickled. Her eyes caught movement. In the shadows, under tables and behind pillars.

A pack of small, wary things.

Umbran.

She told herself to ignore it and go back to bed.

She slid off the hammock to investigate.

The most defined was still incomplete, eyes too large for its head. Bits were missing from its form; fingers, skin, teeth, the patterns of muscle and veins and nerves darkly pulsing and put together wrong. A child's approximation of the human form, maybe, broken apart and put together wrong.

In its mess of discarded, denuded drives, the lieutenant saw a small sphere of frosted glass, a fist-sized bulge of what looked like brain matter inside. The second umbran was curled up around it, holding it like some kind of beloved toy. She realized, with a start, this one was familiar. It was the same one she'd been seeing elsewhere. But before she could ask anything, formulate the questions in her mind—*did you ride the signal here, can you tell me how to break the encryption*—a section of glass bubbled up and pinched off, floating away.

Tharsis caught it carefully, cerebrospinal fluid shifting around the small pinch of synthetic gray matter within. Gray matter.

DNA-encoded data.

"Thank you," she whispered. "Thank you so much."

The umbran blinked, and almost smiled.

Tharsis pushed out to where she'd stashed her bag in the entrance area, tugged out a clean set of clothes. Her boots she left, pulling on a spare set of socks instead, tying down the ends of her pants.

With any luck, tDaer wouldn't wake up while she was gone.

Tharsis found her way back to the port easily enough. The umbran shadowed her, popping into her line of sight here and there, peeking around corners, watching her up ahead from empty doorways. The lieutenant tried to ignore it.

Amalthea rattled through her mind: the screams echoing through the shafts, bodies melting under the blast of mining chemicals, the way Jupiter had hung in the sky, vast and hungry and ancient, so ancient.

The divedrive was dark when she approached, its non-glow muted in sleep. She pushed out to it, catching herself on the hull, working with her fingers through the spiderweb of cracks until a stabilization panel pulled out, opening a straight tunnel into the hold.

Tharsis settled cross-legged on the gentle white curve of the interior, near where she knew the main controls normally came up. Rubbed at her arm. She tapped herself up a small interface panel, complete with keyboard, and made short, terse work of the past forty-eight hours.

REACHED IAPETUS SAFELY. AVOIDED WORST OF RIOTS ON AMALTHEA. NO FURTHER INJURIES. FOUND REQUESTED DATA, WILL NEED QUANT SEQUENCING IN ORDER TO TRANSMIT. UMBRAN ENTITY CONFIRMED ORIGIN TO ME AS NOQUMIUT, NOTHING MORE KNOWN. I DON'T LIKE THE WAY IT'S LOOKING AT ME—I DON'T LIKE THE WAY ANYONE LOOKS AT ME HERE.

Reading back over it, the lieutenant erased the last sentence. It was something she might have shared once with Olin, but he was effectively dead. It was just the Rossen now, and she had no interest in sharing her concerns with him. Satisfied, she dropped her status update into its encrypted tunnel and shot it off.

"Thanks," she murmured to it, patting the panel back down into neutral.

But before she could leave, something else snicked open.

Over the past month or so, Tharsis had memorized the location of most of the craft's equipment panels and lockers. That one, she'd never seen before.

"What the hell?" she muttered to herself and kicked slowly over.

It was definitely the largest hold she'd seen so far, at least a meter and a half to a side and deep enough to comfortably stand up in. Almost all the way out to the outer hull, then, she calculated, and examined its contents. The space was dark, dominated by a series of long titanium tubes that just barely fit, too large for her to comfortably get both hands around. Pulling herself closer, she caught the sight of recessed markings, stamped into unpolished caps.

"Light," she ordered, tapping the hull next to her, and a small nob extruded from just beyond the edge, pulling up over, flooding it bright.

Her heart shot into her throat.

Embossed there was the international symbol for radioactive material.

pU

12.04.07.0728hS

9.531 kg

Tharsis took a quick account, not really believing what she'd found. Twenty-one cylinders, dates inside the last HST year, weight between 9.45 and 9.55 kilograms. Upwards of two hundred kilos of plutonium. In a craft they'd just dove out of a virtual war zone.

"Holy fuck," she breathed to herself.

It had to be what was loaded on in the Trojans. It had to be what tDaer had mentioned, what they were taking out to Noqumiut. What the Arcna had asked for.

Two hundred kilograms of weapons-grade fissile material.

"What is this?" she asked aloud, asked the Flet, pushing out like she had before. "Why is this here? What's going on? What are they doing out there?"

Tharsis waited there then, on the edge of that locker, hoping like hell for some kind of explanation. But none came, and, frustrated, she pulled the transmission panel back up.

TWO HUNDRED KILOS PU ABOARD. ORDERS?

Michael, she found herself thinking, as she hit <send>, *I could really use some help here.*

CHAPTER
THIRTY-ONE

THE UMBRAN WAS WAITING for her the next day.

With dozens of others, some whispers in the back of her vision, some loud and grimy-bright as corporeal toddlers. Unsettling sights, those things, and she'd tried not to look at them. But it wasn't until she came back up from the haze of general anesthesia that the damn things were gone.

The doctor was giving her instructions in the recovery room —"Keep the med pack on, yes, you can still get an ENEX fit,"—but Tharsis wasn't really listening.

She'd lost control of the navigation material.

It narrowed her list of options significantly.

tDaer had taken Tharsis to the clinic earlier that morning. *We need to deal with that*, hen had said, gesturing at the lieutenant's arm, splotchy with fresh bruises. The docs and the vat on Deimos had removed some of the Naven's rock from her arm. But there were still fragments buried in the tissues deeper down; she suspected the Rossen had left it there on purpose. As bait, maybe. Whatever the reason, the scat desperately needed out. Tharsis had barely been able to move the limb that morning.

Tharsis hadn't expected much from the clinic, based on the way tDaer had scoffed at the thought of going, and it had been even worse than she'd imagined. Worn and tired, full of people, with a line that didn't seem to move at all.

"Primary care," hen explained, palming a thick roll of bills off to a nurse. Two thousand in Jovian currency, almost seven hundred MSD. "Riqan's generosity bought you some private attention."

"Did you steal that off him?"

Hen'd shrugged. "We need that scat out of you."

"And you can't steal something for the exogear?"

"That is going to be more than the Nepo's pocket change."

The procedure had been quick and efficient, even if they had put her under general anesthesia to do it. She'd protested that when they mentioned it, telling them she'd be fine with local, but the doctor had just looked confused.

"Look," Tharsis had tried, uneasy about the whole thing, "I know what's in me, I want to make sure I keep positive control of it."

tDaer had just squeezed her good hand. "Don't worry," hen said.

Her worries were vindicated after she'd woken up. tDaer had brandished the little vial of shards and refused to give them back.

Tharsis's arm tingled under the thin med pack they'd applied, but it felt a hell of a lot better.

Riqan and tDaer had just started up another argument about resupplying the craft and the presence of a black market in the ration-happy Cronuan inwell, when the university news turned to Jupiter. They both fell silent, watching. Projected screens were showing time-lagged video feeds of the situation in the Jovians. Amalthea had been brought back under control. Other moons, like Metis, had turned into meat grinders.

Riqan, just done from his own all-night clinic session, looked as ruined as Tharsis had ever seen anyone, skin gray and tired under its gold ink, shoulders heavy. "Fucking savages," he grumbled. "See how they like it when the Onias pulls them all back to Themisto to explain themselves." It held none of his usual arrogance.

"Why doesn't he just drop everyone?" Angakkuq asked softly. "He's got the power to do that."

"Because he's not a fucking god," tDaer pointed out.

"He could summon the Wytt."

Tharsis didn't know if she wanted to slap Ang or give him a hug. He looked wrecked. "The Wytt's not their attack dog, Ang. He can't just go kill people."

"But he has the power to do that. He has the power to destroy those who would defy… he has to. The Onias has to. It's what he promised us."

tDaer snorted. "The Landlords lie, Ang."

"No, it's not that," Tharsis murmured without thinking, and flinched a little as everyone's eyes landed on her. "The Wytt can't show up unless the person's been infected."

Riqan cocked his head at her. "Is that so?" he purred.

Fuck, Tharsis thought, and desperately tried to remember if that was privileged information. Something one wouldn't know unless one had been under the needle for it. "That's the rumor, anyway."

It was a lame dodge, and the Nepo seemed to know it. His smile could have shattered glass.

"The Arcna's unlimited," Ang insisted. "She'll show us the way. She'll make these things stop."

"Come on," Tharsis told him. "Let's go."

THE GREENHOUSES where the exogear fabrication facility was located were, according to the plaques lining the broad hand-tracked passageway, one of the primary sources of breathable atmo for Iapetus's campuses and outlying facilities.

The world beyond the glass tunnel they were being pulled through was a wild, senseless jumble of boles of gigantic, twisted trees, of translucent soil streaked with vast root systems. Those islands of life bobbing, held together in a semblance of planar form by climbing, clinging vines. The canopy was incredibly dense, the leaves broad and greedy, obscuring false sunlight. Contorted fungi grew in the rot.

There were no insects, no creatures of any kind. The sound of water —dripping, pooling, flowing, floating—was the only noise to be heard. There had to be a hundred different types of plants in there, millions of distinct structures, and she breathed in deep the oxygen they were putting off, pumped into the tunnel; it was the best air she'd tasted since leaving the Bulge.

"Do forests look like this on Mars?" Angakkuq asked. "Can you see anything in it?"

"What, like, umbran?" she asked and felt a weight on the back of her leg. The one from the night before, holding on to the rolled-up and belted-down leg of the borrowed pants. Oozing out of the glass bubble, no doubt. Tharsis gritted her teeth and willed it back out of her sight. "Can't say that I can."

"Aren't they created by living things? Or is it the other way around?"

"Only under certain conditions," and she thought about the umbran, leaking out of tDaer's makeshift wetware setup. "Trees don't produce them at all, far as I know."

"Must be great," he mused, "being able to see all that stuff."

"It's not that special."

"It is, though. Access to Udlormiut, your penumbra, the ability to see across the worlds… it's a wonderful thing. All the things they have to teach us."

"Teach us? Teach us what? Truth only comes from one place, Ang, and it ain't them."

Angakkuq was quiet for a moment, and he nodded. "The Arcna. She'll show you."

"No offense, Ang, but that's what I don't understand. I thought she was supposed to be an old-world, hard-line scientist. This spiritualism stuff doesn't really match up."

"She lives with one foot in the penumbra," he said. "Look how the Propagations work. Intelligent things that move and whisper and guide us. Seems like her world's figured out how to dwell there in those higher stages of enlightenment. That's why finding her is so important."

Tharsis thought about how he'd been on the shuttle ride over, collapsed against the glass of the car, curled tight, and changed the subject. "You doing okay?"

"What do you mean?"

"Amalthea."

He didn't answer for a few moments. "The Arcna is going to give us something better. Noqumiut is rising now. She'll make the Tenancy what it was supposed to be. She'll make us what we were always supposed to be. All this suffering is going to wash away."

"You really believe that?"

"Don't you?"

She didn't answer

Sections of glass bubbled off from the main path, where they had to switch hand tacks. Tharsis caught name plaques on the side of some of them. Labs, mostly, specialty reference libraries, chummer and social lounge areas, another student union.

After what had to be three or four kilometers, the forest began to thin. Spreading out, younger, smaller, until they were finally in something of a clearing, where the passage widened and broadened. The smooth layers of glass and organic growth gave way to the natural folds of the moon's surface, the glass terminating sharply. The exogear fabrication facility was positioned inside a crevasse on that cliff face, its bulk spilling like a waterfall from the top of the cliff, far above the habitat ceiling, to a wide entrance of porous, oiled wood.

"They use organics as building material?" Ang asked.

"Looks like it. It's common enough on Mars."

"That's disgusting."

Passing through, the pair found themselves in a dimly lit but airy showroom. Fixed nubs of hand-tempered glass rose up in an irregular sequence from the floor, a winding little path of handrail between them obviously set for maximum viewing potential. Angakkuq smiled and pushed up to some level above. Tharsis just took hold of a handle and let herself be pulled to the first of these vats, hooking into a recessed foothold for a better look.

Inside the glass, a dark mass bobbed serenely, hazy, in a clear liquid. Outside, little plastic reference panels flashed. Curious, she flicked her fingers across that surface, and the projected image of an ENEX came up above the top of the vat. Writing was there as well, but in the near-undecipherable technical jargon Cronuans were infamous for. "Scat," she muttered to herself, and scanned the little panel for anything that looked like a translation button.

"This one," a voice offered, and a hand snaked around in front of her to gesture at a small rectangular key.

Tharsis smiled ruefully, looking at it. It was a rough approximation of the Tenancy flag, the off-kilter concentric rings obvious in their gold background. "Ah," she said, and hit it. The words immediately started rearranging themselves. "Thanks."

"We keep our system set to Crono as a matter of course, but we understand that there are many people who come here for these products. You'll forgive the confusion," the Iapetan who'd helped her said. Hen looked young, dressed in the same nondescript uniforms Tharsis had seen a number of people wearing in the chummer. "You're Martian, right?"

Instead of unintelligible symbols, the projection now had specs listed out. Average pressure, limb sizing, wrapper layer thickness, radiation output, recommended time of usage, even color choice. "I'm sort of on a tight timeframe here, so…"

"All of these are models we can manufacture and prepare for you same day. If you want a premium model, I can get it for you by the end of this sevenday. Very fast." And hen paused. "Umm, I hate to be rude, but before we go any further…"

Tharsis tugged down the collar of her borrowed blouse. "I'm not in the military."

"Good, that's good." And the Iapetan relaxed visibly. "So, what are your plans for your new exogear?"

"Does it matter?"

"Model is determined by function."

Tharsis flicked her fingertips over the plastic controls, sending the light of the projected stats scattering off. tDaer had gone over a basic story with her that morning, and she repeated it to that student. "I'm headed out to the university, you know, civil engineering scholarship. I've been told it's part of the program requirements to have a good ENEX for it."

Hen nodded along. "Ah, Titan? Must be quite the opportunity for you. Don't your people normally use women as breeding stock?"

Tharsis forced herself to laugh it off. "I escaped."

"Very good, very good," the student replied cheerfully, and gestured back to the vat. "So, based on your program, I'm guessing you need something durable for long-period wear. High-radiation environment, temperature extremes. I'd recommend something that's not too restrictive, maybe with a semirigid internal skeleton."

"Well, you're the expert," Tharsis replied, and thought of something else. "Do you think you could make it work with my boots? They're a bit banged up, but the grav-circuitry seems to still be working."

"Shouldn't be a problem. If you want to follow me, I can show you what we have that meet your criteria."

It was an easy choice. Only one model available could be formed to fit her female form, with integrated gravity circuitry installed as an extra.

ASDF ENEX models were mass-produced. Loose in the regions that were difficult to standardize, such as elbows, hands, feet, and head, compressive along the long bones and major muscle groups. And, of course, the xenocyte wrapper was stored in one central location in the backpack. It meant slower emergency deployment, but even violent decompressions granted a few remaining seconds of atmo. The Arran models also minimized direct contact with the skin. The wrapper's digestive processes were still a constant danger, though.

The Iapetan assured her the custom suit would fit like a glove, uniform contact being essential to maintain both joint flexibility and soft tissue integrity under pure compression.

It made Tharsis more than a little nervous.

"It will, of course, be still less bulky than perhaps you are used to in Martian-made suits. The computers do a good job of sizing."

"How does that process work, exactly? I mean, I get the general concept, but…"

"Ahh, yes. Martian suits are so rudimentary." The Iapetan pushed over to a panel on the fitting room wall, bringing up a central projection of a massive three-dimensional loom.

"This," hen said, indicating, "is a fabricator for our standard models. We take your measurements, feed them into our design server, and receive a customized pattern for your body. Where your joints bend, how much your breasts might naturally need to bulge, that sort of thing."

Hen tapped the panel again, and the image shifted to a cross section of what looked like a belly area, colors denoting substructures honeycombed into the suit. "These different areas process radiation, from cosmic rays to your own body's thermal waste, in very different ways. It's essential to keep everything in balance. No chance of merging that way," hen laughed.

Tharsis eyed the Iapetan. "What, like the Rallarhu?"

"Forgive me, I'm doing a research paper on hen right now. Fascinating really. Nobody really knows how hen subsumed into the habitat wrapper as hen did. In fact," and hen's voice dropped a bit, "it's a bit of an industry legend that the experiments on the Rallarhu enabled everything we can do with wrapper today."

"Right," Tharsis muttered, and looked down at herself, flexed her hands, watched the surface of the pattern flow without so much as a wrinkle, and she suddenly felt ill.

She had no intention of using this thing. Going out to the Kuiper. Being anywhere near Noqumiut.

"I'll take it."

CHAPTER
THIRTY-TWO

THE SUIT, she was told, would take about six hours to knit, another twelve to mature. Ready in time, they'd assured her, for a next-morning pickup.

Ang was nowhere to be found, and Tharsis didn't even want to think about what he might be doing. Better he was gone anyway. She needed to deal with the thing in her pocket.

"There a quant I can use anywhere around here?" she'd asked.

"Absolutely. Stuff's scattered all through this facility," the Iapetan student had replied, and drew a complex little diagram of the forest passages. "Shouldn't be more than a fifteen-minute glide out."

Following those directions now, pushing back through the forest on socked feet, Tharsis could see the umbran again. Skipping and bouncing along, sometimes ahead, sometimes behind, and finally stopping at a section of fogged habitat, peering inside intently.

Something small and white and amorphous, a blob of barely-light, clinging to the glass.

She hurried on.

At the end of the scribbled direction, an air lock opened up into the humid warmth of the forest beyond. Onto a small landing, and then a long, flat walkway, leading off into the forest. Tharsis stepped onto it tentatively, feeling the telltale hum of artificial gravity before her foot even touched down. It was a bit disconcerting, but her body adjusted in a few steps, and she was soon striding towards what the placards assured her was the lab.

What it was doing in a place like this, she had no idea.

After a few minutes of pushing—well obscured from the passage's view—the walkway terminated at a large, roundish platform. Without railings or walls, it dropped off sharply into the discreet islands of forest, bobbing softly just out of reach. A large column of poured concrete dominated that artificial clearing, but Tharsis couldn't see a way in.

"You looking for the quant?"

It was a man's voice—definitely male, a marked difference from the campus's general androgyny—but she couldn't see its source. "Hello?"

"Entry's here on the other side. Push around."

Curiosity piqued, she walked over to the edge, throwing her body's momentum around. It carried her over the edge of the platform, just brushing one of the islands, to touch back down on the other side. She grunted a little at the wave of nausea as she hit an unexpected gravity field, miscalculating and falling face-first on the hard metal planks.

"That was as neat as any maneuver I've ever seen an Arran take."

Tharsis huffed a laugh, and pushed herself up to her knees, engaging her gravity. There was a man there, plain and pale, watching her with keen eyes.

"You're the first person I've met outside our inwell to use that."

"What, Arran? I find we have far too many words to not use the correct one when the situation demands it."

Around them, white tendrils reached out of dirt islands, linking and waving through the space, water flowing freely between them, fungi far more extensive and far more visible.

"What is this place, anyway?" she asked. "Atmo facility?"

"Perceptive."

"Why not just use algae, like most inhabitations?"

"Iapetus was the headquarters of the bioengineering campuses, back before the Euphemism." He wandered over to the edge and sat down with his back to her.

"And the Scient let this stand when he torched everything else in the Purges?"

"Oh, there were things here he torched, as you put it," the man said, and his voice was flat. "Things that lived in the darkness. Nightmares. So many nightmares in those days."

"Umbran?" Tharsis asked—because there it was again, perched sideways on the outer wall of the round room in the center of the platform.

That word seemed to intensify the stranger's interest. "Why? Are you seeing them here?" Tharsis hesitated, winced. "I'm not going to mock you, Arran. I'm truly curious."

"Look, I'm not—" but the umbran moved closer. She bit her cheek. "I'm not seeing anything."

"My apologies. I didn't mean to make you uncomfortable." The strange man gestured loosely. "Don't let me keep you or anything," he said, and before she could ask how to access it, an entire side of the seamless column slid neatly open.

"Thanks."

Inside, the sequencer was a sleek-skinned, straightforward thing, a slot accepting the spiked nub of glass and gray matter with ease, the touch screen asking for data delivery options. She ordered a chip, and the thing chimed at her, directions flashing across the screen to have a seat, watch the forest, and wait. A far cry, she thought, from the bulky server banks in their subterranean caverns beneath the Academy, from those biology coursework days.

"Why is it out here?" she called back to the strange man. "I thought voiders hate this sort of, umm, thing."

"Large organics?"

"Yeah, sounds right. I think I've heard tDaer use that phrase before."

"tDaer? A friend of yours?"

Tharsis honestly had no idea what to say to that. What were they to each other? Friends once, sure, but how could that stand in the face of what tDaer wanted to unleash? "I know hen," she replied lamely, and folded herself down next to the stranger. "Do you?"

"I know everybody," he said. "It's my business."

"You're a gardener, and you know everybody?"

"Oh, this isn't my only garden. My job moves me around quite a bit. There aren't too many of us who prefer sustainment over creation," and he stretched out his legs in front of him, eyes far off into the islands of forest. "That's what Cronuans love best, after all. A unique life. Most of them are so similar, it's hard to tell them apart, though. One of the fascinating ironies of this university." A smile cracked his face.

She smiled back. "You don't seem like most of the Cronuans I've met."

"Why?" he asked bluntly. "Because I called you Arran, or because I actually have a detectable male gender?"

Tharsis blanched. "I didn't—"

"Don't worry about it. It's an unusual thing, around here. The Scient's discarded most of the male donor lines over the years."

Huh. "I thought everyone was supposed to be agendered?"

"That was the original idea. Sexual dimorphism eliminated, along with culture, ethnicity, all ties to the past, every person a blank slate upon which to create themselves in their own image. But the entire thing was a disaster." He shrugged. "Certain funguses can live that way, but there's no way to produce a human that's still recognizable as human without a discreet sexual reproductive system. It's fundamental."

"So, what, everyone's actually female? Why pick that one?"

"Why make everyone's skin blue?" the man countered. "What couldn't be accomplished through genetic engineering was instead achieved with a proper education and certain chemical adjustments. But men didn't take the programming as well, and having both sexes around confused the experiment, so they were eliminated."

"What does that make you, then?"

He grinned, mouth full of straight white teeth, but didn't quite answer her question.

"You know what he's after, don't you? What he wants? The Scient?"

"I don't know. Making some kind of rarified, ascended society?"

"No, Arran, he's not after Noqumiut," he laughed. "And what a lovely dodge that is, don't you think?" He picked up a small clump of soil off the platform. Started flicking small stones out of its matrix, out into the mottled daylight of the forest.

"All the Landlords tell stories, all the Tenancy is nothing but a story, comfort to the masses huddled in the twilight of mankind. Some of them, like yours, are still close enough to be hated. Others have been long-proven false, and so, have fallen. But the Arcna can never be reached, so what she says can never be disproven, and we find ourselves believing in something that all our history tells us is impossible. It's what makes it so dangerous."

"You think it's a lie?"

"Of course. Noqumiut cannot exist as promised," the gardener said, unfolding his legs out in front of him. "If we look at a human mind, we can see a set range of possibilities in behavior, personality, thought processes, things like that. A vast set of switches, these things can be turned off or on, some through biology, some through environment, some more easily than others. But no switch can be taken away without collapsing the biological structure of the physical being."

"I don't understand."

"Transhumanism, young lady, was a failure. It will always be. It is impossible to derive a cohesive being from the human genome that is not human. Just as it's impossible to pattern a human being from scratch."

The lieutenant felt like she was back in some early-morning lecture at the Academy, trying to follow a subject she didn't quite understand. "So what's out there?"

"An obscured reality, far different from what is presented. I would wager that the Rallarhu, your Rossen, did what they did in order to prevent any violation of the Accords. To stop anybody from going out there." He nodded. "To protect another Landlord's narrative that, as members of the Tenancy, they're obligated to uphold."

"Oh, fuck that," she groaned.

"Pardon?"

"I said fuck that," she snapped back, suddenly tired of this and every other conversation she'd had recently. "Fuck everything you just said. The Rossen let millions die just to uphold some fucking story?"

"Perhaps he understood the truth would be harder to swallow. Or perhaps he wasn't free to choose."

"Fuck that too. A person's choices are always their own. Even the Rossen's."

From the forest, the umbran's huge eyes fixed on her, carrying an accusation she couldn't answer, and she sucked air, suddenly scared.

"We often ignore the answer our beliefs would have us give. Something to keep in mind." He nodded back towards the pillar. "I think your sample should be coded by now."

"Oh, right." She'd almost forgotten about that. "Thanks."

"Not a problem," he said smoothly. "It's always good to talk to some young person with a bit of fire in her belly."

He gave her an encouraging smile as she walked away from him. Strange man, she thought as she retrieved the chip and gray matter from the quant, but there was more she wanted to ask him about whatever he'd been on about with Noqumiut.

But he was gone by the time she turned back around.

"This fucking place," she muttered to herself. She pocketed sample and data chip both and didn't think anything more about him.

THE INTERNATIONAL AREA of Iapetus's campus boasted a number of foreign national student unions, including one for the Republic of Mars. Tharsis had never been more grateful in her life to see the horizontal civilian flag, inlaid deep in the front doors of the place.

That meant it was a State Department facility.

Equipped with a conventional radio comm suite. Good enough for her purposes.

She'd taken the risk, making a little detour here. tDaer would no doubt expect her back soon, but this was still easier than trying to make the port again.

The Arran receptionist barely gave her a second glance as she entered, nose hovering over a tablet on her desk. Doing homework. It reminded the lieutenant of her little sisters, and she bit back the thought. She hadn't seen them in years. No good getting emotional about it now.

"Comm room?"

"Down the hall, third door on the right," the other girl said, not bothering to glance up.

Network warnings flashed on the screen as Tharsis spooled up the encrypted silic, listing out Tenancy law about providing material to voiders, about ensuring limited use of their wide-spectrum media nets, how only official educational information was allowed online.

She felt a fresh stab of guilt but shoved it just as quickly aside. "You're fixing it," she mumbled to herself. "You're fixing all of this."

It took five minutes to upload the genetic pattern into her encrypted transmission bucket, another three to confirm it had sent. Seventy light-minutes, give or take, to Deimos or the Inner Shoals or wherever it was the Rossen was.

"Hope this helps," she said as the <sent> indicator popped up, blinking green on the black screen, "'cause I'm on the next transport out of here."

But even then, she didn't really believe it.

CHAPTER
THIRTY-THREE

COLONEL CAMBEL WAS right in the middle of briefing prep when Caleb noticed it.

The figure, bleeding through.

A child, barely a toddler, all baby-fat, little haunches, and overwide eyes. There was something familiar about it, something the Landlord couldn't place.

But Tyr was on his paws, growling, hackles raised, and Caleb realized what it was.

What Tharsis had been talking about in that report.

It had been a strange series of messages from her. An umbran riding the signal, plutonium, Nepos being targeted. With everything else that was taking up his time, he hadn't been able to put much thought into it. He'd shot off a quick note, requesting that she contact him via core comm ASAP, and left the CP with orders to contact him the second she messaged back. The data she'd sent, he passed off to Morray and his team.

But that thing in front of him now made it all crystal clear.

"Jesus fuck," he breathed.

The colonel looked up from his notes, spread across every square centimeter of the cramped craft-side briefing room. They were due to brief HOMECOM staff in just under fifteen minutes, and the senior officer looked frazzled. He'd been taking shit over his handling of the situation; he was clearly eager to get command up to velocity and off his back.

"What is it, sir?"

Caleb walked over and knelt down next to the thing. Little fingers pressed into his leg. It wasn't solid, but his skin's warmth still drained beneath its touch. "They aren't supposed to exist anymore," he muttered to himself, and looked back at the colonel. "Do you see this thing?"

"See what, Caleb?"

The thing blinked, eyes boring into him.

"Colonel, did your boys get Tharsis's information in the quant yet?"

"Of course. The simulation should be running."

He stood, signaling Tyr to stay. "Get the chaplain down to the comm lab. Now."

Since waking up in that med vat on Deimos, Caleb hadn't seen anything. No ghosts, no energy smears. None of those grasping, screeching nightmares of the Euphemism clawed up out of the subconscious to haunt waking dreams. He lacked both the modern Arran sensitivity to the penumbra's echoes and his own time's susceptibility to hallucination.

That left only one possibility for the thing in the conference room.

At the next junction, the chaplain caught up with him. Caleb never attended church services on base, but he had a healthy respect for priests, who qualified for deepvoiders, and what they could do.

"What are we looking at, sir?"

"Myling."

They'd once been everywhere, such manifestations. Thick as flies in Euphemism labs, spilling out through every piece of technology those fucking whitecoats ever developed. He'd seen those things as a young man, those sightless, unblinking eyes staring out at him from the doorways in every city, every house, every corner of every soul they'd had to destroy. A type of umbran. The worst type.

The chaplain's stride faltered. "I thought those were just stories."

"Nobody wants to remember this shit was real," Caleb muttered, bitter, and picked up his pace.

Lieutenant Morray was waiting for them, just outside the lab. "The boss called," he began, giving the priest only a quick sideways look, "said there was some kind of problem with the sequencing..."

"Yeah, that. Whatever it is, it's human-derived."

Disbelief registered on the lieutenant's face. "No, no, that's not possible," he said. "We're seeing a synthetic-patterned algorithm coming up on our decryption hardware. It's pretty obviously a home-grown sort of solution, but..."

The priest spread out a hand against the door. "You're mistaken, Eric," he said quietly. "There is most definitely something here. Human. Searching for something."

"Who?"

"A little boy. Angry, very angry. Whoever he's been searching for, he's been searching for a long time."

Morray was stoic. If he could see it, he didn't say. "How bad is this?"

"It's been a few decades since I've had to deal with a myling," Caleb said. "I'd wager it can decohere the quant. Let's make this fast."

The *Barachiel's* quantum mainframe occupied the prime real estate in the dead center of the craft. Shielded against everything from solar storms to dive-time neutrino interference, the core was a small yolk inside a three-deck-thick egg. Caleb had worked on a similar system on the *Turiel* as a newly awoken corporal, and he was well familiar with its operation. A horribly sensitive thing, that computer, only barely tolerating dives, with far less utility than the craft's battle-hardened silics. Yet quants were essential for a myriad of tasks, not the least of which was decryption, so every deepvoider carried one.

It was one of the reasons why places like Humphryes ran on shoe-string budgets, barely able to keep the atmo circulating. The money only went so far, and it had to be spent on one of the most critical missions first. But if this thing showed him what he thought it would, it would be worth every red cent ever spent for the past eight hundred years.

"Fuck. The guys are running the signal through the quant's biological modeling program," Morray said, stopping beside a large tank that looked to be commandeered from the craft-side clinic. Full of undifferentiated modeling gas, it bathed the space around in dull gray light. Technicians clustered around it, submerging electrode panels in the gas. Makeshift hologram tank. The el-tee tapped one on the shoulder. "Tech Berl here's gonna fill you in on the details."

"You've already got the thing modeled?" Caleb asked the younger sergeant.

"Rendering a graphic projection up would take too long."

"But you're pulling data through the quant?"

"Yes sir," Berl said. "Wherever your source got the genetic sequence patterned, it's a fucking good job. Enough time, and we could probably model the originating wetware."

"And it's not human?" Caleb asked.

"It's completely legal, sir. No chance it's exuding a consciousness," Berl offered.

"Show me."

The network of panels sent a fast laser pulse the full length of the tank, heating pinpoint coordinates and cooling others, causing the gas within to swirl and separate. A low back-light pulse swept through immediately after, the laser cycling up again after a fraction of a second. It was a technique used sometimes for graphics too large or too complex to effectively render on a normal light projector, a negative impression bought out in rapid-fire pulses.

At first, it seemed that Morray and Berl was right. There wasn't a person, much less a child, in that projection field. Just a network of finely wound filaments, clumped and wound about each other in swirls of processor, pulls of cabling, terminating into a center hindbrain server. The image hung for a few seconds until the temperature differences could no longer be maintained, and the whole thing swirled back into that homogenous cloud.

"Looks normal," Morray said.

"Can't be," Caleb grunted, walking around it. "This was stripped out of a human at some point."

"I would agree." The priest looked pensive, arms crossed across his chest. "There is definitely something in this room."

"I don't know what to tell you, sir, I'm just not seeing anything."

"There has to b—"

All sound cut away.

Blinking, Caleb found himself in a small, tight room, a rock-hollow barely sealed, his own body glowing with the subtle light put off by hungry exogear. But his hood was pushed off, the air in his nostrils cold and sharp with something like rot that wasn't quite...

All this...

He turned away from the wall, trying to pick out that voice, out into a space too wide and too dark to see the end of. There was another figure there, crouched down, the myling playing around its knees.

Rows and shelves and tables, power cables snaking around, hooked up to containers of glass and steel, filled with translucent, dirty fluids.

The whore never stopped, somebody was saying, *that seal-fucking whore signed on to the Accords but never...*

Caleb knew that voice.

"Sir!"

The vision broke apart under the shout, darkness crumbling into dust, and he found himself back in that lab, with a myling right in front of him. Its hands dug into the loose knees of his uniform blacks, eyes growing wider in its little head. Tugging.

Caleb staggered back, slamming ass-first into the closest bulkhead, grabbing onto it for support as the little thing started climbing up his leg. Its touch burned. Everybody was staring at him except for the chaplain. Eyes closed, he was whispering Latin over a rosary clutched in a tight fist.

"Morray," he hissed, calm as he could, not taking his eyes off it as it hopped up, dragging down on his chest, "shut the quant off."

"Sir, we're still..."

It was trying to tell him something, Caleb knew, but he couldn't hear it. "We can recompile. Quant's useless if this little fucker blasts it out of phase. Turn it off."

"Sir..."

A phantom hand reached for his face. "Turn it off now!" the Landlord ordered, and slapped a hand through the figure clinging to him, trying to get it off.

The effect was instantaneous.

It let loose a bloodcurdling scream that ripped loose from the penumbra, exploding into the craft. Lights flickered, vents slammed shut, bulbs burst in the tank and equipment housings casings cracked.

Its pitch shifted, higher, angrier, sparking a violent blue electrical arc out of the nearest computer panel.

But just as the noise became unbearable, the myling fell. Sobbing.

They were always kids, weren't they? Guilty now, Caleb sat down on his heels, hands open now. An apology. An invitation. But the thing scooted away from that hesitant attempt at comfort, clinging to the nearest bulkhead. The air vibrated with its grief. Even Caleb could feel it.

Finally, finally, tiny fingers reached out.

Then vanished, just as the emergency backup lighting struggled on.

MESSAGE ME BACK THE SECOND YOU GET THIS. I WANT TO TALK TO YOU DIRECTLY. DO NOT BROADCAST FROM NEPO'S DIVEDRIVE. USE THE EMBASSY'S. GIVE THEM MY COMMAND AUTHORIZATION CODES. DO NOT PROCEED WITHOUT FURTHER DIRECTION.

"Fuck," Tharsis muttered to herself, staring at the terminal in the main comm area. She glanced down at the bag by her side. Her errand for the day. Get their three new, perfectly tailored ENEXs into their craft-side suspension vats in the next couple of hours.

The plan, as it stood, was to punch out to the Kuiper first thing tomorrow. tDaer wanted to take a few more days, hen'd said over breakfast, to make sure the divedrive hadn't suffered any serious damage escaping Amalthea. And to let them all heal up fully.

"With the Rossen apparently active, we can't risk the fucking ASDF getting involved," Riqan had said calmly. "We're leaving tomorrow. Tonight would be better. You should go pick up the scat I ordered yesterday, tDaer."

"You don't give me orders."

"I do when I'm paying your bills."

The fight had been short, nasty, and pointless. The Jovian used his ownership of the divedrive like a cudgel, and tDaer had finally stormed out in high dudgeon, Ang in tow.

"What are you after out there, Riqan?" Tharsis had asked. He'd relaxed around her a little bit, since Amalthea, although she suspected that had more to do with her willingness to swing a machete than burn the rank off her neck. "You're no Polarist, and you don't seem to care about anything the Arcna says."

"Oh, the Family cares. I wasn't the only one interested in tDaer's proposition to go out there. Whatever the fuck might still be alive."

"So you don't..."

"Believe? Fuck no, and I know you don't either. You and I, Tharsis, you and I both know it takes more than pretty ideas to run a civilization." And he'd smiled that arrogant, cruel smile. "But it's lasted this long. Whatever's out there, it's going to be fascinating."

It hadn't been an answer. She didn't like that at all.

She didn't like any of this.

Tharsis read the message from the Rossen again. "Scat," she muttered to herself, and went to go pass the command codes off to the staff.

Even with the clearance level the message carried, it took her almost half an hour of begging, cajoling, and outright threatening for the attaché to agree to set the connection up. After that, it was another ten for the quant-hindbrain translators to clear the static off the line. Every wasted second chewed at her mind.

They were scheduled to leave as soon as she got back with the gear. Not enough time to mount any kind of military response against whatever was waiting out there, and such a move would have been a violation of the Accords anyway.

Olin, the ASDF, they couldn't help her.

It was a thought she couldn't shake.

She was on her own with this. She was going to have to do something.

No, she told herself. *No, it won't come to that.* She'd report in, he'd get her home, and this would all be somebody else's problem to manage.

They set up the connection for her in a back room, some quiet, empty office with an empty desk, empty walls, empty chairs. There was just a handset, ubiquitous and unassuming, with an uploader terminal whirring beside it. All distressingly ordinary. She felt sick.

"Room's yours, as long as you need it," the attaché told her.

"Is this soundproof?"

"You think I'd leave this system just anywhere?"

Tharsis smiled. "Right. Thanks."

She tried to wait, tried to be patient. But she couldn't, couldn't do it. She'd been connected through the voice switch on Deimos. Like a regular radio call.

On some impulse she didn't understand, she punched an all-too familiar number into the keypad.

The line picked up almost immediately.

<Chen residence, Brevan here. Rob, if you're calling about wantin' to court little Jen again, I swear to god...>

Tharsis could almost see him, kicked back at the kitchen table, prosthetic disconnected from the nerve receptor plates in his hip, up on the bench next to him. Of everyone in her family, she'd been happiest to leave him behind.

She also missed him the most.

Her big brother.

Anger is like a cancer in you.

"Brevan?" she asked quietly, summoning the courage to keep the handset to her ear.

Only to pull it away again, as he started yelling.

<Ambera!? For god's sake, stay on the fucking line! Don't hang up on me like you did at Christmas,> he said, angry, and then paused. <If you were looking for Mom, I can go get her. She's out in the barn with the twins. One of the horses breeched backwards...>

Tharsis smiled, despite herself. "I didn't realize it was foaling season."

<Seriously, what's going on? Everything okay?>

He sounded worried. Six months at least, she realized, since she'd so much as spoken two words to him. And, for some odd reason, she was suddenly overtaken by the memory of sun-cut hay in the barn and newborn foals tumbling about on their spindly little legs and Brevan laughing from the porch as she and Dad tried to round them up for cold-branding...

<Sis?>

"Yeah, I'm still here. Sorry."

<Where are you? Are you on a core, or are you on Deimos? You get hurt?>

"No, well, yes, but..." She sighed. "It's complicated."

<Look, sis, I can understand if you don't want to talk to me. I know we've got... anyway, let me at least get dad for you, or...>

"No! No. Don't get somebody else. It's okay. It's good. We never talk anymore."

<What do you want to talk about?>

"I don't know. I don't even know why I'm calling," she admitted. "Everything that's happened... I don't know anymore."

And then he just sounded bitter. <I let you down, I know I did.>

What? "No, Brevan, I..."

<You think I don't feel bad about this, Am? You don't think I hate the fact that you're out there and I'm not? You think I don't feel like a complete bastard for driving my sister away from the whole family, making her hate us because I thought I could deal with that leopard on my own? That I don't wake up, every day, wishing it was me in that uniform instead of you?>

"Brevan, I'm not..."

<Because I fucking do.>

"I wouldn't wish what I've got on you."

<What. Happened?> he demanded, frustration crackling across the millions of miles of void between them, as raw as it would have been together at the kitchen table.

"I fucked up," she admitted, voice cracking with regret. "None of this is your fault. It's mine. It's my fault. Mine. It's always been me."

He was quiet for a moment. <Hey, sis, you know the news? About the Rossen coming back? About the Eighth Propagation starting up? Mom was panicking about it the other day.>

Tharsis's fingers tightened down around the handset. "I'm sorry, I'm—"

<Dad gathered her up and told her not to worry. We all know you can handle it. Whatever happens, I know you'll do the right thing.>

The tears started coming, gumming up her lashes, too thick to brush so easily away.

<Hey, it looks like the folks are back in from the barn. You wanna say hi to everybody?>

Tharsis's mind stuttered, caught between a sudden apprehension and a burning need to talk to her parents. Hear them tell her they believed in her. Promise them that she was coming home.

And in that moment, it hit her full on. The Rossen, Sergeant Olin, wasn't going to save her. He couldn't, even if he wanted to. The voiders had a fucking divedrive; they could disappear in a second and never be found. Only she could fix this. Only she was in a position to follow this thing through.

She hadn't done the right thing when it mattered.

There was one path left now.

Only one option.

"I can't," she whispered.

<Sis, come on…>

"Tell them I'm sorry, okay? Please Brevan… just tell everyone I'm sorry. For everything. I have to go."

<Am, whatever you're thinking, you don't hav—>

Tharsis slammed the handset back in its cradle.

For a moment, she couldn't breathe, couldn't think, couldn't do anything.

Just for a moment.

She let it go. Let everything go. Sat there in that soundproof little space and fell apart. Let herself have every tear, every gram of grief, of regret, of fury she'd felt since walking through Humphryes's gates for the first time. Since the Academy. Since she'd looked at her little sisters one night at dinner and said she'd take the family's commitment on. She let herself cry until her breath burnt in her throat and the tears smeared her vision to nothing and the supernova of emotion died away. Leaving her drained. Exhausted.

Please, she prayed in silence, not really knowing where it was coming from, *please, I don't want to go to Noqumiut, I don't want to see that place…*

The handset started buzzing. Loud. Insistent.

The lieutenant wiped the last moisture away from the curve of her nose, rubbed her temples, tried to gather herself. Tried to force herself to pick up. Answer the Rossen. Let him bring her home. Pull her out of the mess she was drowning in.

But she couldn't.

The comm unit buzzed.

She got to her feet. Looked down at the unit one more time.

And left the room.

Tharsis felt a very real thrill of fear down her spine as she headed out the long hallway, sparking out to her fingertips, making her shake. It was different, somehow, than running from that mob on Amalthea. That had been necessary, but this was a choice. Choosing to walk away from a standing order, to ignore her nation's Landlord, to break one of the biggest taboos in the entire system, for the phantom of a chance to...

He's going to execute you for this.

"Miss? You all done?" the administrator asked, coming to the door of his office as she passed.

"Absolutely, thanks," she babbled, knowing how jumpy she sounded, wincing as he glanced back down the hallway. Scat. She hadn't closed the door, that buzz was carrying...

She picked up her own pace.

When Tharsis was within sight of the door, somebody yelled, "Stop, ma'am, right this second, stop!" and she started running. Held the strap down to her chest and ran, full-out for the door. The Student Center was consulate ground, sovereign territory of Mars. If she got outside, back into the Cronuans, they'd have to petition the Scient for extradition to get her back.

The receptionist was blocking her path, gun in hand, right in front of the door. Tharsis picked up speed, dodged right, smashing the woman's jaw with a wild left haymaker. Dropping with a scream, the gun fell from her hand and Tharsis dove for it. But, when she finally managed to jerk it up and around, it went straight into the administrator's face.

The shock of that ran through them both.

"I'm leaving," she said, shocking herself at how cold her voice sounded, and realized there were a couple of younger students, poking out from various rooms and doors, clustered around that main lobby. She held the weapon steady. "I'm leaving," she repeated, and reached behind herself with her free hand, yanking the door open. "Tell him I'm sorry, but I have to do this."

"We have orders to keep you, Lieutenant Chen," the man warned.

"I'm sorry," she repeated, and jumped back into the moon's mig, letting her momentum carry her out, hitting the nearest footfall, and sprinting off to the port with everything she had.

Tharsis made it almost all the way back. But as she rounded the last curve towards tDaer's hookup, a blinding blue light exploded out into the corridor. Caught in its wash, harsh static killed her momentum, rendering her unable to move.

<STUDENT,> a disembodied voice blasted out from some recessed speaker, <YOU ARE IN VIOLATION OF THE UNIVERSITY'S COOP-ERATIVE BEHAVIOR POLICY. YOU ARE BEING HELD FOR ADMINISTRATIVE ACTION. A SECURITY REPRESENTATIVE WILL BE WITH YOU SHORTLY.>

It was a fight, but Tharsis got her head around in time to see tDaer, dragging a pullover sweater around bare shoulders, an irritated expression on hen's face.

"What the fuck did you do?" hen demanded, almost teasing, but— eyes focused on something behind her—groaned. Pretense dropping away. "Seriously, Tharsis, what the fuck did you do? That's the fucking—"

"Scient," a distinctly masculine timbre boomed. "Good to see you again, Arran."

Fuck.

WHEN THE LIGHT HIT HER, Tharsis had thought she was going to get hauled off. Dumped in an office or interrogation room or lockup. Somewhere private.

Last thing she expected was for the Landlord to settle down in the hallway, gesture the Student Center's administrator and tDaer down next to him, and start the whole thing up right there. With people drifting in from all directions to watch.

And she sure as hell hadn't expected the man who had shown up.

The man from the greenhouse. The one who'd sat on the platform with her, talking so deftly and so respectfully about things that most voiders wouldn't even listen to.

"So," he was saying, dirt on the knees of his pants, "evidently we have a bit of an issue here."

"There's no issue," Tharsis grumbled. Talking in the static field made her chest ache.

The Scient waggled a small tablet in front of her face. "Extradition request, filed via core comm. Very high-level stuff. Says here," and he made a little show of reading it, "that it's a matter of national security."

tDaer scoffed. "That's what the Martians say about fucking everything, Scient."

Saturn's Landlord tsked at hen. "Arrans, T-series. Let's get our terms correct." He referenced the pad again. Iapetans were coming out of every hallway now, gathering around the walls. Tharsis's entire body was on fire from the static field. Scat, this was embarrassing. "Let's see, it says she, oh, she provided a copy of *The Book of Shoals* to somebody." He paused. "I wrote that into the Accords myself. See," and his eyes turned on tDaer, "I pride myself on running a studious, open-minded university. Can't do that if we're polluting it with all that religious Noqumiut fanaticism."

"It's not religious!" tDaer protested.

"What's your name, T-series?"

"tDaer."

"Ah, right, the Daers. Good line. You're doing your donor proud." Hen's smile wavered, his tone hardened. "What is it you wanted to say about *Shoals*?"

"I don't understand why it's classified as a religious work in the first place," tDaer pressed. "I know that the Polarists take it like that sometimes, treating the Arcna like she's some kind of demigod or whatever the fuck, but I could just as easily say that the morning news reader on Channel Three is my messiah. At what point can we separate the speaker from her audience?"

The Landlord nodded. "So your argument is that I classify things as religious not based on their own intrinsic qualities but rather, on the reactions of people to them?"

"Exactly," hen continued smoothly, "and how is that fair? We know that not every person has been taught the analytical skills to listen to something and not—"

"Listening skills?" the Scient countered. "This is an international crime we're discussing here, not some academic argument over which brand of voider nihilism is divinely inspired."

"It shouldn't be a crime is what I'm saying."

"I take it she provided it to you, then."

tDaer's careful calm started to slip. "Hen is assisting me with my doctoral thesis, Scient, and—"

"Ah yes, I suppose you are at that age. I shall have to look up your grant proposals," he mused, and tapped the tablet. "And yet, my personal code of ethics does not allow me to hand somebody over for execution without having exacting proof that said person deserves it. This request does not constitute that proof. So you see students, we have an ethical quandary. How fascinating."

The crowd around them began murmuring.

Tharsis wanted to crawl down a mineshaft and die.

"I find the old Earth philosophers to be quite informative in matters like this," the Scient said, waving down a few rowdier Iapetans who were trying to shout an answer. "Better for a hundred guilty individuals to walk free, than one innocent die." He looked right at Tharsis. "It's your day, young lady."

The light cut out; the field died. Tharsis didn't exactly hit the floor, but her muscles unlocked, and she sagged in the low gravity.

The moment over, the gathered crowd began wandering off again, chatting and laughing as if they hadn't almost witnessed an execution. tDaer was staring at her, but Tharsis couldn't meet hen's eyes.

The Scient waited until they were relatively alone to say anything more.

"Look, T-series," the Scient said, "I honestly do not care who you fuck or who you travel with, even if you're slumming it with a Arran. But this thing with *Shoals* is beyond unacceptable, do you understand? The only reason why she's not headed back to Deimos and you're not off to Titan is the fact that the Rossen did not provide any evidence. You understand? Evidence I am going to go request from him right now."

tDaer nodded. "I know you're obligated to—"

"I guarantee you, you do not want to finish that sentence," he interrupted, curt, and turned back to Tharsis. "Arran, the next step for your Landlord is having your Student Center file a report with the university's administration office, formally requesting extradition. It takes an hour to fill out the form. It'll take, on average, six to ten hours for that to clear the wickets through the Dean's Office on Titan and make it onto my tablet. And that will begin, of course, once I notify him that I did not remand you into custody. Until then, I have no legal obligation to keep track of you. You understand?"

"Sir?" she asked, confused.

"I won't keep you. I know tDaer's got some work to do on hen's doctoral thesis. What is it on, exactly?" His attention snapped to the Iapetan.

Hen looked as sheepish as hen ever had. "Biological data encryption."

"Excellent. Exactly what you've done the last four iterations. I do hope you've studied your past conclusions and found a way to expand upon them. I look forward to reading your thesis," he said.

And with that, the only man in Saturn's inwell caught a footfall and pushed away down the corridor.

Stories, Tharsis thought, watching him catch up with a gaggle of students, *stories are running this whole fucking system.*

"We need to get out of here before that paperwork clears," tDaer said quietly, and glanced at Tharsis. "Having second thoughts?"

"Once he reports this, it's over for me. Let's make that count."

"We will," tDaer told her, practically floating with confidence. "We're gonna show everybody."

Tharsis had never wanted to punch anybody so badly in all her life. As if her betrayal of her country, her rejection of her Landlord—her own sergeant, for fuck's sake—was some kind of beautiful, honorable, heroic thing.

But she didn't.

She couldn't.

"We need to go now," she said. "We need to go right the fuck now."

"Noqumiut?"

"Noqumiut."

CALEB KNEW it was counter-productive to be yelling at the man on the other end.

He didn't care.

What the fuck was Tharsis thinking?

"Sir, we're trying to get her back..."

"Goddamn right you're trying to get her back!" he snapped, and tried to think of what he usually did when one of his enlisted kids ended up in jail downtown. Same thing, right? "Get the local Tenancy rep on the line, get her extradited, and get her the fuck back here to Arran territory!" And, after a moment of consideration, added, "and get me the goddamn Scient. Now!"

"Will do, sir."

Caleb threw the handset back into its extruded column, glowering, and settled himself deeper into the seat he'd tapped out for himself in the tight core space. He could have taken this call anywhere in the embassy, but the place was crawling with civilians, and he wanted some privacy.

The *Barachiel* was in a bad way. The crash of rage from the myling had overloaded the electrical systems. Most of the primary fuses in the interior heat exchange manifolds had blown, and more than one power transformer had melted in its casing. They carried spares, but not enough. The quant itself hadn't decohered, but much of its surrounding wiring was useless. Environmental systems were on separate circuitry, at least, as was conventional propulsion. After a quick consultation, Colonel Cambel had set *Barachiel* on a course to dry dock at INSHOALCOM, a three-day journey at full burn. There was just more damage than could be managed at Humphreys, and Hygeia was well within range.

Cambel had offered to leave part of his Marine detachment, but both the Rossen and Major Lanin had turned that down. Regardless of what might happen at Humphreys, the *Barachiel* was a vital asset, and crippled. A boarding action was unlikely, but potentially catastrophic.

Caleb had ordered work on decryption shifted to the embassy's mainframe.

What was spitting out of the translation matrix wasn't doing much for his mood.

... do not be troubled by their restrictions and their laws. It all means nothing. They mean nothing. You must kill them. You must kill them all...

It didn't take a genius to figure out who she was calling out.

Them. The Tenancy. The Landlords.

All of them.

Caleb had heard all the justifications. That old forms of government were incapable of properly running a void-based colony. How planet-side political systems took for granted conditions that, in mig, had to be painstakingly maintained. The efforts required to sustain human life in the extreme conditions of the void, off-planet, needed vast and all-consuming oversight. More than one colony had fallen—outgassed, gone adlet, just plain vanished—and the blame placed on their governments.

Perfect continuity of leadership, it was theorized, could ensure a colony's integrity. Immortal leadership.

Of course, it hadn't quite worked out that way, like so many other ideas from the dying years of the Euphemism. Maybe it was because the only controls on a Landlord were the other Landlords. Perhaps the whole thing had been doomed from the get-go; hadn't they fought to stop transhumanism, not put its successes on olivine thrones? Or maybe it was as simple as granting that Kuiper psychopath a seat at the table.

But the Tenancy was the only thing holding the Heliosphere together. And if the Landlords were killed, if the Accords were swept away, if that two hundred kilos of plutonium was headed for some kind of weapons facility out there at Noqumiut, well, Caleb didn't want to think about what would happen to the human race at that point. They'd come so close to extinction, to dying out forever, back when he was a boy. He couldn't let it happen now. Not on his watch.

A chime pulled him back, and he looked down, expecting to see the craft extruding the handset back out to him.

Instead, somebody was standing in the dive core with him.

"Long time, no see, Caleb," the Scient replied. "Of course, you wouldn't remember it now, would you?"

CHAPTER
THIRTY-FIVE

LANIN LIKED to think of himself as a reasonable man.

He hadn't complained when he'd gotten dragged back to a scatting terrible post, away from his wife and his children and all that family life he'd had far too little of over the past fifteen Arran years. He hadn't raised any objections to the way his old sergeant wanted to deal with Hinden. He hadn't abused his rank or his standing relationship to unduly influence current operations. He'd done everything an officer in the Arran military was sworn to.

His superiors didn't see it the same way.

If the last three and a half hours were any indication at all.

With the *Barachiel* gone, he'd gathered his notes, gone back to his own conference room, and given the briefing to Hygiea, close enough for conventional radio conferencing.

They'd let him run through the prepared slides, laying out the last couple of weeks' worth of information in a calm and orderly fashion. They'd even accepted his excuses for why the Rossen wasn't there and why Colonel Cambel had to bow out. But the fuckers routed the call through the dive comm network.

Which meant he'd had to brief the Congressional Defense Committee. Commandant General Eisen at Deimos. INSHOALCOM's General Cochrane and every fucking member of her staff. The intel bubbas on Deimos. The Trans-Nep watch-captain on Sinope. Trilan's colonel.

Cochrane wouldn't let go of the fact that the Rossen was active in her command, at the biggest piss-chute of an installation they had, being managed by a major. She was, she'd said, having her fusion drive cessna prepped. She and her staff would be out the day after tomorrow. With a replacement for Lanin.

Things were building. And the ASDF couldn't afford some kind of fuckup in a nominally peaceful region like the Ibbies.

Lanin understood that. But he also understood his sergeant.

"I don't know how much more clear I need to make this to y'all," Lanin said in the most respectful tone he could summon, given the circumstances, "that I've got a long history with the Rossen. I don't need somebody from Hygeia showing up to take over here."

"I respect your previous service, but the issue here is not a personal one," Cochrane snapped at him, irritation coming clearly through the line.

"The Rossen trusts me, ma'am. He's not going to trust some colonel from staff."

"He damn well better."

"General, ma'am, I would advise rethinking your strategy. Caleb's deferring to me out of habit. He's not going to do that for anybody, uhh, anybody else."

In the projection field, he could see General Cochrane's aide-de-camp smile a little. *Yeah, you know what I mean*, the major thought wryly.

"You have a chain of command, Trai."

"Yes ma'am, but the Landlord's authority is absolute and..."

He turned at the sound of the door being cracked, the young corporal on console shift poking his head around the corner. He looked worried, holding up a folded piece of inked-up paper.

"Excuse me for a second, General," he said, and, lifting his finger off the vox button, asked the corporal, "what is it?"

"Sir, I've got a note from Nyes."

PROBLEMS AT THE GUARDHOUSE.

Sighing internally, he hit the transmit button again. "General Cochrane, ma'am, I do appreciate your input. But I'm under the Rossen's direct command here. You want me removed, petition Congress. Until then, I'm gonna do the job I was put on this base to do." And with that, he cut the line, and turned to the corporal. "You know what this is about?"

"No, sir."

Major Lanin thought himself a reasonable man.

But there was nothing reasonable about what was going on in the Heliosphere anymore.

"Well, come on. Let's see what's going on."

"I WANT YOU TO KNOW, I support you on this," Saturn's Landlord said, words clipped, yet perfectly formed. It reminded Caleb of the old text to speech technology from computers in his own time. Which it was, in a way. The Scient had limited biological components: skin, hair, the uploaded memories and personality of the first President of Titan University. The rest of him was entirely synthetic. Another one of the Euphemism's more extreme experiments. "That's why I refused your extradition request. Why I let your lieutenant go."

"That makes no sense."

"We all say what we have to say in front of our people. That's our job."

"Our job's to keep them alive, not tell them what they want to hear."

"But how do you distinguish from the reality that is and the reality we wish there was?"

"I'm not fucking high on Euphie shit," Caleb replied drily. "For starters."

"Neither am I." The Scient tapped his chest. "This construct is very immune."

"Why are you here and my lieutenant's not?"

The Scient ignored that. He chose instead to make a little show of settling against one of the core's smooth bulkheads. His body half sunk into it, and that was when Caleb realized it was just a projection. Must have been all the core could handle at the moment.

"Caleb, your problem is that you haven't been around long enough to understand how it works. You don't have to compromise yourself. You don't have to make the choices like those the Onias or the Rallarhu make."

Caleb snorted. "The Rallarhu lets her Ibbies do anything they want."

"We're wrong, you know. There's something wrong with us, Caleb, with me and you and all the rest of the Landlords. We're all missing something that tied us to our species. Death, perhaps, although that seems overly simplistic."

"No shit. You're a robot."

The Scient ignored the dig. "That wrongness, I believe, is the source of all this dysfunction we see in the Heliosphere today."

"Where the hell is my lieutenant?"

"A man can be blameless for his state; justified in his actions, and still failing his ideals. What you intended for yourself or for your people doesn't change the fact that the Tenancy is killing this system."

"You're just going to keep going until I ask, aren't you?" The Scient said nothing. Caleb tried a different tactic. "We just blew a myling out of the quant. Riding the lines out of Noqumiut. That bitch has human-derived wetware out there. Isn't that one of the things we were supposed to stop?"

"Caleb, Caleb, I like you—"

"Oh, get fucked."

"—so let me explain this to you. You don't have the votes to proceed with a military option."

That, Caleb was not expecting. "What?"

"You're going to call for a meeting. Ask us to authorize you to go out there and blow the Arcna to kingdom come. You push for this every Propagation, and every time, we tell you no."

"What? Why? You knew about the wetware?"

"Well, no, not that. That is concerning. But this, this is something you always attempt, and it never works."

"The Arcna is killing this system."

"And she gets to vote."

That brought Caleb up short. "Excuse me? She has a vote?"

"Of course she does. She is one of us, and we are the Heliosphere, Caleb. We have to act in concert. Unilateral, monolithic action. At least, for something of this magnitude."

Caleb ground his teeth in frustration. "Who wrote the rules?"

"We did."

"And we can't change them?"

"That would take another vote. Her vote. We are not free to act against her, not without invalidating ourselves, and if we do that, everything dies." The Scient ambled around the small chamber. "But considering the fact that she never votes at all, I think we would be willing to ignore those particulars."

"So who votes it down?"

"The Rallarhu."

"She'll agree if she knows about the wetware. Consider that vote secured."

"She's not your captain anymore."

"Yeah, everyone keeps telling me that. But people don't change, not really. You know why? Because they're people."

"You're right. They don't change. Especially not the Rallarhu," and the Scient waved his protest away before it could begin. "Which is why I let your lieutenant go. Why the Flet let her live, I believe. Perhaps why you yourself turned her loose. She is free to act where we are not."

Caleb wanted to punch something. "The Tenancy should not be an excuse for this kind of inaction."

"Believe me, Caleb, I too wish for this situation to end. I would like that voice gone. I would like to recall the exodus fleet. I would like to study our old original DNA, find the corruptions, determine what separates humanity from whatever we've become. I would like the species to be human again."

Mars's Landlord shook his head. "That can't be an excuse for permitting genocide. Letting millions die in the name of some possible future restoration? Fucking hypocrisy."

"Of course we're hypocrites, Caleb. Don't you know? It's a prerequisite for government leadership," Saturn's Landlord laughed, humorless, a bitter smile playing on his lips. "But if we were human again, perhaps we could put it to rights."

"It's thinking like that that got us into this mess in the first place. Let's try one more thing, it'll work this time," Caleb said sarcastically. "But we keep fucking it up. Shouldn't that prove we're human enough?"

The other Landlord nodded, pensive, and held out a hand. "Make a note in your Journals to come see me sometime. I always enjoy these talks."

"How's that?" Caleb asked cautiously, shaking back.

"You always say the same thing."

Before he could ask about it, the earpiece in his pocket buzzed.

<Sir?> his shortwave buzzed. <Are you done with your meeting?>

"What's going on?"

<Problem at the gate. Major Lanin asked me to contact you.>

"Tell him it's going to have to wait," he said. "I've got to go deal with something first."

<Roger that, sir.>

He looked around the empty core once more. Whatever answers there were, he wasn't going to find them here.

"Tharsis," he muttered to himself, and whistled for Tyr to follow, "don't fuck this up."

THE MECHANICS of the main air lock doors ground horribly as Lanin passed into the base's only guardhouse. Nyes rose to his feet from behind the desk. Not for the first time, Lanin was grateful to have him. The Marineris-born cop had cut his teeth on a series of remote assignments in the Jovian Lagrangian regions. He brought Humphryes's compliment of combat-trained personnel to two.

"Sit-rep, El-Tee?"

Kid didn't miss a beat. "Mob, sir."

"Different mob? New mob? What makes this mob special?" Ibbie protests outside Humphryes were common. A weekly occurrence, in fact. Vetted, licensed, and approved by the Rallarhu's Administrative Office of Political Expression, the damn things couldn't be more civilized. "What are they doing?"

"Setting up tents, not talking, just watching us, listening to the Propagation," Nyes said, gesturing at a window. "Fucking creepy."

"Propagation?"

"We started hearing it about twenty minutes ago. Sounds like it's coming through the entirety of the city's Big Noise now. Complete override of the Rallarhu's security protocols."

Lanin glanced out a narrow plate-glass window. The open island in front of the base was filling with Ibbies. "This started at the same time?"

"Yes, sir."

"Any of them known Toks?"

"Nothing in our database locally. I had CP put a call in to the intel bubbas at Hygeia, see if they can dredge anything up."

"Perfect," the base commander said, and glanced back out. It was quiet, that assembly, but hell, were they pitching tents? "What's our defensive posture?"

"Small arms are limited to one per man, gate large-cals functional, ammo for two days of defense." The lieutenant paused. "But the bulk of our ENEX inventory is dead."

Hellfire. Never could tell with the impregnated Arran-made stuff, when the wrapper would die. Notoriously unreliable in terms of shelf life. Humphryes wasn't funded at a level great enough to even start to cover the expense of replacing it at safe intervals. In the HQ logistics system, such purchases were ranked against all the other requests. Which meant it never got bought. For a complex regional command like the Inner Shoals, the items needing funding could easily number in the thousands.

"How about our base shielding?" Lanin asked. "It was due for its maintenance inspection a couple sevenday ago, wasn't it? We find anything?"

"Hinden cancelled it."

"So we have no idea if that's functional either." Lanin rubbed a hand across his brow, trying to think. "We'll increase the base's readiness level, cancel exterior movement for the time being, initiate personnel recalls. Maybe we'll get lucky, and the Rallarhu will deal with this little goat-rope for us." Nyes didn't look convinced. The major smiled with far more conviction than he felt. "It's gonna be fine. We won't be putting your boys to the test any time soon."

Silence rolled in on the curl of New Stockholm humidity. Lanin stayed there in the open door for a moment, just listening. For anything.

"It's gone quiet," he muttered to himself.

He drummed a finger on the atmo seal, thinking about his kids back home.

· · ·

STARING out at the glory of stars, Tharsis wondered which one was the sun.

It was a strange thing.

They were in the middle of nowhere, right on the edge of Trans-Neptunian space, nothing but stars in every direction, the sun itself barely big enough to discern from that backdrop. Headed to dive distance after a last few, frantic hours, escaping from the Cronuan inwell.

She'd had just enough time to stop at the currency exchange in the port. It was a limited-service bank, but still had been able to make a few transfers. Wire the entire contents of her savings account to her family's. Bank paperwork was a nightmare and she didn't think the ASDF would have made freezing her small savings a priority. Nothing she'd need, nothing she'd be able to touch, if she made it out of this alive. She had almost seven thousand MSD in there, scrimped and saved from six years of paltry cadet pay, a year of cheap hostel lodging and outwell cost-of-living subsidies.

Not much, in the grand scheme of things, but enough for her brother to buy the ranch a new breeding ram, or for her dad to put away for her sisters' weddings. Simple affairs, weddings, in their part of the Bulge, but still, most little girls dreamed about silk dresses and fresh flowers from the Lunae design catalogues.

She tried to remember if she'd ever had fantasies like that. If she'd ever seen herself like that, garbed in white and hanging on her father's arm, waiting on the other side of the church doors, excited and happy and in love.

There on the Trans-Nep edge, arm aching, new neck-skin itching, Tharsis couldn't recall. She hadn't started her monthly cycle before that future had died. Extinguished, the morning her brother had snuck out to the high slopes, dog and rifle by his side.

The memory didn't elicit its normal rage. She'd been living with that anger for so long she'd almost stopped noticing it. But it was gone, and in its place, a hole. That anger had carried her this far, through the last of her childhood, through the frustration and the pain and the meaninglessness of the past few years in the ASDF.

Its absence now, there, felt like an open wound. Without it, what was she?

Sitting there on the edge of the inhabitable world, the vault of the heavens spread around her and the unknown depths of tomorrow facing her, the lieutenant willed out a silent prayer.

That whatever was coming, whatever she had left would be enough to do whatever it was that needed to be done. That she have the strength to do it. That she be forgiven for the death of that poor little girl. That she be given the chance to see her family again, let them know…

"We're at range."

Too late to turn back now.

BOOK THREE

ERIS

THIRTY-SIX

NORMALLY, dives were instantaneous, only a slight dimming of the lights and strange humming in the ears to indicate the movement.

Normally.

But instead of mind-numbing smoothness, the el-tee met something entirely new.

When she was a little girl of twelve, the mothers in their schooling group took their military-bound children on a field trip to First Landing, down near the Ophir Mesa. It had been Tharsis's first time in a big city, and she'd loved every second of it. The huge three-story buildings with their carven stone facades, the paved streets and their public trolleys, the bustle of so much humanity at work.

They'd come for the Terraforming Safari, a maze of interactive walk-through holograms chronicling the rise of Mars, from dead rock to flourishing, warm, human world. Tharsis had listened obligingly to the docent telling stories about the Mars Charter, its eccentric founder Peter Donovan. The ins and the outs of securing funding, support, from the long-vanished Earth nations of Australia and Singapore, Norway, and Texas. How difficult it had been to find scientific support for such an endeavor, until the Pacific Holocaust, to get it moving. Boring adult politics, followed by fifty years of bacteria and Arctic lupines and lichens.

But the memorial also contained a replica of the interior of the *Undine Glory*, and that, she'd cared about. Its pilot wired in, drifting in and out of meditative collection efforts, solar arrays with their vast capacitors trailing like jellyfish tentacles on a vast scale.

There had been crew quarters and staff and engines and all the normal elements of an exorbital expedition, but the memorial had just been the pilot's quarters: comfortable, almost homey, pictures on the shelves and books on the floor and Earth-normal gravity for the Earth-born pilot and a quilt Mara Donovan had made him.

Apparently, he'd only used them on the flight out to orbit.

He'd spent the next Arran year in the heart of the craft. And that, nobody had seen inside in almost eight hundred years.

He'd nearly died during the ocean reclamation, that nameless pilot. Even with the *Glory's* vast neural networks to help, the strain of moving millions of tons of water from the outer regions to the planet destroyed him. His body had all but pulped, consciousness fused into the wetware. Under the care of the Golanite monks, he'd endured. A human mind, lending its intuitive qualities to the most baffling propulsion methods mankind had ever discovered.

This was that, she saw now. Not the niceness of the exhibit, but the truth of its aftermath, far worse than she'd imagined it as a child. The gore. The splatter of dying red. The utter ruin of a man who'd given his last molecule for their people's future.

"My apologies. I haven't really introduced myself, have I? All these weeks, and no introductions."

The man from the library.

"You're the Flet."

"One and the same."

He was anchored against the far wall, and from the way his head was tilted, she figured that in his mind, he was looking down. She pushed up next to him, able to feel the subtle shift between surrounded and above in her mind. Not a fight like it had been on Amalthea, not exhausting, like on Iapetus. Now, in that place, it flowed, instinctual. She felt as if she was back underwater, just below the wavebreak of the shoreline, light bubbling in pinpricks through the spray.

"Neutrinos," the Flet offered. "They penetrate deepest into the termination shock. If I slowed your matter down enough, you could watch them evaporate back into the higher regions. Like soap bubbles pop on a hot spring day. Fascinating."

The Flet was talking about important things. Things she supposed she needed to listen to. But sitting there, at the bottom of reality itself, mentally and physically exhausted, worn to the bone, Tharsis couldn't summon anything. "What the hell do you want with me?"

For a moment, the hull around them tightened, pushing in. "I'm not your enemy, Lieutenant Chen. I'd have let you die inwell of Earth if you were."

"So what, what is this? Dragging me all over the scatting system?"

He settled the projected form of himself down next to her on the hull, staring off into the bursts of energy above them. "Do you know, Ambera, who the Landlords are? Really are?"

"What do you mean?"

"Means sometimes I can remember the man I used to be." Unnamed emotion rippled the hull. "I remember the humans we all used to be."

Tharsis stared up at the bubbling edge of the universe. It was easier not to think of them as people, as humans, the Landlords. To think of them as anything but the totalitarian monsters of the Tenancy. Who was the Flet before he volunteered to pilot that mission? There were no records.

"You regret it, what this has become," she realized, rubbing a twinge from her arm. "The Naven gave me this because she regrets it, right?"

"Ah yes." Empty eyes tracked into the nothingness. "Noqumiut. Our great shame."

"What's out there?" She hesitated. "Can you tell me?"

"A dream of an angry child," and the Flet shrugged. "So many people dead for so many useless theories. So many gone."

Quiet grief pressed down on her, echoing from the hull. Tharsis bit down so hard she could taste blood in her mouth. "I am sorry."

"About the Naven? Ah." The apparition of the Landlord just looked at her askance, its empty eyes radiating their own apology. "Time is… not what you think. I'll see her again, even if we have no new moments together. Perhaps you will too. But never mind. You see that? How it's getting thinner?"

278

It was. Like looking up at the night sky through deep water.

"It doesn't tolerate us for long, this place. Detests us, in fact. But the energy of thought extends from the deepest black to the highest light of the penumbra, and it gives us mastery against that repulsion," and the Flet smiled, the grief sweeping away, lightness returning. "Knowing the limitations means knowing where the boundless sky begins. If you..."

There came a jerk and a light that flooded the belly of the craft, washing the pilot's form away. His sentence was lost, as the white illumination of the craft's physical form drowned out the delicate non-structures of the depths.

But, for a moment, before the craft surfaced again into the bow shock of reality, a rogue wave broke on the hull.

A figure—woman's hips, child's fear—cast in front of a massive machine, the deep-set porthole in its center. Frost clung to the shallower angles of dull metal surfaces, melted handprints around the edge of the thick glass viewing windows. Writing, a whole hand scraping loose frozen condensation, exogear gloves hanging useless from her raw fingers. Heedless.

Cold gnawing her exposed skin, raw flesh scraping against stinging, singing machine metal, an overwhelming grief driving, driving, driving the words of that epitaph, ghostly…

… AND IN THIS HEAVEN, I LEARNED THE TRUTH

THAT WE ARE ALL OF US…

"… craft's picked up the gravity well, ion drive on, EM noise distinct from the cosmic background…"

Tharsis sucked air, dragged back, once again, into the present.

Her eyes were wet.

The voiders were talking.

Riqan has his ENEX pulled half-over his heavy muscle, hugging his skin like an oil slick on water. "It say what KBO we're at?"

"No. But it looks like we've got a moon," and Ang tapped the hull transparent.

Stars came into view, and faded, just as quickly. Torn away. Blocked. By a huge, hulking curve of darkness punching out against galactic radiation. Its deformed body seemed some accident of Creation, flung to the outer reaches of the sun's influence by its own defiance, the sun's disgust, wounded and torn by the billions of years passed since. In that moment, it seemed to her like some devil from the darkness, a defiant rebel that had sought for itself escape from God's plan, cast into the torment of nothingness.

Corrupted. Haunted. Scarred beyond recall.

Horrible things had occurred there. Performed proudly. Without regret.

From it, the song of the Lighthouse's electromagnetic field rose craggy. Pitted red.

"Looks like we've got a frozen atmosphere, mostly methane and nitrogen, some trace water, other things the craft can't identify. Low-density icerock interior, no surprise there," tDaer was announcing, scrolling through stats printing up on an extruded screen. "Ice moon, position to the sun… Eris, it looks like."

"Eris," the lieutenant repeated slowly, and the vision curled away, leaving only the more mundane details of the physical visage.

White. A white world. Shining in the far distant sunlight nearly 35 AU behind them.

Looked like, of all things, snow.

Obscuring all the evil that lay within.

CHAPTER
THIRTY-SEVEN

THE EMBASSY, according to the clock in the main rotunda, had a mere half hour before evacuation protocols were initiated. The place had felt full before, but now, evacuations just a little ways off, it was stuffed to the gills. Families and individuals bedded down wherever there was room They played cards in the hallways, joked and laughed and ate as if nothing was wrong, but a sense of uncertainty still permeated the throng.

Riding back with them would make sense, Caleb knew. Head home, deal with this strategically.

But then, things were happening here. This was where the Rallarhu was. This was where the navigation material was; he'd left that precious little vial of bloodstained rock in the command section safe before leaving base, just in case something happened out in the city. And besides, Humphryes and its tiny squadron were his home. The District of Lunae was an unknown, but if experience had taught him anything, it was that the generals would fight like hell to ignore anything he told them.

Better to stay out here.

Exiting the embassy now, Caleb headed straight for the one place where the Rallarhu was guaranteed to hear him. "Eliza!" he bellowed as he marched towards that living statue at the center of the square. "Eliza, why the fuck won't you vote for military action? What the fuck did we leave out there?!"

For long minutes, he stood there, arms crossed, waiting.

Nothing changed.

There was no answer, not for almost a half hour.

A great inrush of air swirled around him as the Embassy of the Republic of Mars ceased to be behind him.

Still, he waited.

The sky went dark. Rain began to fall. The Arcna's voice swelled.

From every window, from the speakers perched on every building, that voice came.

Not screaming this time, or cackling, or anything, really. A soft murmur, entreating, soft. Almost gentle.

<And can we deny it, my friends? Can we continue to lie to ourselves? To let others lie to us? Our freedom lies beyond such lies. We must liberate ourselves from them. We must open our minds and embrace the truths of Noqumiut. Allow me to tell you a story now…>

"Heinous bitch," he grumbled to himself.

In the distance came a telltale rumble of motors, the screech of gears, the bone-shaking vibrations of a great mass shaking off inertia.

Great. Somebody was reconfiguring an island.

The sooner he got back, the better.

THE GOING WAS slow on tDaer's scanning run, the planet's gravity so weak the craft could barely keep itself in orbit. Stabilization panels had to be locked out, burning off excess momentum. Made their ad hoc visual scanning of Eris's surface difficult. Complicating matters further were wisps of sublimating methane; this close to the sun, the atmosphere was still in the process of freezing full back down. The whole place was foggy as a morning in Marineris.

"You know this would have been easier, Riqan, if you'd given me the upgraded sensor package I requested," tDaer said at one point, buried in the controls, sweating as hen shifted the panels like rudders, shifting the inclination another five degrees from the equator.

The Nepo had dug himself a neat little harness into the carbon silk, working atmo-sealant into an extended rebreather lung spread out across his lap. "It was that or the final twenty kilos of cargo," he shot back. "Which would you have preferred?"

"Fucking cheapskate," the Iapetan grumbled.

Tharsis pulled her grav bag from its locker before the argument could begin.

Exhausted, she didn't dream.

Hours had gone by when she woke to the sight of a dark indentation on the northern horizon. Near the pole, according to the window's static projection, five kilometers across.

"Diameter of a standard Trans-Jovian Lighthouse field," Tharsis muttered, mostly to herself, shifting in her bag. "Not much space for people."

"Excellent observation," Riqan said, already hunched into his ENEX. "Thoughts?"

Ang leaned over the scene. "We'll find them below ground. A surface settlement would be insanity in conditions like this. Doesn't necessarily mean it's Noqumiut, though."

"We know the Arcna broadcasts from here," tDaer agreed. "Best place to start."

"Don't take the craft too close," Ang warned. "The radiation can fuck with the outer paneling."

Argon drive firing, the dark region came into detail. Perfectly round, rounder than any crater, and far more shallow, the interior hazy with atmo cling, the antenna forest's upmost fronds waving dully against the ever black of the void. No sign of movement, of life, of anything.

Dead.

tDaer didn't put the craft down, deploying the stabilization panels to keep it in a synched orbit for the moment. A safe distance, half a kilometer above the surface, a kilometer from the forest. Hen fussed over it for long minutes, until Riqan, irritated, told hen to knock it the fuck off.

"Steady as it's gonna get," tDaer said, wiping sweat-damp hands on the soft fabric of hen's pants. "We'll deploy a clip line, make it easier to move gear. Ang, you got that?"

Tharsis zipped up her new ENEX. It clung tighter than her baggy Arran one, but not painfully so, and without those weird pinches in the joints. She checked the incorporated harness, giving her clips a few strong tugs. The wrapper in these was kept not in a backpack, but in a thin reservoir layer within the suit's fabric itself. Deployed through the pores. She hoped it would work.

"I'll go down with him."

Riqan tossed her the anchor gun, with its wicked carbon steel payload and carbon fiber line. "Shoot it deep, Martian," he told her, and went over to help tDaer struggle out some massive package from the storage locker.

As they moved into the air lock of the hatch, tDaer shot them both a big smile before the sphincter locked. The cylindrical space was normally tight; with the gun, it was unbearable. The air was getting colder and thinner, pressure dropping.

"You excited?" Ang asked, grinning.

Tharsis's stomach dropped. "That's a word for it."

The indicator light dinged green. The hatch dilated open to the void. Warmth suddenly flooded her suit; wrapper deployed.

Before she could float off, Tharsis braced herself against the rim of the hull, aiming the gun straight down—out, horizontal—and pulled the trigger. The anchor flew, its bright red line uncoiled, and a small, recessed cubby opened by her foot to store and hook it in.

<Secure?> Ang asked.

It sank deep, carbon silk flowing, locking in place. <Secure.>

He clipped himself on and kicked down, the small thruster pack between his shoulder blades firing a defiant blue against the screaming light from distant stars.

She followed.

When Tharsis made the bottom, she engaged the gravity emitters in her boots for a moment. The voiders, she knew, would want to move out on thrust-pack, but her brain needed her feet on the surface to orient herself.

They'd anchored above a small hillock, the gentle slope of which was entirely covered in white methane ice. Details were lost to wisps of thin gas. Eris's atmosphere, still in the process of freezing back down after its long, slow perigee. The albedo was painful where the mist didn't obscure it, the stars bleeding into it at the edges of the close horizon, breaking only against the Lighthouse's heat shield.

With eyes on that snowfield, that pitted wall, the lieutenant found herself thinking not of the voice that had tortured the Heliosphere for centuries, but the Bulge. The snows across the high mountain pastures. Her family's ranch, nestled back in the hills.

Would they still hang her stocking for her this year at Christmas? Set a place for her at dinner?

<Beautiful, isn't it?> Ang asked across the radio.

<Yeah. Beautiful,> she sent back, choking back the tightness forming in her throat. Her family would disown her memory. The only thing she had left was the planet beneath her feet, the Lighthouse before her eyes, and stopping whatever task the Arcna had brought them here to perform.

It had to count. She had to make it count.

Tension rattled the line in her hand. Riqan, coming down. She let go and stepped away, taking a few steps down the slope to the other side of the hill, staring off across the fields.

<So, this is what snow looks like?>

<After it's fallen, yeah, but not quite as…> she began.

And didn't finish.

Because there, across the atmo-draped plains, was a figure. Walking.

A figure. Small, bound up in the thick yellow ENEX normally reserved for heavy radiation exposure. Striding as easily at it might have in Mars-normal gravity, tugging a bobbing, bulky sledge behind.

Something rolled off, bouncing into the snow, and Tharsis could feel the figure's irritation as it stopped to retrieve it. Manhandling it back onto the carrier, a glimpse of a marking decal on its side.

The international symbol for radioactivity.

<You okay?> Ang's voice asked, breaking the vision apart, the yellow and the black fading into nothing.

Tharsis blinked. <Yeah. Yeah, fine. Just thought I saw movement.>

<Tuurngait?>

<It was nothing,> she lied, and made a little show of adjusting the focus on the outer rims of her goggles. <Fog and snow have a way of doing that.>

<Family's got some areas on Themisto that emulate it,> Riqan said, unclipping himself from the line. A hundred kilo mass-belt around his waist kept him from floating off. <Doesn't look this nice, though.>

<Who gives a moldy scat what fucking planet-bound weather looks

like?> tDaer replied, off the line now as well, and impatient. <Let's go.>

Hen had a thrust-sled in hand and Tharsis automatically trudged back up to help wrangle it into configuration. A modular skeletal frame, it had seats for five, one of which was occupied by straps and secured with little gear bundles they'd built on the way off Saturn: cameras, water, extended atmo bottle.

The last were somewhat foreboding. A standard ENEX bottle held enough oxygen and recycling compounds in its matrices to rebreathe for eight hours, the exact amount of time for safe wear of the suit. Margin of safety provided another two hours in an emergency, but the possibility of extended wear was terrifying.

Riqan slid into the control seat, tDaer's eye roll almost visible through hen's goggles. Tharsis bumped hen's shoulder lightly as she climbed on, trying to tell the grad student to lighten the fuck up. Last thing any of them needed was more infighting.

The sled's thrusters fired in silence.

Echoing up into the penumbra.

It was startling to hear it, feel it, so clearly. Nothing else around, though, nothing else for dozens of AU. Just them, and the rock, and the utter deprivation of sound. Even the sun was too far away—a mere speck in the sky, barely larger that the pad of Tharsis's thumb—to provide much interference.

The dark edge of the Lighthouse's heat shield became a wall, not all that imposing, but still too high at six meters for the sled to navigate over without losing the ballast they'd need to get down the other side. Riqan killed their momentum with a quick three-second forward burn, coming to a halt ten meters from its edge, antennas clearly visible above. The atmospheric snow was piled gently against its base, but only the first half meter or so looked to be part of the heat shield.

The rest had been built with rocks, heavy and dry-laid. Like the sheep-walls they put up back home, Tharsis thought, but with far less skill.

<Well, this is interesting,> the Nepo mused, drumming his fingers against the steering yoke. <Thoughts?>

<We can head over on suit thrusters, leave the gear,> tDaer suggested.

<There's got to be a gate or something,> Tharsis said.

Riqan nodded, and fired the thrusters back up again, steering off along the curve of the precariously stacked wall.

But they'd hardly started—two hundred yards, maybe less—before he pulled up hard again.

<What the fuck is that?>

Tharsis caught a glimpse of something moving in front of them— yellow, black, gone.

Heart pounding, Tharsis took a deep inhale of cold oxygen. Hit the gravity in her boots.

Set into the wall was a gateway. Not a clean gateway, but one badly mangled, metallic shards blown out across the snow. A chasm, yawning out biolight. The penumbra swirled thick against tenuous static atmo shielding.

And above, a word, melted into the lintel. Badly scrawled, hand-writing almost indecipherable.

<What's it say?> Ang asked, pushing up alongside.

tDaer, in hen's black-pressed wrapper, was unreadable. "Noqumiut. It says Noqumiut."

STIFLING a yawn with the back of his hand, Lanin trudged back up the stairs to his office.

Between General Cochrane's impending visit, his deployment orders, and whatever the hell those Ibbies were doing outside his air lock, he was struggling to keep his equilibrium.

His body was screaming for exercise, though, and he'd figured that an hour reading on the incumbent bike rather than at his desk was a good way to split the difference. With any luck, it would improve his focus. He'd been averaging four hours of sleep a night since his return to Humphryes. He was exhausted.

Which was probably why it took Lanin a full ten seconds to realize what he was looking at when he opened the door to his office.

His secretary, who should have gone home hours ago, on her knees in front of the open safe, rifling through the compartments.

She shouldn't have known the combination. That was his. His

alone. And that was strange enough. But then he caught sight of what was in her hand.

He shouted—stop, maybe, he didn't really know—and she turned. Smiled the evilest smile he'd ever seen.

"Glory to Noqumiut," she laughed, and lifted it to her mouth.

Lanin covered the distance in a flash, knocking her to the ground, driving a thumb into her jaw, trying to scoop out the little twist of glass before she could swallow it. No good, though. It was already down.

She screamed, the sound piercing, and twisted loose, trying to run. But there was no chance of her winning; not an Ibbie, not against a man born in a planetary gravity well. The worst she did was knock the handset off the desk, smashing it against the wall. It brought Anders running out of his office next door, just as Lanin wrapped an arm around her waist and slammed her body into the ground.

"Call the guardhouse, tell them to send a team up here, now!" he yelled at his chief.

The secretary kicked out, catching him in the stomach and knocking the air from his diaphragm. In response, he jammed her head into the tile, twisting her arm up in a brutal joint lock.

"Cheria, I was raised never to hit a woman," he told her firmly, digging his knee deep into her back and pushing her shoulder up until she yelped, "but if you don't fucking stop right now, I just might forget about your residual reproductive organs."

With one last whimper, she went limp, and he started sweeping his hands down her body, trying to feel for anything out of the ordinary. Muscle, bone, skin all seemed right…

"Sir?"

Lanin looked up to find a brace of enlisted cops, confused, sweaty from their run.

"Arrest her, scan her, put her in lockup," he ordered the lieutenant, pulling himself and the Ibbie woman off the ground, finished with his preliminary sweep. "Chief, call her family in and arrest them too. Chris is Arran. We have jurisdiction. I doubt he left with the embassy."

His chief's worn face contorted. "I'll handle it personally."

"And one of you give me your handset," he said to the cops. "Bitch broke mine."

Lanin moved to the side to let one of the corporals slap handcuffs on her wrists, and he accepted the handset wordlessly. "Charge her with Tok involvement," he said flatly, and pressed the channel on the radio for the CP. "This is Major Lanin. I want an encrypted comm bucket to the *Barachiel*. You've got five minutes."

"That big of a problem, sir?" Anders asked, as the enlisted boys wrangled a limp Cheria from the room.

"Better safe than sorry," the major muttered.

She'd eaten that slip of Noqumiut. Thank fuck the thing was in hermetic glass; maybe they could get her to vomit it out.

But it should have been safe in the safe. How the fuck had she known about it? Had he said anything about it to Cheria? And how in the fuck had they missed Nalatok tendencies on her background check?

"Need anything else?"

"Just deal with her family, Chief," he snarled, and headed out.

Junia had the comm bucket up for him when he arrived. "What's going on, sir?"

He ignored that and started typing. "Call INSHOALCOM, tell them that Humphryes is compromised. General Cochrane's cessna needs to divert back to Hygeia. We can't guarantee her safety. Can you get the Landlord on shortwave?"

"I'll try, sir."

"Fucking lovely," he grumbled, and perhaps sensing his mood, Junia left him alone.

Lanin worked on the message, fast as he could, one question burning in his thoughts. Where the hell was the Rossen? The embassy wasn't that far. He should have been back by now.

RIQAN WAS DRIVING one of the last tent stakes down when tDaer returned.

Thoroughly disgruntled.

Itching to get out of her own exogear and into the relative security of an enclosed space, Tharsis was working fast to unload the contents of the last sled run into the structure's shallow entrance cavity. Almost seven hours now.

<Anything?> she asked tDaer.

<We got the pressure on yet?>

<Yeah. It's still inflating, but .16 ATM ought to be fine. Take your time with getting out of your suit.>

The Iapetan pushed up into the air lock wordlessly, sealing it up behind hen.

Tharsis glanced over at Riqan, who just shook his head, exaggerating the gesture so it would read through his suit. <Take the scat that's in there inside with you,> she added through the headset.

<Obviously!> tDaer snapped back, and hen's radio went dead.

<Ang.> Riqan tapped his ear, sending a pounding noise through the line. <What crawled up her ass and died?>

<No signs of surface life,> the other Jovian replied.

<No scatting way. Only idiots build on the surface.>

<Imagine what kind of beauty's going to be down there if we can only——>

Tharsis switched off her own earpiece and grabbed for a nearby handhold on the tent's outer structure, pulling herself around. If she was going to sleep in the damn thing, she wanted to know it was secure.

Matte-black, ribbed in emergency-beacon yellow, and beautifully manufactured, the pressure tent's only resemblance to her old training kit was function. Collapsed, it had taken up a single deep locker on the craft. Inflated, it measured eleven meters from end to oblong end. Thick wrapper layers protected the outer shell, the space within highly pressurized to offer structural stability and more efficient atmo-scrubbing. The living space inside was programmed to a survivable .278 ATM.

Tharsis wasn't thrilled about having to use the damn thing. She'd never forgotten the fear from that last night of void training, back on the *Centrifuge*. She'd been convinced, then, that she was going to die. She didn't want to revisit those memories. But they could anchor a pressure tent much closer to the antenna field than the divedrive, which meant less transit time for surveys. Riqan had assured her at least twice that he hadn't purchased anything substandard, "considering I'm staying here, too."

Tethered a good ten meters off the ground, a hedge against the horrible cold, it looked more like a Cimmerian pleasure dirigible than an exo-condition level five protective shelter. She was surprised he'd actually had enough wrapped carbon-fiber line to anchor it so high, but Riqan had just shrugged, and told her that paranoia sometimes paid off.

<Won't protect us if something really wants to get up here,> the lieutenant had pointed out three hours before, when they'd started unrolling the thing.

<They won't be able to pull it loose, cut it free, or slice through it,> he'd replied, and gestured back at the sled. <And that should take care of anything that wants to try.>

He'd brought a wide-scatter, high-velocity shotgun with him, the kind voider security forces were so fond of. Tharsis was familiar with its mechanics thanks to her dad, who'd brought one home with him from his own time in the service and had let her fire it a few times back before she'd left for the Academy. The butt absorbed the recoil, the barrel worked to provide a specific field of fire. The rounds she'd watched Riqan load into it, back on the divedrive, were shelled in green plastic, the international code for phosphorus.

<Don't suppose you brought two?>

<Now why would I do that?> he'd sneered back.

tDaer couldn't have missed it, Tharsis realized, which meant something was seriously wrong with the Iapetan; the very sight of a weapon should have sparked off an argument.

Upon finding that rough, hand-scrawled word in the lintel—disquieting in its crudeness—the group had held a quick discussion. Or rather, Riqan and Angakkuq, conversing in sliding Franco-Jove tones, had grown increasingly loud over the vox channel, until the Nepo was practically yelling at the Trojan in their own language. Tharsis caught the curse words, tDaer everything else, and hen silenced the whole thing by screaming an obscenity over the line.

<I'm going in there,> hen had snapped, when they'd both fallen silent. <Take some photographs, look for heat chimneys, whatever. Anybody who wants to come is welcome.>

Ang, predictably, had gone. Riqan had suggested he and Tharsis use the time to set up camp.

The integrated light above the air lock went white, indicating it was free to be used, and Tharsis pulled the last of the supplies off the sled. <I'm heading in, unless there's anything else that needs to be done out here?>

<I'll come in with you,> Ang replied, but it wasn't until they were inside, with the pressure equalizing, ENEX hoods down, that she understood the tension she heard in his voice.

He looked worried.

More to the point, he looked scared.

"So there's really nothing out there?" Tharsis asked, easing a sticky corner of her rebreather out of her mouth. She'd retracted everything that could be retracted, her lungs straining in the too-weak air. Worth it, though, to have the exogear deactivated. The dormant parts clung to her skin like slime.

"Nothing active on the surface," the Jovian agreed, and nudged his ENEX hood back into its pouch at the base of his neck. "Did you, umm, see anything?"

"In the penumbra?" He nodded. "No. It's… it's really quiet. Like, nothing."

"You sure?"

She hesitated. It wasn't that she hadn't seen anything. The image of that figure wandering across the methane snowfields was actually strongly impressed in her mind, playing over and over until she'd blocked it out.

Other things she'd barely noticed before were coming into sharp focus, though. Aural energy of the expedition's members, heat bleeding off the tent skin, the faint thrum of momentum in the sled or in the artificial graviton field put off by her boots. It was as if she'd been blind all her life and was now being forced to understand things for which her brain had no frame of reference.

And there was something else she was seeing, something almost broiling in the planet. Some kind of arcane, decaying energy. Tharsis didn't have enough experience to identify it by feel alone. But whatever it was, it was wrong.

None of that, she suspected, was anything the voider in front of her wanted to hear.

"No umbran."

"There will be in the antenna forest." He sounded pleased.

She checked the pressure gauge again, not meeting his eyes. "Another thirty seconds."

Inside the tent's main room, tDaer had one leg thoughtlessly hooked into a hammock, a huge tablet pulled out wide across hen's lap and hen's camera hooked into its data port. The two-dimensional images were flicking across the screen.

"There are signs of activity," the Iapetan said as Tharsis leaned in, catching the pressure-thermos of electrolyte water Ang threw over to hen with barely a glance. A long finger tapped the screen, stopping the progression, highlighting an area of the ground. "Like this. You see that, the mound?"

Tharsis nodded and accepted another thermos from the Jovian as he sidled over. tDaer laid out the flexible screen in the space between them. A few more manipulations of the image, and stats scrolled up alongside it. "About three meters in diameter, two high, and roughly spherical, with dirt and rock built over the top. Hollow. Antenna forests are designed with flat ground—"

"—especially in a place where heat shielding has to be used," Tharsis agreed.

"So it's a construction."

The photo wasn't the best quality, the haze of the forest's atmosphere thicker, denser, than it should have been, but something about that round pitch seemed familiar to Tharsis. Something from that haze of nonsense over Earth. "There any more of these?"

"Lots. Mostly clustered towards the center, where the antennas grow thicker." tDaer flicked to an image pocked heavily with the hillocks. "Hundreds."

"And there's nothing moving out there at all?"

"Nothing. Not even temperature variations," tDaer said, looking at a readout in the corner of the screen, and frowned. "That can't be right. We should be seeing some kind of…" And hen stopped. Cold. "Tharsis? Can you take a look at this for me?"

A bare strand of light had smeared up the bole of one of the antennas. Not the blue of biolight, but an uncanny gold. Pinching the image wider, Tharsis could see depth to it.

"There was nothing in this grid."

Ang cocked his head at it. "Tuurngait can impress up into the visible world, given the right energetic conditions, can't they?"

Tharsis rubbed a hand over her mouth, trying to remember what Gran had told her. "Yeah, but it's rare."

tDaer huffed. "We're gonna go check."

"Right now?"

"Well, we gotta give our suits time to cycle back down, but as soon as they do? Fuck yes, Tharsis, you and I are going back out there." The grad student nodded, tagging the photo and scrolling on. "We came here to find Noqumiut, and that's exactly what we're going to do."

THARSIS TOOK THE SHOTGUN.

Riqan had dumped some of the ballast off the sled, allowing them to bring it up, skim across the top of the heat shield's upcurved edge, and as they zoomed out across it, Tharsis had a sensation of gradient movement, like they were somehow going back in time.

She squeezed her eyes shut behind her goggles, praying a quiet, desperate prayer. *Please don't make me look at this scat. Don't let me see.*

With the sled thrusters at full power, they burned their way to the spot in mere minutes. Anchoring via small harpoon cable to the nearest antenna, they had a wide patch of ground beneath them clearly visible.

<Anything, Tharsis?>

<No. Nothing.>

It wasn't quite true. Faint heat pulsed out of the antenna bole across the penumbra, illuminating the exhalation of its bark, a flutter of lichens clinging to its base, the dim rumble of energy far beneath the crust of the ground.

tDaer, silent, unhooked from the harness and shoved down to the spot hen'd photographed hours before.

Joining hen on the ground, Tharsis crooked the shotgun in her elbow and tapped the gravity in her boots to a half setting; enough to push off if something came for them, but still strong enough to let her move normally.

All around her, the mounds rose in dust-covered silence, inward sloping walls yawning open into pure darkness. There were little paths between them, worn places in the hard rock and the dirt, where feet or hands might have fallen.

On the ground, not five paces away, Tharsis could see claw marks.

Left by dogs, moving fast.

The Arran could almost see them, impressed in the memory of the antenna forest's subtle magnetic fields, tearing past, howling in pursuit of some twisted thing.

She didn't say anything about it, wiping the marks away with her own boot as she stepped forward, closer to the mounds, where tDaer was already collecting material samples.

<Looks like adobe,> Tharsis commented, watching cracks spread out around tDaer's little scoop.

<Ado-what?>

<Building material. Mud or scat mixed with binding fibers.>

<Your people use scat to build dwellings?> tDaer laughed back and

scraped a bit of the surface of one into a tube. Capping it, hen took a photo and moved to another area, repeating the process. <It effective?>

<It can be a pretty good insulation technique, done correctly and thickly enough,> Tharsis said, unwilling to pass fully into the cluster.

<This doesn't look thick enough to cover anything, does it?>

<I don't know. Can't see,> she replied, distracted.

Nothing was moving in the haze. But there was something there. Curiosity, rippling across the penumbra. No malice. Just pain.

The evil wasn't there in the forest with them. It was below them. Inside. In the dark.

Cackling in cavernous filth.

<Tharsis? Need your help,> tDaer said.

Shaking herself, the lieutenant trudged over to the grad student's position, slinging the gun back into tactical carry as she went. tDaer had the thick fingers of hen's glove pulling at an exposed top corner of one of those gaping doorways, the other fumbling with the controls of a small plasma cutter.

<There's something weird about the material. Need a sample.>

Holding the exposed tent still, the lieutenant caught her breath hard. All around her, there was a strange glow, just barely discernible, lifting up from the mounds. Fireflies on a warm summer night, the eerie white of—

Scattered to nothing again by the brilliant blue of the arc cutter.

tDaer worked fast, but not fast enough. The fingers of Tharsis's gloves, thick and compressive, offered little tactile feedback. So, she didn't sense the building tension, and before she realized what was happening, the adobe gave way entirely.

The mound collapsed in a rush of particulate, clogging Tharsis's field of vision, obscuring the immediate area. She jumped immediately, tapping the gravity off just as she started to fall again, catching herself about three meters up, above the billow of murky cloud. <tDaer?> she called over the radio.

<Yeah, I'm here,> the Iapetan said, popping out of the dust cloud. <I didn't think we were cutting that much.>

<Thing looked ancient. Fuck only knows how unstable they all are.>

tDaer itched at the integrated air line through hen's suit, the thing moving like a protruding vein. <Need to move the dust out of the way, see what's inside.>

<It's just going to hang there, isn't it? Unless you can move it?>

<Sure,> tDaer replied, voice registering in cracks across the line, and pushed up to the sled, coming back down with a spare atmo tank. <Can you shoot this?>

<Are you insane?>

The Iapetan released it carefully, the tank hanging motionless in the air. <Know a better way to get a breeze down here?>

It worked. The resultant explosion was violent but brief, pressurized O2 bursting out with hurricane force. Pieces of carbon fiber tank shattered out, one disassociating straight through tDaer's stomach. Tharsis caught the ripple of its impact only just, the piece floating out of the Iapetan's back, momentum totally redirected by the wrapper.

<You okay?> she asked.

But the grad student's attention was fixed to the now visible ground.

On the contents of that broken shelter.

<Is that—>

<Yeah. Yeah, it is. Human bones.>

An umbran moved in the haze, and Tharsis saw it.

What had happened there.

She pushed up to the sled, strapping in, eyes fixed on the sky. Willing tears back. She didn't want to fog up her goggles. tDaer went down and took a few more samples before heading back to the tent, wrapped in hen's own thoughts.

Her brain was hitching on what she'd seen back there, unwilling to even process it, unable even to summon tears. If things like that had happened, if the people here had descended to that, there was no telling what might have welled up. What might have formed. What could detach from that hovel and follow them back.

As they waited for the pressure to equalize in the air lock, Tharsis closed her eyes and turned off her radio, whispering aloud a prayer they'd been taught in Sevenday School. A prayer to Michael. To ask him to shut out the things that crawled out from the true depths, seeking the ruin of humanity.

"*Defende nos in proelio*," she whispered in the momentary quiet, utterly isolated, where the voiders couldn't hear, "*contra nequitiam...*"

She could only barely remember it and didn't know if it could do her any good anyway. If he even existed, or, if he did, if he would listen to a woman who'd betrayed her uniform and her country. But the Latin calmed her, and that, whatever the source, it was appreciated.

CHAPTER
THIRTY-NINE

THE *BARACHIEL* COULDN'T BE RAISED. Whether that was just a problem with their radio equipment or something had befallen them already, nobody knew.

That was the bad news.

The Rossen was on his way back, though.

That should have been the good news.

Except for the fact that everyone in the CP had just heard the same orders come through the radio. Lieutenant Junia looked shocked. The sergeant on duty had pulled up a copy of *ASDF Guidance Document 1.1, Rossen Support Authorizations,* and was frantically scrolling through it. Looking for a way for Major Lanin to refuse.

But the base commander didn't have much hope of even that sticking, and he depressed the talk button slowly. "You can't be serious, sir."

<What part of what I said didn't make fucking sense?>

"I think it was the part where you asked me to administer an internationally controlled hallucinogen to my secretary—"

<Your Landlord's ordered you to interrogate a Nalatok operative. Time is critical.>

"Sir," he warned.

<I have a couple of pre-measured syringes in my quarters. Upper left drawer in the desk, small PIN-locked carbon steel box. It's programmed to automatically destroy its contents if it's tampered

with, so you're going to need to take down the sixteen-digit number exactly.>

Lanin sat down, rubbing a hand over his face. "Anything?" he asked the duty controller, who just shook his head. "Caleb, we're still trying to get her to throw up. If we don't get that scat out of her stomach—"

<Stop stalling. You and I both know the options here. Every second you argue with me is a second of response time we're losing.>

Yeah, Lanin knew the options. He'd never liked interrogations of any sort. At least when the Landlord had put Tharsis through this, Lanin hadn't had to deal with it himself. The scat shouldn't have even existed anymore. One of the nightmares that should have been left on Earth.

But Junia and Winters were looking at him, and he remembered his words to Caleb. There was an order to things in the military, in Arran life, for a reason. For a purpose. It had to be respected. Not for the sake of the system itself, but for everyone who served within it.

He sighed. "Where do I inject her?"

<Fleshy part of her thigh. Don't disinfect. The strain's purposely weakened. Iodine might kill it. Ready for the number?>

"Hold on a second. Let me grab a pencil."

And ten minutes later, with three of his sergeants holding down the screaming Ibbie woman, Lanin watched the first tendrils of blue unfurl from the still bleeding injection site and wondered what in the hell was going on.

THARSIS HADN'T SPOKEN since they left the field. Hadn't eaten. Wouldn't let anyone touch hen. Just curled up in hen's grav bag the second they got inside and hadn't come out since.

tDaer couldn't understand why the Martian was acting so void-burned bitchy.

Noqumiut was here, within their reach, and it was like hen didn't care at all.

Hen hadn't known what they would be getting into, out in the Kuiper, and contrary to what Riqan seemed to believe hen believed, hen had considered the possibility of finding less than optimal conditions. Ruins of scat-hovels weren't exactly in the portfolio of theories, but at least hen had the equipment for analyzing it.

The field silica dinged for the third time, the little door on the chem analyzer plug-in sliding open, offering up the sample hen had stuck in there half an hour ago.

The others, scraped from the sides of the little structures, had confirmed what the Martian had said about possible building materials. Inorganic dirt, mixed with hair, of all things, and human excrement. tDaer had isolated some of that material in the containment box, for carbon dating in the isotope unit.

But what the computer was telling tDaer now made no sense.

"Tharsis!" hen hollered, breaking the uneasy quiet. "Get out here. Now!"

"What is it?" Angakkuq asked, looking up from the mess of spare parts velcroed to a makeshift workbench, spread across half the tent. Hen was jury-rigging a surveillance wasp for building a workable map of the antenna forest. tDaer had done as much research on the things as possible, but even their first cursory foray revealed significant differences that would have to be studied, catalogued, and uploaded to suit palm maps.

Riqan, lounging against the outmost wall, headphones sealed over hen's ears, glanced over with curious gold eyes.

"I don't know," tDaer said, and swung over to grab the roll-out imager, flicking back through the photos she'd taken of the collapsed site. "Doesn't make any sense... Tharsis!"

"Fucking what?" the Martian's mumbled reply shot back, and a moment later, hen's long, tangled braid emerged from the sleeping bag. "What do you want?"

"What did you see out there?"

"What do you mean, what did I see out there?"

tDaer held up the sample bag. "This is skin. Human skin."

Something dark crossed that ruddy face. "Yeah, I know."

"You saw it? In the penumbra?"

"What do you want me to say? It's fucking thick down there."

This was not the way things were supposed to go. tDaer needed the data, needed to know. "Why the fuck didn't you say something?"

The Martian pushed out fully, that annoying mig-binder hastily wound around hen's heavy planet-born chest.

"They were chewing it," hen said, digging the heel of a palm into the bridge of hen's nose. "Chewing the fat off. The skinned body was hoisted up on one of the antennas, up… up beyond the atmo, where it wouldn't rot."

"What?" the graduate student demanded, mind starting to spin. Adlet activity? Here? No, that was impossible.

"It wasn't even cold when they started stretching it for the roof," the Martian snapped, and through hen's anger, hen's eyes were starting to leak. "Do you want me to tell you how old they were?"

tDaer realized hen's own mouth was hanging open, and swallowed slowly, staring at the sample bag. Ang looked devastated.

Riqan, normally unreadable, was visibly concerned. "It's human?"

"The fuck did I just say?" Tharsis said, voice strained now. "Yes, it's human."

Ang opened hen's mouth. Once, twice, before the words came out. "Did… did you see anything else? Like maybe this only happened just that one time. Adlet activity's hardly uncommon with—"

"There are hundreds of those things out there!" Tharsis exploded. "Hundreds of those fucking structures! Do the fucking math!"

"This whole place went adlet?" Riqan asked, oddly intense. "Interesting."

"At least on the surface," the graduate student said, grasping, as always, for logic. "It's entirely possibly this was an unfortunate passing phase."

"A fucking phase?" Tharsis demanded. "Going adlet? A phase?"

"Plenty of voider societies have had their experiences with it," tDaer retorted. "Not every Landlord executes for it on the spot, like yours does."

"I'm not going back out there until one of you confirms there is nothing alive on this rock," Tharsis muttered. "No fucking way."

"Tharsis, come on."

"You don't have to look at it!"

Nobody had a response for that, and nobody tried to come up with one. Tharsis went back to her tablet, Ang and Riqan to their wasp. tDaer replaced the samples into their holder, and went over to help them program a flight path for it, along with the proper commands for the robotic actuator on the camera. Eight hours, and they'd have a workable map of the complex beyond.

Launching the makeshift little thing marked the end of their first day on Eris. As they started settling in with food and bags and the tent set to its maximum security settings at Tharsis's quiet, angry behest, tDaer felt uncertainty building around them.

"We need to check the interior," the Iapetan told Tharsis, and made to zip their bags together. Their own comfortable little world, that's what hen needed right now. Fit those soft Martian curves against tDaer's own angular lines. "That's where it'll be. What's up here is an aberration."

"If there was something underground, it would have come for us by now," Tharsis replied, sounding very far away. Hen's back was to tDaer. "That's why we've been here for over half a day now, and we haven't seen so much as a whisper of activity from below."

"We will," tDaer promised, and snapped the zipper in. "We will."

But whatever hen had been looking for that night from hen's Martian lover, it wasn't forthcoming. And when tDaer finally awoke, hen was alone.

"WHAT'D YOU FIND OUT?" Caleb asked softly, not bothering to look over at where the Wytt had projected himself. The visual didn't matter. He was nothing more than an impressed presence on the surface of Caleb's mind. As much as Caleb resented the intrusion, it was what it was.

He'd arrived back at the guardhouse not five minutes ago. It wasn't a long walk normally, but with the Arcna's voice already pouring into New Stockholm's streets, he hadn't wanted to take any chances. He'd stuck to the back ways. Avoided everyone he could.

"Not much," Lanin told him quietly. "She's part of a Nalatok cell. Overheard us talking about the navigation material when you gave it to me, figured she'd get her hands on it."

"Did you get it out of her?"

"We couldn't make her to throw up. Doc's going to try again. The vial's hermetically sealed. Should be okay."

"So it's still in there," he mused. "She tell anybody else what she was planning?"

"Her cell knows."

"That all we can get? Can't trace it back further?"

"There's nothing to trace, Caleb. There never is. No leaders, no organization, no control of any kind. Financiers and fighters and sympathizers only. Even if she knew who was funding her cell here on Vesta, she wouldn't know how far up it goes." The shadow vision of the Wytt shrugged inside his mind. "What else do you want out of her?"

The Ibbie woman was sweating, blood congealing on her neck and around her manic eyes. Under the extreme stress of whatever it was the Wytt was subjecting her mind to, her body was forcing it out through her pores.

"How deep did you take her?"

"She wasn't cooperating, mind slamming shut in a thousand places. I dislike that game, and you didn't give her a high enough dosage for me to override it," the Wytt replied. "You know her people are only afraid of the Rallarhu."

"So you what? Projected her into the sucksuck?" He squatted down next to her still shaking body, wiped a bead of thin red away from her forehead. "Fuck. Is she still there?"

"I suggest you let me continue," the Wytt replied, and pushed Caleb's calloused hands away with his own insubstantial ones. "Or I risk her breaking loose, needing to start over."

Wiping his fingers on his uniform pants, Caleb rose. He knew what she was going through, knew how bad it could be, but he couldn't summon any compassion for her. No anger. No emotion of any kind. Like it wasn't even a person he was looking at.

Huh, he thought, and the Wytt cocked his head in silent question.

"I want to know who she's working with, where they are, what they're doing."

"You can't take care of it yourself, Caleb. Not on Eliza's rock."

The Rallarhu. Another problem that needed his attention. Why wouldn't she answer him? Fucking Tenancy.

"Nyes? I'm done here," he called, and the lieutenant peeled himself off his vantage point down the hall, keys in hand, mouth set in a thin line.

Spasms began wracking her petite body once again.

The Wytt's expression was almost tender.

"There won't be any permanent physical damage," Caleb told Nyes, and then, to Tyr, "Stay here until the Wytt's done."

Tyr, still seated motionlessly outside the door, looked almost pleased.

In the next cell over, a scruffy-looking Hinden regarded him with wary eyes. "Don't they let you fucking shave?" Caleb quipped, unable to resist.

"No, sir," the captain muttered back.

"We aren't allowed to let the prisoners have razors, sir. It's in the giddies," Nyes said, and then added, more quietly, "Normally we don't have somebody here this long."

Caleb looked the captain over. A sevenday or two in lockup had done him a world of good. The characteristic arrogance was completely gone, like air from a deflated balloon, replaced with a vague sense of regret. Shame was a great place to start fixing attitude problems. Maybe there'd be something to salvage from this guy after all.

Not that the Landlord felt obligated to tell him that.

"You're off uniform giddies," he decided. "Fix it."

Hinden's grudgingly little, "Yes sir," followed him up the corridor to the main room of the guardhouse.

Where somebody else was shouting.

"Chris, please. You've got to calm down—"

"Calm down?" the red-faced pub owner bellowed at the corporal trying to talk some sense into him. His pale-faced daughter was right behind him, retreating as always, dark hair spilling like silk around mig-thin shoulders. "Calm down?! You have my wife in there!"

Nyes pushed past Caleb. "Your wife is under arrest, sir, suspicion of working for a Tok cell. Your family is subject to the same treatment until we ascertain what the fuck's going on."

"Fuck what I'm subject to! My wife would never do this!"

"Sir, the evidence is utterly incontrovertible at this point. I'm sorry."

Caleb's eyes drifted over to the window next to them, the one that looked out over the wide street in front of Humphryes. That mob was still out, still silent. Unnerving.

His eye caught movement, snapping his attention over: that daughter, so innocent in her voluminous clothing, eyes overlarge in that pale face. Backing up now, clutching at her arm, fingers moving on her clenched palm, as if...

"Caleb!" the Wytt's voice snapped into his head. "Caleb, it's—"

He lunged for the girl, catching her wrist and neck, and slamming her down against the guardhouse's wide counter. She screamed, thrashing, and Caleb dug in with every gram of Earth-born strength he had. The bones of her arm ground together, rougher and tighter than they should have been. Metal. False.

Forcing his fingers through hers to keep her from sending a command up through synthetic nerves, the sergeant yanked the limb as hard as he could. The pop as the joint dislocated brought another, higher scream, and she was fighting him now to try to get her fingers back, blunt teeth snapping for his skin, rage in her eyes.

"Nyes," he barked over his shoulder, at the stunned lieutenant who was only barely holding on to the enraged father. "Nyes, knife! Now!"

"Rossen..."

"Her arm's packed!" he yelled.

The lieutenant moved instantly, not questioning a second more, blade flashing out and down snake-fast, severing the false limb completely away. Under the force of the blow, it went flying, barely missing the female private working the counter to crash back behind her.

The daughter passed out; Caleb, contemptuous, let her body hit the floor as her father rushed to her side. The Landlord hopped the counter, over to where the private was staring at the still twitching prosthesis.

"You ever seen one of these before?" he asked her quietly.

She shook her head, clearly shaken.

Caleb crouched down for a better look. "Tok-make. Kilo or so of explosive alloy. The coating on the bones serves as additional shrapnel. They amputate the healthy limb and graft on the artificial one, stretching the skin back over. No metal components."

"Common out in the Jovians. But they've only got a two- or three-day lifespan before necrosis sets in," Nyes added. "What do you think it's..."

But the lieutenant didn't have a chance to finish his sentence.

Because the front wall of the guardhouse exploded in white-green fire.

Almost before the shock wave hit the back wall, static shields shot up across the hole, sealing it away. Curled up behind the counter next to that young private—skull split in half by a raw chunk of glass—

Caleb barely recognized the sound, the impending rush of air across his body, for what it was.

Emergency fire suppression system.

He only just managed to grab onto the underside of the counter before the ceiling vented open, blasting out atmo and fire alike. Papers, rubble, loose bits of body surged upward into that stream, and Caleb slammed his eyes shut, forcing himself to count out the seconds as his skin started to burn.

The Landlord got to six by the time the ceiling closed up, ten by the time enough air was pumped back in, and twenty before the pressure equalized enough for him to draw breath. At twenty-six, he was able to get his footing and push up. There was a sense of movement he had, like people running by him, but he couldn't figure out what that was. Beyond, he could dimly hear the base siren wailing.

When he finally forced himself to his feet, it was to devastation. The room was a disaster zone, scorched and pitted, body parts scattered everywhere. Caleb willed himself not to look at those and grabbed one of the A-24 rifles stashed under the counter, heading back for the Tok he had locked up in a cell.

What he found was a battle.

Tyr, bleeding from one flattened ear, with his jaws around the throat of an Ibbie, a second already dead on the floor. A small cutting charge, abandoned on the floor behind. A Tok posse in balaclavas, almost comically bright, fleeing through another hole on the other side of the dog.

Caleb managed to get off a shot, but too late. The Toks were gone already. The dog snapped the neck of the one he had, growling at the body, hair standing up along the ridge of his spine, and his eyes flicked up to Caleb. Wanting to give chase.

He nodded to the big animal and turned back to the cells as Tyr tore out after them.

"You hurt, Captain?" he asked, already knowing the answer. Hinden wasn't bleeding, but he was in the initial stages of shock, eyes glazing over, skin going white. "Answer me!"

The captain roused himself enough to croak out a "yes."

"Cheria?"

The Ibbie woman was worse off, Laying at the base of the bars, she bared her teeth at him. Blood leaked from her mouth. Internal injuries, then. Further diluting the possibility of getting the rock out of her gut.

He didn't have time for this shit.

Considering his options, Caleb huffed out a breath. And then shot her clean through the head.

The shot rang loud in the harsh dust of the ruined guardhouse, but she died in silence. Brain matter splattered on the ground beneath her.

Hinden scrambled to the back of the cell. Lanin came around the corner.

"Get the scat out of her," Caleb ordered, curt. "Cut her open, pull it out. That's the last chance we have of getting to the Kuiper, I'm not fucking losing it!"

"Olin..."

"Do it!" And he took off through the broken wall, Tyr howling in the distance.

Out in the streets in front of the base, the extent of the damage was clear. The poisoned phosphorous charge, still burning in places, had splattered a huge swatch of the boundary wall. The main air lock gates were on emergency shutdown, and base sirens were wailing. Whatever they'd used had been aimed well; the small hangar just inside the base boundary had been hit as well, the base's only rockjump obliterated. The mob was scattering in flurries of silk and pale skin and abject fear. Some were screaming, clutching at their own injuries. Fires burned along the wide cobblestones; the air reeked of thallium.

Caleb took it all in in a second. Then Tyr bayed. Scent found. The dog tore out towards it.

The chase lasted long, long minutes. The Landlord had to keep his uniform on full gravity compensators, just to keep his body moving properly. He didn't have a prayer of catching up to Tyr, though, the dog much more accustomed to running in low gravity and a hell of a lot more sure on his paws than he was on his own feet. He could hear the howling, and he followed.

Wasn't the first time they'd hunted in such a way.

The streets widened, the spaces between the building breaking apart to reveal open water, and Caleb realized he'd been led all the way down to the fractures at the edge of the city. Always moving, adrift on the ocean, this collection of islands formed the fuzzy delineation between the mainland on which New Stockholm proper was built, and the amorphous archipelago beyond.

The harried Toks were there, on the last of the islands before the open sea, pushing back, engines firing below the water. Retreating.

His feet carried him to the island's edge, street falling into bounding sea, Tyr tearing alongside. Caleb switched off the gravity in his boots. His dog howled.

They took the leap together.

Earth-born muscle carried them easily over that hundred or so meters. Even with the gravity differential, though, pain screeched through Caleb's legs as he hit.

The Toks were on him before he could respond, whooping and screeching, dark cloth concealing their faces like shrouds as they tore at his body with broken glass. Tyr snarled as he tore into them. Caleb had his combat knife on him, but against a hoard, it did little good. It was like fighting water. They bore him down. A curve of glass, longer than his hand, drove into his gut.

The sky roared.

An organic pillar of bluish-green light crashed.

The burning reek of the void burst over his senses.

The Toks were gone.

Caleb lay there for a moment, stunned, blood oozing out around a broken bottle , the island slowly drifting out into the ocean. Tyr was standing over him, panting hard, and, taking a handful of his fur, the Landlord pulled himself to standing.

Only to see the Rallarhu, falling to land, pinching off from the sky.

Mars's Landlord didn't pull the glass out. Just stared at the ruin of his old captain. The oil slick curve offered only an illusion of the woman he'd once known—dark-haired, grim, beautiful in her rage.

They were all angry, back then.

"Tyr," he said quietly, the animal's ears perking even at the low sound, "get back to base, bolster the defenses if it comes to it. Shit's probably going to get ugly."

Not a protest. Not so much as a twisted ear at the command. The dog huffed comprehension and ran full speed towards the back of the island. Kicking off at the very last possible second, he took the now almost two-hundred-yard distance like it was nothing.

Tyr sat back for a moment, howled an acknowledgement, and was gone.

Caleb watched, smiling a little to himself, and then faltered, blood slicking through the inside of his blacks.

"Hello, Eliza."

"You better take care of that," she told him. "Wouldn't want you to bleed out."

"Yeah, you think?" he replied, sarcastic. It hurt to breathe.

She didn't reply. Just blinked once more, and the illusion of her fell apart. The flimsy xenocyte construct died in the atmo. A soap bubble bursting on dry grass.

Blood still pumping out under his fingers, Caleb turned his attention to the small pavilion in the middle of the island.

The place seemed more park than city. The Ibbies didn't have many of those, and judging by the single structure on it, it must have been somebody's private escape. Excess wealth wasn't common, but certainly wasn't illegal. He wondered whose it was, if they'd been funding the Nalatok cell that Cheria must have been part of.

Time for wondering would come later. The wound in his side needed immediate attention. He was losing too much blood.

The open-air pavilion was mercifully well-stocked with both food and medical supplies. If he looked further, no doubt he'd find a weapons cache as well. Maybe a bomb-maker's kit somewhere as well. Definitely a cell safe house.

He tore open a med pack. Bracing himself, Caleb yanked the glass free at the same time he slid the pack onto the wound. Caleb gasped as the cool gel grabbed hold of his wound, painkillers flooding his system. The bleeding stopped immediately.

Legs giving out, he slumped down against one of the pavilion's smooth olivine glass walls. A grayness was stealing over his vision, narrowing, pulling him away.

He'd be lucky to wake up, he thought, and then it took him completely.

"HE DIDN'T AIM, Major. Just looked at her and fired, and then he was gone," Hinden babbled.

Standing in the ruin of his guardhouse's little lockup, the chaplain's enlisted aide scraping the gore from the walls of the main room, two people dead and Nyes in critical condition, Lanin didn't know what to tell the captain. He'd never heard the younger officer sound so off-balance.

The whole thing was surreal.

Static shields were holding, at least, granting time for fast-growth alloy patches to stitch themselves across the in-blown walls. Not a permanent solution by any means. It'd take a day to patch-weld in a proper fix, but it would most likely hold. Lanin didn't anticipate another attack on that level. The depleted uranium shells they'd been hit with were fucking expensive, very rare. They weren't likely to see those again.

The streets were empty, the earlier crowds gone.

Out-facing security cameras had reported skyhooks, two clicks or so to 'roid south.

Lanin would have been tempted to declare the incident over, but for the Arcna's voice, still echoing through the city.

Nothing would be over, nobody would be safe, until that stopped.

But that was the least of his problems.

The fucking navigation material was still in Cheria's stomach.

Fuck, the major thought tiredly, staring down at the mess that had once been his secretary. He'd liked her.

No matter. Toks were Toks. Pulling his little utility knife from his pocket, he squatted down over the growing puddle of blood to tear away her blouse. Nothing Lanin hadn't done before, during slaughter season back on the family farm, but this was no lamb for the larder.

"He does things like that."

"It was… it was just…"

Lanin had wondered, from time to time, just what Caleb's life had been like, what horrors the Euphemism had held. There were so many stories. Now, though, wasn't really the best time to worry about it.

"Shut up, Captain," he muttered, and sliced her open, solar plexus to belly button.

It took mere nerve-wracking moments to locate her stomach, but when he reached it, incised it open, there was nothing.

The glass cylinder was broken.

Dripping goo. Empty.

The delicate crystalline matrix of the minerals had completely dissolved.

He sat back over his heels, reeling. There was no way of knowing how far molecular breakdown had gone, if there was anything recognizable left in there, but the Landlord's orders had been clear. And he wasn't stupid enough to think that the man would tolerate something like that being disobeyed.

Distantly, Lanin heard the sounds of the rushing medical crew, and bit his cheek.

Putting me through it today, aren't you? he thought.

As he re-emerged into the main room, Lieutenant Nyes—both legs and one arm completely gone—was being loaded into the base's stasis unit. Guided by synthetic wetware, the emergency medical system effectively ejected its contents from the gradient, slowing relative time within to almost nothing. A sevenday outside was less than a second in the bag.

Their only stasis unit.

Fuck. Of course.

"Stop! Don't seal him up!" he ordered, hating himself.

The two medics attempting to manhandle the lieutenant's shattered, still breathing body into the bag froze.

"Sir, if we don't get him in this, he's going to die. We don't have the facilities to deal with a triple amputation."

"I know," he replied, tense, and took a knee next to Nyes's barely living form. "Take that setup back in the cells and load Cheria's body."

One of them shook his head. "Sir, she's already dead…"

"Do it!" he growled.

The med tech who hadn't spoken nodded once and made to obey.

The first pursed his lips and went back to working on the lieutenant. They'd clamped the major veins in what was left of his legs, arm stump bound up in an emergency tourniquet, blood replacement drips in place; that blue-gray liquid wasn't so much leaking as it was running out.

Lanin tried to tell himself that even with the bag, Nyes was terminal.

It almost worked.

"Is he conscious?"

"Barely."

Lanin touched his lieutenant's forehead, his neck, and then squeezed, hard, on the drip bag. Nyes's face was in tatters, bleeding from a dozen deep shrapnel cuts, but his eyes blinked open, shiny with whatever they'd doped him up on. The base commander was glad to see it—no man deserved to leave the world in that kind of pain.

"Nyes," the major said, weirdly calm, "listen to me. I'm not letting the doc bag you. I need Cheria's body intact. We lose that, we lose our only chance of stopping this Propagation."

The lieutenant swallowed, blinked—once, twice, very slow. Lanin closed his hand around the dying man's remaining hand, and Nyes squeezed back as hard as he could.

Lanin stayed there as the medic kept working, as the chaplain administered last rites, as his lieutenant's hand slipped from his, limp on the blood-slicked ground. As he pulled Nyes's eyelids down. As the subtle white of death light smoked from his body into the guard-house's already murky penumbra.

Four, his mind whispered to him as the chaplain opened his catechism to the correct prayers, *you've lost four of them today.*

CHAPTER
FORTY-ONE

"ARE you sure that's the official word from Command?" Lanin asked Lieutenant Junia, down in the CP the next morning.

Exhausted, the lieutenant shook her head. "I spent three hours on the line with the Warfare Operations Center last night, had the guys get on as soon as the new shift started up there at District of Lunae. There's nothing. Nobody they'll send."

"They know the fucking Landlord is here, right?" He'd ordered them not to say anything about the fact that Caleb was missing. Lanin couldn't be entirely certain that some political ass back in District of Lunae wouldn't actively try make the situation worse for them. The Landlord wasn't the most popular figure in Arran politics; his mere existence grated on national sensibilities. "The Landlord, who is missing?"

"Humphryes isn't a high-priority location."

"We got hit yesterday."

"Everything's getting hit right now, sir," and she waved her hand down the console. "The morning ops report the WOC sent over for you is something like fifty pages long."

"Junia…"

Winters swiveled around in his chair. "The lieutenant's being diplomatic, boss. WOC says HOMECOM is not diverting resources towards protecting a man who can't die."

Yeah, that was about what he'd expected. Still. "There are two hundred and nineteen troops stationed here who can."

"That's what they said, sir," the sergeant confirmed.

A lifetime of practice let Lanin could keep his temper in check. He forced himself to look at this coldly, logically. A gray, cold rain had been falling since last night, an effective dampener of both Tok activity and the endless wasp of the Arcna's voice. The Rallarhu had a police presence out in force as well. So far, the base hadn't been hit again. Maybe it wouldn't be.

"What about the *Barachiel*? Have we heard anything yet?"

"Nothing, sir. They could have been re-tasked, or something might have happened to them. INSHOALCOM doesn't know where they are either." Winters paused and squinted at one of his screens. "Sir, I've got something from the gate."

"What is it?"

"Tyr's back."

ROLLING her shoulder to loosen a tight spot in her rebreather cord, Tharsis stared at the door in front of her. It looked, for all intents and purposes, normal. Tall, squared-off, metal. But there was no seal on it, no suction barrier to prevent out-gassing, and gouges stood out in the otherwise shining finish.

It stank of corruption.

"Here," tDaer had said that morning, once the silica was done compiling the makeshift wasp's data. A long finger, tapping the screen. "That's where the thermal readings change. That's where they'll be."

She had not wanted to leave her grav bag. She'd even gotten irritated enough in the middle of the night to unzip tDaer's sleeper off hers and curl up as far from hen as she could. Fuck all of that. Fuck this entire expedition.

But her once-friend had whined and cajoled over breakfast.

How can you stop them if you don't know what they're up to? she'd figured. Thought about the plutonium. She'd agreed to go.

The forest had been thankfully inactive that morning. Tharsis had had an occasional flash of gunfire, of shouting, of the howling of dogs and the inhuman cries of a people, she was beginning to understand, who had no language of their own. Shadows played across the ground, twilight twisting out from the boles, ill-defined umbran flitting near, but never drawing close.

There was no blood, no bodies, no signs of any kind of battle. She'd only had one glimpse of a corpse being hauled away, bobbing and twisting in the thin air and low gravity, bloody, skinned.

Adlet activity.

She was grateful she hadn't seen more.

But there was one thing that she caught outside the Lighthouse, bright as a backlit window at high summer noon: the figure. The one from the snowfields. Walking through the antenna forest. Tugging its load behind it. Leaving footprints that hadn't yet been obscured. Other sets that had long evaporated.

Seven of those.

Overlaid, in intent if nothing else.

All leading to the same place.

This place.

A door. A broad and hard door of pitted, stained, rusting steel. It didn't look like it needed explosives to open. A sharp kick would have sufficed.

If blowing something up made Riqan feel better, Tharsis couldn't have cared less.

<Martian? You still with me here?>

tDaer and Ang were doing another loop through the antenna forest. They'd looked into a couple more of the shelters on their way. A morass of gnawed bone and crumbling man-leather those might have been, but both voiders were convinced there was more going on.

Noqumiut, Tharsis thought sarcastically, and wished she could spit. Her fingers itched. <Tell me again why you only brought the one gun? >

<You know as well as I do what we're going to find in here,> he said, and attached a thermite charge to the still fastened latch. <Whole planet's a tomb.>

<We don't know that.>

<Habitats don't go adlet out of fun, Tharsis. Family's never seen an instance where the population was able to sustain itself longer than ten years after that starts.>

<Ten years?>

<Well, Hilda-892 was a bit of a special case. Average is eight months.>

They'd brought a large bag of Jovian float-lamps, little things that ran on nuclear batteries and were practically indestructible. Tharsis only had the one switched on, the silica chip inside anchoring it a comfortable half meter above her head, throwing out a four-meter sphere of light.

<Is adlet activity normal in the Jovians?> she asked, and ran a finger down the outside seam that held her Arran-make knife. The rock machete's sheath was strapped firmly to that same leg, adjusted so she could still reach the inner pocket if she needed to. A gun would have been better.

He was quiet for an unusually long time. <When a habitat destabilizes, food production is the first life-support system that fails. It's designed that way.>

<Yeah, that's not cruel at all.>

<What would you prefer, Martian? The atmo scrubbers?>

<But you let it go for ten years?> Silence. She snorted. <I thought the Tenancy was supposed to eliminate habitat failures.>

Thermite hatched into life, eating through its thick-packed oxygen yolk. The Nepo's bulk stood black against it, the faint glow of his aural energy momentarily obliterated by the burn. <Over a thousand habitats orbit Jupiter directly. Many times that many out in the Lagrange. Even with the Family, it's too much territory to watch.>

<Yeah, but—>

<It's a fucking miracle that the system's held together as long as it has,> he replied, sounding pensive for the first time since she'd met him. <The tech's old, our currency's manipulated against the MSD, we have to literally mandate that families grow babies. Nothing's organic anymore. Without the Landlords propping it up, humanity would have died out a long time ago. Eaten itself. Just like this place.>

The glow of the thermite burn died, revealing a half-eaten door twenty centimeters thick, glowing too hot yet to touch. Beyond it, the darkness beckoned.

<Not on Mars,> Tharsis told him, and punched in a command on her suit's static palm pad, sending a floater through the gap, into the

outbuilding. It was just a room, bare, empty, extending to the outside walls of the building. Nothing remarkable at all. And somehow, that only served to make her more nervous.

<You think you're immune to human nature because you've got a planet?> A derisive grunt sounded over the line.

<Why are you out here?>

The Nepo gestured at his ear. <Switch back to vox,> he said. <Your girlfriend's calling.>

Tharsis rolled her eyes but switched channels anyway. tDaer's voice immediately broke through.

<You two found anything yet?>

<Yeah,> Tharsis replied, and looked back to the door. Riqan was prying it the rest of the way open. Static shields, enough to hold atmo, crackled beneath his fingers. <We're inside.>

<On our way,> the Iapetan ordered, and hen's line fell quiet.

Muted, not off, and Tharsis told herself to keep a lid on further adlet talk. The grad student was punchy enough as it was. The lieutenant was worried about what would happen should a member of their party snap.

tDaer and Ang caught up just as the door fell away. And without any ceremony at all, tDaer pushed up and over the still glowing metal, into the antechamber, and disappeared.

The Jovians followed.

The Arran lingered.

Behind her, she could feel eyes. Hundreds, thousands, of eyes. Watching her. Waiting to see what she was going to do. The faded shades of a twisted past, caught in the energy currents of the forest's radiation, never to escape. Hungry. A ceaseless, undying hunger that could never now be satisfied.

What do you want? she wondered but was grateful that the eyes didn't follow her inside.

The whole place needed a fucking exorcism.

They passed into a narrow room, then a mud-clogged tunnel, falling into a vast dark space only barely illuminated by the spreading floaters.

Tharsis felt as if she was suspended underwater, in the ruin of some ancient cathedral.

In contrast to the desperate crudeness above, the foyer of the sealed complex was civilized, almost beautiful. Smooth stone tiles sealed the icerock in patterns of alternating shapes and color. Clearly set out on an inwell design schematic, the floor and walls and ceiling were all discernible, a neat spread of hallways yawning into the first main chamber in which they were hovering with mathematical precision. Archways stood out in relief against the harsh glow of the mechanical fairy-lights, shadows pulling back as if burned by the sudden influx of energy, after all their time in the cold dark of the Kuiper.

Riqan's voice kept echoing in her ears.

This planet's a tomb.

Oxygen levels were badly depleted in the underground's atmo, temperature deathly low. Only slightly better than those outside. Barely enough to inconvenience the xenocyte in their ENEXes. Tharsis's palm readout looked like the summer weather report for the upmost accessible regions of Olympus Mons.

<Right below the death zone,> she muttered.

<What do you mean?> Ang asked.

<Conditions are only barely survivable,> the lieutenant explained. <Even professional mountaineers wouldn't try something like this without exogear.>

<What's a mountaineer?>

Riqan's wrappered hands twitched on his gun. <Switch channels or shut up. tDaer? Thoughts?>

<Should have brought a mapping wasp,> tDaer mused into the radio, turning henself around with minute little flaps of a hand. <This place could be huge.>

<I'm only seeing one heat reading that's significantly above ambient,> Angakkuq replied, and flicked up a projection on his palm pad. <Half a kilometer down.>

A round portal was set deep in the floor below them, rimmed with blasted, broken metal, as if the door had been blown out. And the lieutenant had a sudden flash of the figure from the snowfields drifting down towards it, a heavy burden in tow, silent. Grieved.

<How big?> tDaer asked.

The Trojan twisted the image, considering. <Large enough to be a reactor. She could be there.>

<We should split up, do a thorough search,> Riqan said. <Just to be sure we don't miss anything.>

<We can't. What if—>

<There is no what-if, tDaer. The human population is long dead. Might as well figure out what's around before we go confront the spider in the basement.>

<I refuse to believe that. This is where the species succeeded, where all else failed.> Even over the radio, tDaer sounded frantic. <This was the perfect society.>

<Maybe the perfect society is one that's fucking dead, then,> he shot back, and gestured at Tharsis. <You go with your girlfriend. I'll take Ang.>

<I am not a fucking girl, Ri—>

Tharsis hit mute on her radio and hit the gravity on her boots to descend.

Somebody, she figured, was going to snap.

ARRANS, Caleb had been told, lacked the ability to dream.

He still could, though. He often did. Of the Rockies under winter snows and summer breezes, of greased gears in atmospheric aircraft bays, of clouds gone black under the weight of their loads at the top of the sky. Of monsters with human faces, howling even as they died. Of dark hair and sad eyes and soft hands tucked into his own. Of a woman he'd loved desperately, quietly, without ever saying a word to her about it.

People, places, long vanished from his life. Memories. Slippery, flighty things that almost always vanished before he woke.

But he dreamed most often of her, and even though he couldn't see her face in his mind anymore, he'd always known who it was.

She was there now. Standing next to him before a wide window, ice stretched out in front of them, curving away off the edge of the world, a stealth-hulled craft rising away from it, visible only where its mass sliced through the starfield.

Her hand was in his. Clammy-cold. Squeezing hard enough to snap bone.

They were both in uniform, and he didn't understand why her heart was breaking.

It was the clearest image of her, of Eliza Rallison, that he'd had in years. Had to be important. Why else would it be coming through so strongly? But he couldn't remember, not clearly, not in waking, why they had been there, what they were watching, or why it was forcing its way through now.

Made all of this harder. Made it all that much more difficult to understand.

He woke in considerably less pain than he'd been expecting.

It took effort to rouse himself, overcome the murderous ache in his gut, but it took no time to take stock of his surroundings. The island was less than an acre wide, the area around its little house seeded with soft, low vegetation. Hardly natural, though. The island was something that Ibbies could win in yearly government lotteries or buy outright. Settle. Use as they pleased.

These places were stashed far away from the urban sprawl. The city's central spires were only barely visible on the horizon, and then, obscured by the thick rain falling there. But even as far out to sea as he was, he could still hear the Arcna broadcasting. It was insane. She normally took breaks, sometimes days of breaks.

The Rallarhu had left him there. For what reason, to what end, he had no idea.

Fifty years he'd served by that woman's side, he'd been told, but his Journals spoke of nothing but rage between them now.

What had they seen in Noqumiut?

What the fuck had they left out there?

He probably had organ damage, and his abdominal muscles had been sliced open. Neither injury could be fixed by a few hours in a puddle of goo. He wasn't going to die any time soon, but he needed surgery, time, and rest. Caleb didn't regenerate like one of those not-humans in his granddad's old comic books; as long as he was alive, he had to have his injuries conventionally treated like everyone else.

Beat up like this, he couldn't swim back.

Tyr would have gotten back, at least. Nothing stopped that animal when he wasn't of a mind to be stopped.

"Fuck," Caleb grumbled, staring off at the iron pinnacles, retreating into the distance. He went back to the little house, to see if he could get the island's engine working.

He got lucky. An hour of uncomfortable maneuvering inside the little wheelhouse got everything moving again back towards shore, and whatever the hell it was the Rallarhu was trying to hide.

CHAPTER
FORTY-TWO

THOSE HOURS SPENT CRAWLING through Noqumiut's underbelly were the most unbearable of Tharsis's life.

The spaces spoke of what the stories did—human activity, human community, striving towards the Arcna's perfect society. Alive and vibrant in some distant past. Abandoned now to the detritus of human existence. Toothbrushes were still snapped in their holders in the shower room they found, mold growing half-dead in the grout of the tiles. Towels were still wrapped around their hold-bars. Trinkets floated gently in faint air currents. Equipment stood as if abandoned mid-use, and instruments bobbed in sterilely packed containers. Amino combines lay in ruins, gaping, shattered.

It was all disconcerting, terrifying in the vague way that an abandoned hospital might have been terrifying. But there were none of Ang's tuurngait, no umbran, no echoes of any kind. Nothing resembling the montage of nightmares lurking topside, in the forest.

Not that there weren't still physical things that whispered of horrors. One hallway boasted labs, deep rooms of empty medical vats and smashed silic processors. Another was sealed tight ten meters back, the plug harder than concrete. Bullet holes and dark stains riddled tile surfaces, and evidence of chemical fires was burned into hemispherical containers that seemed to be everywhere. One room held nothing but bones. Another, empty oxygen tanks. Still another, broken-down engine parts, horns and pipes and magnetizers rusted beyond use.

Most doorways, however, were empty voids, blank spaces staring dumbly into the temporary illumination of the search. Empty. Useless.

<Looks like a pop-'n'-play facility to me,> Tharsis commented as they passed another such room, continuing on down the fourth hall. <Look at the design. It had to have functioning gravity and everything at one time.>

<Prefabricated?> tDaer asked from above. <So, they, what? Excavated part of the forest, built it into the ground?>

<Probably. Or maybe the facility was built with this in mind, like there would be people out here taking care of the Lighthouse. It sort of looks like something the Silicone Age would have built. Maybe...> the lieutenant began and stopped.

In front of them was a wall. With the largest door yet. Two and a half meters high, arched, made of what looked like real wood.

<Library,> tDaer said, shining hen's own flashlight over a brass plaque. <Odd design.>

<Old Earth,> Tharsis replied, and stepped forward, pushing ancient pine wide.

It took six floaters to throw enough light into the space to get a proper look at it, and even then, it made no sense, richly appointed in dark woods and leathers and plush wool carpets. Nothing was bolted down, as it had been in other locations, so it was a floating mess of furniture and books and ends of lamps. tDaer went paddling through it quietly, radio generating only static as hen caught books and released them again with what was no doubt a frown.

Tharsis cast around from the floor, trying to catch a glimpse of anything that might help. A few of the titles she recognized, but most were written in unfamiliar languages. One book completely disintegrated as she touched it.

<See anything?>

Another flash, the penumbra ripping open in the center of the room, and that figure coming in, unburdened now and faster. Moving towards a central shelf, far in the back.

<Over here.>

tDaer met her, swimming down as Tharsis trudged over, gravity fluctuating painfully.

<What is it?>

<I don't know,> the Arran replied, and reached out for it, sensing her hand pass through others—bigger, smaller, older, younger—to pull it free.

The bookcase groaned, the furniture shifted. A hard current of cold air poured out around them.

A dark room, set behind the wall.

More cave than chamber, the feel of the ground uneven, the shape oblong. Sending a float-lamp into the narrow space did little to alleviate the darkness. The white light seemed to die, splattering to exhaustion across the spray-sealed surface of the hewn icerock. Penumbra energy. Stained with grief.

That figure from the snowfields was there, seated in a floor-bolted stool. Spread out in front of her was a book.

Fairy tales, bedtime stories.

In the ruins of Noqumiut, in the end of the Heliosphere itself.

<Fuck,> tDaer breathed, hissing air through hen's rebreather. The sharp poke of it in her ear drew Tharsis's attention up, up to where the voider was, wedged in between the termination point of that smooth surface, and the rough expanse of ceiling.

<What is it?>

In response, tDaer sent up a float-lamp across the surface, scattering light through the contents.

A tank. It was a tank. Nearly three meters long and filled with some half-frozen substance leeching blue.

Over a weave. Organic. Biological. Like the roots of some weird tree, spreading and twisting in all directions, some thinner than hairs, other thick as fingers. All of it, radiating out from one central point-cluster, the shape mimicking the shape of a human body.

<Wetware,> Tharsis growled.

tDaer made a strange noise.

Riqan cocked his head. <It looks organic.>

<Probably is,> tDaer said. <A human-derived system will assume that body pattern, the nervous system still thinking there's a physical body that needs to be maintained…>

Tharsis's mind was spinning. That, right there, was the purest violations of the Tenancy Accords there was. If the Rossen knew, if he could be told, if proof was offered…had he not seen it when he came here? <That entire discipline was destroyed in the Scient's purges.>

<Obviously not,> tDaer said.

Walking around to a cluster of electrochemical data converters in the back, Tharsis found a plaque. A strange, obtuse little thing, plasma-cut from something completely different and welded. The lack of sensation in her fingertips from frustrating; running her gloved hand over it, Tharsis couldn't tell if it was plastic or metal. It was wrong, though, and so was whatever was written on it, some type of odd glyph-forms that seemed to fade when viewed directly.

<What is that?> tDaer asked, over from where hen was examining the control system, data displays, screens long since cracked apart, rubber components brittle. <Found something?>

<I don't know,> she admitted, and tapped the glass. <Is this thing still alive?>

But before she could check for a reaction, the radio crackled and Riqan's voice filled their ears.

<Ladies, we found something you both should see.>

tDaer's body stiffened. <Riqan, for the last fucking time, I'm not—>

Tharsis groaned. <What is it?>

<Get out here. Follow the lights.>

<What. Is. It?>

<Don't worry, Martian, you're going to love it.>

She gave the tank one last glance as they left the room. But if the wetware was still alive, it gave no sign.

No mylings.

The Jovians were down one of the hallways exactly opposite, oriented away from the heat shield. At the end of it, a vast room gaped out into the icerock, crowned with a steel-hard ceiling of methane snowfall.

A room full of tiny, coffin-like capsules.

Those hemispheres they'd seen everywhere in the facility.

Each and every one empty.

The same name tagged on each.

USSF Padua Anthony

That acronym was familiar. One of her old history lessons. Which one though, Tharsis couldn't recall.

<Stasis pods, Euphemism tech,> Riqan said, from the entrance. <Thousands of them.>

<The stories are true. She brought down an exodus craft,> the lieutenant breathed, dread welling in her.

<None of these are big enough for a fully grown person,> tDaer said. <Must have been children. Young ones, too, if the size is anything to go by. I doubt you could get an Earth-born kid over four or five into one of these.>

<That can't be,> Ang said, something wounded in his words. <All the stories indicate that people came to her of their own free will.>

<No, no, it makes perfect sense. She was setting up a perfect society. You can't do that with adults. Children would be a better choice. It's what I'd do if I were trying to build it up. Start from scratch, take away the contamination of previous socializations.> There was wonder in tDaer's voice. <This... this is how Noqumiut was born. The eggs from which it hatched.>

<Doesn't answer the primary question here, though,> Riqan said. <Why'd your perfect little Noqumiut fail—>

<—and where the hell's the Arcna?> Tharsis finished, sick.

They spent half an hour amid the stasis containers cracked open like mussels breathing in the shallow waters beneath thick sea-ice. It was an eerie place, long cold, long dead, with barely a whisper of energy to it. But here and there, Tharsis caught a glimpse of children.

Curled up in deep hibernation.

Being leveraged out with cold, uncaring hands.

Dragged away naked, covered in suspension fluid, screaming.

Seeing that last part, she shut off her goggles, struggling to keep herself together.

<Hey,> tDaer said, pushing next to her, squeezing her shoulder hard enough to read through the suit. <You okay?>

No, she wanted to answer, and knew that none of them would understand. <I've been six hours in my gear. I should head back.>

<Not alone,> Riqan said quickly. <tDaer, you go with her.>

<Like fuck I'm leaving this before I have to,> the Iapetan retorted.

<I'll go,> Ang said, oddly subdued. <I'll go. It's fine.>

Despite the fact that thruster fuel was running low in both of their ENEXs, Tharsis insisted on altitude once they hit the forest. She couldn't face them: those wordless umbran, ghosts of wordless children torn from safety, hope, into this horror. Echoes in the energy, nothing sentient left, but still more than she could handle.

Angakkuq didn't speak until they were back in the air lock. Hood pushed back a little too soon, eyes closed, he so unlike that confident, wannabe philosopher-Tok she'd come to know.

He looked scared.

"What do you suppose happened to them?" he asked, hoarse from sucking pure oxygen for the past seven hours.

"I think they died. I think they all died."

"Not the kids. I mean, the people who came here to help her bu—"

"It's the same fucking thing, Ang. Same fucking answer."

He didn't ask her anything more. Just took a couple pills of something and crawled straight into his bag when he got fully inside, not even bothering to seal up his exogear first.

Tharsis changed out her thruster fuel-bottles and oxygen filters and dunked her ENEX back in its tank to knock the xenocytes back into dormancy.

After she was sure he was asleep, she threw her gear back on and headed out, fast as she could.

THRUSTER TANKS in her suit changed out, it was an easy trip back to the divedrive. Tharsis kept her eyes firmly up and away from the snowy wastes. Away from that figure trudging on, endlessly.

Stop thinking about it, she ordered herself, and pressed on.

Inside the divedrive, she tapped up the comm system, opened her bucket back to the *Barachiel,* or wherever the fuck the Rossen was.

Despite the inevitable consequences, she wanted to dive back. Tell them.

Flee.

But that would sign the voiders' death warrants, something she couldn't do. And the plutonium had been off-loaded with the rest of the gear, a big black package tied to the base of the shelter. She couldn't leave them here with that. Not until she knew what the fuck was going

on. Whatever had happened to the children of the *Padua Anthony* here
—whatever had happened to the dreamers of Ang's fantasies, or the
heroes of tDaer's theories—the Rossen had allowed it to stand.
However unthinkable. However illegal.

Had he known? About the wetware?

Tharsis couldn't see Sergeant Olin, who'd grown up in the dark
days, just permitting this.

Something else was going on.

So, she dropped her message in its comm bucket and headed back.

No sooner had she closed the shelter air lock, pressurization cycle
initiated, than a frantic call came over the radio.

<Both of you, get the fuck back here!>

Tharsis held her breath. Fuck. Fuck…

<Tharsis! Ang! Somebody pick up the void-burned line!>

Sweating, she tapped her earpiece. <I'm here. What the fuck?>

<Good, Tharsis, fuck. Where's Ang?>

<Right here,> a sleepy voice answered.

<What is going on?> Tharsis demanded, loud as she could, over
any potential questions about her whereabouts.

<Problems.>

<You find the Arcna yet?>

<Stop wasting atmo and get your asses down here. Now.>

THE ROSSEN'S dog had volunteered to help fill the chinks in the patrol detail. He was sitting in the dead center of the air lock, staring out at the streets beyond, ears pricked, eyes fixed, and Lanin found himself just watching the big animal as he sipped at his own very human coffee.

It had taken the chaplain and one of the sergeants whose family bred dogs to get the story out of Tyr, when the dog had finally limped back. Once the initial blast of hunt-rage cleared. Animals were not good at narrating events. There was a reason it took two full semesters to get through *Wardog of Mars*.

The gist, once through, was bad.

The Rossen, taking a broken bottle to the gut. Getting skyhooked by the Rallarhu. He could have been floating around out there in the void for all any of them knew, and with no way to retrieve him if he was. The base's only rockjump was scrap now, destroyed in its guardhouse hangar by the explosion.

Outside, despite the rain that had been falling off and on all day, the crowds were starting to gather again. Ibbies, mostly, but quite a few outwellers as well. Trojans, for the most part, stunted and yellow-eyed. He was no sighted man, but Lanin could tell the energy coming off the mob was no good. He could feel it in his bones.

He'd ordered a couple of the heavy artillery guns brought up out of storage.

All two of them.

It was their only base defense weaponry. And like everything else, they were old. But Nyes had run a tight shop, so they were oiled, clean, and fire-ready that morning.

Tyr, from his low-level imagery grumble, agreed with that assessment.

The Arcna was still talking. It was one of the many things about this Propagation that made no sense. Normally, she took breaks, a few hours of transmission a day, and no more.

She hadn't stopped for nearly a day and a half.

The whole thing was fucking strange.

The radio on his belt buzzed.

"Talk to me."

<Major. Hope I didn't worry you too much.>

Thank fuck. "Caleb, good to hear from you," he drawled, smiling a little. Nice to have some good news. "So, what's goin' on?"

A pause. <Oh, you know. The Rallarhu flung me off onto some island. The usual.>

<Good to hear. You enjoy your break?>

<Not at all. Look, the islands are all being moved, shuffled around. Nervous tenants, I'd guess. But it's a maze right now. Can't find my way back.>

"I'll get a mapping wasp out."

<Thanks.>

"And Olin?"

<Yeah?>

"I'm glad you're not dead."

<Me too. Get me that wasp. It's foggy as fuck out here.>

ANG HADN'T ASKED where Tharsis had been. Just popped into the air lock, exogear rendering his face emotionless, gloved hand waving vaguely in the direction of the forest.

Nothing more came over the radio, no matter how many times she asked.

<At least let me know you're alive!> she finally said.

As they reached the facility's main entrance, Riqan's voice came back. Tinny. <We're alive. Get down here.>

The bottom pit doors yawned wide as they descended through the static field and in. Scattered float-lamps revealed a corkscrew stairway, spiraling down into the planetoid's heart. Without a word, they both engaged thrusters, diving down, diving in, her plane of reference shifting to accommodate.

A shaped charge had ripped through the metal portal, she could see, a long time ago. Ahead of them, below them, falling into that darkness, was a figure.

Traveling alone with that heavy burden.

Grief-rage clung like dust to every imaginable surface.

It burned Tharsis's lungs, sent her mind reeling.

<We must be near the bottom of the heat shield,> Angakkuq observed as the shaft bottomed out.

<We're near the reactor, right?> Around them was another series of archways, leading away at painful angles, their alcoves lit by hesitant float-lamps, equipment shattered and covered in dust, placement mirroring those upstairs. Old gravity plating tugged at them in every direction, fighting with the natural mig.

Her brain jammed up; the lieutenant grabbed for the wall to breathe through it. Ang, born in the mig of some lonely Trojan 'roid, had no such orientation issue, and pushed clean past her. Silent. Towards the only open door, backlit with so many floaters it was almost too harsh to look at.

Alone, Tharsis caught something. In that glow.

Silhouettes. Three. Standing in the threshold in eternal echo.

Her curiosity overcame her lack of balance, watching them. Bizarre, that such a small little moment would impress so much more deeply than anything else.

The tallest of them stared back into the room, the one on the left slumping back against the doorway, hand on its forehead. But the last of them fell to hands and knees in the thick dust of the floor, ripping off its hood and rebreather.

Screamed, dark hair freezing in the space around it, world-ending despair ripping loose, shaking the very foundations of the forest...

<Tharsis?>

The knife's edge panic sliced the penumbra echo away.

<I'm here, just disoriented by the descent,> she replied, and knocked the gravity on in her boots, forcing herself to stand on the surface beneath her, see it as floor, not wall. To move into the chamber beyond.

Tharsis had seen that place before. Her dreams that weren't dreams.

A vast room, lit only by the weak glow coming from the windows of some vast, heavy machine, riveted together with bolts bigger than her arm, skin configuration familiar, alien.

On its side, in the chill dust that clung to it, somebody had scratched out an epitaph.

WITH HOPE WE LAUNCHED THEM

WITH FAITH WE BUILT THEM

BUT IN THE END, WE DAMNED THEM

TO LIVE THE NIGHTMARES THAT OTHERS FANCIED DREAMS

AND SO IN THIS HEAVEN I LEARNED THE TRUTH

THAT WE ARE ALL OF US...

<Hypocrites,> she whispered, finishing the sentence, staring up at the words. The same handwriting that graced the entrance lintel. Tharsis could almost see, almost perceive, who'd written it. It wasn't the Arcna. She could feel that in her bones.

<Excuse me?> tDaer replied.

Tharsis blinked, her vision snapping back to the present. The voiders were clustered around a control panel. <What is this place?>

<Power bank,> Ang supplied. <It's a Silicone Age–style nuclear generator. Fissile. Radiation is harvested along with the electricity to feed the field. Heats the place too.>

<Generator,> Tharsis echoed. <Who's been resupplying the fuel rods?>

<Excellent question, Martian,> Riqan said, and he sounded somewhere between bemusement and anger. <I'm sure the answer will be fascinating.>

tDaer rapped hen's earpiece. <Riqan, we need some thermite.>

<Found something?>

<Yeah. The control room, I think.>

It took an hour and a half to cut through a thick steel door, half-obscured in the far wall, behind the battery's machinery. Enough time for Tharsis to notice the little things about it. How the dirt was piled against it. How it looked as if it had been locked from the outside. How the footprints ended there—but only one set.

The lieutenant didn't understand it.

Until she did.

Inside, in the Lighthouse transmission system, tucked away in the deepest, safest part of the entire facility, there was a body.

Anchored in an ancient hammock.

A decrepit, mummified body, teeth marks scraped against the bare, jutting bones of its lower legs and left arm. The right was mostly intact, fingers curled around the radio's mic. Hair trailed away from its head like cobwebs; tatters of clothing only barely clung to its wasted chest.

And in front of it was the control panel.

A wall of blinking, self-renewing lights, the bulbs reminding her of that tumor from Humphreys's auditorium ceiling. Another time, another place, it seemed, so far away as to be almost nonexistent.

Cables wove through the panel's bulk, electrical and chemical and biological pathways weaving in and out of each other, held together by age-cracked rubbers and careful, more recent tapings. It had been repaired more than once, the lieutenant could see, but her knowledge was limited, her perspective narrow. She could see it, but she couldn't quite see what it was doing.

<Tharsis?>

She picked out one line. One trace. It stood out to her for some reason she couldn't quite place, and she pushed around the desiccated corpse for a better look.

An indicator bulb, different from the rest. Blinking.

<It's all wired in,> she said, checking the labels on the panel, the Silicone English markings starting to make sense. They were old and hand-etched into the metal facings, right over the old phonetics. <Everything, I think, it's all routed through here.>

<What do you mean?>

Transmitting, the silic said. Transmitting, with nobody talking.

<I'm no expert on this scat, but it looks like she rewired the entire panel for broadcast to every repeater, every end station in the

network.> She pulled the float-lamp down for a better look. <She's got a feed set for every channel possible, flooding the spectrum.>

<So, this is the Arcna?> Ang asked, tone odd. <This is her?>

<It can't be,> tDaer replied tersely.

<It is,> Tharsis said quietly, and nobody spoke for a while.

Confronted by the corpse, it seemed impossible that somebody could do this to themselves. It must have taken the Arcna years to record all the broadcasts, all the speeches, to ensure that it would be deployed just so.

Why? What had she been hoping for? Had she believed in her message? Had she known what kind of chaos it would bring? Had she been hoping for endless conflict, or had she thought her words could truly remake the Heliosphere, their very species, if they were just repeated long enough?

The deception was shocking in its enormity. Tharsis was struck by how premeditated it must have been, how much effort would have gone into it. The entire *Book of Shoals* amounted to over ten thousand hours of recordings. Ten thousand hours of grand visions, anecdotes, philosophical ramblings. Spoken, all of it, by the same person. Ten thousand hours. More, most likely, if there were recording yet to be broadcast.

Must have taken her years to compile it all, program each clip to some discreet value, key it for just this situation or that input coming in off the networks. That must have been what the wetware in the tank was for. Intelligent sorting of ever-more delirious insanity, reliable memory for the Arcna as her own body broke down and her mind failed under these extreme conditions. Encryption, too, probably. Or maybe…

There were no answers, Tharsis realized. Maybe there would never be answers.

Her Gran would have said that was fine. Contemplating evil was a sick game.

<I'm gonna go find tDaer,> she said, and turned away from the backlit decay around them.

<What?> Riqan taunted. <None of that famous Martian agony over the departed? That famous mercy for all sinners? You aren't going to pray or something?>

He couldn't have cut her deeper if he'd hit her with that damn machete; she clenched a fist, trying to keep her own anger down. As if there was any prayer that could fix this. Eight centuries of horror. Eight centuries of pointless destruction.

<tDaer's not here. On the off chance hen's decided to strip down and walk into the void, I think we should go look.>

<Suit yourself,> he said, and nudged a distraught Angakkuq. <Come. I want a second look at that generator.>

Tharsis found the Iapetan collapsed in a dark corner of the main rotunda, head between hen's hands, ENEX stripped to hen's waist. Hen's knuckles were white, squeezing tight into hen's bare scalp, broken nails a deathly gray. Cobalt skin was beginning to take on the first waxy flush of frostbite.

"I couldn't leave it on a second longer," tDaer explained, words barely audible and body curled, defeated by more than the weak atmo pressure. Utterly, fatally, raw. "I… I couldn't spend another minute in that place. The Arcna… all these years… all the work… for this…"

<You are going to freeze to death,> Tharsis told hen firmly up over the top of her own raging confusion at the sight. She kicked around, pulling at the edges of the Iapetan's exogear. <Put your fuckin' suit back on.>

tDaer lashed out, throwing Tharsis into the opposite wall with enough force to knock her lungs empty. "What difference does it make?" hen screamed. That voice, normally so confident, was shrill, thin, in the weak atmo. "What the fuck difference does it make, Tharsis?! Why should I care if I'm dead?! I never wanted any of this! "

Tharsis took a deep breath, gathering herself, checking the outside temperature on the palm read-out one more time. 215 K, .35 ATM. A minute wasn't going to kill her, just hurt like hell.

The killing squeeze of cold was almost unbearable as she unsealed herself, the air reedy, too thin, barely breathable. But she'd been cold back home, every one of Mars's endless winters, and she just managed to keep herself from shaking as she pushed to sit down next to tDaer.

"I didn't expect this either, you know," she replied, trying not to look at her once friend's ashen skin. "This is the last fucking thing I expected to find out here."

"That's not what I meant," tDaer grumbled through waxy lips. "I mean, to put up with all the scat in the system, to deal with… deal with this."

"What are you talking about?"

"Life!" the Iapetan snapped, rage breaking in the cold. "Who the fuck had the right to bring me into this fucked up world in the first place? I never asked for any of this!"

"Nobody ever asks to be born. It doesn't work that way," Tharsis replied, confused.

"Yeah, other people make that fucking decision for us, don't they? Our fucking Landlords, thinking… thinking they have the right to just make us any way they want, make us into anything they want, when… all the answers here…" Those normally bright spots along tDaer's neck flashed darkly. "It's all scat. It's always been scat."

"So what if this is Noqumiut?" Tharsis replied, forcing it. "Fuck it, fuck the Landlords, right? They don't own us." She reached over again, pulled the Iapetan's ENEX up over hen's freezing skin. Her own fingers were starting to ache. The lack of atmo would kill them before the cold did. "They don't get to decide what we are. They don't have to be obeyed."

"Yeah, fuck 'em," tDaer replied, face pinched, words hollow. "Fuck Noqumiut. It was only the one place that was supposed to actually be worth a void-burned thing, where there were answers…"

Tharsis rubbed a cold, naked shoulder. Her lungs were burning. Her lips were starting to crack. "It's too goddamn cold for this spider scat."

"You're still missing the point."

"Yeah? Explain it to me once we're not in danger of dying."

CHAPTER
FORTY-FOUR

WHEN THEY FINALLY ALL rendezvoused back at the pressure tent, Angakkuq was in a bad way.

Their Trojan had dissolved into a weird fugue state, barely talking, barely moving. Tharsis had had to strip his exogear off him, and once she had, he'd grabbed the silic and the chip out of his suit and tucked himself half into his sleeping bag and lost himself. Refusing even the heated, sweet amino smoothie Tharsis pressed into his hand.

Somebody was going to snap.

The only question was who was it going to be.

Tharsis would have been more scared if she hadn't been so goddamn cold.

Riqan couldn't have been more visibly indifferent if he'd tried, though he tucked into his own meal packet with little gusto. tDaer had barely pulled henself free of that strange mood on the thrust back and hadn't even bothered putting hen's exogear away. Tharsis felt as if she'd been wrapped in raw, greasy wool, straight off the shearing. Dark and airless and numbing.

Odds and ends of their gear floated freely about the shelter, a single float-lamp turned on as if by afterthought, the entire scene one of defeat.

"Okay," Angakkuq finally said, "I think I've got a theory, if anybody cares to hear it."

tDaer, still wrapped up in hen's own little world, didn't reply.

Riqan, lounging back with an almost offensive casualness, just waved a hand. "Go."

Still in his bag, Ang pushed over to plug his handheld silic into the projection unit. The space between the scattered members of the expedition lit up with a linear diagram. "The, uh, wide-spectrum scans support an internal structure, umm, consistent with that of a Euphemism-Era nuclear battery station. It's got some kind of weird time lock on it, like it's only accessible at certain points in the decay cycle, which is really unusual. It's open right now, so maybe that doesn't matter…"

"Just get to the point," Riqan ordered.

The smaller Jovian cringed. "Anyway, umm, I've got the silic calculating power requirements, decay rates of the various chambers inside of it, all that. I'd guess, based on how much material this thing needs to run and the energy requirements of an average Trans-Nep Lighthouse array, it's ineffective once the plutonium falls below the first half-life value."

"What's that mean?" Tharsis asked, forcing bites of dinner down her own throat. She wasn't hungry—her stomach ached, actually—but if she'd learned anything at the Academy, it was to eat when one could.

"Getting our plutonium was extremely difficult. Took me a year and a half to coordinate it, and even then, they were charging me expedited rates."

"The Naven," Tharsis said quietly, and they all looked at her. "It'd be my guess. Who else?"

"Or maybe it was others, like us, catching the signal like I did and coming out," tDaer said, dull. "Does it fucking matter?"

"What's the half-life on this particular isotope?" Riqan yawned.

"283?" Ang asked. "A little under ninety years."

"That's more than the time between Propagations."

"Significantly more, in some instances," tDaer said. "Ang, you're reaching."

The rail-thin Jovian retreated back into his calculations, and Riqan, rolling his eyes, picked it up. "Eighty-nine-point-seven years could reasonably be expected from a system that's running on perfectly refined plutonium. Older stuff, maybe something pulled out of a reactor or weapon system elsewhere, it's possible that the actual battery life is much lower."

The lieutenant groaned. "Like the seventy year gap we saw between the Third and Fourth Propagations? Or sixty-three, between the Fifth and Sixth." And a single piece fell into horrible place. Dinner bubbled in its heater by her knee. She couldn't have cared less. "She tied the signal into the battery life, created a hostage situation. Keep her signal alive or lose the exodus craft."

"Lose the remnants of the original human genome," Riqan added.

"Fuck the genome," tDaer said dismissively, and turned back to Ang. "We have what we need to rest the system, right? How much time do we have?"

"That's what I'm trying to figure out right now. But we're already at, what, seventy-five years? I guess…" He glanced back down at the silic. "I take it back. No guesses. Critical power levels will be reached in less than a month, maybe sooner. At that point, like Tharsis said, the forest is going to die, and we lose her word forever."

tDaer nodded, short, tight. "Tomorrow, then."

Tharsis held up a hand, cutting in. "What?"

"Well, we have to reset it."

"Fucking why?" she demanded, and looked around at the voiders, hating them all. "Heliosphere-wide totals on Propagation deaths exceed a hundred and fifty million. That's like a tenth of the people who have ever lived under the Tenancy. Dead, because some madwoman locked herself in a room and ate herself to death. And you, what, want to continue it? Doesn't that strike you as insane?"

"Why's it insane? Her theories, everything that's obviously set up here, are sound."

The lieutenant forced herself not to groan. "Sound?"

"Sound. Complete isolation, control of socialization from conception, perfectly descriptive language, a whole host of volunteers dedicated to the idea—"

"Those were toddlers. Babies. They didn't volunteer for scat."

"We'll do it right this time!" tDaer shot back, defensive, manic. "Maybe… maybe she didn't have the resources out here to handle it. Maybe the other Landlords didn't keep their own obligations to her on—"

"Resources? Babies are not resources for experimentation," Tharsis snapped, rage building in her chest. "She fucking tortured god only knows how many kids to insanity and death and—"

"That's your theory."

"All we have are theories, tDaer! There are no answers here, none! You're just substituting what you want to believe for what actually happened!"

"Ladies—"

"Fuck off, Riqan, I'm not fucking female! Tharsis, look—"

"Ladies!" the Nepo roared. "Where'd Angakkuq go?"

The Trojan's bag was empty, silic abandoned.

The indicator light on the air lock was blinking red.

In use.

"Fuck," Tharsis groaned, and pushed out of her hammock, fast as she could. The controls offered her no options for an emergency open, no way to get to him until the system reset. "Ang!" she yelled, banging on the stiff plastic seal. "Angakkuq! I know you can hear me, what are you doing?"

No answer, except for a faint yellow-gray glow drifting back to her, through the penumbra. The color of despair, she remembered from somewhere. She keyed on the radio.

"Don't do anything stupid! Wait for me outside!"

"What are you doing?" Riqan asked dryly, sipping at his dinner as Tharsis began yanking on her own ENEX. "I mean, really?"

She fought the main zipper up. "He's just had his entire belief system blasted to dust. You think he's not going to do something stupid?"

"What if he does?" the Nepo challenged. "It's his own business."

"His own business? If he goes out there and kills himself?"

"I don't own his 'roid."

"So, just like that, he's worthless?" She looked over to tDaer in disbelief. "Come on..."

"Riqan's right. His life is his to take if he fuckin' wants. What difference does it make?"

The light dinged white, and Tharsis pushed back into the translucent plug of space as the hatch spiraled open. "It makes a difference," she said, knowing how she must sound to the voiders and not caring in the slightest. "Makes a difference to me."

Depressurization took thirty seconds—an eternity—and when she was finally spit out above the snowfields, Tharsis despaired.

He'd taken the sled.

Zooming towards the forest.

<Ang!> she yelled into the radio. No answer, not even static.

The lieutenant hit the thrusters in her boots and took off after him.

It was no contest between the sled and her own weak jets; he was soon out of sight. Still, she pushed, burning fast and hard, until his contrails came back into focus.

After that desperate push, Tharsis almost overshot him, static-tethered dead center over the forest, holding on to the edge of the sled. Bobbing. Looking for all the world like some diver on the Vastitas Ocean back home, contemplating the Lyot Depths.

The look of a man who had a long descent before him.

The radiation of the boles rose up around them, glowing white-green in the penumbra. Within it, umbran were watching, knowing, malice rolling up into the waves of energy. The lieutenant's stomach clenched hard around the few bites of rehydrated lamb she'd choked down.

<Ang,> she tried again, managing to hold herself a meter or two away. <Angakkuq, you should come back to the shelter.>

He rotated down, goggles to the world beneath them. Despair flooded the void around him. <I loved her.>

<I know.>

<I wanted to believe, that she... that there were answers. That things could be different.>

<There are, Ang, it can be. Just come back to the shelter.>

<The tuurngait here, Tharsis, you see them. Do they know her mind? Is she here, among them, speaking her glory?>

<There's nothing here worth knowing,> Tharsis said, as carefully as she could. <But there are other things out there. Things worth learning. Worth dedicating yourself to.>

He flung himself into a slow spin, back around to face her with the blank space of his hood. <No,> he said, <there's not.>

He dug the fingers of his suit under the edge of his hood and zipped the whole thing open, neck to groin.

<No!> Tharsis screamed, and fired and dove, but she overcalculated and overshot, struggling to get control, to slow, to turn. Precious seconds wasted

Fifteen, exactly.

Too long.

Death light was already rising, white and dark at the same time, ghosting in the currents of the forest's radiation. His exposed body was already turning blue, eyes iced, moisture boiling away. Catching onto a rail, Tharsis reached out with an unsteady hand to try to close them, but the lids were frozen in place.

His expression was empty.

Stiff. Extinguished.

Buzzing, the earpiece cut through the numbness descending back down on her. <You found him, Martian?>

<Oh, yeah, I found him,> she snapped back so loudly she could hear the feedback crackle in her own earpiece. <Walked out into the void. You happy?>

<You bringing the sled back?>

<Jesus Christ, give the dead a moment, won't you?>

A strangled little sound hit the line. <He's nothing but meat. Cut him loose. Bring the sled back. Fuck your girlfriend for me, she's downright unmanageable right now. Silic came back with power levels dipping to emergency in less than twenty-four hours. We're doing this, whether you like it or not.>

Before Tharsis could answer, put all the boiling disgust she felt for the Nepo into words, she caught a glimpse of the divedrive.

Sleek and graceful against the starfield.

The sun only barely discernible beyond.

Twenty-four hours.

Would it be possible to get a team here in that amount of time? A deepvoider, something, to come dismantle this insanity? The technology was ancient, but it was still operational. Somebody had to know how to fix it, how to stop it. Olin—the Rossen—was a capable technician, wasn't he? He could fix this. Maintain the forest, the connection to the exodus craft, win the Arcna's sick little game.

But he hadn't. He'd shot himself instead. Why?

"He wouldn't compromise," she whispered into the humid pinch of her rebreather. Not the sergeant she knew. Not that man.

<What's that?>

Riqan. Tharsis blanched.

Over thirty lifetimes ago, Caleb Ross had made a choice to leave this place alone. Maybe Sergeant Olin deserved his chance at it.

<I'm gonna need some time,> she said, locked on the sphere of the divedrive in the distance. <Just give me some time.>

CHAPTER
FORTY-FIVE

ON A GOOD DAY, it took no longer than a few hours to get to the edge of Old Town from Humphryes.

That day was not a good day.

Passing through the tight, twisting slots that made up the administrative heart of the Inner Shoals, Caleb noticed workers battening down windows, locking doors, retreating into their buildings as if they were fortresses. The streets were studiously empty but for police, whose presence seemed to increase with every block. Cobblestone pavements, heated from beneath by rumbling engines, were smoking, and between that and the rain, fog clung to every surface.

The neon was dark. The little cafes and shops and pleasure-places lay empty.

He passed one, a bar, where two Ibbies were loading bottles of liquor into a deep handcart. Employees maybe, or looters. Didn't matter. They just stared at him, almost daring him to take some kind of action. But Caleb merely held up his hands in the international gesture for *no problem here* and kept moving.

If looting had begun, if the Landlord had chosen to withdraw, it wouldn't be long before the entire place erupted. *A thin veneer,* he reminded himself, and closed instantly down against the assault of memory. If his youth had taught him anything, it was just how fragile civilization really was.

Approaching the edge of Old Town, facing the bridges into the city proper, Caleb was acutely aware of his lack of weaponry. To say it made him nervous, being unarmed, was an understatement. He was no stranger to urban unrest, an old and unwelcome friend; he knew how fast things could go bad.

The Arcna's voice droned on, telling some kind of extended story that seemed to have nothing to do with anything. But it hardly mattered. He could hardly hear it, sound muffled by the gentle fall of rain around him, a mob-mutter rising in the distance to overtake it. In the distance, an explosion was rising green and heavy through the mists, above the rooftops.

Rain and tight streets were making it impossible to visually scan for any incoming threats. Caleb halted at the edge of the bridge. It was an exposed structure, open and wide, with no hiding places, designed for the defense of Old Town, and he pursed his lips. As paranoid as the Arrans could be, and as much as they disliked his presence, he'd never worried about them coming to get him.

A sudden thought hit him. Could Eliza be killed in her present state?

Don't think about it, he ordered himself, eyes trained on the problem at hand. That bridge. Two hundred meters of exposure. Two hundred meters of fuck-you. *Stop thinking about her.*

Ibbie looters wouldn't be a huge problem.

Ibbie Toks, on the other hand…

He made it almost to the other side—moving low, as close to the rail as possible, the still closing wound in his side an agony—before he saw movement. A silent, grim-faced mob, bags slung over their shoulders, balaclavas tied around their faces.

Caleb dropped as far as he could, crouched over his heels tight to the solid railing, stillness blending his black uniform to the facade of dark stone. They passed meters from him, eyes forward, a kind of blazing indignation there that he recognized so well from so many years ago. Police were filing out, falling in line against the iron railings set into the edge of the island.

Nothing ever changes, he thought grimly.

The bridge erupted in gunfire.

Caleb started running.

• • •

"FUCK," Tharsis muttered, poking a strand of greasy, unwashed hair back in its bun, fingers itching over the extruded keyboard.

But what to say?

The bitch fucking ate herself like she's eating all of us seemed a little dramatic.

MILITARY RESPONSE NEEDED IMMEDIATELY, she typed instead. ARCNA CONFIRMED DEAD. NOQUMIUT CONFIRMED DEAD. LIGHTHOUSE POWER SUPPLY RIGGED, HAVE CHANCE TO PREVENT THIS AND ALL FUTURE PROPAGATIONS IF...

"If what?"

Her heart plummeted as she turned. Saw.

Riqan very casually standing behind her, machete in hand. tDaer, right there, hand over hen's mouth, more lost than Tharsis had ever seen hen.

Fuck. She hadn't heard them come in. Hadn't even bothered to check.

He came around, peering down at the screen. "Yeah, that's definitely what it says. What do you think, tDaer? Think the lieutenant here was trying to contact her people?"

The Iapetan scratched at a temple. "Hen's not a lieutenant anymore."

Riqan was wearing that rock machete. There was no point in denying it. And Tharsis couldn't. Didn't want to. Not now. Not anymore.

"What?" she sneered, summoning every bit of rage she had left to cover up her own swelling fear. "You think we fuck once or twice and I'm going to betray my planet? Just like that?"

tDaer's expression contorted. "Your people... what the hell does that even mean? What makes them so fucking special? You said you were with me on this. You said you were with me."

Tharsis swallowed, and pushed up to her feet. This moment, she knew, ended in blood.

"We found nothing out here but death, tDaer. We were never going to find anything but death. Don't you get that? All her ideas, everything she says, she had to know they weren't working when she started recording, she had to know she was going to fail..."

"Hen didn't fail, hen just couldn't make it work. Hen didn't have the right tools, hen made mistakes. But we, we can make it work."

"No we can't," Tharsis said, watching the voider's face contort in a way that, despite everything, cut her to the bone. "We can't. We have to let it go. We have to stop this. Too many people have died, and for what? For nothing."

"It's not nothing," tDaer replied, backing away. "It can't be nothing…"

The lieutenant took another step towards hen. "tDaer…"

"Enough," Riqan groaned, jerking her violently backwards, hand in the scruff of her hood, fingers creeping around to encircle her throat. Tharsis felt the tip of the blade caress the line of her hip, the hot, fetid breath of the words against her ear. "I've really, really been looking forward to this, Lieutenant."

Tharsis kept her eyes squarely on tDaer, still shrinking back. Her fingers worked against her own hip pocket, her feet shuffling ever so slightly off center. The Nepo was taller and stronger, far more attuned to moving, fighting, in microgravity. There was only going to be one shot at this.

"tDaer," she pleaded, heart speeding, adrenaline flooding, "listen to me, get him under control. Nobody needs to die here today, okay? We don't need to do this."

Those dark eyes blinked. Once, twice. And narrowed.

"Yeah," hen said. "Yeah, Tharsis, we kind of do."

The steel-hard hand on her throat tightening, the blade pressing down, Tharsis popped the last of the seal on her pocket, sliding her fingers inside. Breathed out, just once. Slapped her hand on the nearest patch of hull, willing the gravity projection on.

And, as the sudden force knocked the voiders over, she struck.

As she ripped the knife free, she stabbed it as fast as she could into the big Nepo's thigh. Twisting back against it, she the force of her blow to throw the mig-adapted bastard back and around. His body couldn't react fast enough, and she dropped her weight hard, pulling the blade towards herself with all her strength, shearing open wrapper and flesh, clean down to the bone. Up the leg, seeking the groin.

Blood fountained.

tDaer was screaming.

Before Tharsis could reach his femoral, Riqan hit the craft hard, knocking the gravity off and the Arran off with it, hip-checking her with vicious force. Buried deep as it was, and horribly off-balance herself, Tharsis lost her grip on the knife, sailing off to strike hard against the far side of the curve. The wind knocked loose from her lungs. She wheezed, pulling herself up.

Blood streamed out and around him even as the ENEX began sealing itself over the gored wound and knife alike.

She threw herself into a roll in the mig, fast as she could, making for the equipment locker where their thermite charges had been kept. Her hands dug into the hull and ripped the door free. She managed to grab a charge and looked up.

Only to see him rocketing towards her, momentum carrying him impossibly fast from the other side of the craft's belly.

Machete cocked back. A killing strike loaded in his arm.

Tharsis only barely managed to miss the blow, twisting on the subtle friction of the hull's inner surface, blade sinking in a few centimeters from her head. He ripped it free and took another swing, and another, driving her deeper and deeper into the hull even as she tried to scramble backwards. Catching him around the waist, Tharsis pushed up with all her strength, barely managing to keep him from crushing her, sinking her down into the psychoreactive carbon almost to her eyes.

He raised the blade. Grinning.

And over the panic screaming through her blood, Tharsis caught something.

A line. A hairline crack, all around her. The hatch. But there was no way the native programming of the craft would let her tear it open, she knew, no way, unless…

Moments away from being gutted like a fish, across all the AU between herself and Pluto, she screamed one simple word.

"Flet!"

And drove the charge into the hull beside her, priming the fuse with a desperate flick of her thumb.

The hatch flew open, void sealing her into the safety of her suit as she was sucked out.

A hairsbreadth later, the thermite detonated.

Between the high oxygen environment of the spacecraft's interior and the tug of vacuum, the effect was devastating. The thermite in the charge aerosolized, catching the atmo on fire. The skin of the craft near the hatch turned red, melting.

As she flew backwards, she watched Riqan struggle his way through to the hatch. His suit was on fire; it hadn't sealed in time. She caught one last glimpse of his face, bone exposed.

What happened to tDaer, she couldn't see.

The hull buckled, rippled.

Just for a moment. Before the craft's panels shot out, overloading, loosed magnetic fields ripping through the hull's interior mechanics.

The divedrive tore itself to pieces. Debris shot out in all directions at subsonic speeds, tearing across the airless void of Eris's sky. One stabilization panel caught Tharsis hard in the chest, trapping her inside its curve. She was able, just barely, to scramble back through to the leeward side and away before it could drag her out into deep space.

The dwarf planet's gravity had her. Below her, she could see the antenna field. Pieces of the destroyed craft were still traveling, charging hard past her, but she was falling back into the white of the snowfields.

In the distance, she saw a massive blade of shrapnel tear through their shelter, splitting it apart. Precious atmo lost to the void. Along with the ENEX suspension vats.

<—arsis!> she heard yelled over her radio, and she looked out just in time to see tDaer's ENEX whipping past her. That was panic, unlike anything Tharsis had ever heard in tDaer's voice before.

How in the fuck, she thought, but managed to throw herself around. Despite the rain of killing-force projectiles, Tharsis stuck out a hand. <Grab on!> she yelled back. <tDaer, come on, grab on!>

The Iapetan's fingers brushed hers, desperate, reaching, grasping, slipping.

Gone.

Rolling, Tharsis only just caught the sight of a gigantic piece of outer hull slicing right through the Iapetan's suit.

For a moment, it looked like the exogear would be able to handle it. Disassociate.

For a moment.

Blood boiled as it hit the open void. tDaer's body was limp, sliding apart. Drawn out, into the outer darkness of the Kuiper.

Tharsis fell.

There was no sound.

Despite the low gravity, despite the best efforts of her suit thrusters, Tharsis still hit Eris with punishing force. Her momentum bounced her hundreds of meters across the snowy crust. Dirt and methane ice-slush sloughed off as she tore across the planet's surface, drifting up to the stars.

When she finally ground to a halt, body buried half a meter into mercifully disassociated icerock, the lieutenant just lay there, too stunned to move, body aching from the fall. She managed to turn her eyes to the read-out in her palm. Barely a minute had passed. Barely a minute.

Turning her head proved one motion too many. Her stomach heaved, and she forced herself out of the hole her body had made, forcing her lips around the suit's water tube and opening the one-way valve just in time to vomit out every bite of food, every drop of bile, her stomach contained.

Nausea passed over her in a wave as her body turned inside out, her ribs and chest aching anew, and she turned on the barely working gravity in her ENEX for some stability. She fell back against a clean patch of rock, sucking cold oxygen, throat on fire, heart beating so hard it seemed as if it would just fall out.

Time passed—she wasn't sure how much—with her staring out at the planet's close horizon, the tendrils of the forest waving above their heat shield. Miles away, maybe.

It occurred to the lieutenant, in that moment, that she was the most distant human being in the entire Heliosphere. Nobody further from the sun than she.

Nobody more alone.

An Arran girl from the Tharsan highlands in damaged exogear.

But the fear that had been growing in her gut ever since they surfaced here had finally subsided. In its place, certainty.

For the first time since leaving Earth, she understood. What the Landlords had brought her here to do. What the Naven must have wanted her to do.

Or maybe she was just extraordinarily unlucky.

Either way, she knew what she had to do.

"Okay," she whispered into the squeeze of her mask, hauling herself to her feet, the acrid taste of digestive fluid still clinging to her tongue. Burning in her throat. "Okay."

CHAPTER
FORTY-SIX

"SIR? You don't have to do this."

Coming out of the mercifully intact armory, Major Lanin wasn't all that surprised by what he saw. Graben, Chief Anders, a few of the more senior NCOs, Hinden.

Clustered in the remains of the guardhouse.

Well, Hinden was a surprise. The captain had been strangely quiet during the quick briefing Lanin had given him on this. The major had thought he'd be happy, getting his command back, but then, maybe that was a fucking ungenerous thing to think.

Lounging in the air lock, Tyr's ears were pricked.

The rain had gotten stranger; the sea had started to pull up the edges of the sky. In Lanin's four tours out in the Inner Shoals, he'd never seen anything like it.

Rain and darkness. Darkness and rain. It was like every bad warstory radio serial Lanin had ever listened to as a boy. Somehow, it fit.

Maybe that was the whole point.

Maybe the Rallarhu was doing it on purpose, just to fuck with them.

No telling with the Landlords.

"Who else is going to do it, Lieutenant?" he asked bluntly. There was nothing else to be done. The Arcna was still out there, still broadcasting, howling for the blood of the rest of the Tenancy, and fuck only knew what would happen to the Rossen if some Tok cell got their hands on him. Cheria had likely given them everything on him. "He's still out there and the mapping wasp couldn't find him."

"Sir," and that was Anders, "you know we all respect the hell out of Caleb, Landlord or not, but this…"

"What do you mean, Ike, Landlord or not?"

The old chief didn't flinch. "Major, he can't die. You can. Don't go out there and get yourself killed for him. Caleb wouldn't want that."

Lanin nodded, pushed the last bullet into the last clip. Five, loaded to capacity at fifteen rounds each. It was all he could manage in grays. For the first time in years, he missed his deepvoider kit. Armor, emergency oxygen, everything a man might need. Instead, he had an ill-fitting tactical cuirass and a dog whose ENEX vest took two standard A-24 magazines.

"I thought about that," he replied, keeping his voice as neutral as possible, moving out ahead into the air lock. Tyr scrambled to his paws. He'd already explained the situation to the animal, who was of the same mind as he was about what needed to be done. "And then I decided that was a coward's answer."

"He's the Landlord, he'll just—"

"Come back? You so sure about that? The Arcna is screaming for their deaths out there. If they've caught him, if they figure out who he is, they can tear him apart."

"Chief, if the Landlord's gone, we're all fucked when the rest of the Tenancy decides to vote us into oblivion," Hinden said, from behind everyone else. "We can't lose him."

Huh, Lanin thought.

Anders pressed. "That doesn't change the fact that you're the senior-ranking man on base, Major. What happens if we lose you out there?"

"Let's deal with this situation one problem at a time."

"Major Lanin…"

He waved them all silent. "I am not willing to sit on my ass and do nothing while one of my sergeants, and Caleb is one of my sergeants, gets his ass killed out there."

Lieutenant Graben shook his head. "You can't go out there by yourself, sir."

Making a little show of checking the safety on his rifle, Lanin tried to think of how to respond to that. He knew the tone he heard in the kid's voice: the desire to do something, do something real for once, instead of filing more fucking paperwork.

He knew that feeling.

He also knew there was no kind way to answer it.

Olin was his friend. This was his burden. He wouldn't ask anyone else to die with him.

"I'm taking Tyr with me. I won't be alone."

"Sir—"

"This isn't a vote! Michael's fucking ballsweat, follow a fucking order!" But at seeing the look on the young man's face, he softened. "I have to go. You boys make sure that Cheria's body stays in stasis. That's our only chance of getting out to the Kuiper. I want her intact for when I get Caleb back and the *Barachiel* arrives, you understand?"

Graben was making to say something else, but Chief got in front of it. "It's been a pleasure, boss."

Lanin tapped the secondary mag back into his weapon. "I'm coming back, we're going to get support in time, and no one else on this base is going to die," he said, mustering the words they needed to hear, and leveled a finger at Hinden. "Captain, like we discussed, you're in charge until the *Barachiel* gets here. Chief, he does anything stupid, you have my permission to shoot him." He was only half-joking. "Did you clear the intersection?"

Chief Ander's face twitched. "Yes sir."

"Beautiful. Now somebody go open the fuckin' air lock for me."

Outside the gate, the tents had been abandoned. The gathering crowd had become mobile, melted back into the rain. No targets. Lanin wasn't sure if that was a good thing or not.

Not that he enjoyed killing. Hated it, in fact. It was one of the reasons he'd left the deepvoider fleet, retrained into base support. His wife had been the other, but he put her from his mind. Not the time.

Tyr sniffed the air cautiously and gave a low affirmation.

No active phosphate weapons. No human scent. No enemy presence.

"We'll track him from Old Town," Lanin muttered to the animal, and, A-24 at tactical, the pair of them set off into the crying twilight.

· · ·

IF SHE WERE some character in a radio play, Tharsis imagined, or a priest, or hell, even her own grandmother, it would have been that trudge back to the forest in which she would have seen everything. The whole history of Noqumiut, laid out before her.

Seen craft land, bearing the Heliosphere's disillusioned, looking for a better way of life, the first stirrings, the early attempts at creating something new, something unique.

Watched them struggle, come to face the harshness of the environment, realities that couldn't simply be hand-waved away by wishful thinking.

Heard the conversations and arguments and fights.

Seen the *Padua* make planetfall.

Witnessed the experiments, the attempts, baselining a new society from the seeds of that which had already been destroyed, pure humanity captured and manipulated into something that could be seen as ideal, as liberating, liberated.

Viewed even that failure, tweaks becoming twists, liberation becoming oppression, until finally, the Arcna fled from it and locked herself in the radio control room, spinning her web of ideas across the Heliosphere to some finally revealed end.

Found the answer for why the Naven—for who else could it have been?—carried that burden of fuel rods out here again and again and again.

But Tharsis wasn't a radio heroine or a priest or half the woman her grandmother was, and she saw nothing. Just the antenna boles growing bigger and bigger in her goggles' field of view.

Whatever had happened here, only the forest's radiation remembered now. And it wasn't speaking to her.

She put her head down and moved as well as she could.

The suit had disassociated her through the worst of the debris, kept her from any mortal injuries. But her body was still groaning, the equipment still damaged. Her grav-boots were barely functional. Tharsis took the distance in leaping bounds, just thankful that it hadn't been the atmo tank.

Not that that's going to save you, she reminded herself. Approaching the wall, the palm read-out listed her as having barely an hour before hitting the safety limits in the suit. Ninety minutes before it dissolved the upper layers of her skin past the point of repair.

It should have been more time. She'd only spent two hours trying to get back from where she'd crashed, four since she'd pulled it back on. With few breaks over the last few days, the scat hadn't been hibernating properly.

Didn't matter much anyway; with the divedrive gone, she was going to die on Eris, one way or another. Unlike void training as a cadet, nobody was coming to rescue her.

She tried to put it out of her mind.

She had things to do.

There wasn't much left of the shelter, not that she'd had much hope of that, after watching it burst under the wreckage. A few scattered items, tatters of tent material driven into the ground by shards of the divedrive. Tharsis spent precious time digging through the mess, just in case there was something useful there. Like water for her burning throat. She found a bottle, half-full but still sealed. Pausing to hook it up to her intake tube, the lieutenant bagged up a few surviving food packets in a scrap of tent and looked up to the end of the tether.

It hadn't snapped, amazingly, and was still taught, pulled out by the mass hanging on its end. That black bag containing the plutonium was still there, swaying gently on its anchor line.

Staring at it, Tharsis wondered if she should use it. Install it. Save the forest, get a message out somehow, or leave one, making sure that for the next Propagation, anyone who came out would know what needed to be done.

But even as she weighed that option, the Arran in her wouldn't accept it. Too risky, too much left to chance. If she didn't fix this problem now, she'd be leaving it to somebody who knew even less about it than she did. Millions more might die. No telling what the next Propagation would bring.

No. It had to end. Everything. It had to end.

Cutting the fissile material free, Tharsis started into the forest, the words of one of her dad's favorite passages running through her mind. *Though I walk through the valley of the shadow of death, I will fear no evil, for you are with me...*

"Michael, if you've got a minute to spare from watchin' over the troops and whatever the hell's going on back in the Heliosphere," she grumbled into her mask, "I could really use some help right now."

Because while she might not have seen anything out on the plains, she was seeing it now. All the umbran, shades of the people who had lived and died here, impressed into the field, watching her. Paper cutouts, the drawings from some child's book, abstracted from whatever they had been in life. Making them more human in some cases.

Less, in others.

Dangerous, Gran would have said.

The lieutenant wondered if she was going to be joining them. If tDaer had. If they'd have—as Ang had believed—any secrets to tell.

Don't think about it, she thought, and ordered her exhausted body on.

They were everywhere, in everything. Shades of people, echoes and memories and full minds, still trapped, still screaming into death. But even the ones busy reliving those last moments stopped to stare at her. Behind them and within them were other things, Eris's own inhuman penumbran emissions, wandering in. They didn't approach, didn't get near, but she could feel them, all of them, bent on her, flitting through the boles and around the terrible little mounds, shadowing her progress.

The plutonium was the draw, she realized about halfway through, the plutonium. It would recharge the fields generated by the antennas, renew the radiation.

Keep them there.

Tharsis didn't know what they were going to do with her, if they figured out she wasn't putting it back in its place. Or maybe they'd welcome it.

She reached the clearing below the sled. The little craft was still anchored above her. Ang was still anchored to it. Tharsis looked around one more time at the eyes watching her from the shallows of the penumbra.

Switching off the stuttering gravity in her boots, she floated up.

Untangling Ang's body was going to be impossible, she realized, without breaking off his entire hand, frozen solid and still gripped tight to the rung. Tharsis couldn't do that, and wished she knew a

Polarist prayer for the dead, something proper to say, to offer. Death, ever close on Mars, was treated with utmost respect.

But there was nothing of his own she could give him.

So, she said one of the prayers she did know. A prayer for souls in purgatory. And she hoped it would be enough.

It took time and energy to secure the plutonium to the sled, to jam the controls. Outwell escape velocity for a planetoid of Eris's size was minuscule; the sled would be more than adequate to take it a hundred kilometers or more. Hopefully more—if anybody came back, she didn't want them to have any possibility of recharging the batteries.

She watched the thrusters fire with little satisfaction.

Tharsis lingered after they were gone, not wanting to look down below. Not wanting to see those umbran again.

Yet, after long, long minutes, when she finally descended, struggling in her damaged gear to lose the altitude, it was something quite different that she found.

She found nothing.

Like a switch had been flipped. On the planet, in her head, she didn't care which. All of it, the emotion, the figures, just gone.

No whisper of anything beyond the visible spectrum. No hint of background static. Nothing. Not even a hole, where all those things had been. Just a warmth, and a certainty, and a courage that felt far too strong to be her own.

She almost smiled, and whispered a *thank you*.

Her palm read-out told her she had ten minutes before hitting the safety limits on the suit. Yet judging from the tingle that had started up just under her skin, the timer's estimate was optimistic. The wrapper was waking up.

Get moving, Chen, she ordered herself, and headed across the curve of the static field, back down to the gates.

IN HIS DECADE AT HUMPHRYES, Caleb had made a point of learning the area off base as well as he could. Most of the islands here were set, anchored to the bedrock and to each other, cables rusting in places after so many centuries of immobility. Little changed, even if the periphery shifted quite often, and he was well familiar with most of the streets and bridges and elevated catwalks.

But now, mobs—Tok or otherwise—were cutting the cables, slicing them off, most likely, from inside the island structures themselves. Entire blocks were shifting and tilting, loosed on the waters. Few were moving, but those that were groaned into each other, sending waves of wrapper-coated water splashing across cobblestone and wall alike.

Furtive shapes dodged in and out and between, some loaded down, others hidden behind balaclavas and those shiftless garments that gave nothing away of the individual within. Fires were ripping through the streets, the stench of them carrying on cold atmo, phosphorous undeterred by the weather. The only blessing in that, Caleb supposed, was that it was likely keeping the thallium down—some of the smoke was rising green above the city's delirious spires.

Definite Tok activity, Caleb knew, and wondered why in the hell the Rallarhu's police forces weren't cracking down harder.

Wondered, until the next bridge answered it for him.

A mob was attacking a Tenancy administration building, smashing the main floor display windows, hurtling makeshift Molotovs in through the shatter. There were police among them, firing bursts into the structure above the howls. A couple of them were on each other's shoulders, chipping at the Rallarhu's insignia, inlaid in the plaster above the door.

If the police were rioting now as well, the entire 'roid was as good as gone.

"Fuck," he muttered to himself, balancing over his heels for a moment, considering the options. He needed to get past them, and nothing was going to be achieved by staying in his current position.

But creeping around behind another building, he ran into another group. Proper Toks, dressed all in black, recognition dawning on their faces.

Cheria must have given them all my face, Caleb realized.

For a moment, nobody moved.

And then they all did.

Whoops tore out of the throats of the Toks as they chased him, pouring out around him from narrow alleys and high windows, coming in from all directions, impossible to determine where or how, swarming like locusts through the island. He evaded as best he could, his core muscles screaming their unwillingness to obey the commands coming from his nerve endings, the tear still not quite healed. Somebody bodychecked him around the edge, tackling him into the pavers and scrambling up his back. Caleb barely shook that off, and, switching off his gravity, tore away.

He took the cleanest leap he could, but the streets were tight and the buildings an impossible maze. Unable to stop the parabola of his own momentum, the sergeant crashed hard into a low wall, tumbling over the side.

Something dark loomed over him, blocking out the rain.

Caleb braced himself.

But instead of a gun in his face, there was a hand being held out, and a wet nose pressed to his shoulder.

"Come on, Caleb, get off your ass," that familiar voice chided, echoed shortly by strong-pushed anxiety from the dog.

He grasped it, letting the major pull him up. "What are you doin' out here, Trai?"

Lanin shrugged and passed him a fresh A-24. "Thought I'd see the sights one last time before the fuckers set it all on fire," he replied, laconic.

"Eh, it was a shithole anyway," the Landlord replied, and held out his hand to his dog, giving his hard-set ears a quick pat. "How far are we from Humphryes?"

"About three clicks."

Another column of smoke, bright as emerald in the rain. "We should get moving. Tyr?"

The big animal padded ahead with a soft acknowledgement, tail level and fur plastered flat to his back.

CHAPTER
FORTY-SEVEN

PAUSING on the edge of the radio room, the Arcna's body cast in harsh silhouette against the float-lamps still burning at the top of the ceiling, Tharsis wondered if what she was planning was worth the effort.

Her exogear's biological equilibrium had tipped in favor of the xenocytes now, not her. It refused to retreat into its protective layer, but it wasn't dying yet like it should have. The atmosphere was weak here, and the ambient radiation substantial. Her skin was on fire. Tharsis had no idea how long she, or it, would last

But she wasn't going to just lay down and die. Arrans didn't accept zero-sum outcomes. That was what Dad always said. Wouldn't be the right thing, going out without trying to do something about this insanity.

Tharsis spent long minutes pouring over the details of the radio controls. She couldn't see much, though; the cases would have to be cracked in order to really get at the innards. Probably to no end. The screws bore signs of stripping, some so utterly ruined that nothing short of an ionizer would have pulled them loose. Somebody had worked on this thing before—the Rossen, most likely—and come to the conclusion, somehow, someway, that it couldn't be done. It, its message, couldn't be disconnected.

Extortion, she thought contemptuously, but went back to the main panel anyway. Even if there was no way to undo what the Landlord had done, her own deserved to know what had been done out here, and why, and how.

The Arcna's body wasn't frightening, Tharsis realized, plucking the microphone from a desiccated hand, and she didn't hate it. If anybody deserved that kind of death, it was the Arcna. By rights, she should smash the mummified remains into dust. But the lieutenant felt only a swell of pity for it.

Pathetic, that thing, that death. Lost and pathetic and meaningless.

It was also responsible for killing a sizable fraction of what remained of the human race.

"What the fuck's wrong with you?" Tharsis muttered to herself.

There was no way to remove the body from its harnesses, to move it from the room, but it was fairly far back, enough to keep it from bumping into her if she stood at the main console. Tharsis kept an eye on it as she traced the wires protruding from the panel, ripped the mic assembly free, forcing her brain through the struggle of Silicone English. Thinking she had the sense of it, the lieutenant pulled a few cables, flipped a few switches, made a few emergency splices with ancient electrical tape from a nearby cabinet. Prayed.

And, with one last deep breath, unsealed her suit.

As before, the cold was unbearable. The thin air burned as it hit her face, and she realized that was the radiation. She didn't dare take off the rest of the suit. She made the mistake of touching her head; a clump of hair pulled away under her fingers, bloody.

Tharsis raised her breathing mask back up and took a few deep breaths

The divedrive blowing up had sealed her fate. She'd known that, But, for some reason, it was that—her hair, of all the damn things—that made her realize.

She wasn't going home.

Tears welled up in her eyes, moisture icing up in her lashes, and she dashed it away.

No point in grieving.

Sucking another quick breath through cracking lips, Tharsis switched her rebreather off and depressed the <talk> button.

And—wonder of wonders—the system crackled into life.

"For anyone who can hear me," she began, wheezing a little, "this is Infrastructure Lieutenant Third-Class Ambera Chen, formerly of the 589th Sustainment Squadron, Contingency Base Humphryes, 4Vesta." Her lungs, bruising under the force of drawing the mortally thin atmo, seized; she lifted the dying gear for another breath. "My current location is the Eris Lighthouse, Kuiper Shoals. Noqumiut. I repeat, I am at Noqumiut. The Arcna is dead. According to carbon dating we did, she's been dead for seven hundred years, before the First Propagation." Another lungful. "Her words are nothing more than a recording in a computer. She ate herself. This world ate itself."

She paused, taking a few more breaths. Her lungs were already aching. Tharsis knew she was risking edema, but at this point, what was one more thing?

What to say? *The Arcna rigged the system to broadcast, fucked the Rossen over. I can stop the Propagations, but at the cost of the exodus craft.* Command, the Rossen, would know that if they picked this up. She didn't have the air to give it voice. Barely had the time to think about it.

But maybe there had only ever been one answer. One other decision.

"My… craft blew up, no way to bring navigation material back. I'm ranking officer on scene. My call. Power out here stays off."

Tharsis took another long draw before continuing. "If anybody in the ASDF is picking this up, tell my family I'm sorry… sorry I haven't been home in so long. Should have come home last year."

She glanced at the mummified corpse. Did she have family, before? Did the people who came here, her happy brigade of volunteers? People who cared for them, who they threw away? It all seemed such a waste.

"Tell my brother… it's okay."

Her lungs couldn't force any more air through her straining throat, and the words trailed off to nothing, the pressure of the room hardly adequate to force air into her, so she could force them out. Tharsis clamped the mask back over her face, breathing deep as she could.

Careful over the dirty, bloody mat of her dark hair, tearing off her head now—and why had she ever bothered to keep it so long in the first place?—she tugged her hood back on.

The burning in her skin didn't subside as the ENEX sealed up, changing from tiny pinpricks of sensation to a full, spreading dullness. She slumped down against the bulkhead of the console, mind swimming, body screaming for some rest, exhausted from the effort of breathing.

"Soon enough," she whispered to herself, and wondered if she had the energy to make it up to the surface, out of the forest, onto those open plains. Lay down and look up at the stars and just wait. Better than dying in this place, already so deeply scarred, body stuck next to the Arcna's for eternity, or until somebody came out to investigate the claims.

Seeing the stars one last time sounded nice, she decided, and with a herculean effort, pulled herself back up.

OF THE TRIP BACK, Caleb couldn't distinguish much of anything.

There was rain, and darkness, and unhinged laughter. There were more mobs, more firebombs, more rushes, more skirmishes in tight alleys and frenetic streets. The minutes pooled and bled, time slipping away as Tyr, nose to the air, led the way back to their own territory.

Nobody spoke. No need for communication, not in those conditions. When it was still, when the space around them was empty, senses instinctively trained outward, on every little sound, every misplaced splash, and every distant crash. When they found themselves again in a bubble of chaos, muscle memory took over for both man and beast. His dog, especially, cut a bloody, furious swath through the Ibbie gangs that crossed their path.

It was almost funny, watching them flee when they realized what they were up against.

Caleb moved easily enough. Kept his gun sights moving, kept Tok targets dropping in the streets, when they were stupid enough to present themselves.

The strain wore on him, though. His side ached. The med-pack had ripped off, the uniform already too soaked with blood to be effective. Mostly closed, he judged the tissues, but it wouldn't take more than a hard knock to open it back up again. He tried to put it out of his mind, but his body wasn't that young corporal's any longer, and in the cold of the rain, leeching into his very bones, everything had started to hurt. Joints to skin.

Through the haze of it all, words crashed over from the Big Noise, the Arcna still talking. Still droning on. What was the point of it? What did she want, truly? Did she honestly think she had the recipe for human perfection? Or was she just like the rest of those deep green Euphie fucks from the old days, wanting to just kill and kill and kill until there wasn't a single human left alive?

Lanin, however, was still moving fast, faster than Caleb had seen him move in years, and while his own hands might have been shaking, he didn't seem to notice.

"What the fuck's going on out here?" he huffed, as they scrambled over the wide bridge that led into a familiar square. The entire island had tilted, canted sideways, loose bits of cafe tables and vendor carts crashed to the lower end. Stress fractures were still spreading through the paving stones in geometric webs.

But Caleb knew it. This was the Wardog's island, and the sergeant shoved out of his mind the uneasy grief for his dead friend. Only about half a click or so from Humphryes. The still unbroken dome of its sky was visible, high above the buildings of the outer neighborhood they were passing into.

And just in time. They only had one cartridge left between them, Lanin's knife notched near to uselessness. The fur around Tyr's mouth was thick with drying voider blood, and the normally sure-footed animal was beginning to stumble. Caleb knew how he felt. Low-gravity combat was the worst. Not enough pull to move normally, too much to cut free and swim it out. Keeping one's momentum in control was exhausting, and even with the emergency suture pack, he was barely staying on his feet.

"Fuckers are cutting island anchor lines," Caleb grumbled. He looked up at the sky—dark, the rain obscuring any hint of the stars, any promise that Eliza might drag herself away from whatever the fuck she was doing. Deal with the fucking situation on the ground in her territory. "You seeing anything, Major?

"You mean, like…"

"Yeah. Like that."

Lanin glanced up, water beading down the neck of thin grays.

"Death lights," he said, teeth almost bared. "Swirling like fog up there."

Caleb couldn't see it. He'd never had the average Arran's familiarity with the penumbra. But if Lanin said it was happening, it was.

Tyr was out ahead, scouting. He was limping a little from a lucky strike by a looter across his left haunch, but nothing beyond his limits.

Lanin's words were easy, hands tight on his gun's short stock. "These people, the Ibbies, they're about as close to useless as you can get. Lazy and happy…"

"Doesn't take a big percentage of the population being true believers to fuck things up royally. Five, ten percent, maybe," the Landlord replied. "That's all you need."

The major stopped, hand on Caleb's arm, pulling him up.

Caleb looked up.

A pair of black-garbed Toks, standing on the bridge behind them, long, dark tubes slung over their shoulders.

Before any of them had any time to react, Tyr, coiled to strike, strung out from the prolonged retreat from Old Town, turned off his own gravity and pounced. Moving too fast for Caleb to call him off the prey, the dog tore down, jaws locking into an Ibbie throat, shaking the human bodily, even as the man tried to fight back with another cloth-wrapped lance of broken glass. The second figure broke loose in a mad dash for the bridge.

Lanin, however, calmly snapped his A-24 up and exhaled one slow shot. The Ibbie's body crumpled, brain matter exploding out the front of the skull, the sharp report of the bullet echoing through the square.

Tyr started limping back, slow, ponderous, back leg tucked up into his body. Caleb wanted to yell at him for attacking without the command, but before he could form the words, a new mob started pulling into view from the rain, and Tyr started hobbling faster.

Every side street, every alley, every doorway, was suddenly alive.

They were surrounded.

Lanin's face twitched. "Caleb…"

"I see it," he snapped back, and whistled to Tyr, casting about for some patch of city that didn't look infested.

"They've got phosphorous charges," he warned. "Fuckers are glowing with it."

"Coming for the base," he agreed, finding something that might work. Behind them, of all the damn places, was the pub. Three stories high, sixty yards away. He nodded back at it. "Can you make that jump, Trai?"

"Maybe. We weren't all born on Earth."

"I'll throw you." A soaking-wet muzzle was pushed into his hand, pain rattling out from the animal into him. "Stupid move, boy," he murmured to him, but the answering ripple of agreement didn't do anything to settle the Landlord's mind. Caleb switched the gravity off in his suit, the grip of the world beneath his feet fading to almost nothing. "The count of three, we break for it."

Lanin nodded once, tight. The Ibbies were starting to enter the square.

"One."

The fur stood up along the ridge of Tyr's back, clear down to his tail.

"Two."

The black masses of them were pressing closer, closer, the defecting security forces moving to the front, captured weapons from those who may have been more loyal coming to the fore. Closer, faster, starting to jog, starting to run.

"Three."

They barely made the roof.

Even with his physical advantage, Caleb could barely summon the energy for the final bound, and the force of it ripped the still-unhealed wound in his side completely open, blood and abdominal fluid flooding his already soaked uniform.

Lanin was right. Even with his own gravity off, he barely made the landing on the second floor, and from there, there was nothing to grab onto, nothing to pull himself up with. Caleb leaned as far over the edge as he could, hooking a foot into the railing and letting himself fall over, Lanin missing his hand by inches on his next jump, bullets hitting the olivine brick around them. Shrapnel took Caleb in the arm, and he pulled himself back up with his good hand, cursing.

The major would have been lost, if not for Tyr. The dog had held his ground against the encroaching mob, only letting himself be pushed back barely, tail bristled and fangs bared wide, bloodlust rolling off him in waves. Caleb's voice couldn't carry over the roar of the throng below to call him back. From his own perch on the roof, it looked grim.

But when the bullets started hitting the store walls, something in Tyr clicked back into place, and he twisted around, heaving the bulk of his body back and around and up, launching in a high parabolic arch. His front paws hit the edge of the landing where Lanin was pinned down, teeth digging into the major's collar, and back paws pushing off again—straight up—in less time than it took to blink.

Both Tyr and Lanin hit the roof hard, the dog collapsing as the human rolled hard into a mass of piping, dead center on the rough surface. Keeping low below the lip, ignoring his own injuries, Caleb hurried over to the seventy kilos of wounded animal, pulling him off his injured side to get a better look.

"He shattered his leg," Lanin gasped, pulling himself up into a crouch. The fall had scraped a good deal of skin off his hands and fore-arms, dark spots spreading against water-soaked sleeves. "I heard it."

"Shh, shh, boy, calm down," Caleb ordered, one hand on the bare patch of tattooed rank, the other trying to feel down that left leg. Lanin was right. Broken in three places, tendons snapped. Under his own numb fingers, the dog's huge heart was racing. He glanced at Lanin "Fuck. We're not... we might not be able to get him back on a busted leg."

The mob was still roaring beneath them. Louder, louder, louder.

Lanin rubbed a hand over his mouth. "We're not leaving him here."

"Fucking right about that," Caleb growled, and tore open the first aid kit from Tyr's vest, looking for a compression bandage. "You have anything, Trai? Working radio, anything?"

Shaking his head, the major held up the remnants of a now smashed handset. "Guess Humphryes doesn't qualify for the hardened stuff."

"The fall?"

"Part of it may be in my hip," he said, and winced a little as he pulled himself back up to his knees, sliding the clip out of his A-24, and ejecting a round clearly jammed in the chamber. Winced again as he shifted up closer to the edge of the wall, leg dragging. "Definitely in my hip."

370

"It bad?"

"Nothing that heading downstairs for a drink wouldn't fix. Think those fuckers have gotten into the booze stores yet?"

The dog's head propped up in his lap, hands busy securing the splint around the worst fracture, Caleb only barely glanced over at him. "Keep your gravity off. Ought to help a little."

"Way ahead of you there," Lanin replied. "I'm amazed my boots are still working at all."

"Guess there's one thing they issue you that holds up," Caleb joked back, trying to smile a little, and Lanin huffed out a small, pained laugh.

"Yeah, our illustrious acquisitions process. Why haven't you fixed that yet?"

"Money doesn't just grow on trees, it's gotta get pulled from…" and he fell silent, some new noise rising up over the din below them. A hard, heavy, whump-umphp, like a cannonball being dropped into water. "Was that…"

"Sounded like a paralytic suppressor blast," Lanin said, and pushed himself up a little, eyes scanning the dark sky. And he laughed a real, happy laugh. "Look at who finally decided to show up to the party."

Barely visible through the slide of water across the darkened dome of the sky was the form of the *Barachiel*, blue markers glowing. Caleb smiled grimly to himself. If the deepvoider had gotten here, if Yip's Marines were off-loading…

"How far are we? Half a click?"

"Straight? Probably. But I'm usually not straight-up, stumbling out of here."

Caleb thought of better days, drinking down in the pub beneath them, laughing and joking with the owner. Poor Chris. Idiot, marrying a Tok. The sex couldn't have been that good. "They'll have a ground team out if they're using crowd suppressors, right?"

"Sounds about right."

"But we've got no radio."

Lanin shook his head. "They'll have at least a two-canine contingent on the ground team. His pack."

"Yeah, but—"

"Vocal range of ten kilometers."

"Trai, that'll draw in every Tok in the fucking city."

"They already know we're here. Our own boys don't." Lanin smiled, obviously forced. "All they need is your body mostly intact."

Caleb sighed and looked at his dog. He sent him the image, the impression, of the craft and its pack. "Get up. We need you to call them down."

Tyr struggled, back leg slipping on that injured leg, paw unable to get any kind of traction. Cursing, Caleb dialed the gravity in his vest completely off, started pulling on him.

Lanin tightened his hand around the stock of the gun as the screaming below them got louder. "What happens to him, Caleb?"

There was no need to ask what he meant. Caleb knew—he knew from the second he'd hit the roof. None of them were walking away. But only one of them wouldn't get up again.

"Same as me," the Rossen replied, and, wrapping hands under the animal's chest, yanked him up hard, tearing his own stomach muscles open wider, fresh blood gushing out. Tyr whimpered, but managed to stay upright this time, swaying on his good paws. "Wakes back up."

The animal's eyes were pained, fully aware and yet pleading, innocent. *All the death we've seen together, boy*, the sergeant thought, and hoped to hell that his dog's memory was as leaky as his own. He'd never known what Tyr remembered and what he didn't.

"He'll be back. He always is." And he patted his dog's head, scratched his ears. "C'mon, Tyr. Call 'em down for me. Bring your pack, and let's kill these motherfuckers, okay?"

Explosions were ringing out from Humphryes now, the sounds of the deepvoider crew's non-kinetic weaponry crackling into the endless night. At those decibel levels now, the blasts would be lethal. No chances taken. No mercy given.

Caleb loved Arrans sometimes.

"They're coming for you, boy. Pack's out there. We need them here."

A shot rang out from Lanin's rifle, a head exploded in a red haze, raining down on the screaming masses below. Silent for a moment. "Caleb..." Lanin warned, voice shaking.

A howl ripped out of the big dog's throat, soaring above the roar of the mob, above the Arcna's cackling glee, back to Humphryes.

Caleb pressed a useless hand against the life gushing out of his side, wanting to hang on to this time, this moment, this place, just a little longer. It wasn't the end. He knew that, even if his reptile brain was screaming its panic at him.

No. Not death. Just loss. Twenty years of loss. Twenty years of memories and experiences and friends…

"Sorry I dragged you off Deimos, sir," he coughed. "Away from that plum planetside posting you were headed to."

"Yeah, doing what? File papers, run briefings, make the fucking general's coffee? Annoy my wife by actually being home on the weekends?" Another round tore out of Lanin's gun. "I just get in her way."

He could feel it now, life ebbing. Breathing was harder, hurting. "Why… why's that?"

"Can't keep…" another shot, "… my hands off her and those fucking sexy…" another, "aprons of hers."

"Trai…"

Lanin forced the magazine out with unsteady fingers, checking the contents one more time. "Don't," he warned, voice harder than the Landlord had ever heard it, before smiling again. "Don't worry about it. This is what I signed up for."

"Nobody signs up to…" he began, coughing, and then noticed something.

The major must have caught it, too. "Huh."

The Arcna's voice had stopped.

There was an answering howl, rising in that silence, Tyr answering, sharper, higher. Caleb could hear what was in it, but he couldn't bring himself to care. He felt tired. Tired enough to fall asleep.

But, as the blood started slowing, as a chill stole through his limbs, as his hands couldn't hold on to Tyr's fur any longer, the Big Noise screeched awake.

Not the Arcna, nor the Rallarhu, though. Another voice speaking. A familiar voice.

<… *I am standing in Noqumiut, and the Arcna is dead…*>

And, even as a strange grayness crept over his vision for the second time in as many days, Caleb almost started laughing.

It was just—

CHAPTER
FORTY-EIGHT

WITH TREMORS RUNNING through her skin and her suit thrusters low on fuel, Tharsis knew she couldn't make the trip through Noqumiut's forest to the open snowfields. Instead, seized by an idea, she used what little propulsion she had left to make it to the top of the shaft, and then switched back to the gravity settings to make her slow way down the hallway to the weird tidal pool of a chamber, the one containing the shells of the children who had died on Eris.

Tharsis stood in the doorway for a moment, unwilling to go in, to face it again. Where it had gone wrong. Where it had ended, where Noqumiut had died. This place—not the forest or the radio room or anything else—was the true mausoleum of the Arcna's ambitions.

Gathering herself in a deep, deep breath, she started in.

Just as it had been upstairs, in the clearing before the entrance to the facility proper, there wasn't so much as a wheedling hint of penumbra. No echoes, no umbran.

Nothing.

Felt stranger that way. Sadder.

There was no telling where the ice might be thinnest, scraping overhead and just out of reach of her fingertips, but the lieutenant didn't think she'd have any trouble in breaking through it—how strong could it be?

Strong, she realized, her fist landing with jarring force, rocking her back. Frowning a little into her rebreather, she struck harder and harder, nothing seeming to so much as crack it.

On her next blow, the lieutenant's foot slipped, knocking out a section of wall as she fell, and pulling herself laboriously back up, Tharsis noticed a space behind.

Something blinking within.

She found herself scrambling for it, then, as if possessed. Whatever it was, she had to see it, had to know, had to get her hands on it and find out what little sliver of energy had escaped Ang's scans. What it was doing there. What it was.

With shaking hands, she tore at the wall, ripping it away in huge pieces, and it occurred to her that it was metal, bending and breaking in her grasp. It wasn't some cave, then, that they'd dug for the stasis pods.

It was the *Padua Anthony* itself.

After a few precious, frantic minutes, Tharsis found herself with a two-meter hole, the arch of the old doorway obvious in the shattered alloys, leading into a small chamber full of equally shattered equipment, scattered over whatever was producing that central light. She squeezed inside, digging it out much more carefully, turning this piece and that bit over in her gloves, rebellious wrapper licking at their surfaces. Indeterminate, most of it. No voidman herself, she didn't quite know what she was looking at. A navigation system, perhaps, or...

No. Not perhaps.

Definitely.

It was a small globe, barely bigger than both her fists placed together, a small, dull sphere set into a transparent housing, held up on a small pillar of what appeared to be brass, iron spheres placed strategically around it. The light was coming from a series of tiny pinholes around its side. The whole thing reminded her of a planetary compass, the kind sailors might use to guide their way in storms.

Curious, she reached out for it.

The globe sprang alive at the contact, throwing out a rudimentary holographic image, filling the room with discreet splashes of color. Red and gold and blue and white. Cruder than the one tDaer had once shown her—and that hurt, it did—but better, details coming together from the scatter. Planets red, major 'roids gold, Lighthouses blue, and white…

One blue and one white were overlapping, set to just the right angle, if the green positioning line there was HST midnight, and she realized what it was.

Tharsis pulled her bruised hand away, feeling the skin of her knuckles split.

It didn't matter.

Thoughts reeling, her eyes went not to the thirteen white dots, however, orbiting in quiet planes of high eccentricity, but rather to a solitary red one, so small, almost lost within the vastness that the map was clearly meant to convey.

A small red dot, nothing fancy, nothing special, nothing at all remarkable about it.

A single, lonely point in space.

There was nothing that a hologram could show her about that dot, about its rivers and oceans and thermal pools, glowing crystal blue under winter skies.

It couldn't possibly describe the way the newpeat smelled when its tiny blooms opened under the first rays of the long spring, how green it was against the hooves of the dark sheep moving across it, the feeling of it beneath bare feet on sleepy summer days.

The dot couldn't show her the low dome of the family's ranch house, standing proudly in its highland meadow, or the path down to the barns, where the cats chased mice in the hayloft and the dogs slept in the sun in the dirt outside.

It didn't smell of fresh bread or fall roasts or the winter fires when Gran sat everyone down at the hearth and told the stories of the umbran nightmares roiling in the kirabata winds of Olympus Mons's wicked west slopes.

There was nothing in it that spoke of family, of home, at all, but in that moment, it was all the lieutenant could see. And, goggles or no, she wanted nothing more in that moment than to break down, to let the ground of that strange, dead world hold her while her tears drained her dry.

She couldn't, though. She couldn't cry. Couldn't summon anything.

They'll come, that little voice in the back of her mind whispered to her. *They'll come now. They'll find it.*

"Got through it, Brevan," she whispered, and with one last glance, left the room. "Did the right thing."

She picked another spot—as far away as she could get from that precious little navigation chamber—and this time, the ceiling of ice gave way easily, breaking apart after only a few hard, quick blows. It was short work to clear a space big enough to worm through, and Tharsis found herself staring up at a hole to the stars above.

Thinking about the divedrive.

About the Flet.

About home.

And that was an insane idea, she knew, utterly insane. She wasn't qualified, wasn't focused, wasn't hardly alive—her body was screaming at her now, skin on fire.

"What the hell," she muttered to herself, hands on the edge of the hole, boots digging in for a solid push-point in the icerock, a strange calm spreading through her limbs. "You're already…"

But she didn't let herself finish it. Took a firm stance, closed her eyes, and threw herself up into the open void.

As she hurtled away from the planetoid, she forced her brain to stop thinking about rising, about flying. It wasn't about that. It was about falling, falling away from the rock, falling away from the death, from all the evil there, into something pure. Falling.

Just like in the mountain pools back home, playing with her brother and her sisters and not a single care in the world.

Slipping away.

Beneath the surface.

Gone.

EPILOGUE

A snowstorm was threatening in the Olympian heights, lightning dancing amidst the dark gather of clouds, when the Rossen came to call.

Old-wardog-ancestor-smell, the family alpha whined, and Brevan looked up from the hunting rifle he was cleaning.

To the sight of a young man, striding up the drive. Grim-faced, young, dwarfed by the hulking Aonian war dog padding silently alongside. A shock of non-regulation hair fell over his brows and a loose sets of deepvoider blacks wrapped around him. Corporal, judging from the rank emblazoned on his lapels, but he walked as if burdened by far more than the small kit bag on his shoulder.

Straight up the steps, onto the porch, dog protective at his side.

The man of the Tharsan Bulge stood, steady on the mostly functional myoelectric prosthetic that ran from hip to boot, wiping gun grease off his hands.

"You Brevan Chen?" the corporal asked, eyes like obsidian, voice strangely accented.

Brevan stood his ground. "Who wants to know?"

"Corporal Caleb Petrison," the young soldier said, extending a hand. "At your service."

His arm, sleeve pulled up, was scarred blue.

Brevan bristled.

The Rossen made an expression that approximated a smile. "They do tell me nobody has these anymore," he said, rolling his sleeve back down. "Progress, I guess."

"Fuck your progress," Brevan snapped. "Where's my fucking sister?"

He'd heard her. Everyone had heard her—the entire Heliosphere, everyone, everywhere.

… It's okay. Tell my brother that. It's okay…

Then static. Then nothing.

Seven hundred years of history, of theory, of hope and belief and faith, destroyed by his little sister's voice.

He wanted to be proud of her. He desperately needed to be proud of her.

But while it had stopped the Propagation conflict cold, nobody knew what it meant yet. Not for the Heliosphere. Not for the Tenancy. Or Mars. Or the Chen family.

Other than heartbreak.

The ASDF had been silent on the subject—strangely so—but everyone thought she was dead. All the shortwave stations, all the national papers, all the stories that ended with *the Chen family has no comment* instead of the more appropriate *Mr. William Chen threw our reporters off his porch, Mr. Brevan Chen told us to go fuck ourselves.* But they could speculate all they wanted; HOMECOM refused to even acknowledge it had happened.

District of Lunae was in an uproar, evidently. The Lighthouses had been the last link to the exodus craft, and the recovery of those had always been of utmost importance to the Arran people, to their future. Dad said the government was taking out their anger over losing the connection on Tharsis, as if she'd somehow invalidated the millions of lives given to protect that vital link to humanity's past.

Brevan didn't fucking care about that.

Mom still wouldn't stop crying. Dad had barely said two words to anyone since the broadcast. The twins were both wrecks. They all felt like they'd failed her. But Brevan knew where the responsibility really lay in the Chen family. He couldn't even grieve for hating himself.

His baby sister was most likely dead. Because of him.

Nothing was ever going to make that okay.

"I understand nobody's called you," the Rossen said, and there was something in his manner that made him seem impossibly young. "Some news should be delivered in person. And I've had a few other stops to make. Hell of a way to see Mars for the first time."

Brevan found himself wondering, despite himself, what kind of hell the Rossen had been through in the past few sevenday.

"We've been out there, you know, that shithole, Noqumiut," the Rossen continued. "Fucked-up shit, man. Seven and a half centuries, and nothing's changed." And he stopped. "The one thing we didn't find, though, was Lieutenant Chen's body."

Fuck. That was going to break their mother's heart. "Could she have drifted off?"

"We were very thorough. Nothing within a thousand kilometers of Eris." He paused. "We don't know where she is. They've got some theories, insane, but."

"Like what?" the rancher asked, and took a stab. "Skin diving?"

"That's one of the theories that's being floated right—" he began.

But didn't get to finish.

Because at that moment, the screen door banged open.

Mom. In her apron and dusty work jeans. Probably coming to tell him lunch was ready.

But she took one look at the uniform, at the kit bag, and let out a strangled cry like a stuck cat. Brevan barely caught her as she crumpled, wrapping her up as she screamed into his shoulder.

Dad, barging out to see what the commotion was, the twins hot on his heels, wasn't quite so restrained.

"The War Department puts us through hell for the past month, lets the fucking press drag our family name through the mud, and then sends a fucking scat-eaten corporal to tell me she's dead?" he demanded, that one vein standing out on his forehead. "Who's your commander? What worthless son of a bitch sends some kid to do his job?"

"Dad, this is—"

"I don't fucking care if he's the fucking Landlord, we're owed some goddamn answers!" his father roared. "So tell me, corporal, why was she out there? Who the fuck was responsible for that?" The Rossen didn't answer. "Where's my little girl?!"

It hung, heavy and dark, on the sunny porch.

"I was," the corporal finally said, quiet, hand twisting in his dog's fur. "I sent her out there. Her commander hasn't come because he was killed in action, day of her broadcast."

Mom lifted her face off Brevan's shoulder, aghast. Perplexed.

Dad didn't look much better.

"This is the Landlord," Brevan explained. "Look at his arms. It's him."

For a moment, nobody on the porch spoke.

Then Mom pulled back, wiping her eyes on the edge of her sleeve. "Would you like to come in, have some lunch?" she asked, voice unsteady. "We were just about to eat. Your dog's welcome, I'm sure I've got a bone or something in the chiller…"

"Honey…"

"He's probably been living off protein packs for the last month," she said firmly, and turned back to the Landlord. "When's the last time you had a home-cooked meal?"

The kid smiled the sad, twisted smile of an unsettled life. "It's been a few years."

"I'm going to set you a place. We'll eat in five," she said, and, giving Dad another look, swept her and the girls back into the house.

His father waited a moment, until the women were gone, and then turned on the Rossen.

"Answer me this. Is my daughter dead?"

"We have no idea. But I'm going to find her," the corporal promised, jaw set and hand tight in the dog's neck ruff. "Whatever it takes. I'm going to bring her home."

Dad didn't say a word. Just stepped aside, and let the Landlord in.

The Chen males left on the porch exchanged a glance, too many years wrapped up in the moment for either man to say what he was thinking. So, Brevan patted his father on the back, pretended he didn't see the tears in the man's eyes, and headed into the cool of the ranch house.

His myoelectric leg chafing against the scars.

THE ARIUMS OF EARTH
THE HELIOSPHERE TRILOGY
BOOK TWO, COMING MAY 2023

The ocean here, they told him, was boiling.

Boiling so slowly that only the Flet could properly observe the movement. Some kind of convection caused by a freezing layer of water, kilometers below.

To Caleb Ross, the scene in front of him just looked like the frozen north. Norway, maybe. One of those missions up to Svalbard in the winter, or the lab raid where he'd found Tyr. The far north, under starlight. No aurora, no moonlight.

Beyond the hardened glass windows of the abbot's spare office, glaciers drained out into that frozen sea, nitrogen ice sliding forever into the stillness.

Perched on the edge of Sputnik Planem, the Elysium Monestary clung in thick, stepped segments to the nameless mountains. Living modules, communal gathering areas, chapels, greenhouses, laboratories, linked together with enclosed stairs and bridges. Long legs—in some places, over half a kilometer tall - held the entire thing safely above the frozen surface. Over three hundred degrees below zero.

Insulation and heat exchangers kept the monastery from melting the water ice, harder than rock, into which it was driven. Satellite facilities were scattered across the entire planet, he'd been told, as well as three of the moons. Fusion generators, tethered at the equator, provided the energy required to keep the network of habitats alive.

Inside, the structure seemed grand, robust, vast. But at least one dome out there had been cracked open, revealed for the fragile thing it was. It resembled a broken snow globe now, its conifer forest flash-frozen by explosive decompression. A swarm of repair wasps, most of them the *Barachiel's*, clustered around it.

"Beautiful, isn't it?"

The Rallarhu's axilla bud had been quiet since their small party had arrived. What it wanted, what it was after, Caleb had no idea. The thing was unreadable in its sealed pressure suit. But it was at least a fragment of a Landlord, and so the monks hadn't questioned its presence.

He ignored it. He wished it would wear any face, any image, besides Rallison's.

"I'm sorry to see the damage here," the deputy commander said. Stag, if Caleb remembered his call sign right. "Last time I was through, the place was beautiful."

"We can rebuild our facilities. I mourn for the lives lost, though."

The man who'd spoken was older, walking up in a hurry. He was rail thin, the same mig-clouded eyes as the *Barachiel's* Colonel Cambel. Loose robes hung on his wasted frame, over some kind of fitted body suit. He looked much the same as any monk Caleb had encountered so far, except for his age. And despite the low gravity, he walked as though burdened to the very edge of human capacity.

"Abbot," Stag acknowledged.

"Lieutenant Colonel, is it now? It's been a proper few years since you've come through here. My apologies for the wait."

"We have Ops searching for bodies right now," Stag said, obviously ignoring the pleasantries. "Your people indicated there were several who went floating off into the void when that dome was blown out. If they're still within range, we can get them back for you."

The abbot nodded. "What assistance you can offer, we're grateful for. But don't let our problems guide your decisions." Those milky eyes turned on Caleb. "You must have more important things to do."

"We might not be able to leave. That was one of the things Colonel Cambel wanted me to speak with you about. Every dive core, every comm node, across the entire Heliosphere is down. We barely made it here," Stag said.

"Yes, so I heard," the abbot said.

"You have any idea what's going on? Does it have anything to do with the attack you suffered? It's an unprecedented situation and if you have any insight on—"

"I doubt it. We've been hit before, and have never seen a linkage."

"What do you mean?"

And at that, the abbot truly hesitated. "We've observed events like this before. The Flet's consciousness going missing, brainwaves flatlining. Never anything that lasted more than a few minutes. He's never been missing for this long."

Stag leaned forward. "Why hasn't this been communicated to the ASDF?"

"I'm telling you now," the abbot said, and nodded in Caleb's direction. "Because the Rossen is here."

"What do you mean?"

"The Flet is alive, but rarely conscious. It takes an extreme effort for him to manifest as an apparition. We're not sure why, but he's never done so here. We have a text machine set up for him to communicate with us. He uses it rarely. But when he does, it's almost always followed by one of these absence events. And then, it's always the same phrase." The abbot paused. "*Caleb come find me.*"

Caleb glanced over at the axilla, but the simulacrum of Rallison's face gave nothing away. Why would some wetware ghost be invoking his name? "Then I should probably go talk to him."

"Brother Terzio is waiting outside. He'll show you the way."

After both the Rossen and that Rallarhu-thing had gone, the abbot waved Stag away from the wide windows, over to the corner where his spare desk was set up.

"The Landlord of Mars," he said, opening a wall compartment to reveal a large pressure kettle inset in an alcove. "Have you ever dealt with him before?"

This was a part of his job Stag wasn't all that comfortable with. Politics. Talking. Playing nice. But politics were a big part of deep-voider operations. Besides, Colonel Cambel was edging close to miglock; planets were painful for him to set foot on, even one as small as Pluto. Stag supposed he'd be there himself someday, when he made full colonel and had a command of his own. Then he could make his own senior duty officer handle this scat.

Still, he put in the effort.

"For a few sevenday, before he got killed this last time. He seems," and Stag struggled for the right word. The *political* word. "He's young."

"Yes, I would think so." The abbot laughed, and handed Stag a small, steaming cup.

Tea. Not Stag's favorite drink, but he accepted it anyway. There was something about Pluto; the cold crept into a man's bones.

"Young, and has no idea what the fuck he's doing."

"Maybe no idea about the Heliosphere, but he was a soldier from a young age. He understands the nature of our common enemy. Existential as it may appear to us sometimes, it's very real," the abbot said. "Don't mistake his behavior for the ignorance of youth."

Stag looked out the thick glass curve of the abbot's office wall, towards the shattered remains of the environmental dome. It had been one of Elysium's main environmental parks, part of the life support system. The loss of both its atmosphere and water would be a rough blow to the entire monastery. "Doesn't seem so existential right now, Father."

"Indeed," the abbot said, and sipped at his tea. "Now come, tell me, what does Ignace want to ask me? He wouldn't have sent you in person if there wasn't some pressing need."

Stag set his tea aside. "We're missing a lieutenant. Lost out at Noqumiut. Command wants her found, but it's like she vanished. No body, and the divedrive she took out to that fuckin' places appears to have been destroyed there."

"Ahh," the abbot said. "The young lady who ended the Propagation. I was quite fascinating by her broadcast."

"Doesn't look like everybody here was," Stag observed.

"Proving their paradise dead won't stop people from believing in it." He turned to the window. Sipped his tea. "You're asking about skin diving. If she moved herself off Noqumiut."

Stag frowned. "I've heard about it, but-"

"It's not a story or metaphor. Every brother here has done it. At least once." The abbot smiled. "For most of us, only once."

"I've always heard it really has nothing to do with faith in—"

"It doesn't, although that's a common misconception amongst the voider nations. One of the more pernicious legacies of the Euphemism were the repeated attempt to blur these lines. Father Golan's great insight, one of them, was illuminating the distinction between the spiritual realm and the penumbra. He asked us, as members of his order, to undergo this process as a means of comprehending the difference." The abbot ran a thoughtful finger around the rim of his cup. "That is why, incidentally, our order cares for the Flet. Why we host such a large scientific community here. He is… the secular understanding of the larger truths."

"What's that got to do with Lieutenant Chen?" Stag asked. "Could she have done it?"

The abbot breathed out, obviously considering the idea carefully. "Anyone is theoretically capable of it. But it's an incredible act of-"

"Will?"

The abbot shook his head. "If it was just that, we wouldn't need void craft. But we do. As I said, it's a very rare feat. Often it takes years of preparation."

"So…"

"If she had accomplished it, she would most likely be here. And unfortunately for her, she is not."

"What do you mean, here?"

"As you know, in the Silicone Age, it was thought that spacetime was akin to a smooth sheet. We understand the nature of things a bit more completely now. Spacetime is more like an ocean. It has depth, and when we push down into it, the nature of reality tends to shove us back up. We can't exist anywhere but the surface. It's the nature of reality. God's order."

Stag really, really hated this part of the job. "I know, but-"

"There are currents. One of these, the surface current, we experience as the flow of time. But there are others that flow in other directions, under the surface. Most aren't well understood, but we do know there is a significant one that tends to flow here. To the Flet."

"So what, the Flet has some kind of gravity that pulls people in?"

"Our metaphors are clashing now, of course, but yes, something like that." The abbot paused. "As I said, it's not well understood. The person best suited for studying it is the Flet himself, but he is disinclined to do so."

"So where could she be?"

"Quite likely, somewhere he is."

"But he's here."

"Yes," the abbot agreed serenely. "For now."

ABOUT THE AUTHOR

A lifelong science fiction fanatic, E.M. Rensing still managed to surprise her family when she decided to pursue a commission in the US Air Force. A graduate of the United States Air Force Academy, she enjoyed a 13 year career as a Cyber Operations Officer, and has traveled all over the world. E.M. Rensing lives with her husband and daughters in south Texas.

Visit her website to sign up for her newsletter! Get all the latest updates, future release information, and heck, maybe even the occasional Embarrassing Cadet Story.

rensingwrites.com